Dear

Monica

Lewinsky

ALSO BY JULIA LANGBEIN

American Mermaid

Laugh Lines: Caricaturing Painting in Nineteenth-Century France

Dear Monica Lewinsky

JULIA LANGBEIN

DOUBLEDAY
NEW YORK
2026

FIRST DOUBLEDAY HARDCOVER EDITION 2026

Published by Doubleday, a division of Penguin Random House LLC, 1745 Broadway, New York, NY 10019.

DOUBLEDAY and the portrayal of an anchor with a dolphin are registered trademarks of Penguin Random House LLC.

Illustration on p. 30 courtesy of Catherine Vaesca.

LIBRARY OF CONGRESS CATALOGING-IN-PUBLICATION DATA
Names: Langbein, Julia (art historian), author.
Title: Dear Monica Lewinsky : a novel / Julia Langbein.
Description: First Doubleday hardcover edition. |
New York : Doubleday, 2026.
Identifiers: LCCN 2025019827 (print) | LCCN 2025019828 (ebook) |
ISBN 9780385551502 (hardcover) | ISBN 9780385551519 (ebook)
Subjects: LCSH: Lewinsky, Monica S. (Monica Samille), [date]—Fiction |
LCGFT: Biographical fiction. | Fiction. | Novels.
Classification: LCC PS3612.A563 D43 2026 (print) | LCC PS3612.A563 (ebook)
LC record available at https://lccn.loc.gov/2025019827
LC ebook record available at https://lccn.loc.gov/2025019828

penguinrandomhouse.com | doubleday.com

Printed in the United States of America
1st Printing

The authorized representative in the EU for product safety and compliance is Penguin Random House Ireland, Morrison Chambers, 32 Nassau Street, Dublin D02 YH68, Ireland, https://eu-contact.penguin.ie.

The events must be not only registered within [a] chronological framework . . . but narrated as well, that is to say, revealed as possessing a structure, an order of meaning, which they do *not* possess as mere sequence.

—HAYDEN WHITE, "THE VALUE OF NARRATIVITY IN THE REPRESENTATION OF REALITY"

The philosophers and the orators have fallen into oblivion; the masses do not even know the names of the emperors and their generals; but everyone knows the names of the martyrs, better than those of their most intimate friends.

—THEODORET, BISHOP OF CYRUS, FIFTH CENTURY CE

Prologue

A LIFE OF SAINT MONICA

+ + +

Monica Lewinsky was born in 1973 to a noble family of Jews living in the American Empire. She grew up a beautiful and spirited girl and was given a rare position as a servant to the emperor in the heart of the imperial palace. The emperor himself was so taken with her that he began to entreat her with words and gifts to love him and to give him comfort and to kiss and touch him. Monica responded to the emperor's entreaties and indeed felt a profound affection for the emperor, whom she came to know as a person when he put aside his crown and reclined with her and spoke of nothing at all.

Well, the emperor had many enemies, foremost among them a dogged Christian prosecutor named Kenneth. Kenneth hated the emperor because he imagined that the emperor had all the sex that Kenneth denied himself, and so he decried the emperor loudly as a man with no virtue, unfit to be ruler of the Americans.

When Kenneth found out that the emperor and this young noblewoman had kissed and caressed each other in the palace, he was overjoyed. He brought in a younger, prurient Christian assistant who himself loved to drink beer and to exercise his frustrated lust, and that licentious man was called Brett. When it came time for the emperor to be questioned under oath about what had passed between him and Monica, Brett argued that the most explicit questions be asked, and he wrote such questions as would make any good and private person blush to answer aloud. For how many times the young woman was digitally stimulated, and what was said between her and her lover, and how many times her breasts were exposed and caressed, and how many times and when and under what circumstances she had taken the emperor's penis in her mouth to give him pleasure—these details were sussed out by the horny Christians, supposedly to prove that the emperor could not lead America. But America is the horniest place on Earth and loves to put its penis into people's mouths, and the emperor was not shamed, and he held on to his throne, and the people moved on.

But the prurient Christian prosecutors continued to mortify Monica Lewinsky, and gave all the details of her body and its pleasures and penetrations to the legislature, which released the tales of her sexual acts into the wind for no legal reason in the hopes that every person in the empire, and in the world, would read about each and every one of her private physical encounters in order to degrade her as weak, loose, and used, as a shameful accessory to the emperor's own sin.

This was the mortification of Monica Lewinsky at the hands of the most powerful lawmakers during the height of the American Empire. And for many long years, she could not show her face, for her body bore its mortification, and she carried her name like a dirty joke, and she moved countries, but there was no country that word of her body's defilement had not reached.

But more years passed, and while the same factions continued to fight, and lustful Brett was now one of the highest judges in the land and still under the guise of Christian virtue sought to shame and cause physical suffering to women, America began to feel great remorse for the mortification of Monica Lewinsky. And the former emperor knew it and he began to fast, to foreswear meat and cheese as if to say, *I have no more desire. I have mastered my appetites. I too will mortify my flesh.* And he lost so much weight that he looked like a blanched femur someone found in the desert and he talked like a ghost sheep and all the saliva he did not spend on meat stayed in his mouth and formed a mousse and nobody wanted to listen to him anymore. And Monica Lewinsky became exalted as the patron saint of those who suffer venal public shaming and patriarchal cruelty, and she forgave the people with what they recognized as true grace, and they exalted her and looked anew upon her beautiful glossy dark hair and said things like "I saw Monica Lewinsky on *The Today Show*. She's so smart."

Saint Monica Lewinsky was consecrated by the collective force of the American conscience during the second decade of the third millennium AD. It is said that many women pray to her and that she is known to perform miracles.

PART I

✦ ✦ ✦

Prayer & Intercession

Chapter 1

THURSDAY, APRIL 18, 2019
JEAN RECEIVES A MESSAGE

The day that Jean Dornan first prayed to me began for her like any other—with a coffee and a soft-boiled egg and an unspeakable sense of dread. Well, unspeakable in that she never speaks about it, but she could describe its texture in detail: She might be doing something normal, washing her face or spacing out on the train, and suddenly her stomach drops and she thinks, *I have to get back.* But back where? To some juncture where she went wrong.

Mornings, she feels most acutely the pressure to stuff her dead day like a taxidermist into a convincing position.

"Bye, Jeannie," her husband called up from the front door.

"Bye, Michael," she responded sweetly, imagined divorcing him, and felt fine about it.

See, none of your choices make any sense to you. I know this rot, have lived it—this deepening suspicion that your existence is a remnant of an event long since concluded. Maybe you foolishly wandered away from your path. Or maybe—maybe you were *tricked.*

✦

So on this Thursday, Jean sat at the kitchen table and idly looked at her phone. And suddenly, she saw an email that gave her a shock. She had to put the phone down and peer into it as if it were a well. She read the whole email. A racy heat swirled in her sternum and flooded her cheeks; a feeling of doing something wrong, getting caught. The past had been swung into her body like the dull end of a big tree. She murmured his name aloud in disbelief, and his name, voiced, poured out of her with the alarming materiality of blood, of a substance usually withheld.

"David."

Stunned, she drifted into the guest room, which was cluttered with empty suitcases and storage bins. She found her old chef's kit, slipped out the boning knife, and slit open boxes, sliced tape. Her fingers moved quickly. She knew what she was looking for. She shoved aside the wedding album, dug past the tax forms, went further and further back in time. Finally she reached the right sedimentary depth, the right era: She found some photographs, flicked through them, and brought one—a group shot—up close to her face. A dozen or so people, smiling into the bright sun in front of the ivy-covered stone façade of a castle in France. He stood to one side of the group, his public self, affable, enthused. She opened a spiral notebook, filled with flowing script that sometimes gave way to doodles—of people, of shapes; a thick cross drawn in wobbly black pen, dotted with markings.

She thought she knew the story, roughly, its essential beats: the silly girl, the greedy man, the setting so lush and seductive that all of life after had seemed like the hallway outside a theater. But then she settled down to read. And after some time, she encountered something surprising, a figure she had forgotten, lurking in the archive of her notes: me.

This morning I found everyone in the salon watching yesterday's news from home. Clinton admitted on TV to an affair in the White House with a skanky intern, and everyone was saying how stupid they were.

Putting down the diary, eyes closed, Jean made a noise that started as a low moan, like a choir girl holding the bass line, and ended in a high scream that she strained to stifle in her throat.

Then, in a weak pile, she whimpered, "You *idiot.*"

This time she meant herself, not me.

Chapter 2

Jean's day went on in a braid: She tried to read a book, but the memories of that summer cut before her eyes and she had to return to the photos. She put on sneakers and ran, literally ran out of the house as if she could escape her mind like some folk fool, like Jonah, who thought almighty God couldn't track him to Spain. She came back from running clapping her hands as if she were a new person named Trudy from Wichita who only smiles—it was honestly adorable. But the weaving wouldn't stop and in came the thick thread of the past and soon she was crying on the floor or else sitting at her desk, looking nowhere with eyes that were opaque, that saw only inward, like the chalky orbs of an ancient bust.

Michael marveled at her thirst for wine later that night. She brushed it off:

"This Sangiovese goes so well with pizza."

When he talked about the hospital—he's a nurse—she pretended to listen, dispensing ready-made replies like "Maybe you can delegate more."

She has never told him about what happened the summer before her junior year of college because she cannot find words that suit the truth. *Affair*—too glamorous and grown up. *Relationship*—too stable, with a *ship* in the word, the inhabiting together of a big, wooden noun. *Sexual impropriety*—too legalese and small, like shoplifting, like bad manners, like this man had burped at the table with a hand on her ass. *Molested*—too Catholic church, not fun enough. But *fun* isn't the word, either. Nothing is the word.

No words, only the feeling of coming into existence, of the hard plastic casings of her organs popping inside like grapes, good, warm, in their time, running with the juice they were meant to give. All the fallout, all the pain that came with its calamitous end, had been worth it for the sweet center, hadn't it? Her last two years of college had been berserk, unfocused, humiliating. But that's *college,* riiiiight? You partied too much, you woke up in recycling bins and laughed about it, relishing the colorful contrast it would make with your stable, productive future.

But what if the future never stabilized?

She graduated with grades that were beneath her and a major—Modern Languages—that seemed like code for "just talking." At first she could argue that college didn't matter, that her real talent was cooking, anyway, and out of the three people who had trained with her at Le Cheval d'Or the summer after her senior year, she was the only one the restaurant hired. She learned hygiene codes and how to bond a broken sauce, fell easily into cooks' camaraderie, and kept her shit together in the service crush. And the early 2000s were thrilling years in New York kitchens, when high-end food was becoming not just refined but *delicious;* when you'd serve bone marrow—beyond blood, the brown gel that makes blood, what the dog knows to gnaw for—with *gros sel* and rough bread to people in Theory blazers. Jean loved it, could not imagine a life spent away from little pinches, little metal teaspoons all day long of some torched meat, some bashed herb, all these carefully waged violences come good on the tongue.

All the while, an infection from long ago was doing its work—not a physical one, although she worried about her body as she began to puff up from booze and the kind of snacks that only line cooks make (sweetbread lollipops; deep-fried strawberries; shooters of cold cream, vodka, and *orgeat:* They treated the kitchen like a meth lab for flavor). She had strategies for managing her attractiveness: skipping meals, running obsessively. But she couldn't starve or outrun the doubts that undermined her existence. Would she be a lawyer or an architect, would she have kids and a sturdy umbrella, if her filthy little sex scandal hadn't turned her toward restaurant kitchens, this nocturnal, underground arena full of grab-ass men and gratuitous butter? *Maybe I cook because I'm a people-pleaser. Maybe I cook because I'm a pig. Maybe I was destined to do something more sustainable and cerebral, but I fucked it up.* It was easy to be struck with these doubts while doing a bump of coke before the brunch rush, or waking up next to Shlomo the Garnish King in a part of Brooklyn so far out she thought she'd pass fur traders on her way home.

Jean is no dummy. She has always known that David is involved in the self-doubt that accompanies all her choices. And even so, for this first decade out of college, she managed to think of what had happened between them as painful but affirmative, proof of her attractiveness, of her femininity; an unusual but necessary introduction to the sour colors and thick breath and delicious rot that lay beyond innocence.

Until she imploded. In 2009, she had a relationship with another cook, the executive chef of the restaurant where she worked, a sort of gentlemanly divorcé who put work before everything. He was well-meaning but exhausted, and he broke up with her over pastrami that he paid for, explaining that he was overwhelmed, which anyone could see in his stoop, in the purple hammocks under his eyes. He knew nothing of David, the man who had come ten years before and broken all of Jean's bones just as they were hardening. So when the executive chef cut off their relationship, he shattered her along the old fracture lines. Another woman might have taken it reasonably, gotten shit-faced, keyed his car, spent a week crying. But Jean saw that she would never get it right, that she was always doomed: a pest, bothersome, easy, not worthy of the center but pushed to the margin, not a partner for the day but a mistake in the night, not good but greedy. She had to leave, not just kitchens but her life, her skin. She had to find her way, if not back, then elsewhere. She imagined herself boiled like a pickling jar, sterilized. With ten years of knowledge accumulated in her mind, in her hands, in the fine, diagnostic organ of her tongue, having earned the high regard of some of the city's best cooks, she quit.

A period of intense darkness lasted almost a year; she was jobless, lost, desperately trying to purge herself of her sickening drives, of her addiction to the urgent touch, the thrilled palate. At nearly thirty years old, she crashed with her mother, a lifelong dieter, whose habits of self-denial suddenly suited Jean. Special K was the woodchip that might scrape her clean; low-fat cottage cheese squeaked against her teeth, lactating a sour, soapy water. A job-search website identified her language skills and sent her to assist a certified translator at the federal courthouse in Manhattan. The first time she entered the courtroom, she found a pale linoleum heaven: dead, sterile, the opposite of a kitchen, bright and odorless, no one fuckable and nothing delicious. *Safe.*

I will tell you that she could have been an astronaut, alone in the amicrobial void, all shiny tools and mineral dust and pee that floats up, and she would not have been safe. When they get to you young, they're in your blood, in your brain stem. Like Jonah, you're a fool to run. Horrified by her own compulsions, she still fantasized about David, tried to keep him a constant in her mind, to retain the timbre of his voice from so long ago, to lick the old bones of the phrases she'd saved for licking: "You were wonderful, Jean." "How do you know how to do this, Jean?" She refreshed memories with fantasy, put him in scenes art-directed like a Merchant Ivory film: ecru hotel suites, train compartments where silver rattled, a thatched cottage out of Jane Austen's England except with wall-thumping simultaneous orgasms.

Even after she met a nurse at a christening in 2010 and married him (she's doing her best!), she always returns to the well where fantasies of David's affection pool, ready to be slurped up for instant, guilty gratification. But something has happened now, over the past few years: The well is polluted. She tries to pull David out of the armoire of her erotic props and set him up all ready to go in the four-poster bed in the stone room with her crawling toward him on the floor with her big young waterbed boobs swaying, and he'll say, *in her own fantasy,* "I don't think we should do this anymore—don't you understand that I fucked you up? It doesn't feel very feminist." *Take your pants off, for fuck's sake!* screams her subconscious like an angry director with a bullhorn on an expensive set. But the celluloid stand-in shakes his head and moves to get dressed.

The trade-off—he hurt and humiliated her, but he cannot be removed from the white-hot center of her deepest mental pleasures—may be a terrible bargain, but it has always been *hers* to make.

That's a secret. If you asked, she'd say she never thinks about him.

But she thinks about him more and more. Now she is forty—approaching the age *he was*—and when a twenty-year-old boy scans her almonds at Trader Joe's, she looks at him and thinks of the long interspecies distance between them, uncrossable: He is like a spotted salamander, a ropey caloric sinkhole whose skin is shiny with some adolescent slime and whose moves are quick and jerky and who looks at her with animal uncaring because she is, to him, some old brown horse. *How could David have loved me when I was nineteen?* she thinks, staring at the salamander in the Hawaiian shirt who has to ask twice if she wants her receipt.

"No, thank you."

"OK. Have a good day, ma'am."

Then what was it? Pure exploitation? Were my resources extracted? She imagines a pit in the earth, her soul a pretty ore, shimmering like eye shadow, there for the scraping.

Chapter 3

She had forgotten, completely forgotten until David's email sent her tumbling through her old diaries this morning, that she had met him during the *Summer of Monica.* In 1998, when a scandalous and ill-advised affair was on everyone's mind, she never saw the parallels. It represented nothing to Jean but a distant comical blunder, a political circus. How disconnected from politics had she been at nineteen? How ensconced in a private, subjective experience, how naive and immature? How disconnected had she *remained,* only in the past year, when #MeToo had come and gone like a parade two streets over but didn't seem to have anything to do with her? Her love for David was its own creature, a fish too complicated to debone, a delicacy that would always stick in her throat. She couldn't connect it to assaults, harassment; didn't want to see David on a list with hot-handed dirtbags or pervs or felons. It had been consensual. She had loved him.

Jean's husband and friends know she "made out with" her teacher once long ago, and they've all laughed at it collectively as evidence of something doofy and harmlessly libidinous called "the nineties." They have no idea that he is like a god, who created the world of her sexuality by naming it for the first time, a great carved gaping stone mouth who granted her all the desire that she can then bring, secondhand, to humans like her husband, Michael.

So on this morning, it was unassimilable, impossible, that the god who had breathed her to life had written to her the way that Citibank or Aunt Carol did, through her email. Attached to his few words—*would be such a treat to see you . . . may not be worth crossing the ocean for a glass of champagne! . . . hope you've been well*—was a formal invitation to a party celebrating the twentieth anniversary of the Intercollegiate Hub for the Study of Medieval Art and

Architecture in Plaisy, France, along with a Festschrift for David Harwell's retirement as director.

The first time she'd heard from him in twenty years and there were no signs that anything had ever happened between them: It would be "such a treat" to see her. Oh, *such a treat.* He was, to her, a muddy river of nourishment and danger that oozed down the full Amazonian course of her spine and all her limbs, bringing settlement and disease, bubbling with animal breath and sometimes drowning children, and she was to him a Hershey's kiss, a "treat." And the secondary shock of his retirement: that he had aged, that he had gone on living a human life, that he was *sixty-five;* that he would likely die before her, and leave her alone in this world.

"Die and leave me alone," she repeated aloud on the floor in the guest room that morning, mortified by the dumb dog-hearted craziness of it, of her primordial attachment to a man she had not seen, had seldom mentioned aloud, since college.

So at dinner she sat across from Michael working hard to think about anything but the email she'd received even though all the fish were slipping past each other frantically and the crocodiles snapping their jaws in the thickening river of her blood. The only thing to calm them was the wine, the vapor of it like someone else's breath in her throat, the only thing that made sense, that had a hint of the rotten, secret intimacy that travels her bones and clouds her thoughts, the filth that first grew her like a rich ordure.

✦

Later that night, her husband's affable company irritated her.

"You wanna watch something?" he said, from his simpler world where it still seemed appealing to watch a mentally unstable Swedish detective discover which unlikely bureaucrat had strangled a teenage girl.

"I might do some work." She had to be alone.

"Now?" Her work was rarely urgent. Court interpreters showed up, listened, repeated.

"I'm doing a case tomorrow with some new vocabulary. I should probably prepare."

Michael lay on his side in a blue scrubs top and briefs, propping up an iPad. Her lie had been too interesting. "What kind of vocabulary?"

"Construction." He made a noise from behind his nose that indicated the abrupt death of his curiosity and turned back to the screen.

Even then, she waited for him to sleep—*Finally, he's extinguished,* she thought like a killer, relieved to see his face go slack—before she dipped back to the kitchen, grabbed the wine bottle by the neck, returned to the guest room, and opened the old notebook again. On her knees surrounded by an archipelago of documents, glossy photos, ticket stubs, letters, receipts, books, she whimpered in escalating anguish, "Monica, Monica, Monica. I'm sorry, I'm sorry, I'm sorry, I'm sorry." Her words spiraled up to the sky in their repetition, and as they whipped upward, they veered at a new angle, like a tilting flock of birds: "I'm sorry, I'm sorry, I'm sorry. Oh *help me, help me, help me.*"

Her heart lay open, completely open to me, and though her eyes were squeezed shut, her hands moved with a priest's ritual calm from her old diary to a blue book with a kneeling monk on the cover and a woman with a knife in her throat floating above his head. "Dear Monica Lewinsky," she called, holding *The Golden Legend* to her heart, *"please help me."*

And I heard her.

Chapter 4

FRIDAY, APRIL 19, 2019

I'm so embarrassed to be hungover at work, embarrassed that one email from David sent me weeping and slamming wine while Michael slept soundly after healing people all day. I nestle into the little neutral box of the interpreter, at my own desk with my own headset, seated behind the defendant.

"*Sí,*" replies the defendant, pockmarked and heavy-faced, in early middle age.

"Yes," I say. Everyone knows what *sí* means, but this is the joyous brainlessness of interpretation. I don't choose; I must translate comprehensively, so that later, no one can make use of a gap in the record.

"Now if you'll turn to document 16 C 5, please." The lady lawyer who's prosecuting looks at me to make sure I am with her. I am with her. I shouldn't call her a "lady lawyer." That's not feminist. I flinch—a little acid memory of what I had written about Monica Lewinsky in my college notebook comes up. What did I call her? Crazy? Stupid?

Look at the lady lawyer. Dammit, *the lawyer.* She's got a law degree. Should I have gotten a law degree? Maybe I could have done some good with a law degree. She is telling the jury, and I am telling Mr. Juarez, that mortgage fraud is *not a victimless crime.* She is trying to harden everyone against him, because she knows they smell the death and desperation on him, the circumstances, the things he wanted to give his wife and children that he couldn't afford, like a mammogram and some Air Jordans, for fuck's sake—

"Are you unwell, Miss Dornan?"

"*¿Se está usted sintiendo mal,* Señora Dornan?"

"Don't translate that. Why are you translating that?"

Oh god, what's happening? I shake my head, as if to wake myself up.

"Miss Dornan, you seem unable to keep up with the proceedings."

"No, I'm fine. I'm not unwell." I hear myself say it and it's a lie. I called the lawyer a lady lawyer. And I called Monica Lewinsky stupid in 1998, and if I'd been a better person, if I'd seen myself in Monica, seen that she was me and I was her, then maybe I would have had my guard up. Maybe I'd be leading the right life today.

Then the room melts away into a periphery of tears, but the lady lawyer's face remains clear. It softens into a new shape, a beautiful polished oval, and she stares at me and I see her irises are rings of fire and I hear her say, "Be calm, Jean. Do not be afraid." I have cried in court before, but I have never heard voices. My ears fill with heat, and through the heat I hear it again, not from the lawyer's lips but from the air itself, a voice that strikes me as familiar, although I can't name it: "I have heard you, Jean. I have come."

Who? Who has come? Her voice dislodges something in my heart. I feel it unlatch, pop like a button. I am *not* afraid of the voice, although I am afraid of a sudden nakedness, here, in front of everyone—can they see the unlatching? Are my pants still on? Why is my face so *very* hot? Juarez looks at me with wonder, as if I have burst into flames. *Have* I burst into flames? I am opening, I am softening, I—

I am bawling at work.

"This court will take a recess. We need a new interpreter."

✦

I stumble out of the courthouse onto Centre Street, pointing myself in the direction of the subway. But I sense I will not make my train. Reality is peeling away, and the air vibrates with weird possibility. The way that, when you walk, the sun leaps from building to building in the Financial District, tossed between towers like a gold coin—today it shines for me, winks at me, flashes like the barbed metal that makes a fish follow. My legs move faster and faster as I pass the office ladies smoking in clusters by the revolving doors and the tourist families looking up and shuffling on—the voice in the courtroom: Do they hear it? I look at everyone with none of the usual city hardness. I discard no one. *Who? Where are you?*

The guy who is always outside Duane Reade with his boom box is playing "Say You, Say Me," and I feel the hydraulics inside my face start to pump. It takes extreme effort not to let myself weep. What the fuck? It's not even "Tears in Heaven"! *I had a dream, I had an awesome dream*... It's so indecent, the bleeding synthesizer, part machine gun, part maxi pad. And yet! This disgusting song has entered my undefended heart and moved me to a state of compassion for all humanity and I can't help crying, spluttering into my coat collar. I have lost it, lost the layer that lets us function, the sealant that lets us brush past people like piles of hay and not get stuck staring at the face of every child. A woman in a brown terrycloth jumpsuit limps out of Dunkin' Donuts sucking the filling from a Boston cream and almost bangs into me. "Is it you?" I ask her, and she must be someone who has searched everywhere for a familiar voice because she doesn't say, "Are you crazy?" She says, softly: "Sorry, sweetheart."

I keep going, the golden disk of the sun swinging from mirrored panel to mirrored panel above my head, like a mesmerizing pocket watch.

Abruptly the sun stops leaping along the high, reflective canopy of skyscrapers, because they have all disappeared. And out of the cement rises a church, with a green yard and tombstones off-kilter. A *church.* It's so obvious and preposterous that I stop in my tracks and give a little laugh, almost a social laugh, as if I'm already not alone, greeted by the building. The sun breaks like a yolk over the church's red-brown roof and its warm brown brick sides. It is as if the city were a colossal relic, an ancient mistake that rose from the cocaine sands of finance a thousand years ago, now dead and abandoned. The church alone is alive, human, with its quaint elf's hat of a spire and the rubies and hot pinks of its windows—heart-colored, mouth-colored. And at the same time, if all the office towers are obvious, present, "New York," then this spindly, crenelated, baked and buttressed house is out of time, impossible—a magical bubble, a Gothic church where the Gothic cannot be imagined.

Like a hopping sparrow, my hammering heart fills my body completely. I haven't been in a church for twenty years, but I cross the threshold with purpose, with belonging, past enormous bronze doors paneled in Bible stories I'm too frantic to stop and read. "Are you here?" I whisper. "Where are you?" I scamper around the place, my feet swishing on the hard stone floor as I adjust to the artfulness of every surface, the tea-smelling air in the great heights above me. Words I once knew pop into my mind as my eyes skate along the building's lines: *nave, clerestory, chancery, apse. Vaults,* I think as I stare up at the ceiling, vaults, piped like the seams of a gingerbread house, drawings in a storybook I used to know by heart.

But these vaults are mute: They don't hum with the voice I heard. I don't hear her, can't find her. In the brilliant blue stained glass, I find Jesus, obviously, being really Jesus-y (center part, bathrobe) and Luke and Mark and Matthew with their pets, and what's-his-face, and the other guy. But there are no women here, no Marys, no Margarets or Lucies or Catherines or Barbaras, and the only worshippers are three tattered men sleeping in pews. A custodian in a cardigan gently wakes them, to usher them out before closing.

Closing? It's nearing five o'clock. I will be shooed out empty-handed. There was nothing here for me, only more men, lined up radiant in the windows, men sculpted into marble niches, men pooled in bronze relief. The custodian approaches me, but I cut him off, angry.

"I'm leaving. Can I use the toilet first?"

"Downstairs," he says with a hard edge, accustomed to godless opportunists who come here to relieve themselves. He gestures to an unmarked door. "We close in five."

I look at my watch. I can still make my train if I pee and run. I push open the door and trot down the stone steps toward another door bearing a white plastic panel marked with the cartoon symbol of a woman—two cobalt triangles in the shape of a dress. This whole thing has been so stupid, another mark of my coming undone. That I invented a—

Chapter 5

A blast of light.

Blindness. Heat on my face. I fall back.

A thousand holy golden female voices hailing, lifting up, unquestioning, bright, pushed with a joyful breath that renews and renews and renews itself. I cannot see anything, but the sound comes at me like a vision, butter yellow, lit from within. The voices rise, with completeness and fullness like an ecstatic agreement of insects at the hottest moment of midday, and then: silence.

The wall of light ripples and recedes to the periphery
to reveal its center.
Monica Lewinsky sits on a golden throne.

Slowly, my vision expands to include the gray-veined
white marble plinth on which the throne rests.

The marble steps that lead up to it.
The wide marble room, with a large tub to my left,
filled and still.

Monica Lewinsky, dark hair cascading to her waist,
meets my gaze.

Her eyes are brown and warm. A black halo floats
above her.

"Well?" She smiles; she tilts her head. "You called me, over and over." I feel for my body—it is still there. I look down at my two arms, up at her undulating cobalt robes. Did I call her?

I think back. To when I was upset and drunk, after hearing from David, looking through my diary.

"I"—I am amazed to hear my own voice echo in this place—"I was thinking of the woman."

"Were you? Who prays to a woman, a real live person? A person could not have received your prayer. But you called to me, nonetheless."

Without thinking about it, I had invoked something more than a single life. It was an instinct—an assumption—that there was some *greater being* called "Monica Lewinsky." And now I behold her: I could not have imagined fully the sheer power of her, the stillness with which she holds her head—both awesome and familiar, the inviolate aura of her radiance, the amplitude of her voice.

Then, with a pang of terror, I remember what I said about her all those years ago. How little I cared, when I should have. Is she here to punish me? To make me pay?

"Please forgive me. I should have defended you, and instead I was unkind." She stares steadily at me, her chin rising slightly. "I'm *so* sorry."

I look at her face, a face I have known all my adult life—one that has meant a cluster of things: ripeness and error, lust and humiliation. And later, the surprise of survival, of new life.

"I forgive you."

"You do?"

She nods, but her eyes keep me pinned; she's not done with me. "Why did you call me, Jean?" Her voice expands to fill the chamber. It has a brassy beauty to it, a trumpeter's golden control. "You said, 'Help me, help me, help me.' "

I sense that in this place, my usual excuses and justifications will ring with their true, thin shittiness. What is it that I can't tell my husband, won't admit to myself? "A mistake I made twenty years ago has warped my life's course, sapped me, undermined my every choice. But it was twenty years ago! And it was consensual! I—I'm almost more ashamed that I can't just *get over it,* that I let this thing fuck me up for so long. It's exhausting. I'm exhausted," I say, realizing that the truth is actually so simple: "I don't want to live my life anymore. I have no conviction. I'm dead."

"You're not dead."

"I can't move forward, can't choose for myself. The first time I tried to become someone, it was a mistake, so now—"

"You'll dodge being a person altogether." She says this like she knows me already.

"Last night, when I found my old diary, I had forgotten that you were—happening—at the same time. I was cruel about you in the summer of '98." Enthroned, she listens, almost expecting these words—no surprise moves across her face. "If I had had any empathy, any heart, I would have seen the parallels. Where I should have taken your suffering as a warning, I laughed like everyone else. It was a moral test that I failed, and it's led to this—this sham life." She takes it in. No protest from her about my "sham life."

"I got an email this morning," I tell her. "Do you know what that is?"

"I'm all-knowing."

"OK. There's a Festschrift."

"A *what*?"

"I thought you were—"

"Well, I don't speak *German*."

"It's this thing that big-shot academics do when they retire. Everyone comes to a party and reads a little tribute they wrote about the person."

"OK. A funeral."

"Kind of. A professional one. For years, this guy has been the head of a fancy center in France—it's where he taught me originally, although it's grown a lot since then, and now it's run by a bunch of universities. He's retiring. And they're having a Festschrift for him."

"And what, you want me to proofread your thingy?"

"No! I'm not going. It's in France, and it's next week! I don't understand how I got invited." Monica rises, and her cobalt raiment slithers behind her down the steps. She comes to sit on the ledge of the oversize white stone tub. She flicks her fiery gaze at me.

"You *can* go. Or you can ride this downward spiral of poisonous nostalgia and bone-deep shame until you really would rather die.

Up to you." She raises an eyebrow, and the flames around her halo leap.

I look around a little more. There's a toilet off to the side, little toiletries, a double sink, and a logo on the towels: Ritz-Carlton. Some dormant deep knowledge of her life surges to mind, and—

"Is this—is this the en-suite bathroom at the Ritz-Carlton, Pentagon City? Oh my god, this is where the FBI kidnapped you and wouldn't let you call a lawyer." *This* is where you go when you pray to Monica Lewinsky?

"You would look to Jesus on his cross, wouldn't you?" Suddenly everything clicks into place. Saint Monica. She was martyred and mortified and endured and rose again in the eyes of the people. Beatific, powerful, a holy mediatrix, distantly beloved. Hers is a suffering we have all witnessed. Her resurrection is my hope.

"Go to this event in France, Jean!"

"And do what?"

"Tell him the truth."

"What does that mean?"

"Exactly. You *don't know the truth.*"

"No, I know. I'll tell you the truth: I was a hormonal idiot on a study abroad course. I was naive, and I was *had.*" Of course that's it. The words from his email come back to me: *such a treat.*

She says nothing, only listens, and then touches the water in the tub with the tip of a finger. We watch together as the light rippling on the surface shimmers and dissolves into a picture of a young woman, just weeks from her twentieth birthday, sitting on a suitcase at Charles de Gaulle Airport in Paris, biting her nails.

It's me. Dishwater hair, to my chin. Asics. Face completely blank.

"I was nothing special."

"That's not true."

"What I mean is, I was lost in all the normal ways. I was about to start my third year at Rutgers." A silent beat. "The State University of New Jersey."

"I know it."

"It's a good school!"

"No, I know!"

"It is!"

"I know!"

"I grew up in New Jersey, in a town of doctors and engineers, and I did well at school, and I had two best girlfriends. We went to New York alone on the train to see the Smashing Pumpkins and we came back screaming and sober. I didn't want tattoos. I was neutral to myself, I had no particular flavor, I was just trying to say yes to the right things. I was an only child and my parents were divorced but not mean to each other and their houses were mostly quiet, and for fun I went with Dee and Eunice to the mall and spent babysitting money on clothes from the Gap and the Limited. Does this tell you enough?"

"Almost. Did you go to prom?"

"Yes! With someone named Danny DiVito—*Di* with an *i*!—from Maple Borough High. In a strapless mauve dress from Contempo. We went with a big group of Danny's friends. I could always go with the flow."

"OK. Now that's everything."

"That *was* everything! I spent the first two years of college moving between different groups. There was the newspaper, which I quit because frankly I was too nice and I didn't want to cold-call a football player and ask how it felt to be reamed by Virginia Tech. The Game Room people were easy to join because anyone can join a game, but they were so competitive, and it seemed cowardly to hide from life's risks by playing thirty-six hours of Risk. I hung out with a group of drunk girls for a while, but they were always spraining their ankles and they told stories in falsely cool tones about barely sensate hookups that scared the crap out of me. I hadn't had sex yet and didn't want to stumble into it drunk, so I wandered away from them, too."

"Isn't it OK, not to know your place at nineteen?" Monica considers the girl on the suitcase, who has licked her thumb and is using it to rub lint off the exposed end of a roll of Lifesavers. "Not every nineteen-year-old finds her way to a summer in France—you must have had some kind of compass."

"I spoke French because I was raised bilingual—it was an accident; my mother is from Belgium. But in college I just kept taking more languages because I liked the way that when you start a new language, you can sort of *feel yourself being.* It's not automatic anymore. You can't just go with the flow—you have to will yourself to make thoughts; your tongue visits places in your mouth it's never been. You're in Beginners Italian and you roll your *r*'s and suddenly you're a specific lady named Giovanna or Patrizia, even if you're sitting around in east New Jersey picking gum from under your desk. From the moment you choose the fake name in class—*Mi chiamo Giovanna*—it's a simple way to feel like a person. To say: *Voglio comprare questo cappello.*"

"That *is* good. What does it mean?"

" 'I want to buy this hat.' "

Monica closes her eyes with serene forbearance.

"It's significant! You don't just buy a hat. You've bodied forth into the world *to buy a hat*!"

"Because you're Italian?"

"Because you're *not* Italian, so you have to *be* Italian! So that's what I did in college. Learned more languages so I could turn to my neighbor and say, *'Hal tawadu an tashtari mawzah?'* "

"What's that?"

" 'Would you like to buy a banana?' in Arabic."

"OK. We need to go."

"We need to go where?"

"Jean." She looks up at me from under her brows as if to say, *You know.* "You've repackaged this summer over the years—first he created you, then he used you. You lost yourself in the story. He's the only actor! Where are you? *Who were you and what did you do?*" Her voice swells, filling the chamber like steam.

The picture on the surface of the water remains: The girl is there, sitting on her suitcase, Lifesaver raking across her teeth. She's surrounded by a few other students, also waiting to be collected.

"The summer of '98 . . ." The flames flare again around Monica's black halo, and I look closer and— "Is that a beret with the center cut out?"

"Don't get distracted. How did you end up in France?"

"All I'd ever taken was a scattered bunch of language classes. After two years, and with all my teachers telling me I was smart, I started to believe I could do more, maybe major in something more analytical, like English or history. I had this idea that I might like medieval art, because when we visited my grandparents in Belgium, we used to drive from their home in Ath—spelled *A-t-h* but pronounced 'at' like a town that forgot to name itself—to Ghent and Bruges and Brussels and see lots of tall pictures of priests and saints with endlessly knuckled fingers praying and pointing up. A baby Jesus that was dusty and stringy before the Renaissance fed him protein shakes. I liked the churches with clover-shaped windows and lacy lead contours for slippery Jell-O colors. There was something about medieval art that resonated with me. It was awkward; it didn't seem to have itself figured out. It didn't know what a beautiful body was or a loving mother or a rational space. It was the teenager of art history, emotionally unregulated, weeping, laughing at butts, full of heart—sometimes literal heart, in dried chunks, in jewelry boxes. And it needed *me.* I could help figure it out with all these languages I knew for no reason, Latin and French and Spanish and Arabic, keys dangling at my side looking for locks."

"You tried to take an Introduction to Medieval Art course in the spring of your sophomore year, but you quit."

"I didn't have room in my schedule." I'm lying, but hopefully she won't—

"That's a lie. Tell me why you dropped David's class."

I take a deep breath.

Chapter 6

"My parents opted out of the meal plan my freshman year and instead gave me an envelope of cash at the start of each semester to spend on groceries and feed myself. Whatever was left was mine, and if I blew it all, I'd starve. No one but me used the dorm kitchenette, a tiny, unventilated room with a single burner next to the men's showers on the fourth floor of Hampton Hall.

"After my parents' divorce, in middle school, I was alone in the evenings a lot. I learned pretty quick how to make pasta. But when I got to college, I had to change it up. I loved delicious things, but I also knew I'd get scurvy if no one gave me vegetables, so I made creamy pasta bakes with spinach, big eggy messes with cheddar and peppers. I made a lot of mistakes at first because I wasn't using cookbooks, I was just predicting what would happen, and what happens if you cook beans without soaking them is that you get a kind of gas that feels like appendicitis and you have to have a premed student named Daryl palpate your organs and talk you down from going to the emergency room and give you Gas-X while your whole dorm looks on, excited for you to die.

"Cookbooks put me off because the covers always featured beaming fat ladies holding ducks by the ankles or standing confidently by a gorgeous copper pot that would have been laughable in my bean closet.

"But one day I wandered past a used bookstore and saw *Cuisine Économique—Economical Cooking*—in a bin out front. The cover photo was ugly, some pears half stewed in something pink so they all looked like deflated old tomatoes and scattered blindly with some garbage, which turned out to be almonds. Something white, maybe butter, had been forgotten nearby and was oozing. A cook a lot like me was behind this, I felt. Someone for whom 'European' doesn't mean rich or classy; it means a tolerance for bacteria.

Someone sloppy and cheap but with a nose for the good stuff. That was how my food got good."

"What did you make?"

"A cheese soufflé you could prep in five minutes, a lamb stir-fry with cumin that tasted like the work of a cool mom who'd been backpacking. Lasagna that cost about two bucks and would feed you for a week. Stews made from hocks and bones that I sometimes got for free from the Italian butcher like a stray dog. The food was good for me—but bad for everyone else. The boys walked fresh and soft and tacky in their towels out of the dorm showers and right into my steaming emanations of stewing garlic and searing gut, and they made barf faces and waved their bony arms and said, 'Jesus, Jean!' It was regular, reliable, every time I cooked, to hear some distant, genuinely distressed voice down the hall yelling, 'WHY DOES IT ALWAYS SMELL LIKE SOUP AROUND HERE??? I'm TRYING to STUDY!!!'

"Once or twice when a nice person appeared in the doorway and said, 'Hey, what are you making?' and I inevitably showed them a brown thing in a bowl, or a pink thing I was browning, or a paste made of anchovies and oil spread over my fingers and deep under my nails like I'd tunneled out of prison, they would cringe and walk away.

"So when I went to David Harwell's Introduction to Medieval Art lecture in January of 1998, and I folded down the wooden seat in the lecture hall and put my backpack under my legs and pulled out a spiral notebook and sat in the glorious idle intake of the first day of class, David Harwell put his notes on the lectern, took a deep breath, stopped short, and said, 'Is someone here eating hot food?' Everyone looked around. No one was eating hot food. But I had been searing oxtail fifteen minutes earlier, and it was all over me. I went red and sunk into my seat and smelled myself slowly, taking in the sweet beefiness of my own surfaces: my hair, my flannel shirt, my skin the skin of a bull's ass-end, plus carrots and celery and thyme and heat and butter.

" 'Hot food is not allowed in here,' he said.

"And I was hot food."

Chapter 7

"I picked up my bag and shuffled off, and I didn't go near the history department the rest of the year. But on my way out of the building, I saw a flyer on the department corkboard for the Château Plaisy Summer School—a medieval art history intensive in France. If they accepted you, everything was free, even the flight, and you got a whopping sixteen credits, the equivalent of four semester-long courses. Coming back from summer vacation with those credits would mean I'd be able to make up for two years of indecision and declare myself a history major. So I filled out the application and—shockingly—they accepted me. My parents were so impressed: I wasn't just bobbing along; I had been chosen. I was going to Europe with a team of experts."

"Why didn't you take a shower and try another history class?"

"I was too ashamed." Thinking about it now, the smells come back to me, the saturated fabrics of my little dorm room, the nubbly burger-stinking jersey sheets, the garlicky spinach mist in my hoodies. The things I did, the places I touched, greedily, imprudently. I know where this leads, and I can't face it. "I asked for your help in a weird moment—the email from David, it knocked me off-kilter. But I'll be fine now. I won't go to the Festschrift—"

"Do you have to spit when you say it?" Monica dips back, still perched on the rim of the marble tub.

"I promise, I'll just move on. It's an internal turmoil." *Turmoil:* I've never said it before, and the admission makes my voice wobble. "It'll go away with time."

"It's been two decades. It's getting worse."

"I can live with it. I'll contain it." I feel my eyes welling.

"Then what happened in court this morning, before I answered you?" She rises and walks to me. "Internal turmoil?" She puts a finger to my face and catches a tear as it drops down my cheek. "You can't stop weeping, and not just at normal things like the news. At work, at home, in the middle of the night." She rubs my tear into her palm. "Here is a list of things you've wept at in the past month alone, before you even heard from David." She enumerates with her fingers. "Your job, which is, no offense, boring. Commercials for life insurance, pet food, drugs, and diapers (you basically can't watch TV). An aquarium, just point-blank, in a Chinese restaurant. A couple of discarded Christmas trees in the street that looked like they were fucking—which, honestly, should have made you laugh. Keds—Keds sneakers in a window display. I guess they're back. People playing public pianos in train stations, *twice*, neither with any skill."

"That one makes sense!"

"Fine. But Greta Thunberg's voice, anytime, anywhere—"

"It's just—the braids, the moral clarity!"

"You're about to lose your job."

"It's a stupid job anyway! I fell into it when I burned out of cooking."

"Michael. Your marriage. You are hiding so much from Michael, you will wake up a stranger to him." Monica steps back to the tub and ripples a finger across its surface. The college student dissolves, and in her place we see a grown woman in office clothes and a swim cap sitting on a fire escape smoking a cigarette. "You want to talk me through this?"

I redden. "This is me, a few days ago, in the afternoon. I wore a swim cap so Michael wouldn't smell the smoke in my hair, so he wouldn't know I'd been smoking." What was the cigarette for? I don't smoke anymore; I haven't for years. "I wanted to taste the taste of twenty years ago."

"That's right. You wanted to tempt it, to touch just the blue ozone around that world, around those events. You *want* to go back."

"I don't! I was insecure, and I put some naive idea of romance ahead of all the important things."

"You don't remember it right, Jean. It's up to you if you want to scorn your own life, but don't do it based on false premises." She returns to the tub, perches on its rim. "I will be with you. We'll go together. Don't be afraid."

"I can't change what happened." Or maybe—is this why Monica's here? "Can I?"

"No."

"Then *leave me alone.*" The moment I say it, I realize that I never want her to leave me, that her steadiness is slowly fortifying me and her presence is like a single golden star in a black night and either I follow it or I am lost.

"In France, at this party next week, everyone will be writing David's life for him, laying tributes at his feet." Her arm swoops down across her body. "The magnitude of his achievement, now finally visible in its culmination, will be sung in chorus, painted on canvas. Do you know your story? *Your* story?"

Monica taps the water and the picture comes into focus again: There she is, little Jean, nineteen, sitting on her suitcase. An older man with a neat white beard gestures to her and to other students, seated similarly around her. Teen Jean gets up—wide-leg jeans frayed at the heel, a tight V-neck T-shirt—and pulls out the handle of her suitcase and rolls it behind her, following the white-haired man toward the sliding glass doors of the airport.

"Now," says Monica. "Be brave. Come with me. And you might get your life back. I'll even turn this thing off," she says. I hear a click as she holds up a voice recorder and winks.

PART II

✦ ✦ ✦

Summer 1998: Windows

Chapter 8

Professor Neary is in his late sixties, white-haired and white-bearded, rumpled as we all are from our overnight flights. He's the one who held the sign at the arrivals terminal like a hired driver: "Château Plaisy Summer School." When he greeted us, he spoke with a British accent and was curt and cold. Students accrued and I saw David Harwell, the Medieval Art 101 professor from home whose class I had run out of just a few months ago, making the rounds with a clipboard. He didn't recognize me, just ticked my name off a list, introduced himself (he also had a British accent, although different from Neary's), and moved along. In our jeans with our bad airplane breath, America suddenly an anecdote, we students were put in two vans and conveyed, dozing, to a place in the middle of France full of flat green fields, stony villages, few tourists, a ton of cows, and the castle where we were to live for the next six weeks.

I bumped along in the van full of strangers, lulled to sleep by radio fuzz and repetitive scenery of roundabouts and roadside restaurants, overhearing bits of small talk—"Where are you from?" "Raleigh." "Oh wow." If I hadn't been accepted into this program, I would have spent my summer working at Red Lobster with Eunice. I'd have made *tons* of money—Eunice's sister had done it the summer before and told us you could eat other people's lobster if they didn't finish it, and she got so rich she went around the mall smoking weed with the busboys and buying anything she wanted. I remember crying, and Eunice crying, when I told her that we would not share a summer in matching red shirts smoking Parliament lights outside a stucco castle off Route 18 in Wayside, New Jersey, and now I stumble out of a mouth-smelling van before a castle so real, so colorful and majestic, I wonder if *I* am made of stucco.

The castle is not what I expected—nothing out of Robin Hood, no archers' slits or ramparts, but rather a three-story mansion in pinkish-gray stone, with a high, sloping slate roof busy with chimneys and spires, flanked by two turrets, the whole thing crawling with ivy. It's the first of July. Crickets are shrieking, the air is hot and dusty, and even so this place glows with ancient good health. Or maybe that's just a trick the mind plays when it hasn't seen a 7-Eleven in twenty-four hours. No, it's not just not-fake, or not-home, or not-modern; it's beautiful. Imposing but not incalculable. There's something domestic about it, its towers so neatly arranged, like utensils upright in a tin, shiny in the sun, so prettily pointed. A lush and storied setting, yawning, unpeopled, ready for actors as it absorbs us dumbstruck students.

Everyone clusters at the entrance to the castle with their luggage and their questions, so I turn away from the giant double wooden doors and wander toward the driveway, where a scrubby terrier lies on his side in the sun. He senses my approach and rolls onto his back, his paws swaying with his breath. I squat next to him and give him the works—the ears, the tummy, right behind the tail. His lips flop down, exposing his yellow teeth, but I can tell he's smiling.

"His name is Robert. The dog," says a singsong voice in French.

I look up to see a lanky man, maybe in his late thirties, ruddy and relaxed with an oversize tool belt strapped around his waist.

"Robert?"

"Oh, it's a funny name for a sack of fleas. But him, too, he's a Bourbon." The man says this not as a joke but as a fact, and he squints toward the distant landscape, as if surveying everything young Robert will one day rule.

"You're a Bourbon, are you?" I say to the dog, his crusty eyes rolled back, abandoned to pleasure with the entitlement of a louche king.

"I'm Jojo. I take care of the place." Jesus, and the man is named like a dog.

"I'm Jean. Is everyone waiting to meet the prince?" I look at the crowd milling about in front of the doors to the château.

"Oh, he's not here now. He's very busy. But you'll meet him soon. He's a great guy. You're lucky to be here under his protection." *Protection*? From what? The English? The Venetians? Mosquitos? Taxes? "This house has stood for eight hundred years." Oh, time, protection from time, from the contamination of the present. "Come on, you want to see the chickens?"

I want nothing more.

Twenty minutes later, I wander back from the chicken coop with Jojo, with three brown eggs in my hands, to find that everyone has disappeared from the gravel drive and the castle entrance. Jojo skips through the grand doors—I hear him holler *"Allo?"* into the cavernous reception hall, where I see my suitcase clustered with the others. He comes back out, and something catches his eye off to one side of the castle. "Ah," he says, waggling his eyebrows, making a face I'd make if I heard the Mister Softee jingle at the beach. "They're in the chapel." He points to a building nestled into the greenery not far from where we stand, sort of a mini castle of its own, topped with a cross.

I'm jet-lagged and parched and confused by the late-afternoon heat, but when I slip through the front door of the chapel and swat away a burgundy velvet curtain, I'm in a seasonless place, deli-cold, populated by stone strangers in fancy clothes. The sound of Neary's voice leads me a few paces into the church toward an alcove where I find everyone gathered around a white marble sculpture of a woman sleeping.

"She died in childbirth in 1302." *Of course. Not sleeping. Very dead.* "This gisant was originally paired with that of her husband, Hubert of Burgundy, but his tomb was destroyed in the revolution."

"This *what*?" asks a guy my age in a sky-blue polo.

"Gisant," says Neary. "A sculptural figure like this, lying flat on its back."

"Wonder why they spared her," muses David Harwell, standing by Neary.

"She's so pretty," says a small young woman with long, curly black hair.

"Ah," says Neary. "Yes, um, what's your— Never mind. I'll learn names later. It's not an irrelevant point. This is a *tomb,* a marker of *death.* But look at her: fresh as a daisy. Beautiful." Though she lies flat, her robes fall straight down as if she were still standing; her pointed fingers are interlaced at her abdomen, waiting sweetly for her baby to grow. "This religion—Christianity—celebrates death. Welcomes death. Why?"

A stern-faced, redheaded student in his early twenties, stocky and holding a wide stance and wearing a shirt buttoned up to the last button, says, "Resurrection. Death is new life."

"Yes. This is of enormous importance. Romans— *Shoo!*" Neary flings his veiny hands out. "Romans chucked their dead outside the city walls. Christians bring them in. Look at this dog." A white marble puppy, with a short nose and floppy ears, sits folded up at the feet of the noblewoman. Stone, like her, but alive, too. "You could toss him a bone."

✦

Coming out of the church, I start to register who everyone is. The redhead who was very confident about resurrection, his name is Patrick. I didn't even know people this Irish Catholic still existed—he has eleven siblings, I heard him say, not as a joke. My dad's family is Irish American, and I always thought I looked pretty Irish—freckles, sandy hair, button nose. But I feel like a tabby housecat seeing my first Bengal tiger, the true undiluted species of which I am a watered-down descendent. Patrick is a master's student at a place called St. John's and wears flat-front khakis and doesn't say much. He looks at me with deep suspicion. I have the feeling that in his eyes, a lot of secondhand knowledge about "liberal secular young coeds" hangs around my neck, and while for the moment I just stand here in baggy jeans looking lost, moments earlier or moments from now I was or will be searching for penises to put in my mouth and taking the Lord's name in vain.

Patrick does not give this same suspicious side-eye to Caitlin, who's a Southern Baptist, even though she's ten times prettier than I am. She wears nice brown eyeliner that matches her shiny brown blowout and she smiles and says "y'all" all the time. She's a master's student from Texas Christian University and knows everything there is to know about the Bible, which, I'm learning, seems to be a prerequisite for studying medieval art. Then there's the soft-spoken girl with the frizzy black ponytail down her back who spoke in the church. I thought she was maybe even younger than me, but she's a graduate student named Judith who just finished her first year of a PhD at Harvard. She says "Hiii" to me like it's an apology, shrinking, descending, and then she puts her eyes elsewhere and spins away.

Brice and Sam are married graduate students at Princeton. Brice, unsmiling and athletic, studies old buildings and his wife, Sam, unsmiling and athletic, is learning to restore them.

Sigrid is small and blond, a completely incongruous package for what's inside. American, but studies with Neary at Cambridge. Her hair is cropped to the jaw, never styled, and often flopped over her face. When she talks, it's like a bookie—in a low voice, always smoking, telling you whatever she's telling you like it's an expensive tip, like you should take it to the bank. "Watch out for Neary," she says to me outside the chapel, chin down, eyes at the upper limits of their sockets, as if she's aiming a gun at the old professor. "He's a tippler."

"What does that mean?"

"He's in a bad mood until noon. The good news? There's always wine at lunch." She stubs out her cigarette on the bottom of her running shoe, carries the butt to a planter, and buries it in the potting soil like a body. She looks back at me and raises her eyebrows. I nod to acknowledge the tip.

The one in the sky-blue polo who asked about gisants in the chapel is Yoni. An undergrad, like me. Georgetown. There's something of the elegant tourist about him, detached, tracking us all coolly like someone who's signed up for a cultural event and will soon be at drinks. He has a bony spade of a chin and a narrow little bird mouth that looks almost sweet at rest but slices way up into his cheeks like a jester's when he smiles. He's my age but more adult, carries himself like he has a retirement plan. Dresses like a businessman in the Grand Canyon, blazers and shorts; goose-down vests and a hiker's canteen over Brooks Brothers shirts and tennis whites. Maybe I've just never met a classy person from Maine before, but I think he has style.

Then there's David Harwell. Brown hair, average height, quite trim. Maybe in his mid-forties. Dressed like a teacher—khaki pants and a button-down. Nothing remarkable. When he came out of the chapel, he looked at the eggs in my hands and smiled with wonder, as if I'd done something miraculous.

Chapter 9

On the morning of our first full workday, Professor Neary, in a straw hat, gathers us at the foot of the stairwell in the castle's entry and asks, "What are we all doing here this summer?" I am thrilled he has addressed the question. "The truth is, we really don't know."

Oh great.

He emits a dry little cough from the back of his throat, which, it turns out, is his laugh. David Harwell jumps in.

"Let's start with what we *do* know. This region possesses over a *hundred* churches, all stylistically grouped as 'Romanesque' but each one different from the next. Tourists ignore them—this is one of the least touristy bits of France—and researchers have snubbed them, too. Why? Well, first of all, it's a logistical issue: The sheer quantity of Romanesque churches here is daunting. Someone's got to show you where they all are, make sense of their basic differences. And then, to many people, the Romanesque is just the dull phase before the sexy Gothic." He wiggles his hips to *sexy Gothic* and I feel embarrassed for him. "But once you attend to it"—he lowers his voice, is almost secretive—"there's so much to admire in its human scale, so much ambition in its humble harmonies, its odd visions. You'll see all of life—"

"And buckets of death," says Neary.

"Inside and outside these buildings." David Harwell pauses, scrutinizing all of us as if we might faint in excitement, and actually, most of the grad students look like they're about to. "So, someone needs to create an archive, a foundational map, to guide people to the beauty and significance of these churches. And that's what you're here to do."

If David Harwell has made this work seem noble and important, Neary now makes it sound corrupt. "You're being paid for it—not in cash, of course." It turns out that Prince Germain de Bourbon-Saxe is furious that everyone knows Cannes and nobody knows Moulins, and in return for the light we hope to shine on his ancestral region, he will house and feed us in this, his very own castle. "Now," Neary says, "time to get to work!" He is about to read from a paper in his hands when David interrupts.

"We should perhaps say that you won't have regular assignments, as with a normal course. Rather, every day we'll visit a church, and you'll have a job, an aspect of the church to account for. At the end of the day, we'll come back here and collate our research. You advanced art and architectural historians will be well equipped to measure, document, and describe these churches. Those of you who are new to this—we have a couple of undergraduates—you'll learn by doing."

David Harwell looks like he wants to say more, but Neary jumps in: "Can we get *doing,* please?"

"Sorry, James. Go ahead."

"OK," Neary says, turning back to the paper in his hands, "plan and elevation: Sam and Brice." Sam and Brice high-five without making eye contact. They have bags of tools over their shoulders. They are fit and focused, and I envy them.

"Sigrid, you'll take the portals and capitals. Caitlin, I want you on the decorative. Patrick and Yoni, you team up on devotional objects, from ancient to modern."

Patrick, a padded camera bag over his shoulder, nods dutifully; Yoni's head rotates slowly toward Patrick, who does not look at him.

Neary picks up again. "Judith, you'll look at construction and materials." Child-size Judith nods with a grave face, like this is a big responsibility. "And finally, Jean—" He looks up from his list, trying to deduce who "Jean" is. I wave. "You're on apertures." I don't know what this means—*aperire,* Latin, "to open"?

"Apertures," I repeat shakily, hoping he'll elaborate.

"Good." He flings his gaze over the assembled group with something like regret. "There are two vans. I don't care who goes with me and who goes with David, just get in."

Sigrid, somehow already sunburned, tucking her hay-colored hair behind her ears, sidles up to me as I wander out the castle doors toward the vans.

"Openings," she whispers.

"What?"

"Apertures are openings."

"Ew."

She hits my arm. "Like windows and doors."

"Oh. What am I supposed to do with them?"

Sigrid shrugs. "Measure them."

I'm going to be measuring windows all summer? "But why?"

"It's part of the building. We're studying the whole building. Little things can tell you a lot." She levels a stare of deep meaning at me and then cuts me off to get into the van.

✦

Later that night, I lie in a four-poster bed in the circular stone room I share with Judith and Sigrid, staring up at the underside of the wooden canopy, painted in a deep blue with sharp golden stars. Neary and Harwell assigned us this room, two stories up, inside one of the tall turrets; Yoni and Caitlin are in adjoining children's bedrooms, down the hall from us in the body of the castle. Sam and Brice got a marital suite one flight up, and Patrick's alone somewhere with Jesus. I don't know where David and Neary sleep—there must be six or seven bedrooms here I wouldn't know how to find.

The windows in our bedroom are open, begging for a cross-breeze, and we hear the humanlike moans of the sheep that live on the great lawn behind the castle. It should feel strange to share a wide, round room with two other women, to watch them lay their clothes out in stacks by their pony-high beds, our bodies in quiet pursuits open to view, but it doesn't. Something's prepared me for this, some deep history of storytelling about orphans or maidens. I don't know why, but I feel suddenly, intensely feminine. I have always worn baseball caps and been good at math. I'm built like a pillar with boobs, and I feel lucky to be so manly when women complain about their pear shapes and apple bottoms. But now, when I exhale, I feel my ribs coming together, and this gesture of contracting my ribs makes me feel exquisitely small, like my waist is a thing that should be held, held down, held in someone's hands, squeezed. Framed in new geometries, in a room that's a circle and a bed that's a vise, I should be wrung out and pressed with passion.

Sigrid's filled half a bookshelf with books and papers, and now she stacks little aluminum packets on the other half. She catches my eye.

"Pure protein. I'm marathon training."

"Oh gosh, that's impressive," says Judith, loopy and overly kind. Judith sits on her own bed—she took the slightly smaller one without even being asked to—brushing her long, curly hair, making it frizzier. She holds the cascade of hair over her shoulder, running the paddle brush down rhythmically, and I wonder whether she, too, is being changed by this castle, whether she, too, suddenly feels like a princess and is grooming herself to be taken and squeezed. Judith, shy and practical, is going soft and receptive, preparing herself to be consumed. I don't feel so stupid now. After all, Judith goes to Harvard.

Chapter 10

After breakfast this morning, Professor Neary squinted at me and said, "Joan, is it?" I was so surprised to be addressed at all that I said yes. So far, I have only mapped my way to three destinations, starting at the entrance hall: straight through the ground floor reception room (piano, oil paintings, padded armchairs) to the back lawn; down a corridor and up a circular winding stair to my bedroom in the tower; or through a corridor in the opposite direction and down a flight to the underground kitchen. Now Neary pointed me toward a wide staircase leading up from the foyer. "Go to the third floor. Big door—you'll think it's locked, but just push. That's the library. David's there; he's got some books for you."

There must be twenty steps between floors, and you feel the heat accumulate with every step. Panting as I arrive at the summit, I lean into the heavy wooden door and it makes an alarming squeak and I'm in the library. It's not a "library" like where you get murdered in Clue, a fancy room with a wingback chair and a fire; it's actually kind of a mess, a long, low-ceilinged, musty wood-paneled room, under the eaves of the castle, along its central body, between the towers. It's lined with shelves, and books in stacks, and cluttered with too much furniture. David Harwell sits at a desk.

"Can I help you?" It isn't said like a customer service prompt—it is an invitation, genuine, his tone leaping up and landing softly on slippered feet.

"Professor Neary told me to come here and get some books."

"Sure, what are you researching?"

"Well, I don't really know anything about medieval art."

"Ha." A gentle puff of laughter. "I haven't heard someone say that in years. What have you been assigned? What's your background?"

My background? "I haven't taken any medieval courses. Or, actually, I haven't taken any history courses. I applied for this because I saw a flyer in the—" *In the history department after you kicked me out of class for smelling beefy.*

"Ohhhhhh." He nods and looks at me with sudden understanding. "I know who you are."

"You do?" *Beef girl! I remember you!*

"You're the undergraduate."

"I'm the only one?"

"No, actually, there are two of you. And one of you is also from Rutgers."

"It's me."

"But I don't know you."

"No. I haven't taken your classes. No offense!"

"No, no, of course." I'm relieved—he really *doesn't* recognize me. "Well, this is a wonderful place to start learning about the medieval."

At this point, I begin to feel frustrated. "Yes, I know. *That's why I came to the library.* Neary sent me."

"Of course! Sorry. It's the jet lag. I'm not thinking straight. Yes, we ordered some course materials for you undergrads. Let me look . . ."

I follow him around a few makeshift carrels—ornate side tables and gilded vanities moved here and cleared off and paired with chairs of suitable heights and unsuitable styles. The spines of the books that line the walls are all muted and earthy, burgundy and dusty rose; a big atlas sits closed on a stand, blue-gray and glossy like a wet elephant. But he takes me to an open suitcase full of ugly modern books with flimsy cardboard covers and castles on the front.

"So you've done no medieval history?" he asks.

I shake my head.

"What's your major?"

"I don't have one."

He furrows his brow. "What year are you?"

"I'll be a junior."

"So you have to declare this fall."

"Yeah. I thought maybe with these credits, this summer, I could switch to history as a major."

"Seems feasible. Why history?"

"I used to visit medieval churches and museums a lot, with my family. Like, we're not religious, but"—he kneels at the suitcase, rifling, but he looks up at me occasionally to show he's listening—"I always thought the art was beautiful, but also . . . kind of ugly?" I can feel myself blushing, afraid I've said something stupid, but he races to agree.

"Yes! No, you're right. It's a—a cosmology of extremes." He says this half consciously while focusing on his search for the right books in the suitcase. But then he stops and looks up at me. "So if you haven't done any history, what have you been taking?" It's a big university, and my advisor is someone whose name I saw on a slip at orientation and whom I have never met in person. This conversation suddenly feels sensible. I'm being cared for.

"Languages."

He laughs again, although I have no idea what's so funny. I can't believe how easily he laughs at the things I say, like I'm a foolproof fit for his sense of humor, like nothing I say can go wrong.

"What languages?"

"Spanish, Italian, Latin, although I dropped that. I started Arabic. I took a course on hieroglyphics. That was cool."

He starts to laugh again but finds himself surprised by his own interest.

"Could you speak—what is it—"

"Well, spoken Egyptian is lost. The closest you can get is Coptic."

"Of course."

"Which I haven't studied. But I could decipher a Middle Kingdom inscription. With a dictionary."

"That *is* impressive. All this must feel very modern, then." I don't know what he means.

"These churches. The medieval."

"Oh, that's OK, I don't mind." This time he smiles and narrows his eyes as if to see me more sharply. Then he draws a quick breath and stands up. He hands me a few books with university press insignias on the back, all shields and swords and snakes.

"This probably seems like a lot, but just—here—" He leans his head to the side a little so he can read the spines and he points to one of them and says, "Start with that. For the purposes of this summer, you want to understand the general framework of patronage and the dominance of religion in daily life. Why is there an expensive, architecturally ambitious church every five miles around here, on this flat farmland?"

I stare at him. He's close to me now and I can smell him and I'm a little scared. He doesn't smell like aftershave, abstract and applied; he smells like animal warmth, like breath after bread. I've only ever seen him from a distance. At the front of a lecture hall, at the other end of a hallway, disappearing into an office. So far on this trip, he's always been with Neary or one of the graduate students, arms folded, like a portrait of himself. Now he's touching my fingers and his intake of breath is slightly stuffy and he wears a scuffed gold wedding band. There's nothing overly surprising about any of it, just frighteningly vivid, David Harwell being a person in the world very close to me. I feel like a city person suddenly close to a horse.

"It's intriguing, isn't it?" he continues. "Who wanted these churches here? Who paid for them? Why is each one such a jewel box, so different from the next? What if you had competing skyscrapers in a place where society was predominantly poor and agrarian—I don't know, Indiana or Arkansas?" He's slipped into teacher mode, his questions lovingly articulated. He's gotten a little carried away, been lifted a centimeter or two off the ground by his passion for this subject, how badly he wants me to see it. He twitches out of teacher mode, lands back on the ground. "Where are you from?"

"Indiana."

He bellows a big "HA! No!"

"Yeah. And then later we moved to Arkansas."

He tilts his head. "Come on."

"I'm from Monmouth. New Jersey." He looks at his watch.

"Gosh," he says. "I have to get back to work, but so do you, I should think." He points to the books in my arms. "I won't assign you pages per day, but you'll need to get familiar with some architectural and iconographic terms."

I'm ashamed of my stupid joke. Is that why he suddenly dismissed me? At first when we spoke I was effortlessly funny, and then I tried too hard and ruined it and he had to feign looking at his watch to get rid of me. *Stupid,* I think. I wish I'd said less, wish I'd been simpler and easier.

"Aha! Here we go . . ." He leans down and picks up one more book. "Speaking of iconography. This book is the key." He lays the paperback on top of the stack in my arms. On the cover is a bald guy on his knees, staring up at a smiling woman in a starry blue sky with a knife in her throat: *The Golden Legend.* "After the Bible, this was the most widely read book in Europe for five hundred years. It was the lives of the saints compiled in *The Golden Legend* that everyone knew, that everyone told and retold. You'll see these stories come to life in stone, in wood, in stained glass." I'm barely listening, I'm so relieved that he called me back. But I won't make the same mistake; no more stupid jokes.

"OK, thanks!" I say and run away. Just before I push the massive door open with my hip, I hear him say, "Hey!" I turn around. In a few steps of his long legs, he reaches me.

"This will also be a help to you here," he says, and David Harwell gives me a Bible.

Chapter II

> In the beginning when God created the heavens and the earth, the earth was a formless void and darkness covered the face of the deep, while a wind from God swept over the face of the waters.

That's actually better than I expected. Although if it's formless, how does it have a face? Yeah, this sucks.

I chuck the Bible off the bed and wince as it lands with a recriminating thud. My hand dips down to the dark wood shelf beside my bed. There are books on local monuments, a genealogy of the Bourbons, a wine lovers' magazine from 1992—and a lime-green hardback, sized for a child's hands, with a picture of a white mountain dog on the cover. *Belle et Sébastien.* I flip the book open to the first page, where there's a scant ink illustration of a twisting female form, her dress whipped by the wind. I read the French text:

> When the woman had crossed Saint-Martin, no one had paid attention to her. Who would have believed that she was off that high, toward the pass, with her big gypsy skirts, her bad low shoes, protected only by the shawl that covered her from head to hips?

Now *this* is a good beginning. God can't compete with this story. There's no way into his showstopping allness, his windy preexistence. I feel stupid about it, that I can't fit the obviously important book in my mouth, can't taste it; that I want a gooey after-school snack instead. But this wandering woman, nameless, in bad shoes—*low* shoes: I wrap my mind around the alpine wind that bends her skirts. I can follow her. I find her footsteps in the snow. I read on.

Chapter 12

It's our fourth evening here, and every evening has been the same, which is to say equally magical. A banquet table twenty feet long and dark and grooved that seems important and ceremonial, seems like it should come out once a generation for weddings, lives out on the lawn behind the castle, and the sun stays up late, but it loses its edge and the grass gets a bit blue. Jojo the groundskeeper and his wife, Victoire, make dinner. (You never know who'll get a human name around here; Victoire passed a sheep the other day and said, "Move it, Maurice.") There's always wine at dinner and often at lunch, as Sigrid promised. The first night, dinner was a terra-cotta dish the size of a paddling pool with about fifty chicken thighs in it, and huge sprigs of thyme and whole lemons. Then whitefish stew with tomatoes and rice on the second night, and cubes of pork with black olives last night.

Neary and Harwell sit at one end of the table, always, and the rest of us have settled into hierarchical seating like good subjects without even being told to. The older grad students—Sam and Brice (academic Barbie and Ken), Catholic Patrick, intense Sigrid with her blond bob and bookie's tips—are up near the kings. The younger grad students and us children—Harvard Judith and Southern Caitlin, me and Yoni—are at the other end, so far away from Neary and Harwell that we can't hear them.

Because I can't follow the thread of the conversation, I see the overall patterns: David Harwell's geniality slowly brings Neary out of his fatigue. The wine must be working, too, because almost every night, David revs Neary up to a state of something like openness, then relaxes, settles back into himself, and smiles with genuine appreciation as Neary tells stories. Harwell seems like a good friend, a good listener.

I see myself as part of a tableau of gabby girls at the far end of the table, joyful and carefree. I do not want to be seen raising a chicken thigh to my mouth, slapping grease and lemon on my chin. I time my bites; they're small and intermittent. I don't eat as much as I would if I were alone with this hot savory joint, if I were holding it over my knees in my dorm room, its fat smell permeating my bedclothes. What do we talk about, the little girls at the table? The content doesn't matter—it might as well be pantomime—but here's a sample: Caitlin the Baptist gospel singer from TCU has a boyfriend named Trent whom she misses so much that she has to plead with David Harwell about making long-distance calls from the castle—apparently there's a telephone in the library, but it's not for student use.

I watch the grad students around Patrick argue a point, interrupting each other, but he sits with a stillness so unusual, so unperturbed, I can't tell whether he's tending to profound inner fires or whether he died of a stroke five minutes ago and if you pushed him, he'd tip over.

"Do you think Patrick believes in evolution?" I ask.

"No way!" says Yoni. "He thinks the communion wafer turns into Jesus jerky in his mouth. You know they believe that?"

"Y'all," says Caitlin, guiding us toward kinder chat. Caitlin's teeth are shiny. Her face smiles at rest. Her boobs are wobbly and good. She's the freshest person I've ever seen. I must be hard to see next to her. I must look like I need polishing or paint, like something wood next to something gold. I look down the table and see Judith smiling in a sickly, ambient way, her chicken untouched.

✦

Every night is like this, and it builds. The first night, I was just happy to be outside eating. But over the next two nights, I became more and more aware of this spread, this structure. Stranger, I started to crave it, to crave the long separation between me and David Harwell, so that I could look out over the scene and fret him with my gaze, uncaught. I don't know why this is happening. I have no thoughts about him—we have barely spoken. It is something structural, it belongs to the scene, it is a thin piece of gut tied across the wooden bow of the table, simply there, tense and thrilling, but nothing I've strung up for my fun. It belongs to the grass, to the table, to the group. I never imagine that any part of it comes from David.

The movements of the sheep on the property are completely unpredictable. For some reason, the sheep have chosen now, maybe nine o'clock, to come wandering over to us. Some days they are all clumped together, frightened, far from us, down by the lake. Sometimes they're chill, roaming, brushing against our legs like faithful hounds. They have numbers on their wool, in blue marker, as if a child that scribbles on carpets got to them. 24, 9, 3. Number 24 came to see me when I was reading a book in the afternoon. I thought it would be afraid of me, but then it ate the page I had just highlighted.

JEAN: I'm so surprised.

MONICA: I know, they'll eat anything.

JEAN: No—surprised by the way I used to read.

MONICA: Without glasses?

JEAN: Without a clue. Without an ego. That student-mindedness, where your job is to be open: I could sit on a garden chair and just chew up a book on—what is that?

MONICA: *Carolingian Civilization.* It's one of the books David gave you.

JEAN: I just gobbled it up like a sheep myself—not worried about whether it was the right kind of feed for me. I would be afraid of a history book like that now. I'd think it was indigestible for me, wrong for my species.

MONICA: You're reading about Charlemagne's four wives and many concubines and you can't even vaguely imagine where on a map you might find Alamannia or Lombardy, but you love it nonetheless. You savor names like Hiltrude of Wormsgau and later that night, you patter about it to

David, and he shapes what you said into an observation about "crises of succession."

JEAN: It was never the same after this summer, the blind confidence with which I could learn. [Turns to Monica] Are you trying to tell me David's responsible for that?

MONICA: I'm not trying to tell you anything, only that you can still read *Carolingian Civilization* if you want. I'll order it for you right now.

JEAN: No thanks.

MONICA: It's beautifully illustrated. You can find it used for a dollar online.

JEAN [with a heavy sigh]: So we're not here to review a case of coupling, to consider dirty little quiet bits of contact. It's about all of this, isn't it? I can have them back, I can play with them, all the ideas in the dollar bin.

MONICA: All the ideas in the world.

It's our first Saturday here, and Neary stands up at the end of the meal. "Look," he begins, "today happens to be the Fourth of July, so you can head into the village if you like, go sing your Yankee Doodles"—I hear someone go "*What?*"—"but keep it civilized. We are guests here. And for *god's sake,* don't mention Bastille Day—that's next Tuesday. Our host has decreed it *strictly* off-limits." There are some giggles and David Harwell half stands next to Neary without stealing his pulpit and adds, "He's not kidding, guys. This castle is the home of a living Bourbon prince. Obviously, they've been—what's the word—"

"Beheaded?" says Brice.

"They're not *in power,*" says David, "but they're still a very old and noble family."

"Rich as Croesus," mumbles Neary.

"I know you haven't met him yet, but believe me," says David, "the prince takes this very seriously—he considers Bastille Day a celebration of murder. So. You know." He puts his finger to his lips: "*Shhh.*" He drops back into his seat.

"Now," Neary resumes, "Jojo and Victoire take Sundays off, so our feast days must be suspended. We'll have to work for our supper. I've made a rota," he says, holding up a piece of paper, "and we will take turns, in pairs, making dinner for the whole group, tomorrow and the five Sundays after that. Two rules: Don't burn the place down, and don't poison anyone. Some of you may have more experience than others, but you're all A students. Just keep it simple. *Via trita, via tuta.*" Some people laugh, but I'm barely listening, I'm too overcome with a lightness, a feeling of excitement, of destiny having come for me. Neary begins to sit down, until someone calls out, "Who's first?"

"Oh yes: Tomorrow . . . Brice and Sam." The two of them nod with confidence.

Chapter 13

The next day, Sunday, is full of little jokes: "Shouldn't you be out plucking a goose, Sam?" and "What's on the menu, chef?," but we all go very silent over dinner, a giant omelet full of snotty, runny strands, unseasoned and hiding hard bits of potato and unrendered lardons. Bowls of plain pasta, cooked to the consistency of wet felt, unbuttered and dried into clumps, disappear quickly given the options. We tear up and ravish the baguettes like battlefield crows. You catch people concentrating on swallowing. Sam and Brice do not acknowledge that it's a disaster, so no one else can, because Sam and Brice are beautiful and competent and not used to failure, especially a wide civic failure like this. David and Neary got a TV set up in the large, formal salon downstairs to watch the last few matches of the World Cup. There's a big game at nine p.m., so it's easy to pretend that our appreciation of the meal has to be rushed and cursory because of that. We thank Sam and Brice and clear the table, carrying continents of globulous wet egg back to the kitchen to be trashed.

But if there's a subtle, unspoken disappointment among the group that night, I am beatific.

MONICA: You are. You're glowing.

JEAN: Something emboldened me—some knife-wielding, golden, brave person appeared in me and told me to find David Harwell that night.

It must be around ten o'clock. I put myself in my best outfit, red bell-bottom sweatpants from Urban Outfitters that cost four hours' worth of babysitting money and a waffle-knit J.Crew "boyfriend Henley" that I stole from Eunice three years ago and still lie about and that shows the perfect amount of the top of my boobs.

Monica's face hits her palm.
Then she looks at the scene again with new attention.

MONICA: You know what? You've done something really beautiful here. It's like a corporate cotton Venus de Milo—the way it drapes.
JEAN: I think so, too! It's like, the best outfit.

Monica snaps her fingers and is suddenly in a cobalt blue version of the same outfit, Henley front-tucked into the bell-bottom sweatpants with a drawstring dangling at her waist, the pants draped perfectly around her hips, like a luscious, precious blue vase. She beams with satisfaction.

There's still an amber evening light leaking into the castle through the wooden shutters, making the stone walls blush, the parquet floors glow. First I wander around the castle corridors, reaching the kitchen door, touching it and turning around, rehearsing in my mind what I'll say and how I'll appear saying it. I look down at my own breasts as if with David's eyes, at my own thighs in rich red swinging down the stone passages, warming up. I look into the big salon, where everyone else sits in ornate bone-colored armchairs watching soccer on TV, Neary shouting insane things like "HE'S MADE HIM LOOK A MUG!" or "STICK IT IN THE MIXER!" David isn't there.

I make my way up the three flights to the library, pause to catch my breath, and push the creaky door open. David looks up straightaway. His hair is mussed from holding his own head in frustration. His hands hover strangely by his ears, and he looks at me with a blank face.

"Hi," I say quickly, and for some reason I sort of skip over to him. I trot. I did not plan to trot. I instantly feel out of control. He actually moves back a little in his chair as if I were planning to skip *over* him like a show-jumping pony, but I freeze a few feet from the desk where he works in front of a big black laptop with stacks and stacks of xeroxed papers.

"Hi," I say again, both too casual and too loud.

"Hi. What's up?" He looks at me with profound confusion, not like I'm a person with unclear motives but like I'm a silver hologram, a squirrel in shoes, a monstrous incongruity.

"OK, well." This is also not how I planned to start. I drafted a speech. An appeal, to be delivered as a silken gift: *David, I can help you. I don't know much about churches, but I can cook.* Instead I find myself saying, "Um. I was thinking. Maybe you could move me up in the rota."

"Sorry?" He looks annoyed—I've interrupted him. I have to make sense now.

"I'm just saying I would like to be the person to make dinner next Sunday."

"Oh! Sure." He shakes his head free of the confusion. "Didn't know *what* you were on about, Jean."

He knows my name. It's been nearly a week, so of course he knows everyone's name, but this is the first time he's spontaneously said mine, released it, warm and soft, like a little mouse, from the box in his throat. "Sorry, my head's elsewhere. I think next Sunday night was supposed to be me and Patrick, so I'm *more* than happy to let you take over. I've got mountains of work to do."

"Is it a lot of work running a summer program?" It doesn't seem like it—there's no homework to grade.

David sighs. "No, I have a book to finish. I should have finished it about four years ago."

"Wow. That's really overdue."

"I *know*!" It comes with a regretful laugh, and he pushes his chair back and sits curled over, staring at the floor, at piles of books and photocopies. "I *know*. And in that time, my wife has written two books and about six articles."

"Woooowww."

"Will you stop it with your 'wows'?" His exaggerated plea crisps his eyes at the edges and makes them a new, thrilling shape, the eyes of a completely new handsome person, and my heart sends one quick pump of something cold and corrosive through me.

"Um. Well. Good luck, I guess." I pivot and run away.

MONICA: Was that part of your plan? To run away?

JEAN: No, I think I meant to say "Have a great evening" and kind of swing my butt a little as I walked out slowly.

MONICA: Maybe it's better that you ran.

Chapter 14

A LIFE OF SAINT LUCY, VIRGIN, KILLED IN THE YEAR 310, FROM *The Golden Legend*[1]

✦ ✦ ✦

Lucy was the daughter of a noble family. Her mother suffered from an incurable flow of blood, but Lucy prayed to Saint Agatha and Agatha appeared in a dream to Lucy and when she woke, her mother was cured. In the name of the saint, Lucy begged her mother to give all their wealth to the poor, which she did. This act of charity drew the attention of the consul Paschasius, who commanded Lucy to sacrifice to the idols. She refused and declared that the Holy Spirit spoke through her: "Those who live chaste lives are the temples of the Holy Spirit." Paschasius threatened to take her to a brothel to defile her body, but she said the body could not be defiled without the consent of the mind. "As for my body, here it is. Ready for every torture."

So he summoned procurers to invite a crowd to rape her. "Let them abuse her until she is dead." But when they tried to carry her off, she was stuck to the ground and could not be moved even with a thousand yoke of oxen. Paschasius thought urine might chase away her magic, so he had strangers piss on her until she was drenched. Still she was stuck to the ground.

---

1 Author's note: The texts of the lives of the saints included here have been condensed, edited, and partially paraphrased for style and clarity. However, the names, places, events, and sequences in these stories are unchanged from *The Golden Legend*, compiled by Jacobus de Voragine in the thirteenth century, and from *The Lives of the Saints*, first compiled by Alban Butler and published in the 1750s, and regularly updated with newly canonized saints.

Paschasius became enraged, so his friends stabbed Lucy in the throat because they did not like to see him upset. With a knife in her throat, she declared that, far across the empire, Diocletian had been driven from the throne. The words she spoke were true, and at that instant Paschasius was seized by Caesar's envoys and dragged to Rome to be tried for corruption. Lucy was buried in the ground. Above her dead virgin body, they built a church.

Chapter 15

Now in the middle of our second week, I'm getting a sense of what we'll be doing all summer: We split up into two vans and we drive to the Church of Saint Someone—Sainte Marthe, Sainte Brigitte, Saint Étienne. Neary told us the churches often claim to have some of the dead saint's bone or flesh in the basement, which they are very proud of, although to me it feels like the start of a *Dateline* mystery about a missing housewife. Mostly the churches are in small villages, sometimes barely more than a dirt intersection. The villages have long, complicated names like Bézélmy-sur-Soave, but I just made that up because they're impossible to remember. Neary gives us a little intro. It's a hot, landlocked part of France, always baking in the sun, and we gather squinting and sweating in the gravel parking lot or the grass patch in front of the squat stone church, and Neary picks a subject. Sometimes it's the church itself—"Well, this *is* a grand portal for so small a structure" or "He used a drill, the stonemason, on this capital"—or it's something else. "You have to imagine you're a peasant farmer, and the bells, the bells that chime from *this tower,* tell you when to start work, when to eat, when to put down your tools and contemplate. Anyone who could hear these bells was bound to a rhythm of life. And we're going to ring them!" He almost never smiles, and when he does, it looks difficult for him, his eyes remaining fixed in diabolical scrutiny but his lips peeling back to reveal old brown teeth and flashes of metal. David stands nearby, nodding, or staring, pleased and intrigued by some aspect of the church he alone has noticed.

✦

At today's church, David finds me wandering around.

"You look at loose ends."

"I'm apertures."

"And what are you supposed to be doing?" This almost makes me angry. Nobody told me!

"I don't know!"

David's demeanor changes; his eyebrows leap up.

"Oh god, I'm so sorry. No one ever—instructed you." I shake my head. "What did you do at the previous site visits?"

"I wandered around looking at the windows and the doors. Sigrid gave me a tape measure"—I pull it out of my crossbody purse, where it's been living unmolested next to cigarettes, lip balm, and the novel I found in my bedroom—"but, like, I can't reach most of the windows."

"Right. Oh dear." He looks at me with concern. "Let me check with Neary. Be back in two shakes."

His little Britishisms. His linen blazer flaps as he spins away from me. The copper beginning of a beard on the side of his jaw flashes in the sunlight.

I sit on a rock that hurts my butt in front of the church, but I'm suddenly aware—I can't place this awareness; where did it come from?—that I might look adorable sitting on this rock with my face in my hands waiting to be "instructed," so I stay there. I know David Harwell will soon return, and I imagine this is a charming sight for him, me, dopey but eager, alone in front of Bézélmont-sur-Buttrock. And return he does, with a stepladder. I let him observe me on the rock for a moment and then I spring up to meet him.

"OK, Jean, it's very simple, really." His hand rises, pointing at the church. "East face. You know churches always face east, right?"

"Yeah," I say blankly, and then I know I can't get away with lying and am just starting to say "No" when he says:

"You don't know *anything*, do you?"

"I *told* you, Mister Harwell—"

"Oh, come on." A gentle laugh—I've been absurd. "David."

"David." Me, too, now, I skate on a little pleasant laugh with him, although I don't know why. I guess because I called him "Mister" like a newsboy, which I didn't even know was funny until it amused him.

"You *did* tell me! And as I said, that's *wonderful.* You stand to learn so much."

"Great."

"So, as usual, Sigrid was right. You note the number of windows and you measure their width and height, and you do the same with the doors."

"Measure? Just like, in centimeters?" *I'm an interior decorator suddenly?* I glance at the church, its sides punctured at regular intervals with openings that are tiny, I now notice, and arched, the shape of the bottom of my Bic lighter.

"Yes, in centimeters." He sizes me up. "You're pretty tall." He holds up the ladder. "Still, this should help."

"And I do the doors, too?"

"Yes, same, get the dimensions. Look, observe. Were they bigger than the last church's? Can you notice patterns in terms of aperture size and construction date?" Now that I have the details of my mission, it seems obviously stupid.

"Can I just ask, why does it matter? Like how big the windows and doors are."

"Ah!" His head ticks to the side, and he narrows his eyes. "What do windows tell us?"

An image of a window, a little box in a children's story, flat and plain, appears in my mind. The more I try to make meaning of it, the more the window seems moronic and mute. "A *window* has never told me anything."

There it is again! David Harwell laughing, a laugh that seems to surprise him and to make him happy. A big, sudden *HA* from which he recovers with a sigh and a moment, again, of considering me with his squinting blue eyes.

"Well, pretend you're building a structure. You have to think about not only illumination but also stability, and defense. How *open* can you afford to be?" He's about to say more when we hear Neary call his name from around a corner, the sound flowing through the church whose holes I'm to measure. David takes my wrist and threads the stepladder over my arm. "You can ask the grad students for help," he says, our eyes locked. "Or you can come find me." He dashes away.

I feel sort of loopy, but I don't know why. It takes me a moment to think what to do next, but before I can, Yoni's standing in front of me.

"Do you want to see the *gayest* thing?"

✦

A few seconds later, Yoni and I are in front of a painted wooden sculpture of a rakish hot guy in a peaked hat with a butt chin who lifts his tunic to show a chiseled thigh. But then I notice there's a spaniel jamming his nose into a big red splotch on the guy's quad.

"Dude, he has the plague."

"Oh, gross. I thought it was a dog bite." The saint has a smattering of an auburn beard along his square jaw, and something quick turns over in my stomach. "He looks like David," Yoni says.

"I was just thinking that!"

"But David's only PLAGUED WITH HOTNESS!" Yoni shouts into the empty church. I smack his arm.

"Oh, he knows it. Everyone knows it. All these bitches are in love with him."

"Stop it. Judith?"

"Oh yeah."

"Caitlin?"

"Wants it."

"Sigrid?"

"Sigrid's gay."

"She *is*? How do you know?"

"Please."

We wander outside and find Sigrid hammering something: "Guys, I found a hammer."

Chapter 16

It's been a week of waking in the mornings in my four-poster bed to the sound of commotion. The hollow clunking of Judith's plastic bottles in her wire caddy coming back from the shower, her pencil-sketch curls now an inky wave. Today, Sigrid, as usual dressed before everyone, reclines on her bed with a difficult and arcane paperback (*Marxist Materiality and Transubstantiation*), chewing a protein bar, checking her watch. Caitlin glides by in a towel, "Mornin', y'aaaallll" echoing down the long, cold hallway.

"Where are we going today?" I croak.

"Sainte Lucie," says Sigrid. "She's a beaut." She puts her book down. "How's apertures?"

"Good," I say. "I know what my job is now, and I have the tools." I can see her weighing very obviously whether to do something generous. She sighs.

"Here, I'm gonna help you." Sigrid grabs a notebook from her nightstand and comes over to my bed. She sits down next to me and draws the outline of a chunky cross. "OK, this is a church. Nave, transept." I've overheard the grad students using these words, and I've seen them in one of the books David gave me. I like them—they are like a foreign language. When I use them, I become a colder version of myself, a specialist of form and structure, a woman with pleated pants and a nude lip pencil. I feel myself building something when I say them: *Vault* draws an arc in my mouth; *apse* snaps shut around a place to pray. "Some of them are gonna have gross fucking add-ons from the nineteenth century or whatever, but pretty much they all have this shape." I'm learning that for most of these medievalists, anything built after about 1400 might as well be a Fisher-Price jungle gym. She jams the tip of the pen into her floor plan. "So for each church we visit, you draw yourself this little outline of a cross and go *tick, tick.*" Here she puts dashes along the church walls. She shows me how to key all the dimensions to the windows in the sketch. "Voilà. You can keep the notebook."

I was listening to Sigrid, but I was also stealing glances at Judith, who is now in underpants and a bra, still toweling her long hair. Her ribs are all visible, her waist scoops in dramatically under them, and I can see the mechanics of her hip bones, their straight sides, their sharp corners tilted out toward me like the corners of a window box. Simultaneously I feel something is wrong with her and I envy her. She must not be like me, greedy and vulgar, a scullery maid with garlicky fingertips. She smells like the invented, the dreamed silky smell of Suave shampoo, and she goes to the school for the smartest people and is going to write knowledge-shaping books about architecture because she likes dry things like symmetry instead of curdled things like cheese. She isn't distracted all the time by appetite. Why do I think that she's lucky, looking at her, when I also see that she's sick? She doesn't seem proud of her thinness, or self-satisfied. She doesn't wear tight clothes or swish around showing off her angles. There is a large gold-rimmed mirror on the gray stone wall by her bed, but she turns away from it toward the window as she pulls her shorts over her stomach, which is concave and, it strikes me in the morning light now, downy.

Sigrid sees she's lost me and follows my gaze to Judith.

"Jesus, Judith, eat a sandwich."

Judith folds forward in a warm laugh, her bony forearms crossing over her middle. "I know," she says, but we don't seem to have touched a nerve. She's goofy about it, she knows it, she possesses this. She loves it? Yes, she is smiling bigger than before. Some secret pleasure of hers is out.

✦

A breakfast of baguettes and salted butter, soft-boiled eggs, jam, coffee, and cocoa is laid out every morning on the rough central worktable in the kitchen, which is half underground, as if pounded into the earth by the turret above it, on the far side of the castle from the turret where I sleep. It's my favorite place in the castle, cool but coal-smelling, with a brick barrel ceiling and a huge stone fireplace and all the copper pans hanging like polished gongs against the back wall. I find Victoire there opening an electric gadget that boils a dozen eggs at a time. She yelps and hisses as she picks up each egg with her naked fingers and throws it angrily in a wicker basket.

"Victoire," I say.

"Ouiiiii." She is deep in battle and doesn't want to be disturbed. But I, too, have my field map, and I need to move my soldiers into place. I need her help. I hand her a piece of paper.

"What's this?" She glances at my writing.

"A shopping list. For Sunday. I'll be the one cooking."

"Smart," she says—it's the respect of one cook for another—as she brings the list closer to her face, reading. She sucks in her cheeks for a moment and says, "Fine, all fine. It'll be in the kitchen for Sunday." It's only Wednesday, but when I think ahead to Sunday, a confidence rushes through me, as if all the meals I made for myself in my dorm were rehearsals for this. I find I can think clearly; I can see all the moves. I have chosen an inexpensive dish made of obvious, easy ingredients. Nothing difficult to source. No one need visit the fowl-butcher or the fishmonger. I am not the fleshy feeder holding the duck by the feet; I am an economist. I am here with the household manager, talking infrastructure and expense. This skill that was so embarrassing back home fits here, finds its perfect theater, its right tools, its just aims. I will impress these scholars and it won't cost a dime. I am happy that no one was in the kitchen yet to catch this exchange between me and Victoire. I want my effort to look effortless, miraculous, a feast for the hungry that sprang from the stone where I touched it.

Chapter 17

A LIFE OF SAINT ANASTASIA, VIRGIN, KILLED IN THE REIGN OF DIOCLETIAN, FROM *The Golden Legend*

+ + +

Anastasia was born into a noble Roman family but raised as a Christian by her mother. She was betrothed against her will to a young man, so she pretended to be weak and sickly so she would not have to see him. But when her betrothed found out she'd been secretly ministering to the needs of the poor, he kept her imprisoned and starved her, hoping she would die, but miraculously he died instead.

Meanwhile, she had three beautiful servant women, all Christians. A local prefect desired them, and when they refused his advances, he had them shut up in a kitchen closet full of cooking utensils. He entered the closet in order to rape them, but God deprived him of his senses and he caressed and kissed the stoves and kettles and pots instead. He satisfied himself with these, and then he went out covered in soot, his clothes ripped. When he found out what had happened, he had the three servant women brought to him and ordered them to be stripped so he could enjoy the sight of their naked bodies. But their clothes clung irremovably to their bodies. The three virgins were finally killed and crowned with martyrdom.

Meanwhile, Anastasia was handed over to another prefect, who tried to rape her and went blind. Then he died. So she was handed to another prefect, with great warnings of her danger. She was thrown in a prison to starve to death but was nourished with food from heaven by Saint Theodora, who had recently gained her martyrdom, and survived. Finally, Anastasia was tied to a stake and burned alive, one of two hundred virgins killed in various ways on the island of Palmaria. A Christian woman buried Anastasia's burnt virgin body in her garden, and above it, built a church in her honor.

Chapter 18

Yoni and I stand outside today's church, arm's length from its cobblestone walls, with our necks craned. Distractingly huge magpies chitter like monkeys and steal branches from a parched vineyard that covers the small slope between the church and the road.

"How am I supposed to measure these windows? Even with a ladder?"

"Beats me." He turns around, leans against the church with his arms crossed. "I'm supposed to be keeping track of devotional objects with Patrick, but he does all the work and barely grunts at me when I try to help." I look confused and Yoni mouths *Homophobe,* then closes his eyes for a moment as he enjoys the morning sun on his face. "Let's just hide behind a tombstone and fuck off."

"Neary and David don't seem to care that we're not doing any work."

"Oh, I'm a poli-sci major. I know anarchy when I see it."

"Did Patrick say something mean to you?"

"No, it's more subtle. He doesn't look at me, he doesn't talk to me. It's so dumb. What does he think I am? I don't even know."

"He's not crazy about me, either."

"Oh, he thinks you're, like, a *jezebel.*" We laugh at the mere sound of the word, gloriously rhinestone-covered to us both. "Wait." His eyes pop wide open. "Did you know he's from *New York City*? Rome for gays!!"

I don't want anyone to be mean to Yoni—Yoni with his alert amber eyes, his gentlemanliness and polish that you're dying to watch crack into mischief—but I'm vaguely aware that our growing closeness owes something to a common enemy, that Patrick has his church and we have ours.

"Come on, help me measure this window," I whine. I put the ladder up, step shakily to the top, and reach as high as I can. My hands still barely reach the bottom of the window. Now Yoni's lighting a cigarette and looking around. The stones in the wall before us are all mismatched, bean-shaped or brick, the color of peanut butter, shoved into mortar that crumbles at the touch. There's a gaping hole in the round chapel wall to our right.

"This church is a piece of shit."

"It's called a *ruin,* Yoni," says Brice, swanning past with a roll of blueprint paper under his arm.

"*You're* a ruin," Yoni shoots back. Then to me, "I'm starting to think that architects are like, to-tal cunts." I wince at the word—my friends don't use it, and it feels nasty and strange.

"Judith's nice."

"She's not an architect, she's a historian. What's up with her, anyway? In the past four days, I've seen her eat one egg white." He lowers his voice. "She's also always in the bathroom."

"What does that mean? Isn't she always just brushing her hair?"

Yoni rolls his eyes. "Where are you from? Inside the rainbow?" Yoni has decided to run with the joke of my being Irish. He likes to call me "Jean McHoulihan!" or "Jean O'Shaughnessy!" in an outrageous Irish accent. The truth is, I like it. I like having an inside joke, feeling known and silly and companionable. Sometimes I suspect I'm supposed to keep the joke going by calling him Jewy Jewburger or something, but then I think there's a five percent chance I'd get it wrong and end our friendship so I just take it.

"Well, what does it mean that she's always in the bathroom?" I ask. Yoni fake barfs on the lawn, and I can't believe I didn't put it together until now. I'm ashamed that I've been so blinded by my own mealtime excesses, I haven't noticed Judith's self-denial, the timing of her disappearances.

Just then Judith comes into sight with David. They're examining the cornerstone together, and I envy their connectedness to each other, to this significant place.

Looking up at the window again, I have an idea. The exterior wall of this church is thick, at least a solid foot across. If I can climb up *into* the window, sitting astride the wall like I'd sit on a horse, then I can balance easily and get the dimensions. The window has one brick in the middle of the sill, like a newly sprouted bottom tooth in the mouth of a baby, but I figure I can either use that as a handhold or hoist myself over it. "Yoni, I need your belt."

"Oh my god, you're gonna kill yourself," he says, gamely removing a tan leather belt. He hands it up to me on the stepladder and I fasten the belt into an "O." I toss it up over the rectangular stone in the middle of the window and pull. Yoni covers his eyes.

"This is insane."

"No, it'll work!" I say, one foot now on the wall as if I could scale it vertically. But I can't get my second leg up; I'm too heavy. I look up again, my hand still on the belt like a subway straphanger's on the strap. This time I choke up on the belt with both hands, hold tight, squat on the stepladder, and jump as hard as I can. I launch myself so high that I have just enough time to whip my hands out from under me and throw them up into the windowsill, gripping the inside of the wall and pulling myself through. My torso falls heavily across the threshold, and the lone brick drives into my chest: "Owww."

I manage to pull myself up and swing a leg over the threshold. I straddle the windowsill, sort of like I planned, but more scratched up, aching and disoriented. For a moment, I sit proudly like an equestrian, both hands on my mount. A farmer across the road who has been watching us from atop his slow-moving tractor shakes his head.

Yoni incants *oh-my-gods* and looks at me through cracks in his hands. "Oh my god, you *did it*."

"I think I broke a rib."

"I think you broke the church." It's only now that I look between my legs and see that the stone at the base of the windowsill has been dislodged. It's askew.

"No, I didn't—" I go to touch the stone and it tumbles off, hitting every step of the ladder and landing at Yoni's feet in the grass.

He's speechless, his jaw dropped. He looks at the stone in horror. He whips his eyes back up at me. We are both frozen. Suddenly he bursts into laughter. I like the idea that I'm funny, that this is a great story, but I'm also red in the face and scared and my throbbing chest confirms that I've done something weird and violent. I have to get down; I have to fix it.

"It couldn't have been important, could it?" I'm asking, seriously.

Sigrid appears from around the chapel wall. "What are you doing up there, you knucklehead?"

Yoni lowers his voice. "Jean broke the church." He bends down and picks up the stone. "This used to be part of the window."

"Yeah, I know."

"How do you know?" I call down to her, wobbling nervously, the hard corners of the stone wall jamming into my butt cheeks.

"Because there's one in every window. Except this one, now." If I lean out to look, I'll fall, but Yoni steps back and scans the wall. "Ohhhhh my goddddd," he says, covering his mouth.

"It's a twelfth-century adaptation of the techniques of decorative billet molding to defense."

"Whaaaat?"

Sigrid takes the brick from Yoni. "Use your eyes, guys. Look down the wall. You can see that this billet was one of a line of them all down this particular seam, running at the level of the windows. Yeah, the other half of the church is in bad shape, but this part was very well preserved—that's original twelfth-century masonry."

I put my head in my hands.

"Get down, get down," Yoni whispers aggressively like a fellow criminal. He motions for me to toss his belt down, like it's evidence we have to hide. Now Judith wanders over with a carefree "Hiii."

"Jean broke the church," says Sigrid, unfortunately taking up Yoni's phrase.

"Oh *noooo,*" says Judith, as if the church is a friend with a sprained ankle and she's about to ask if she can run and get ice.

Now Brice and Sam roll up. "What are you *doing,* Jean?" and "Oh my god," they say simultaneously. Brice: "Are you *holding* a *billet molding,* Sigrid?"

"Yeah," she says, and then everyone joins her in unison: "Jean broke the church."

"You guys!" I say. "It must have been *ready* to break! I barely touched it!"

"I don't know," says Sigrid. "It made it nine hundred years. . . ."

"Someone should tell David," says Sam.

"Definitely. I'll get David," Brice agrees, and I watch him pivot away in his bad bootcut jeans with ugly carpenter loops and inside my head I think, *You* cunt, *you FUCKING CUUUUNT.*

I wish I could climb down, but I can't; it's too far to the ground, and I need help reaching the ladder. After only a few moments, I watch with an almost suffocating panic as Brice returns with David and, to my horror, Professor Neary. Neary sees me in the window, sees the missing stone from a mile away, and just says, "Oh, for fuck's sake" and peels off. He won't deal with this. David approaches. I'm still up there, straddling the windowsill, my perch now smooth and toothless. I preempt the mob:

"I was trying to get up here to measure and . . ." Suddenly the heat in my face, the eyes all looking up at me, the guilt, the deep feeling of wrongdoing, compounded by being heavy, so big and horrible and ungainly that I've cracked ancient stone—it all becomes too much. I feel a flood coming to my eyes. I want to stop it, but I can't. I pull my shirt up over my face.

"Guys—everyone—just—can you all go away?" David pleads. No one moves. "Everyone get out of here," he says severely. "The *tabac* is open." My eyes are squeezed shut, but I can tell from the dip in the volume of David's voice that he's turned to face the other side of the road. "Go get coffees, go smoke." I am trying not to sob, but a little hot-kettle whine comes out instead. All I see is the navy blue of my T-shirt through a blur of water. My chest is pounding.

"Jean? Jean, look at me." I drop my T-shirt from my face and look down to see David stepping one step up on the ladder in his sensible brown leather shoes. "It's OK. Let's get you down from there," he says, holding the ladder steady and extending one hand up to me with gentle formality, like a practiced squire. Sniffling, I pick up the bottom of my shirt again and wipe my nose with it. Then, with a deep breath, I swing my left leg over the sill, so I'm not astride it like it's a horse but sitting on the ledge like it's a bench. I lean down and take David's hand and drop onto the top step of the ladder. He leads me to the ground, letting my hand go. My chest burns with bruising.

He looks sidelong at the starburst of snot in the middle of my T-shirt and fishes around in his pocket for a tissue. “Here, come with me,” he says, and we walk over to his canvas tote bag, which is marked with some academic logo and conference date, leaning against a rock. He pulls out a pack of tissues and hands them over.

“I feel so stupid,” I start to say, completely lost to myself, unable to straighten up, to stop crying. He guides me to a bench, where we sit while he waits quietly for me to catch my breath.

“It’s OK,” he says when I’m calm enough to listen. I breathe deeply to combat the hiccupy sobs. “I mean, it’s not great. We’ll have to take responsibility. . . .” He looks at me and realizes this is the wrong tack. “I once knocked down an entire rood screen, right into the chancery.”

“A *what*?”

He laughs. “Oh, I keep forgetting. You’re new at this.”

“How could you *forget*?” I say, turning and gesturing at the church as if I’ve burned it down.

He laughs again. “Well, quite.” Then he leans in and whispers: “We’ll come back at night with some superglue. No one will know.” I imagine us in Sam and Brice’s carpenter pants, heaps of glue on trowels in the moonlight. I almost believe we’ll do this, and it comforts me. He sees I’m calmer. “Come on, let’s join the others,” he says. “Shall I get you a coffee? It’s abominable coffee at these places. Tea?” A beat, a naughty twitch of the eyebrows: “Pastis?” We are walking, and his hand is lightly on my back. I’m aware of an intimacy born of my humiliation. *You’ll learn by doing:* Welcome to Medieval Art 101.

Chapter 19

We are in the van, on the way to another church. There are long-bodied white cows with dangling throats out all the windows. Shania Twain is singing. It's Caitlin's choice. We take turns offering up CDs from the plastic-pocketed CD books we all seemed to pack, flipping through each other's in the van. I get the impression that everyone is competing for David's approval. He vetoed Sigrid's Toad the Wet Sprocket—"The name alone, Sigrid!" he objected.

"You don't know what you're missing, David."

"Toad. The WET. Sprocket." David wrapped the ugly amphibious words in a trumped-up aristocratic version of his British accent, rolling the *r*, all of us laughing. "I mean, it *is* repulsive."

So instead we will hurtle toward Saint Whatever to the plucky ululations of Shania Twain, which would have been worth fighting about except that the minute the CD slot swallowed the silver disc, Caitlin opened her mouth and released a stunning series of harmonies. Listening to her wrap her notes above and below Shania's melody like a velvet garland, I think it's the most beautiful sound I've ever heard, and I watch David carefully in the rearview mirror to see how entranced he is. Patrick, who for no reason hates me, says to Caitlin, "God gave you a real gift," and she says, "Aren't you a sweetheart," and I see David nod.

"You should sing for everyone back at the castle some evening," David says. "We'd all love that."

"Aw, it'd be my pleasure," she says, making eye contact with him in the mirror. She goes back to singing, and without moving my mouth, as a secret experiment, I begin to hum, to test my own voice, to see whether I, too, might make luxurious harmonies if I tried. I want to hear myself sing beautifully, but I want my melodies to be audible only to me, as a personal reassurance, to tuck them underneath the elegant current that Caitlin controls. I hear my own voice braided up with Shania Twain's and Caitlin's and I think maybe I am good, maybe imperceptibly I am making this whole concert much better, maybe I have a really good ear for—

Suddenly Caitlin stops singing and I am still singing and it sounds like a whine, mechanical, like a power tool encountering difficulty. It's just a second or two and then I stop. No one says anything, but suspicious glances dart around the van. Caitlin starts up again. I stare at the cows, quiet.

✦

A few minutes later, I wander down the aisle of a church. As in all the other churches we've seen, there are little platforms all over carrying figurines—Mary with baby Jesus, Mary with dead Jesus, a murdered virgin, a dude in a brown dress. It's dark and cool and smells like blown-out candles. Everywhere we go, we arrive just before or after a celebration; we are stepping on confetti or in the puddles of water that tumbled off a baby's head.

The stillness and coolness, the feeling of being in between significant moments, makes me momentarily sad, as if my peers and I will never have these happy things: We're a forensics team, we're analysts, we're too smart to light the candles, to live a little life in a little French town. I walk over to an iron bank of hundreds of aluminum-based votives, all extinguished, their charred wicks toppled. I pull a lighter out of my shorts pocket, locate a candle with some wax left in the bottom, and light it. I don't know how to pray; no one has ever taught me. But as the wick takes the flame, I think, *Who for?*, like I have a little gift to give. *Who for?* My dad has sciatica. My mom is depressed. But they'll be fine. They're ticking along. Me? I'm lost. *Give me a life,* come the words. *Give me love.* I want to happen, not just study what happened. I want to be an event.

Monica shudders.

The church is so dark—these are some tiny windows, as I'll definitively document in the course of the day—that the candle's light is hyperbolic, impossible to ignore. It is the only thing happening in the world, this dancing flame. I think I am there a long time looking at it, but then I hear a scuffing of feet and I look to my right. The summer day through the open door is bright behind him, and it's just his trim silhouette, his hands in his pockets. David is watching me. Shafts of light streak toward me through the gap between his arms and his torso, from between his legs, around his head. My eyes adjust and I see something I did not expect, I cannot explain. The way he is looking at me: drinking me in, unaware of himself. He suddenly inhales as if he had been forgetting to breathe, and an arm comes up. He waves me toward him. I re-emerge into the daylight a few steps behind him, squinting. Everyone is still outside, gathered around Neary. They're talking about the capitals, the big carved blocks at the tops of pillars.

"Why these pagan motifs?" Neary asks. The memory of David Harwell's gaze is so fresh in my mind that I don't want to think of anything else, don't want to spill the holy water I'm transporting in the cupped hands of my memory. But "pagan motifs" sounds sexy, so I look up to see what they're talking about, hoping for a snake-headed monster or Zeus with his penis in something. Disappointingly, it's just a man's face and some grapevines. No one answers Neary, so he says, "Look, *look*" almost frantically, angrily, and I look again at the capital although it's a very simple carving and I can't imagine there's more to see. But now I realize that the vines are growing into the man's ears, out of his mouth; his eyes are wide like he's choking. It's not just a motif, it's moving—you can see the vines slithering past his lips; you can feel the ropes crossing, the grapes swelling.

"Sigrid?" says Neary. "Capitals. This is you."

Sigrid doesn't fret. She takes a deep breath and begins, "Yeah. Well. Is this guy dead or alive?"

Yoni starts to say something, but Sigrid didn't want an answer.

"If you really look, he's both. He's returned to nature, he's been *penetrated*"—you can tell she *loves* this word, jamming it into everyone—"by nature. Like a body, like the Christian bodies buried right there." She points to the cemetery. She's not talking like a bookie now, she's blaring her learning, full-throated and confident, a baby David. There is even something a little thrilling in seeing her adopt this masterful tone, this small flaxen-haired woman from Wisconsin, living proof that authority is learned. "But this tracery—the sheer energy that it demands of your eye as you follow it, the animation of the figure; this capital is coursing with life. It's about cycles of death, rebirth. Seasons. As in the vines and the fields; as in the Savior." I look around: Should we clap?

"Good, Sigrid," says Neary, and then David picks up the thread. "We'll see again and again how Christianity takes ownership of the elements of the pagan world, of nature, of death, of birth, of the body itself. This is what makes this religion so successful—it resides in the material, in crosses that you kiss and tombs that stare at you and carvings that drink the wine you made. It is not something the mind believes; it *is* the very flesh—"

"Interpenetrating," says Sigrid, drilling every syllable.

"Thank you, Sigrid," says Neary, tipping quickly from satisfied to bored. "Now," he continues, "I have a lunch booking for us in precisely one hour. Get beavering, you lot. In the van in FORTY-FIVE MINUTES or I will leave you." Most of the students chuckle because they have a fondness for Neary's moods, but I remain plainly terrified. Neary ambles into the church. Everyone else disperses to get to work while Yoni and I sink into a bench and smoke cigarettes, watching them.

"Are you gonna do some work today?" I ask.

"Are you gonna break the church today?"

"This one just has a couple of low, rinky-dink windows. I can estimate the dimensions from here."

"Quality scholarship."

"I can't believe you're a poli-sci major. Why are you even here?"

"This program is worth so many credits, it knocks out all my arts requirements in one go. I can do all politics for the next two years."

All politics? He seems too smart and funny for this. "What, like, treaties and stuff?"

"No, you dummy. It's *people*! You understand a lot about the world if you understand that Yeltsin is a fat fuck with daddy issues.

I like looking at these complex dynamics, the individual in relation to the system—the interplay."

"Interpenetrating," I say in a Sigrid impression.

"In-ter-penetrating," says Yoni, sitting up, jamming his fingers into each other. I burst into laughter and am loving laughing on this bench in the sun, the cigarette making my circulation hum, but I am also aware that a process that began here shortly after my arrival, maybe during mealtimes in the evening, has culminated in a cracking, a split. Part of me has sailed away, has been chipped off me and is hovering nearby like the chunk of earth that became the moon, dangling, looking on. I am seeing myself now from a distance with Yoni laughing on the bench. I am observing myself making a scene, laughing loud about interpenetration. It's good, yes; it's good to look like you have a friend. If David sees you, this is what he'll see: you on the bench looking joyful, looking beautiful in the sun and joyful and likable. He'll want to come find you and then you can get a little more of what you need, of that look on his face just moments ago when he drank in the sight of you. I find I am completely and totally competent at doing two things at once: being Jean, and watching Jean. Yoni has no idea that part of me is monitoring myself for David, arranging myself for his consumption. Yoni only sees me joking with him and being feckless and waiting for lunch. But I am calculating. Something was lit in that dark church today. A belief in a future. A desire for disaster. I hum with anticipation for my own death at David's hands, to vomit vines, to be full of him, to be stuffed up in the mouth with him. *It's not something the mind believes; it is the very flesh.*

Chapter 20

A LIFE OF SAINT AGATHA, VIRGIN, WHO DIED IN 253,
FROM *The Golden Legend*

✦ ✦ ✦

Virgin Agatha was highborn and beautiful, living in Catania, Sicily, where she worshipped Christian God all the time. Quintianus, the consular official of the Roman empire in Sicily, was a libidinous greedy pagan who wanted to have sex with her. He had her brought before him, but when she refused him, he had her given over to a horny brothel-keeper and her nine horny daughters. Agatha resisted them all, even though they promised her pleasure and threatened her with pain. Quintianus ordered her stretched on the rack and tortured, to which she said, "These pains are my delight! It's as if I were hearing good news or seeing an old friend or found treasure." So he ordered the executioners to twist her breast for a long time to cause her maximal pain and then to cut it off, which they did. "In my soul, I have breasts untouched and unharmed, with which I nourish myself," she said.

An old man offered to heal her wounds, saying, "Do not be ashamed, I am a Christian," but she refused, saying, "How could I be ashamed, since I am so cruelly mangled that no one could possibly desire me?" The aged man smiled, for he was Saint Peter and suddenly Agatha's breast was restored and healed and the jailers fled in terror. So Quintianus had her rolled naked over broken pottery and hot coals. At that instant, an earthquake shook the city and the populace shouted at Quintianus because they thought the earthquake was a divine rebuke for his treatment of Agatha. Quintianus stopped torturing her but sent her to prison, where she prayed to Jesus Christ to take her and he did.

Chapter 21

Like an ancient farmer with a dull brown life of animals and dirt, I have looked toward Sunday all week. Only one more day to wait: Tomorrow will change things, reveal things.

This morning I wake up late and my bedroom is empty. I pull on some sweatpants and go down the hall, poke my head into Yoni's and Caitlin's bedrooms. No one there. I check the downstairs salon where people watch TV, and the crumb-strewn kitchen, both empty. *Where* is *everybody?* Have I missed a site visit? Have I got the day wrong? I open the front doors of the castle, awakened by the slap of fresh air and my bare feet on the cold, creamy stone. I note that both vans are still there, but then I am transfixed by the sight of the front lawn, stretching out in a luminous green oval, a magical half acre of royal caprice, organic and expensive. Sometimes it calls like a dollar, engraved by the shade, and sometimes it's as mute as the dirt. Sometimes it's pea green and foamy like a poisonous pond, and sometimes it rolls like a crop, a gift you should collect to the last blade. Today it squirms with sunlight, vivid, ectoplasm you'd believe was ten feet deep. Has it drowned everyone? Do I live here alone now?

Then I remember the one place I haven't looked: the library. I climb the three flights and shove open the door, and there they are, everyone except the professors and Sam and Brice, gathered at the window, looking out over the back lawn. People declaim in disgust and bafflement—"Yugg." "Gross." "Ugh."

"What's going on?" I ask, still a little groggy. My eyes scan the desk where David works in the evenings, abandoned now, stacks of papers marked with his writing. I feel something like affection for these things, as if these messy drafts held the temperature of his body.

Sigrid pipes up from the front of the crowd, closest to the window. "Sam and Brice are doing capoeira."

"Doing *what?*" I squeeze in among the others to get a glimpse out the window—Sam and Brice circle each other menacingly, thighs and buns and smothered balls catching the sunlight in hi-tech biketards.

"You don't know capoeira?" says Sigrid. "It's an Afro-Brazilian martial art."

"Can't they just play Hacky Sack like normal douchebags?" says Yoni.

Caitlin and Judith cannot tear their eyes from the scene. Even Patrick is there. He simply shudders, his mouth curling down behind his rusty beard.

"Is the goal," Judith asks sincerely, "to touch each other in the crotch? Is that how you get . . . *points*?"

"Is it a fight?" asks Caitlin.

"Yeah, or are they gonna bone?"

"Yoni!" Caitlin smacks him.

"Come *on*," says Patrick, sounding exhausted by the effort it takes him to pardon us all, all the time.

An absorbed silence.

A collective "Ewww!"

It was too crowded at the window, so I've meandered around to David's desk. Sigrid looks over at me, and then her gaze rambles over his splayed materials.

"He's under a lot of pressure."

"Who?"

"David."

We all turn to Sigrid, who saunters away from the window to survey the scene of David's struggle. She picks up one of his books—I didn't dare touch anything—reads the cover, says, "Mm-hmm," and puts it back down.

Judith's big eyes follow Sigrid's every move. "What do you mean, 'pressure'?"

"Yeah, what's the dirt?" says Yoni.

"You guys know that David and his wife, Ann, were both Neary's grad students at Cambridge fifteen years ago," says Sigrid. I'm not sure anyone knows this, but we all nod to encourage her. "Both stars. And since then, Ann has written two well-received books—one of them groundbreaking—and David hasn't even gotten his first book out. He's done some articles, he's won some teaching awards, but no one cares about teaching."

"Why not?" I ask. I want David to get credit for the things he's good at. *Me;* he's good at me. He made sure I had the right books; he's taken time to explain things without making me feel stupid; he comforted me when I broke the church. Is what he's done worthless? Is our contact worthless? Our contact: Even when I'm alone with the books David gave me, I'm scissoring out little ideas to take to him later, ideas I know will interest him.

"It doesn't really matter if you're a good teacher. I mean for getting tenure. For securing your job. It's all about the publications."

"Why doesn't he just write his book, then?" asks Yoni.

"No one knows," says Sigrid. "It's probably intimidating watching your spouse just chuuuurn it out." She dangles her fingers and types frantically in the air, her eyes narrowing as she embodies the machinic, manic Ann. "Honestly?" Sigrid drops her hands. "He's got the yips."

"The what?"

"He's in his own head. Been working on the same material too long. Lost confidence. Second-guessing everything. Look at this." She pulls up the top sheet of a printed-out draft. "He crossed out this sentence, then crossed out *his crossing out.* He's going in circles. Stuck."

"You guys, we shouldn't be doing this," whispers Judith. "This is his private stuff."

"Look at all the ink, the Xs. The arrows!" As if arrows were a sure sign of pathology. "This thing is scarred all over, bleeding." We look at the red ink as if it will drip down off a corner of the page.

"Aw, David," says Caitlin. "*You can do it.*"

"Well, he better do it," says Sigrid, who plops herself in the high-backed wooden chair where David works. "Or he'll miss out on the gig of a lifetime. This summer isn't just a one-off—it's a pilot program. Neary and the senior faculty at a couple of other big-name universities want to turn this château into a major research center—I've heard this from Neary himself. David is auditioning to run the place, showing Neary he can fundraise, handle the prince, manage students." Maybe we don't look impressed enough because Sigrid pauses, leans forward in her chair. "When I say research center, I mean a twenty-, thirty-million-dollar building, director's salary in the six figures, tons of prestige."

"You guys," yelps Yoni from the window, "she kicked him in the dick and he's down!"

Everyone—even Patrick, laughing like a chimp—returns to the window, except me and Judith. Later that night, Judith and I sit alone on the front steps of the castle, facing a lawn that skitters with starlight like a field of broken glass. She's so small that alcohol rips into her, and she sways slightly as she says, "David. I hope he gets what he wants."

Chapter 22

Finally, Sunday.

I was in a goofy mood all day. I went for a wander in the woods by the castle, to work out the last details of the menu in my mind, and I saw Sigrid in the distance coming back from one of her runs. I hid behind a huge chestnut trunk, and when she passed, I jumped out and scared the shit out of her. She sprang in the air, her legs spinning. When she landed, her face went red and angry and she charged me and play-punched me all over, but I could tell she was impressed. We walked back together, laughing about yesterday morning, squatting like Brice and Sam and trying to slap each other's crotches. Then she told me about how someone pulled a knife on her when she was an undergrad at Columbia and she ended up taking the knife. I imagine, as we stroll back to the castle, that I am her apprentice. I won't be like other women; I'll be like Sigrid. I'll take the knives that people want to carve me with.

"People who are obsessed with each other are so gross. I could never be like that," I say, trying to bait her into being my guru.

"I don't know," she says, pausing to wipe her face with the bottom of her T-shirt. "I've never worn a fucking singlet, but I've rolled around on some lawns with people." A crooked smile, a suggestive little tick of the head. "It's a good time."

I nod in eager agreement, but I can't shake how pathetic Judith was last night: *I hope he gets what he wants.* And Judith isn't alone. Caitlin, despite her commitment to her banjo-plucking beloved, wants David's attention; she loves his praise. Disciplined, hard-nosed Sam tries to make herself pretty and ingratiating when David leans in to inspect her floor plans. Brice, even! A grown man! Glowy and gregarious when David checks in. I don't have a special connection with David Harwell. David Harwell has an effect on women, on *people.* I see you now, David Harwell. You are a charmer, and I was charmed. Now that I've identified David's warping, prehensile powers, they've diminished. They won't work on me.

Sigrid is panting; her heart is slowing. We march toward the castle in tandem, vines underfoot. She will be hungry. I will feed *her.* I will feed this corps of scholars, and I will not care inordinately for him among them.

David announces that he is going to take a van to town. Trips to town are rare, and the town itself is a heap of old stones, one café, a grocery store, and a *tabac.* Members of our élite squad of academics often just loiter outside the *tabac* while one of us buys a pen. Caitlin goes off to mail a letter to her beau and buy more stamps, Sam and Brice want to stock up on mineral water for their room, and Judith slips quietly into the front passenger seat. I stay back at the castle. It's 2:30. The kitchen is mine.

The World Cup final between France and Brazil is at nine o'clock tonight and I don't want anyone rushed, so I aim to have dinner on the table at six. The kitchen is cold and empty. There's a gas stove with thick dials, an enormous oven, lots of stockpots. Heavy copper casseroles. I know what to do with all of them, what they'll feel like in my hands, how they'll behave on the heat.

JEAN: I did *not* know how they would behave: That oven was basically a crematorium. I burned everything, including myself, at the beginning.

MONICA: In about sixty seconds, you're going to unhook a sauté pan from the wall and it's going to land on your foot with the sound of Big Ben chiming one o'clock.

JEAN: I remember that! It was so painful! Can we warn me?

MONICA: No. You still have a hairline metatarsal fracture from that pan.

JEAN: I do?

MONICA: [Holds up an X-ray] The point is, you're not lying to yourself, Jean, you're leaping forward with dumb confidence. Nobody achieves anything without a naive leap.

JEAN: Is my toe OK?
MONICA: Ironically, you've got a bunion on that foot, which is taking the weight off your fracture.
JEAN: Is it hard being all-knowing?
MONICA: Can be.

Walking into the kitchen feels a little like walking into one of these churches—cooler than the outside, full of altars and equipment. I don't know what to do in a church, what to touch, what to think. It tells me to worship, and of course I try. I look up at the angels in the stained glass, their golden swallows' wings pleated behind them, and I think, *I'm here, I'm human, I'm no smarter than Isaac Newton or Dolly Parton or* all *the presidents.* Just believe, accept your Sky Daddy! Have two billion new friends!

But there is a hard, almost arrogant confidence in me. Little new me. Not two thousand years old—not even twenty! A mere girl who can't even measure the hole in a wall and says "fuckin' A" when she reads a cool fact! Yes, I know better. I know it's all stories, however much I like you, you angels, with your yellow Twizzler hair, that incline of your head that says *We are always listening.*

MONICA: You didn't need them yet.
JEAN: Not that Sunday. I walked into that kitchen and I got to work.

Jojo the groundskeeper passes through at three o'clock to clear out the trash and finds me chopping onions again after tossing a burned batch.

"At the stove already?" he asks.

"It's the game tonight," I say.

He nods at me. He has a liquidy gaze that moves all the time. His eyes swim around the kitchen for a while, and then they land on me. "You can use the garden, you know. The prince would be very happy to know it was used." *The prince.* Talk about Sky Daddy! Who *is* this absent, beneficent lord? This man who gets credit for the herbs that Jojo clips and waters? Does this prince, wherever he is, even know there's a garden? Jojo possesses nothing—even his own goodness he must attribute to the prince. It reminds me of my parents, how when my mom stopped working and didn't earn any money, she couldn't be generous. Handing me a new backpack and saying "Daddy got this for you," when Daddy had no idea.

I follow Jojo to the prince's garden, with Jojo's beautifully organized raised beds. Trellises hold up tomatoes; ropey vines sag with yellow squash. I spot eggplant, as dark as the dirt but shining like polished boots, frilly lettuce, radishes bursting out of the soil. Jojo talks incessantly while we're there, naming everything, putting everything in its cycle for me—"The rhubarb's almost done"; "The carrots will be coming in"—and tsk-tsking at the snail who turned a squash leaf into lace. My compliments are genuine, but also: A new voice has awoken in me, competent, even ruthless, and single-minded. This Ruthless Jean knows she needs access to this garden for the next six weeks.

"You can take what you need," says Jojo.

"I wouldn't want to take too much."

Oh, I would take it all.

✦

I close the oven, check my watch—it's four-thirty; perfect—and sit down for a moment, so hot I have to pull my apron off. My eyes still burn from the onions, and I'm ragged with sweat, but I'm aware of a stillness, a quieting of the usual questions, in this half-buried chamber. I feel as if the barrel ceiling is the arch of my skull, the heat that I command the manifestation of my thought. The sound of wheels crunching gravel breaks my trance; through the little window facing the lawn at ground level, I see the van pull in. I make my way up the steps of the staff exit from the kitchen to the driveway. The kids have all spilled out of the van and David is walking around the hood with newspapers under his arm.

"Hey," I say to David. I know how to be now that I've decided I'm immune to his charms. I'm very manly and businesslike.

"Hey," he says, mirroring my tone, severe.

"Dinner's at six tonight. A little early, for the game."

"OK, great. I'll let everyone know." I pivot back toward the kitchen. "You're very organized, aren't you?" he adds, and I—

MONICA: What did you do?
JEAN: I made a gun with my fingers and pointed the gun at him and made a clicking sound with my mouth.
MONICA: Because you had no feelings for him.
JEAN: Exactly. This is what you do if you have no feelings for someone: you make a finger gun and you go *"tchck tchck"* with your mouth, like professional people at their jobs.
MONICA: You think you were foolish here, but actually—you're working hard.
JEAN: I tried. I tried to think my way out of it, out of him.

For an hour before dinner, all you hear is "What is that smell?" Ancient stone walls are no match for the exhalations of stockpots, no match for the ghosts of dead tomatoes, singing on their way up. The inhabitants of this castle are going crazy, but it's not with disgust like back in my dorm. They salivate, they hover, they gather at the kitchen doorway like I dreamed they would. "What are you making?" "Can I have a taste?" I am sure of what they should do here; I am commanding: "You can get the plates out," I tell them. "Get out of my way and open some wine."

✦

It was part of my plan for the dish itself to be unprepossessing. No garnish, no pheasant with aluminum booties, spilling thyme. No, just two big, stained casserole dishes, with browned cheese bubbling on top. It's the stuff of team dinners, of big families, of fat moms. A spatula tossed casually by. A side dish of summer squash. The wooden table set, everyone sitting, the early evening light strong but keeling sideways, licking us all up one side of our faces like a dog's tongue. Bottles of red sitting out, now gushing sloppily from one glass to another.

"What is this, Jean?" asks Neary.

It's lasagna.

MONICA: You're a fucking genius.

Of course it's lasagna. Because lasagna is a hot sarcophagus of deliciousness. She lies back in her stone bed, a queen gisant. She's been returned to the earth but set on fire, oozing with red, white bones melted, meat disintegrated. A body, dead and alive. She wants to stay intact when you cut her; she reaches for herself, her melted bones distending, heat curling out of the hole you made as you cut her and pull her apart. You *devour* her.

No one speaks. There are strange snuffles, as if they can't eat fast enough. The acid sweetness of the tomatoes and the blank embalming fat of the mozzarella, the béchamel go-between, the good Charolais beef, the near-funk of it caramelized in the tomato paste, Jojo's basil a racy zap of summer heat. I tossed the squash in a mustard vinaigrette that slaps your mouth for looking away from the lasagna and makes you look back.

"Jean . . ." people say, but they don't finish their sentences.

Finally, David says, "How do you know how to do this, Jean?"

"It's just something I do." This I deliver perfectly. "*Via trita, via tuta*": The beaten path is the safe path. It has been three solid hours of work, but I shrug as if I found the lasagna in a cave. I hide my effort to heighten their pleasure. Until this moment, he has treated me like a schoolchild with lice, but now James J. Neary, with a whisker of mozzarella stretched across his chin, raises his glass to me. When I put a bite in my own mouth, it is not to fill myself but to know what everyone else is tasting, to disperse myself on their tongues and supervise their enjoyment. My great garlicky mouthful is the way David's eyes fall on me as Neary raises his glass. The look is level, direct: Now he will know me. He has to know me more.

MONICA: Where did you go that evening?
JEAN: Nowhere. He came to me.

I sit cross-legged on my bed, holding the *Golden Legend* open in my lap, but I'm not reading. My eyes are made of stone. I'm a carving, I'm a statue of an exemplary woman, reading her Bible (for this performance, I've hidden *Belle et Sébastien,* which I *have* been reading, under my pillow). It's late by now, past eleven, but David has taken the night off from his writing for the World Cup final. I know the match is over because the screams from the town can be heard in the castle from across the fields, and the fireworks are so bright and loud that the sheep panic and thump all over the lawn. Listening to the townspeople shout and light fires, I sit on my four-poster bed like a princess who will soon be married or killed, and wait and hope and listen. Judith and Sigrid are both still downstairs with everyone else, watching the after-match coverage.

There's a knock and the door opens slightly.

"Jean, there you are." He's been drinking more than usual but isn't drunk, just a little rosy-cheeked. I wear a white tank top and no bra and ribbed pink leggings from Old Navy.

"Am I interrupting?"

"I'm reading what you told me to."

My tone is hard but also *I'll do what you tell me to do.*

"And how's it going?" He enters the room in small footsteps, earned with each of my answers.

"Good," I say, flatly. He takes another step toward me.

"Good," he repeats. *I know what you are, David,* I think. *I know you charm people. I'm uncharmed, unharmed. I'm not hungry for you.* "Look, I think it's obvious that you—" I'm not smiling. My eyes were functionless opaque orbs a moment ago when I pretended to read, but now I act mildly annoyed, eager to get back to my book. He seems unsettled, starts over. "Without wishing to *overburden you*"—I have sixteen empty waking hours every Sunday, but I will roost here in my sudden importance: *No, you wouldn't want to burden me, David—* "Neary and I have been discussing—it seems like you know what you're doing in the kitchen, and we're wondering if maybe you could . . . take charge of Sundays—of every Sunday. Of feeding everyone." If he steps any closer, he'll have to sit on my bed; he'll be under my canopy, on the blanket of braided cream that tops my bed like a casserole.

"Oh," I say, knitting my brows, as if I had completely forgotten about dinner.

"It would be such a service to all of us"—he lowers his voice—"to keep Sam and Brice out of that kitchen."

"Ha." Now it's my turn to be delighted, his turn to delight. I think for a moment, looking away so that he can take me in, on my bed, in my youth, in my hot, wobbling, unconsumed body. My gaze returns to him, limpid, casual. "Sure."

"Wonderful." He swallows. "Well, I'm sorry to interrupt." He's backing up now, facing me. I am royal. I'll be crowned and poisoned and I'll make decisions I'm not equipped to make. I'm a beautiful royal girl-child, and he's not allowed to turn away from me.

"It's no problem." *You may go.*

"Well, good luck reading now, with this noise. Or sleeping, for that matter."

"I'll be fine," I say. "I always sleep well." And I stretch, shoulders back, elbows behind me.

And he looks at my chest.

MONICA: You wanted him to see you like that, to see you more completely. And then you felt scared.

JEAN: I felt terrified of what I'd done. Of what I'd done to him. What I'd shown him, what I'd fed him. What I'd lit in him, as the fireworks whistled and boomed, as the heavy door closed behind him as he left. Do you know what Patrick said when he had finished his first plateful?

Jean, you're a saint.

Chapter 23

A LIFE OF SAINT PETRONILLA, VIRGIN,
FROM *The Golden Legend*

+ + +

Petronilla was the daughter of Saint Peter the apostle. She was so beautiful that in order to preserve her virginity, her father willed her always to have a fever, so she did. One day, the disciples were eating with Peter and one of them said, "You can cure all kinds of illnesses, so why do you leave your daughter sick?" He said, "It's for her own good." But he didn't want his friends to think that he was unable to cure her, so he said to Petronilla, "Petronilla, get up now and serve us!" She served everyone their dinner. Then Peter said, "Back to bed," and she went back to bed with a fever.

A count named Flaccus, overwhelmed by Petronilla's great beauty, asked to marry Petronilla. She said, "If you want to marry me, send some maidens to accompany me to the altar." While he gathered the maidens, she took up a regimen of fasting and prayer and in three days she died of starvation, a happy virgin.

Chapter 24

Weekday mornings have become routine now, the smells of everyone's soaps and shampoos trapped in the humid corridors, the slow drift through the kitchen for coffee and bread, the warming up of our minds together. I wait for Judith before I go down, holding the door for her. (Who knows where Sigrid is; once we went to the van and she'd been there since the crack of dawn reading a history of the Abbasid Empire with her feet up on the gears.) I am sitting with my coffee and my egg, staring out the kitchen windows, which lie at ground level, where the dew is so close to the glass it swirls up the pink sun and sandy soil into a single entity and gives it breath. My heart leaps into my throat as Professor Neary appears suddenly before me, hatless and harried.

"You." I open my eyes wide. "And the other one."

"What?"

"The undergrad."

"Oh, Yoni."

"Yes. You don't seem to be doing very much."

I look down at my egg, confused. Neary never talks to me. Have I broken a breakfast rule?

"I realize this is partially our fault. David and I. We thought the undergrads could just tag along with the graduate students and you'd pick up their skills, but it's not working. You and the other one are flagrantly idle."

Just then Yoni descends, fresh in a bright white V-neck and khaki shorts, holding a newspaper.

"YOU!" Neary barks at him, too loud in this domed, hard space. Yoni nearly slips off the step. Neary waves him over.

"What are you on?" he asks Yoni, and I can see Yoni weighing whether to make a ketamine joke. "What's your *job*?"

"Oh, I'm Patrick's partner," he says cheerfully, wishing Patrick were there to hear it. "Devotional objects."

"I'm apertures," I say.

"Oh, I know what *you* are," Neary says to me, pointedly. "You're being reassigned. David and I need to give you some kind of grade at the end of this, so as much as you're doing a crackerjack job consuming tobacco, you need to produce some work. Therefore, you will write a guidebook. From now on, during our site visits, you will write a concise account of each church—using the appropriate vocabulary, and supporting your analysis with secondary sources. You will write like a historian, not some *nincompoop.*"

He says "nincompoop" with irrational menace, as if nincompoops were a dangerous invasion, alien body-snatchers dressed as mailmen.

"Can we do it together?" I ask, pointing at Yoni.

"I don't care," says Neary. "And, finally, in the five weeks that remain, you'll each need to write one term paper of about ten pages on a theme adjacent to our work here. Is that all clear?"

We both say yes.

"That should put an end to your *Olympic* faffing."

I can sense Yoni's face tensing next to me as he swallows a laugh. Neary concludes by giving us each a stern look over the rim of his glasses and then marches away soundlessly in his ancient hiking boots.

"Fun!" says Yoni. "We're writing a guidebook!"

"It opens with a warning about *nincompoops.*"

"He's a nutcase," says Yoni.

Our attention falls silently on Patrick, who has entered the kitchen looking like an overgrown child in a brown sweater-vest, made dry toast, and is now whispering to God about it.

"Everyone here is a nutcase," I say.

My attention goes from Patrick to Sam and Brice—staring into each other's plastic Furby eyeballs silently and eating bran flakes they bought for themselves—to Caitlin, smiling for absolutely no reason at a wall.

"Is *everyone* here Christian?"

"Aren't *you,* McShanahan?" asks Yoni, extracting his knife from the soft tissue of a baguette and pointing it at me.

It's hard to describe Northern European Christianity to Americans. It never seems to be about more than braided bread. My Belgian mother spends zero time thinking about what Christ did for whose sins, although even after my parents split we always went to church together on Christmas and Easter, always a Catholic one—it felt like treating ourselves to name-brand Jesus and not the Walgreens kind. But if any of us had spoken of healing, of solace, of transcendence, we would have embarrassed the others.

Yoni slams his espresso cup into its saucer and turns to me with sudden animation. "Oh my god, have you read that book David gave us? *The Golden Legend*?"

"No, I haven't started." I won't tell Yoni how I pretended to read it once, on my bed, as David watched. My mind goes guiltily to how engrossed I've been by an illustrated novella about a little boy and his dog. Maybe Patrick's not the only overgrown child.

"It's *cccccrazy,*" says Yoni, gripping my forearm urgently.

"What are you guys talking about?" Sigrid manifests out of nowhere. "Jacobus de Voragiiiiine?" Why is she talking like Humphrey Bogart?

"Who is Jacobos Borabeen?" I ask.

"A pervert," says Yoni.

"De Voragine," says Sigrid. "He compiled *The Golden Legend.*"

"WHY IS NO ONE IN THE VAN?" roars Neary from the driveway. Every dish in the kitchen suddenly drops and we all bolt for the massive arched door.

"We'll read it together later," says Yoni.

✦

As an act of defiance against the Jean who calculates, I put myself in Neary's van—*I don't need to be near David.* Because Patrick is wary of women and thinks Yoni is the gay devil's foot soldier, his preferred company is, of all people, James Neary. It's almost startling, to see Patrick relentlessly put himself beside Neary, in conversation with Neary, as if the two of them had spent twenty years side by side manning a lighthouse, when it is obvious to the rest of us that Neary wants to push him out of the van. This morning Patrick is talking in business tones about his studies—"That's not what we find in Julius Africanus, for example, not in the Latin"—and Neary, whose face I catch in the rearview mirror, displays the doleful stamina of a woman at her husband's funeral.

Caitlin is next to me on the middle bench in the van, unconsciously humming in perfect harmony with the radio, and I can sense that she is calmly, sweetly available for connection, her eyes shimmering. I'll bite.

"So what were you doing with your summer? Before this?"

"Charity work," she says.

I instantaneously feel like an asshole. "What kind?"

"Bringin' Bibles and song out to people who need it."

"Oh, OK," I say, relieved. She's not *that* much better a person. If she's just bringing Bibles and not soup.

"We do a big pot of soup in a shelter over on the north side and we keep the pantry there stocked." Dammit. "But we get to know people there. You know, they're all great people just down on their luck. That's how I met Trent." I should have seen this coming. All roads lead to Trent.

"Was he homeless?"

"No!" She slaps my thigh. "He was working there, too. I just miss him *so much*," she says. "You would love him, Jean. He's a hoot."

"Totally." I bet he sucks.

"It's hard to be away from him. We just got engaged."

"*Engaged*? How old are you?"

"Just finished my junior year. I'm twenty-one."

"Why are you engaged?"

"I want my life to start." Oh dear. Do I not want my life to start? Was there an "On" button I forgot to push? Do I have to marry a human butt-cut named Trent and have lots of little baby butt-cuts? "I'm ready," she continues. "I'm gonna teach the history of sacred art at a great university, and sing, and raise a couple kids, and have a blast." She sounds so convinced by this last part, like the paper cups and paper plates and the red-checked tablecloth of her life have all been set out and all she needs to do is show up hungry for pie and *have a blast.*

What do I want? Just like, devil things? Am I Team Devil? I'd really like to have sex with someone. *Virgin* is such a gross word, all veils and oils. *Extra-virgin olive oil* is so arrogant about the purity of its extra-virginal olives who stayed in clusters and sang hymns and hid their holes from the hairy humping bees. I don't care about purity! I just don't want to detach from the party and go roll around on a pile of boxers in a pestilential dorm room with a man I know only as "the Brad-Master."

MONICA: And you said you were insecure!

JEAN: No, no, in the context of American college life, I was frankly ambitious.

Chapter 25

Yoni, sitting on my bed, reads from *The Golden Legend.*

"Agnes was a beautiful girl of thirteen years. When she was coming home from school one day, the prefect's son saw her and fell in love. He promised her jewels and wealth if she would marry him, but she said 'Go away, you spark that lights the fire of sin, you fuel of wickedness, you food of death!' "

"So that's a no."

"That's a no." He reads on: " 'Because, she said, she was already engaged. But she meant to *Christ.*' " He looks up at me—"Her boyfriend, Christ." Back to the book: " 'When the prefect discovered this, he had her charged with Christianity, and had her stripped naked and brought to a brothel.' " He looks at me. "I am not making this up." He turns back to the text. " 'But God made her hair grow so long that it covered her vagina and no one could rape her.' "

"Oh my god."

"That's what *she* said. It goes on. 'The prefect's deputy had Agnes thrown into a fire in front of a crowd, but the fire leapt to either side and burned up the crowd and Agnes was fine.' "

"Take that, assholes!"

"Yeah, stupid pagans. 'Finally, the deputy had a soldier stab her in the throat with a dagger and thus her'—and I quote—'heavenly spouse consecrated her his bride.' "

"Oh my god, congratulations!"

"The bride wore, um, a fully charred body and a knife in the throat."

"Then what?"

"Well, after they murder the virgin, they always build a church in her honor, which is so fun for her. But this time there's more! 'So they built a church of Saint Agnes, and one time a priest there was tormented by temptations of the flesh so he wrote to the pope to ask if he could be married. The pope gave him an emerald ring and ordered him to go before a beautiful statue of Saint Agnes in the church and to command her to be his wife. When he did this, the statue of Agnes put out her ring finger, accepted the ring, and retracted the finger.' "

"Like a dog's boner," I say.

"Like a dog's boner," he replies. We sigh next to each other on my bed, peasant imaginations sent spinning by blood and miracle. "I think we should make our guidebook *way* more disgusting."

Chapter 26

Later that night, Yoni, Caitlin, Judith, and I are all drinking in lounge chairs on the back lawn, looking down past the dining table to the pond in the distance, breathing in its marshy smell. At our backs are the double doors that lead to the salon with the TV. It's a warm evening, so the doors and most of the windows are open, and we can hear the others watching *Braveheart*. Surprisingly, Neary is in there, too, occasionally yelling at the TV. "They've made EDWARD the SECOND a POOFTER! What a load of BOLLOCKS!" We whoop with laughter because the work is over for the day and there's nothing to worry about and we've all chipped in for the half case of wine, so why not?

Caitlin, as usual, has dragged the conversation toward Trent. This forces me and Yoni to take increasingly extreme measures to stay entertained.

"So do you and Trent have sex?" I ask. "I mean, if you're engaged, is that good enough?"

"No, ma'am," she says. "There's more than *sex*, you know. We do plenty together."

I picture them necking: it's hour three, and Trent is wincing as his hard-on sucks the blood from his body and his organs shrivel and scream.

"When's your wedding, Caitlin?" asks Judith.

"Next summer. Right after graduation." Judith, who like me has never had a real boyfriend, asks boring questions about Caitlin's wedding dress and I stop listening. I light a cigarette and lean back to look up at the piercing stars in the dark country sky, and even though I'm a virgin, too, and Caitlin's the one 24/7 handling Trent's flaming hot boner through the oven mitt of his stonewashed jeans, I feel somehow unwholesome next to these women. The wine is loose in me, making me agitated, with nothing to do here but track sheep and learn about a distant, weird historical past of toothless peasants and the crazy shit they believed. Surrounded by people who still believe it! *But why should their belief make* me *feel unwholesome?* I start to wonder. *Aren't we all university students here? Aren't we rational intellectuals? Aren't we here to learn to think, to sort fact from fiction, to find ethics in reason?* I look at Caitlin, who's describing a lace bodice with her hands, and I suddenly think, *You're the enemy. I have to fight you.*

"I guess you're also scared of sex," I say, ripping through their happy chat, "because you're probably anti-abortion."

Yoni rolls his eyes. "Jean . . ."

Judith freezes.

"That's true, yup. I'm not *scared* of sex; it has its place. But I am pro-life, yup." You wanted the fight, Jean? What now?

"Well. I hope you never need an abortion." A swing that misses.

"I won't, don't worry." The conversation is suspended and she looks ready to get back to her dress.

"Well, you don't know what other people go through." Yoni looks at me as if to say, *What are you doing?* "Seems like you think you can tell other women what to do with their bodies."

The problem with this, as I can tell from Yoni's pained face, is that it's simply boring. We all know in advance what everyone can possibly say: Caitlin will say the unborn have a right to life, and I'll say that women die when abortion is illegal. So I'll make it a poll.

"Judith, what about you? Are you pro-choice?"

"Yeah, I am," she says apologetically. "But I understand that it's very complicated and I can see why—"

"Yoni?"

"Come on, you guys. Why are we talking about this?"

Caitlin pours her pancake-syrup eyes into mine. "I think you are a *great* girl, Jean, and I have been having a *blast* with you," she says. Oh, I'm invited to her cookout of a life, invited to listen to Shania and use deep conditioner and find a husband who shares my beliefs? *Never.* And now I see an opening. She thinks I'm a great girl? Well, I'll cause a crisis in her, then. That's all I need to do.

Make this smooth woman worry, make her choose. It comes out as easily as if it were true, because in this moment, hot on wine and deep in the fight, I almost believe it.

"I had an abortion," I declare.

Silence. I wasn't ready for the reaction. It's so *caring*. I thought this was a fight, but now I've just wounded myself to wound her, given her an image of my body, seeded and full and then robbed and bloodied. No one says anything, but Caitlin looks at me with sympathy, not judgment, and Judith puts a hand on my arm.

"Yeah. Sophomore year."

"Last year?"

"Yeah."

"How far along were you?"

"I don't really want to talk about it." I don't know anything about abortions, literally not one thing. I ignorantly assume they are done with a crochet hook, like a tiny version of the ones that pull performers offstage. I've been to a gynecologist once for a Pap smear and instead of resting my heels in the metal stirrups I put my feet *through* them and the doctor had to get help from a nurse to yank them out without hurting my ankles. "I'm just saying," I continue, "you shouldn't judge people."

Judith sees the possibility of something that we may need to tend to and bravely asks, "Was it . . . was it with someone you—"

"Yeah, it was with my boyfriend." I'm not going to invent a rape. A fake abortion is completely reasonable, but I'm not a psychopath.

"You've never talked about your boyfriend," says Caitlin, sounding almost cheated, as if we've missed the chance for some fun girl talk.

"Well, now you know why. It was just an accident, one time when we were having sex." Yoni looks queasy. Caitlin and Judith listen with wide eyes. "You know, these things happen. I'm not a bad person."

"Nuh-uh, I know that," says Caitlin. "And I'm so sorry for you, for your loss. That's so hard." Caitlin walks over to my lounger and gives me a hug. Judith lays the orchid stem of her arm across my back. Oh god, Caitlin has tears in her eyes.

"It was fine," I say, too casually. It's quiet for a moment and then, from the salon, we hear a horde of Scottish warriors screaming. Neary shouts, "What ROT! What absolute ROT!"

We burst into laughter, but suddenly the laughter catches in our throats. We hear David Harwell's voice, clear as day.

"Hey, how are you? . . . Good, I'm good. Glad I caught you."

We all twist around and look up—he sounds impossibly close, but he's up in the library; he's been there all night, working with the windows open. I didn't realize how clearly sound carried between the third-floor window and us, with nothing to dampen it along the neatly shorn lawn, the hard castle wall.

My stomach drops. If we can hear him this clearly . . .

Caitlin has the same thought: "Do you think David heard everything we said?"

Yoni and Judith freeze. David's words drift down to us, crisp and intact: "Do you think you'll make it down here? I think you'd love it . . ." I see him holding a phone receiver to his ear, the cord spiraling behind him. I catch his eye, and he holds my gaze, slack-faced, unreadable—maybe displeased?—as he reaches out and pulls the double gables shut.

"We're such dicks," whispers Yoni.

Caitlin winces. "He's trying to work and we're here carousin'. And the others with that loud movie . . ."

And me, spinning maudlin stories about my body, the opposite of the effortless delight I want to be—I can be—with David. As he recedes into the library, out of view, I think, *Team Devil, I really am Team Devil.*

The strings are soaring and it sounds like Mel Gibson is finally getting decapitated. Neary alternates between cackling and protesting—"Longshanks died in CUMBRIA, you NUMPTIES"—and as the secondhand pathos of the swelling soundtrack flows distorted into the night, now, in the form of a rushing sadness, I have finally learned a thing or two about windows.

Chapter 27

The French won the World Cup, *for the first time ever,* on their own soil, two days ago, and now it is Bastille Day and the country has come to a stop. All of France is exploding, juicing itself, running in the streets with exuberance. Already this morning, as we tried to work, the distant pops of firecrackers took us unawares: Sam threw her compass in a spasm of shock at a loud noise and nearly took Brice's eye out. Neary kept saying "Oh, shut up" at the shrieks of revelry that reached us from across distant fields. Although it's Tuesday, nothing was open: no shops, no kiosks. But we are under strict orders from His Never Actually Gonna Be a Royal Highness—whom we still haven't met—not to celebrate Bastille Day. So while all of France peeled through the streets and drank and honked and sang, we plugged our ears and measured stone.

Jojo and Victoire seem distracted, too, and put together a paltry spread of boiled eggs and anchovies and sandy salad, and we all ate dinner eyeballing each other. Who would crack? Who would say, *God has given the French an orgasm on their birthday; they won the Oscar for Best Country; fuck our princely host, let's be with them.* Frenchness is a cake today in the People's mouths, sugary and blood-thinning and official and sweet, and we are collectively getting more and more curious to taste it. We can hear them getting louder, from every direction, shouting and screaming.

We are milling around, clearing dishes, when David drops a stack of plates on the table and says, "This is ridiculous. Come on, let's get the lay of the land."

We check each other's faces—what exactly does he mean?

"I'll take *one* van into town. We'll have a little look-see and we'll come back." Yoni and I gasp. "Let's finish tidying up, and then meet me at the van, if you want to come." Neary and Patrick wave the whole thing off as distasteful and Brice and Sam want to stay and do some homework they've given themselves, but Caitlin and Judith and Sigrid and I wash and dry plates double-quick and then dash inside to change and put makeup on at the idea of "going out," although the plan is to go stare at screaming farmers for fifteen minutes. Soon we are all babbling and laughing and singing "MAN! I feel like a WOMAN!" which David has adorably popped into the CD player without being asked. Seldom-worn perfumes, mingling in the van, make us exciting strangers to ourselves. The guilt of our expedition, the joyous insurrection of it, is delicious—the way David tiptoed to the van, joking about wearing mustaches, pretending to be Canadian, whispering that we musn't let word get back to the prince that we went to sing with the Republican rabble.

Careening out of the driveway, David asks, "Which bar?"

"The one with the gambling machines?"

"No, that one's seedy."

"What about the bar in the town with the fountain that Neary hit with the van?"

"*Grazed*, Yoni!"

"Oh, can we go all the way to La Flèche?"

"Ooh, the town with the parking garage?"

"Yeah, La Flèche!" As if it's Hong Kong, a glittering citadel, burlesque performers dangling by their mouths from the ceilings.

✦

After two weeks at the castle, this crush of strangers at a café-bar-post-office called To the Good Oxen feels like the center of civilization, the bazaar where we all go for our grain and wives and news. In this crush, we are a little liberated from our usual roles: Sigrid can't know it all here, David can't hold us together, Yoni can't finish my sentences. Caitlin covers her ears and grips her purse protectively. We are crammed, jostled, our arms rubbing the whole length of strangers' arms as we reach toward the bar extending wads of francs and lifting precarious pints.

I tap Yoni and pull him outside for cigarettes and air and to my relief David comes, too, not to smoke but to escape the moist, mobbed interior. The outdoor tables are full and drinking has spilled into the parking lot, over a low stone wall, onto a lawn, and while David and the others hang back, I morph into my French-speaking self and am absorbed into the scene. A man named Cyril draws me into the center of his group of friends in tight jeans and blue T-shirts baying with their chins up and lifting me in the air as if I've done something wonderful. All that matters to me is that I'm in my cute black Express miniskirt laughing hard with locals. The locals have a magic tonight that we don't—they are overcome, filled from the inside with vibrant, wild hope. The future has changed for them tonight; they felt history twist like a lock in their hands and they can be all new people now, anyone's friend, anyone's lover. But David and the Americans aren't able to touch this feeling. David, stuck in English, stuck with the students, is forced to keep a distant, seigneurial eye on me. I'm a little scared of reinforcing the idea that I'm skanky after what he heard last night, but something about this scenario pulls me in deeper, satisfies the demands of Ruthless Jean: I'm being warm and flexible, connecting with another man before his eyes, spinning through this cyclone of triumph like a native seabird.

I have told the French men where I live—at the castle—and this has become a monumental joke, and everyone is calling me Princess, Duchess, Queen. Sometimes one of my academic colleagues comes to join us, but they can't keep up with the French so they end up standing there, watching, smiling effortfully until they eventually wander back to David, tourists who can't break in. Judith is deep and Caitlin is pretty, but David, can't you see that I'm more alive than them? That I can be indigenous here, part of the landscape you study? I speak the natives' throaty babble and I make their menfolk laugh: Would you take me by the waist, take me by the neck, push me into paper, and preserve me to study like all your pilasters and your portals? This Frenchman is a real authentic specimen: good jaw, some acne for character, unwashed hair, and a sweater that shouts in imbecilic capitals across the front "CHAMPION TIME NOW"—and you know that he wears this sweater *every day*, not just today, and that like a broken clock, it is accidentally accurate. Jealous, David?

It's only been a little while, two pints in, maybe, when Yoni grabs my sleeve and says, "David's driving back now," twisting his lips in disappointment. I tell the French boys I have to go and they erupt in protests, and tell me to order my men to stand down: "Off with their heads!" they bark.

Cyril says he has to be up for work early, so he won't be out all night—I can stay awhile and he'll drive me back.

"You sure?"

"Sure."

I take him over to David, as if David were my father. "David, this is Cyril."

"*Bonsoir,* Cyril," says David with exaggerated courtesy.

"Can Cyril drop me off on his motorbike a little later?"

"Ees no prob-LEMME," says Cyril.

"Jean, it's really not my place to say no, but . . ."

"I promise I'll be back safely in a couple hours."

David sighs.

Even though Cyril understands little of what we say, I lower my voice and talk out of the side of my mouth. "He's cool. His dad runs the garage in Froussac." David hesitates. "Maybe he can be of service someday if your van breaks down." Like I'm a diplomat at court, a fulcrum for throne-saving favors and trades.

David assesses Cyril, who stands proud.

"Fine. Jean: Don't you make a headache for me."

Caitlin seems distracted and weepy and is happy to cut the night short, but Judith and Yoni look on with peevish little stepsister eyes as I get permission to stay at the ball, and Sigrid winks at me, making a low fist and jamming it back and forth, a gesture I completely ignore and hope David did not see.

I trot off with Cyril, who, the moment David's van disappears down the country road, becomes uninteresting to me. One of Cyril's friends steps up on a wall and leads some chants, and I find myself belting refrains with my hands up, but I'm a figurine, empty. The Jean who watches me sleeps now. Nothing I do here matters, unseen by David. But it is good; she's pleased, this Ruthless Jean. She rouses herself an hour later and taps me on the shoulder—the last thing I should do is make David worry. I tell Cyril, "I should go."

JEAN: *Nothing I do here matters, unseen by David.* It's got nothing to do with sex, does it? If I wanted sex, I could have ridden this sweet French yokel on any number of hay bales.

MONICA: Most certainly. Really would have made his night.

JEAN: I'm coming to life for David. I have a new will, new energy. A new—devil?

MONICA: Oh, Ruthless Jean. She's the part of you that's fixated on David. Wily, determined, amoral.

JEAN: I can remember it now, how good it feels to want someone. How it gives you—

MONICA: Powers. Oh yeah. Watch out for Ruthless Jean.

Cyril puts a helmet on me. I wrap my arms around his waist and soon we are flying through the night, his headlight picking out haunches and hides and the hovering paired silver retinas of the cows. He slows down as we approach the castle, where the driveway is pitch-dark, all the castle's flood lights tilted toward its own façade, to display its beauty, not to guide visitors.

Cyril parks, we hop down, and he takes a long, respectful look up at the castle; I half expect him to bow or kneel. Then he gives me a kiss—I find his tongue suddenly in my mouth like a little creature, a frog I wish would leap back out, and it does, leaving nothing but a trace of tar and possibly some sort of ham product. My mind doesn't map Cyril as we kiss. My heart is like the flood lights, shining up toward the castle. *David, do you see me? Do you see me being kissed? Do you see the young man—from a distance maybe he seems hot, threateningly hot—bowing to me, calling me "your majesty," and getting on his* moto*?*

As Cyril takes off, his engine pops loudly, and I suddenly fear

I've woken people up, I've been inconsiderate. Now panic zips through me: Was this a miscalculation? Given what David knows of me, what he heard, do I seem imprudent or alive, slutty or sociable, needy or magical? *Which, David, which do you think I am? Tell me what I am.*

Chapter 28

Caitlin is going home early. She misses Trent too much. The slow letters, the tricky long-distance phone boxes, are too narrow a conduit for the thick bean soup of his love, and she is starving, starved of Trent. Off she goes. "We hardly knew ye, Cait," I say, and a big sheep moans. The sheep are all over us this evening—I can barely see Judith and Yoni in the lounge chairs over the sheep's filthy matted backs. Judith is petting one down its black bony snout.

"Such a waste of time," says Yoni. "She's not going to get credit for any of this. She wasted the spot."

"Oh gosh, I hadn't thought of that." Judith gnaws at her nail. "Someone else might have really wanted to come." She looks straight into the sheep's eyes: "Do you want her spot? Huh? Number"—she checks its side—"fifteen?" The sheep dips down and pulls at the grass with the sound of fabric ripping at the seams.

✦

Before Jojo drives her to the train station at Moulins, Caitlin gives us a long-promised gift. We assemble at the big table and she stands at the head of it and opens her mouth to sing, unaccompanied.

Blow the wind southerly, southerly, southerly
Blow bonnie breeze, my lover to me.
They told me last night there were ships in the offing,
And I hurried down to the deep rolling sea . . .

Very quickly I go through the following emotions: deep embarrassment for her ("southerly?" da fuck?), then superiority because I would never do anything as self-exposing as opening my throat and pouring out a desperate, earnest love song from my private fuchsia-tissued uterine depth. Then as she keeps going I move toward an irresistible enjoyment of the goldenness, the wholeness and wet rolling lushness of her voice. Then I forget who I am and I'm only a sensation of being inside her song, my heart throbbing with hope for southerly winds, and then when I've adjusted to her triumph over me, I hate her.

"Amazing." I clap with the others when she stops. I look at her face, happy that her eyes are slightly too close together for her to be truly beautiful. "Like, *amazing.*"

"Caitlin, gosh, you show us that and then you go," says David. "You're really breaking our hearts."

Out, out with you, cross-eyed hick. Ah, but that's Ruthless Jean. The real me, the kind me, will miss her, enjoyed being hugged for no reason, enjoyed the purple palette of her wardrobe and her stories about foreplay and football. But Ruthless Jean wants her, the only other young woman here whose butt looks juicy in jeans, out of the way. *I shouldn't care about my butt!!!* I scold myself, sighing loudly in front of everyone—only Yoni catches it, looks at me quizzically.

I have to recommit to *not caring,* remind myself that David's affection is a mirage that everyone sees—look at Judith, tracking David with her soupy eyes. *Via trita, via tuta:* Stay safe, resist attraction, don't be like these silly women who lead with their hearts, losing time, losing energy, wasting opportunities, wasting away.

Chapter 29

A LIFE OF SAINT MARY OF EGYPT,
FROM *The Golden Legend*

✦ ✦ ✦

Saint Mary of Egypt was a prostitute in Alexandria from the age of twelve. For seventeen years she was a prostitute and never refused her body to anyone. One day she met some men going to Jerusalem to pay homage to the holy cross and Mary wanted to join them. When they asked for her fare, she said she had no money, but she could pay them with sex, so she did.

In Jerusalem, she tried to enter the church, but an invisible force pushed her back from the door and would not let her enter. She realized it was because of her licentious lifestyle, so she beat her breast, prayed to the Virgin Mary, and promised to renounce the world and live chastely. The doors opened.

Mary wandered into the desert, where she lived for forty-seven years on the few hard loaves she had brought with her. All her flesh melted away and her clothes fell off and she was naked and never saw another human soul, thereby conquering all temptations. One day a monk wandered into the desert and saw her and did not know whether she was a man or a woman for she was little more than a skeleton, burned dark by the sun. He offered her communion. She said, "Come back next year," so he did, by which time she was dead, but a nice lion came and dug her a grave and then left.

A church rose in the sand.

Chapter 30

"This one's really trashy." Yoni and I process down the nave of a church whose interior was once painted in bright colors, stripes and zigzags, now faded. "I feel like she's got bad tattoos."

"Write that down," I say. Yoni scribbles in the notes for our guidebook. We turn a corner and Judith rushes up to us, her jaw dropped.

"What?" we ask.

She tries to talk, but her jaw won't close.

"Ich kuck," she manages to say. "My daw ich kuck."

"Your jaw?" I ask, in disbelief. She nods.

"Wait, you literally *cannot close* your mouth?" says Yoni. Judith shakes her head in a panic, her jaw out like a shovel.

"Holy shit," he says.

It's a small church. Sam and Brice are only a few feet away, poring over their drawing, and Patrick's not far off, identifying and photographing chipped plaster saints. The hot guy with the plague boil on his thigh—that's Saint Roche. We know him now; he's around every corner, always walking his dog, lifting up his skirt, begging you to look at his holes. These martyrs are all over: Sebastian run through with arrows, Lucy holding the knife they slit her throat with, Catherine smiling next to the wheel they broke her body on. Like Torture Barbies: pretty, long-haired, well-dressed, pumped, perforated.

"We need some privacy," says Yoni. "Come on." He leads us downstairs into the crypt, the creepy central basement where you find saints' relics and sometimes a toilet. This church's crypt has a cramped room with a microwave, an angel-themed wall calendar two years out of date, and, behind a locked iron gate, a dusty altar and a piece of Saint Anthelme's finger. The finger looks like a rabbit poop on a velvet cushion inside a jam jar with a golden lid on a golden pedestal, top and bottom inlaid with pearls, like a sea monkey kit made for Barbra Streisand. Saint Anthelme, Neary told us as we all stood outside the church only fifteen or twenty minutes ago, was a local bishop who had supposedly swiped his finger across the place where Christ's body had lain after coming down from the cross, and that's why Anthelme's finger was so important. We stood outside the doorway of the church, and it was Judith who took the day.

"What do you suppose is going on here?" asked Neary, pointing to the carvings around the door, roughly feathered with angular strokes. "Unskilled craftsmanship? It can happen."

Silence. David walked up, ran his hands over the stone, which I thought was boring—no pictures, no people, no animals, just this allover texture, scraped, clawed. He looked closely, his fingers following rivulets; he emitted a little "Mmmmmm."

"Wear and tear?" offered Patrick. "Vandalism?"

"It's uneven, but the pattern within the markings is too systematic."

"It's skin," said Judith, quietly.

David whipped around to her. "Go on," he urged.

"Um. Well, Christ lay on the stone. His skin touched the stone in the cave—what's it called?"

"The Cave of Resurrection," said Patrick with intense casual familiarity, like a rich housewife might say "Short Hills Mall."

"Yeah," continued Judith. "So then Anthelme touched the spot where his body had been and transferred that holy touch to the stone here, to the church."

"His finger's here, in the crypt," added David. "You all should look at it. Sorry, Judith, please continue."

"Well I just wonder whether . . . maybe this church is all about surface, skin. They don't want a smooth stone surface, they want it to be rough, *activated.*" Her little hands flew out wildly here, and she clawed the air. I could see her smarts, and I loved her for it. "They want the surface to be imperfect, like skin. Oh—maybe even wrinkled! Aging! With"—she seemed embarrassed—"holes."

"Penetrated," added Sigrid, nodding.

Neary looked briefly skyward.

David beamed at Judith. "I think you've cracked this, Judith—there's an *activated* awareness of the surface as you exit and enter."

"In-ter-pen-e-tra-ting," Yoni whispered to me. I giggled, and David shot me a disapproving glance. It hit me harder than he meant it to. Ruthless Jean scolded me: *It probably fits his new image of you as thoughtless and impulsive, after that stupid abortion story, to see you snickering like a moron.* I took a half step away from Yoni.

JEAN: I'm such a turncoat!

MONICA: Ruthless Jean can be very persuasive.

Judith's sweet voice picked up again. "Maybe the church builders wanted to make people think about touch, think about the building as a person . . ."

"To feel embraced by Christ," David added. He looked Judith in the eye, and she nodded in agreement, lost and blissful in her connection to him.

Now, in the crypt, her smile is gone and her tongue is flailing.

"Has this happened before?" asks Yoni. Judith nods, reluctantly.

"Kee-eng-gay."

"What?"

"Kee-eng-gay!" She points to her jaw.

"TMJ!" says Yoni. She nods quickly. "TMJ! Oh my god! My cousin Shira got that from chewing Hubba Bubba. But she can shut her mouth, thank fuck."

"Do you want me to get David?" This is sneaky of me—of course she won't want David to see her like this, grotesque, gaping.

We've been so focused on Judith that we haven't noticed an old man in black—a priest, maybe?—descend the stairs and start puttering in the little room with the microwave.

"What do we do?" I whisper to Judith.

"Gonk geh Gabid."

"Don't get David?"

She shakes her head vehemently.

"Ih jyuss dakes dime . . ." Yoni and I look at each other.

"Time?" Yoni deciphers.

"Oh, *it just takes time.* OK. You have to stay down here with us, out of sight," I tell her. She nods, sways a little closer to me, and wraps her arm around mine.

"OK, well, while we're here." Yoni pulls up the notepad. "Basement full of creepy shit."

"I think you mean 'reliquary in the crypt.' "

"Oh my god, we're *learning.*" We high-five. Suddenly there's an audible click and a gasp and Judith's mouth closes. She rubs her jaw in relief.

"Oh, thank god," I say.

"That was crazy." Yoni assesses the side of her face like he's a bike mechanic. "Does that happen a lot?"

Judith seems both exhausted and ashamed. Her eyes, I notice, are bloodshot in a way they weren't earlier this morning.

"It's happened before," she says. "Not that much." She thanks us, says she has to do her work, and runs off.

Yoni and I face each other, alone in the crypt with Anthelme's shriveled finger and an old man in nurse's shoes. I think about Judith's locked jaw, her red eyes. "Do you think she was giving someone a blow job?" I ask.

"It's 11:35 a.m. and we're in a church, Jean. No. Also, it's *Judith.*"

"Have you noticed the way she looks at David?"

"Oh, like a hungry dog?"

"Yes!"

The priest turns on the microwave, smiling at us, and the place fills with soup smell.

"Let's get out of here," says Yoni. We make our way out of the church, and turn around together to look at the east face, at the rows of gouged columns on either side of the door.

"Maybe that's why they painted the interior! All the stripes and zigzags match the patterns on the portal!"

"*Yes.*" Yoni writes in the notebook. "Tattoos . . . match the piercings." I hold this nugget of an idea happily in my mind—I'll deliver it to David at lunch. He'll love it.

We watch David come around the side of the building with Neary. They both stop at the portal, and David, again, runs his hands along the surface while Neary scribbles in a pocket-size spiral notebook.

Yoni and I move far enough away that they can't hear us.

"Poor Judith," says Yoni.

"Why poor Judith?" says Sigrid, suddenly right behind us. We both jump.

"How do you *do* that?" says Yoni in genuine wonder.

"Where did you come from?" I ask.

"Cemetery," she says, waving toward the gated lawn behind her, as if this is a cool place to hang out.

"Why 'poor Judith'?" Sigrid asks again, but she doesn't wait for an answer. "You guys want to see a dead dog?"

"No," we both say.

"OK, well, there's one in the dumpster, FYI. Looks like a stray. You can see his ribs."

I picture Judith's body the first time I watched her get dressed in our room, like a woodshop project, all planks and joints visible through the skin. I don't want to be like Judith, called to David by some ineluctable feminine weakness in me. I have to rip David out of my mind, the awareness of him, the hope for his attention, the intensity with which I wait for dinner, to be seated at the opposite end of the long table, aware of the tangerine sky and the docile sheep framing the view of me for him, serving myself to him. Listen to Yoni and Sigrid: *Everyone loves David.* And yet you foolishly think you've planted some desire in him? That you're special to him, that he wants to know you, that he wants to run his hands over your skin, know where it's warmest, where it divots, where it gives? He's twenty-five years older than you, important, doing Important Work and married to an Important Woman and you're one of a dozen little girls who look at him with hearts in their eyes. You *have* to be like Sigrid, not like Judith.

"I want to see the dog, Sigrid."

"You do?" she says, energized.

"Yeah. How do you think it died?"

"I just think no one fed it."

Exactly.

Chapter 31

It's the middle of the night, but huddled by my bedside lamp, I finish the book—*Belle et Sébastien*—and have been so deeply engrossed in the story, I didn't realize I was weeping. I don't want to wake Sigrid and Judith, so I put the book under my arm and slip out the door. There are little plastic night-lights in some of the sockets along the floor that lead me through the corridor of the main building and downstairs to the kitchen. I burst the door open, thinking that, far from the bedrooms, I am free to sob liberally, but to my surprise, David and Neary are sitting at the round table in front of a bottle of whisky.

"Oh, for chrissakes," says Neary. "What's *your* crisis?"

David looks embarrassed for me. I must be ugly, my face splotched red, wearing a big dumb Grateful Dead tour T-shirt and wide-leg sweatpants and mismatched socks.

"Next year we're running this program with two or three advanced PhD students, no more undergrads."

"James . . ."

"What is it? You, too, miss your boyfriend?"

"No, it's *Belle et Sébastien.*"

"Who are they?" Neary turns to David in horror. "Have we got mixed up with locals? *You* took them to the bar, David."

"No, it's a book. It was on the bookshelf in my room."

Somehow David's whole face changes without moving; his eyes become keen, and a receptiveness inhabits him invisibly like a spirit. Neary puts his forehead on the table with a *clunk.*

"What's the book about?" asks David.

"Um—"

"You can sit down," David says. "I don't know if you want"—he gestures to Neary's whisky.

"Certainly not," says Neary, forming a defensive wall around the bottle with his arms.

"I don't want any," I say, slipping past them to the cabinet and then the sink, filling up a glass with water. Then I slide onto the low wood stool on the other side of the table from the men, set down my glass. "Um—it starts with a poor, nameless woman climbing through the Alps, and she collapses in a barn, where she has a baby, and then she dies. It was the feast day of Saint Sebastian, so the people who find the baby name him Sébastien. And since he's all alone in the world, he gets taken in by an old mountaineer with a granddaughter."

"Oh, I see where this is going," says Neary.

"It's about children and dogs; no one's banging."

"Ah."

"And on the night of his birth, on another part of the mountain, a white dog is born, and just traded and abandoned and used by people—not monsters, just self-interested people—until she learns to stop loving. She gives up on humans, and because she doesn't try to please them, they think she's psycho. They keep her caged, treat her like shit."

"Jean," says Neary, "must you swear so consistently?"

"Um. Are you saying I should swear less? Or like, less evenly?" I am truly trying to answer Neary, but David smothers a laugh and Neary says, "Never mind. Go on."

"Anyway, so one day the dog escapes and is seen in the village and Sébastien, this little six-year-old boy, hears about her and knows, instinctively, that she must be alone and scared, and he goes out into the mountains to protect her. He finds her and they sense each other's loneliness and they instantly connect. And little by little, Belle—that's the dog—comes to trust people again."

Now they're both listening closely.

"So one day Belle comes into the village and steals some meat from the butcher."

"Oh no," says Neary.

"She was hungry! She didn't hurt anyone. But all these violent, small-town losers, they're sure that Belle is dangerous, so they form a posse to kill her, and Sébastien goes out again to the mountains to protect her. But when he's out there looking for her, there's an avalanche."

"Oh no," says Neary again.

"And everyone thinks the boy is dead. They hike out to find his body. And then, even though Belle knows everyone wants to kill her, she barks from under the snow. They dig her out and she's covered the boy's body with her own"—I wrap my paws around an invisible boy—"and melted the snow above his mouth with her breath so that he can breathe. Because she loved him, and she would do anything to keep him alive."

Neary is staring at me, chin down. David has his elbow on the table, a hand covering his mouth, watching me.

"But when the posse see her, they raise their guns. And the grandfather says, 'You touch this dog and I'll kill you.' "

My eyes feel hot, vaporous.

Neary's sleeve goes up to his face.

"He becomes courageous, just like the dog, and faces down all these people." Neary's eyes are about to spill over and I'm working hard to draw breath through my closing throat. "Because the boy *loves* the dog, and love should be protected."

Neary raises his glass shakily to his lips.

"Gosh," says David, who is aware of Neary losing his composure next to him and seems to want to change registers—as if Neary's dignity has to be protected. "Who's it by? What's this story called?"

"The author is"—I turn the book over and read—"Cécile Aubry. *Belle et Sébastien.*"

Neary sniffles, uses the beat David gave him to tidy his feelings away. His voice is hardening, recovering with a slight quiver. "Saint Sebastian, you know, they—"

"Wait," interrupts David. "Pop quiz. Have you been reading the sources I gave you? What happened to Saint Sebastian?"

"He got shot full of arrows."

"That's right. By?"

"Diocletian."

David beams.

"And?" asks Neary.

"It sucked, I assume."

"He didn't die," says Neary. "He made a miraculous full recovery. Hallelujah." He briefly looks skyward and makes withering jazz hands. "So your Sébastien, he's cheated death, it seems. Like his namesake. Lucky lad."

"Let's hope he survives the sequel," says David. "Let's hope *you* survive the sequel," he says, laughing warmly at my emotion.

The Ruthless Jean inside of me who is always aware of my status in David's eyes is swollen with joy, ecstatic. The smile I give them upon David's last words—*Let's hope* you *survive*—glows with a shy acknowledgment of the way my heart can be made to swell and secrete by the stories I'm told. I am a deep reader, what they wish for in every student. Here I was in my pajamas, bringing them morsels of heart, the two men, yet revealing nothing tawdry, holding my dignity in my breast. Yes, this was a win.

"Off you go," says Neary. "We're not long here, either."

Feeling, triumphally, like I've been patted on the ass, I turn and go.

Chapter 32

MOULINS MARKET SQUARE

I'm cooking later this evening, so Victoire has taken me to the open market at Moulins for supplies. I'm agog at all the vendors; one guy just does melons. There's horsemeat! The fish stalls alone, all the different places a fish can have an eye—on its back, under its jaw. The cheeses laid out like a plaster model of a sprawling city, chalky white towers, pyramids, silos. Victoire is in line for the *traiteur*—under a glass case, the whole pig laid out in parts, even the snow-white hooves, with white velvet skin up to the severed elbows like opera gloves. *These are my people,* I think, looking at the market vendors with familial love, even though they are killers and salters, merchants, with broken veins in their noses and cheeks, exhausted. It is even with some fear and fatalism that I feel this kinship, feel that while the others go on to make webbed maps of ancient vaults, I will be a lady who moves pig parts, who wears a hairnet while maneuvering a blade through a meniscus, waiting to smoke.

As if she can hear me thinking, Victoire surveys me with narrowing eyes and says, in French, "You're not like the others." At the castle, I've attributed a maternity to her because she wears aprons and looks after us, but here, in her jeans, with her cigarette breath, greeting acquaintances at the market, Victoire is suddenly just a middle-aged woman running errands.

MONICA: She's what—
JEAN: Oh, thirty-seven.
MONICA: Max.

"Not like the others, how?" I ask. Victoire sucks on her teeth a bit, holds her list in one hand, leans a hip against the vendor's case of pink pieces. "I don't seem as smart as them?"

"That's not it." Her head falls to the side. "You're not a snob." She doesn't know it, but what she means is, I'm not as smart. "How old are you, eighteen?"

"Nineteen. Almost twenty." She raises her eyebrows with surprise. Everyone always thinks I'm younger than I am, even though I'm not small. It is infuriating, consistent, this way that I can't find the button marked "woman," can't flip the switch.

"It's us," says the vendor, an incredibly intimate way of telling you it's your turn to buy ham.

Poitrine, the French word for "chest" and "breast," what you put in your bra, is also the word for "bacon." I want some. I have a vision, and Victoire, showing the vendor with her fingers how thick we want the bacon sliced, is helping me realize it. It's weird how close we are, without having spoken much. Without any ego, she is pleased that I seem to want to learn from her, which I do; but what's truly miraculous is that I suddenly know so much already.

Sometimes you need to show them the luxury, woo them with goo, with cream, with meat, with proteins that have given up like a public self and been coaxed in the dark to split, and gone viscous and punchy with their own heated blood. But sometimes, my wakening instinct tells me, you get them with a cold hello, with a straight back—with a salad. You will get David by performing good health and simplicity, no tawdry sauces, no scallops queefing steam, just Jojo's lettuce, each leaf a complete waterfall in a kerchief of green cellulose. And I'll salt it up with those wrinkled black olives Victoire uses all the time, and I'll get snipping in the herbs—tarragon and parsley and all that. But then hiding in there will be what he thinks is "bacon," that brown strip that cartoons eat for breakfast, but it will be hand-cut *poitrine.* An unbelievable, unexpected gift of fat, of unction, a pleasure so intense that you feel it behind your ears, on the outside of your throat; you feel touched by a hand on your forehead.

"What's for dinner, Jean?" they'll say, and I won't look at him, because I am cool and not a snob but smarter than all of them, gathering power in my hot little crypt, pulling the current of events toward me like a tablecloth, bringing everything I want with it.

"Just a salad."

Chapter 33

The two Sundays I've cooked so far have conferred a kind of status on me; I get the impression that if Viking marauders demanded hostages, I wouldn't be the first one shoved out the castle doors (bye, Patrick). But the strategist inside my mind who fixates on David finds a new advantage: the term paper.

Yoni and Caitlin were in adjoining singles, so now that Caitlin's gone, Yoni's taken over her room as his office. But between my shared bedroom and the busy kitchen, I have nowhere quiet to work. Evenings now, I need the library.

I push open the heavy library door—still astonished at the volume of its squeal—and David looks up.

"Jean. Can I help you?"

"Um. Can I work on my paper here?"

"Of course," he says. He looks around at the flotilla of side tables and vanities and dining chairs. "Do what I've done—make yourself at home." David has created an alcove by walling his desk off on two sides with five-foot-tall bookshelves.

I take a little desk in the corner, a repurposed sky-blue vanity with violin-shaped legs, because it's far from David, and I don't want him to think I will bother him. I remember what Sigrid told us about the pressure on David to increase his academic output, and even if she hadn't, we can all sense that when dinner ends, David becomes anxious, distant. Even during the day sometimes, in a spare moment—at a local café-*tabac*, crunching into sandwiches while Sigrid explains to the rest of us how a guillotine works—you catch him staring off with a face that sees catastrophe.

"There's a laptop here for student use. Can you and Yoni arrange to take turns with it?"

I nod. "I don't know what building to choose, for my paper. I'm really not that interested in buildings." There it is again—I'm not trying to be funny, but my simplest, most straightforward thought delights him.

"It's about time you came clean."

"Well, it's true. I like a lot of the art. But . . ."

"You don't have to write about architecture. I understand it can be a bit technical. I'm sorry, I should have thought of this sooner." His gaze probes me. "Look, I'll tell you something, but you can't tell the others."

"OK."

"The reason you and Yoni are here— The truth is, we got extra money for including undergrads. The funders love it. No one wants to give money to a bunch of navel-gazing grad students, but when we brought you along, suddenly it looked like a school. So, you're here, but Neary and I haven't properly figured out where you fit."

"Well, there are only two of us."

"Exactly, and you're both brilliant." *Brilliant*—I see myself through David's eyes, holding chalk in front of a complex equation on a blackboard. "My god, that salad!" I replace the chalk with tongs; he also sees that he's somehow detracted from his earlier compliment and he stammers a bit. "Wh-what I mean, your *generosity* aside, is that I think you *are* learning a lot, aren't you?"

"Oh yeah," I gush before I can even think about it, because I want to be supportive, I want to give him a good grade. Then I review my mind's more recent acquisitions: pork fat and billet moldings and a person surviving on dog's breath and Saint Agnes, charbroiled. "Yeah, absolutely."

"So for your paper, do like the grad students do." He gestures at the boxes of books at our feet. "Read around. And then propose something. Any aspect of visual culture. You're just writing for me. I can work with you." *You're writing for me:* My paper will be a secret I whisper to him, a conversation had across a pillow.

The sun is setting earlier but still late, and the evenings have a warmth about them. The pigeons, unbelievably fat, coo and tuck in among the ivy just outside the window. There might be a groan of wood on wood as David leans back to reach a stack of papers behind him. Sometimes the door howls open and Yoni sticks his head in to grab a book or wave a cigarette at me. But mostly David and I just sit there in the quiet doing our work. Nothing seems unseemly, and even the secret choice I've made to read his wife's book—no one sees that. We seldom speak, but the little exchanges we have, over the hours and days, they accumulate.

"You making progress there, Jean?"

"Mmm."

"Good."

"How's your book?"

"Book is good."

Standing to stretch his legs and step away from his computer, he asks, "Why's your French so good? Sometimes I forget you didn't come with the castle."

"My mom's Belgian."

"Belgian? How did that happen?"

I give him the outline—my dad, working for a chemical company in Brussels, gets a rash, and my mom is the pharmacist who sells him ointment. *L'amour.*

"And does she like living in the United States?"

"Nnnnno."

"Do you think she wants to go back to Belgium?"

"Nnnnno." How to start on my mother? How at first I thought it was my fault, that a charming and sociable woman didn't seem to want my company. Her personality was like the cocktails she swirled with a long spoon, a ruby-toned juice for grown-ups that children got scolded for trying to taste. After I'd gone to college, I got the strangest call from her—she was all excited to invite me to dinner just the two of us at the Palm steakhouse in midtown Manhattan. We met, and she handed me the drinks menu with a wink. I realized she'd never wanted *children,* wasn't interested in them, and was ready to meet now on a plane of adult friendship and ideas. She had been a beautiful woman, with sort of a puffy upper lip that was very glamorous and which I got a bit of, and now we could march into the night side by side like bright high beams. Nobody hanging off her, looking for snacks in her purse. But it didn't work; a soggy silence hung about us. I didn't know her taste in jokes. She looked bored when I talked and swatted at my hands when I bit my nails. We watched businessmen bring meat to their mouths, wishing we knew them so they could anchor us there. She would know what to say to *them.*

"My mom's kind of a sad sack."

"I can't imagine that," says David.

"Oh. That's just an expression." I didn't mean to, but again I made a warm laugh rumble from David.

"No, I know what a sad sack is—I mean it seems very different from your . . . constitutional delightedness."

My eyebrows shoot up. This seems to only make him laugh more. But now we've hit some border I didn't know was there and he gets serious, has to drop me.

"Come on," he says. "Back to work." And the silence, as blissful as the conversation, because we live inside of it together, takes over.

JEAN: My god, I'm my mother.

MONICA: Welcome to the club. This dress was $39.99 from T.J. Maxx—bet they still have them in your size. Should we go?

JEAN: She had nothing against family life. But she had been trained, somehow, to engage men, to please them, and nothing counted until she was reactivated by one—any man, an optician, a friend's dad.

MONICA: And here, you see that little Jean's training is under way with David.

JEAN: How significant Jean feels when he's watching, how purposeful. And when he's not, she goes slack. I thought my mother and I were so different, then: she was oversexed and obvious, rifling through a bathroom drawer of thirty-five lipsticks, while I huddled with my girlfriends, laughing at other people's crushes.

MONICA: There's a pretty simple explanation for why you let David train you.

JEAN: What?

MONICA: It was his job.

In the pile of secondary sources, I found David's wife's book. I picked it up with a sense of juicy scandal and hid it within another volume at my desk, but boy is it dry. I don't understand much. It's having an argument with writers I haven't read; I don't know half the terms. (How is "pyx" a whole word????) It feels illegal to read her words, as if I went into her laundry basket and put on her nightie. But when I do, the craziest thing happens: I stop taking notes on the veneration of relics and start to write the thoughts running through my head, sitting across the room from David yet possessed by the imagined intimacy of a spouse.

Your breath is coming out of you ten feet from me—I can steal it from the air, lick it up without asking you. Can you sense me here? Can you hear me thinking about you? Can you feel me tracing the line of your arm across your shoulder, around your jaw? What are the words for the back of your head, the line of your shoulder up your neck? I'm choking on your shoulder in my mouth. Please can I put my mouth on it? Please can I bite it? Someday, if there is a God, if all those guys are right and there's a God, he can kill me right after, he can take the car that my mom was going to give me, and all my favorite clothes, and the people that care about me, Judith and Eunice, he can take them, and my health and my future, take it all, put a period down right after he lets me do it and end the whole sentence, but let me. Let me have you. I know you would like my boobs so much, more than Manny Maiolo and Elliot and that guy at Eunice's sister's house party. They just squeezed and slobbered. David, you would be so happy with my boobs in your mouth—

"What are you reading, Jean?"

"Oh. Uh. Anthony Cutler on ivories."

"Ah, classic. Carry on."

In your mouth, David, in your mouth, put my boobs into your mouth please Christian Jesus if there's any pity in you and any goodness or sense on this earth, please let me, let me.

MONICA: Wow, you were really focused on the breasts.

JEAN: You forget how that's typical of a virgin. In her ignorance of the advanced pleasures, she fixates on the first ones.

MONICA, THOUGHTFUL: I suppose that's true.

JEAN: But maybe that's a kind of virgin wisdom. Because boobs are great. People should spend more time on boobs!

Monica nods with a teacher's pride as if I have just solved a math problem and turns slowly back to the scene.

The silence David and I occupy in the library together is insidious because now even when I am alone, brushing my teeth, or walking from the kitchen to my room, or slamming the rickety toilet door behind me and looking into my face in the tarnished mirror of the café in our town where we've had a thousand bitter coffees, I feel him there, I see him seeing me. When the world was a formless void and darkness covered the face of the deep—remember then?—before families and farms, before weddings and schools, we could have spent infinite time together, lying on a nameless rock, side by side, laughing. I know this! So why don't we? Why aren't we always together? Why does he ever have to go and sleep, wash himself, work, without me? I hear that childish line from the Lord's Prayer: *for ever and ever.* We should rent a room, not for a day but *for ever and ever,* rent a room and lie next to each other on a hard bed and talk. We could fill the time—it would go quickly—and then in my mind, he turns to me, he rolls onto his side, he puts an arm over me. In real life, my stomach drops, I quiver, I blur. Until now I haven't let myself imagine his touch, but now I break. I have to give myself this, fill the space between the formless void where we have each other and the real world where we're nothing.

Chapter 34

"Are you sick?" asks Sigrid.

After we got back from today's church—bright white and kind of tall, with long, narrow columns, a style Yoni and I described in our guidebook as "Glenn Close-y"—I went straight to bed. You wouldn't know what was in my head to look at me, lying like a gisant under my white blanket, and thank god for the stone wall of my skull, because inside my mind I let myself have him, I let myself be had.

"Not sick. Just tired," I say. There's no competition from the real world; everything is happening in my mind now. There's no reason to be awake, standing, eating.

"It's dinner in five," she says. "Are you coming?"

I will go because he'll be there, but I need a little more time. A few more rounds, in my imagination, we'll go together, my body awash with chemical responses to the unreal, my organs darting and dashing in me, responding to the story my mind tells: his mouth on mine, my back against the library door, my bones and all the meat on them gifts for him to palpate and unwrap. He could put any part of himself into me and I would take it, that's what I told him in our meetings in my mind. *I'll do whatever you tell me.*

When I go down to dinner, it's almost a shock to see David there, in his material reality, sharing pretzels from a bowl with dour orange Patrick. I feel guilty I've puppeteered him with wanton psycho perversion in my filthy mind in my princess room in my four-poster bed. But the guilt is contained and I know it won't keep me from going back, and soon, for hours of it.

I sit at the far end of the table, flush from my fantasies, and I don't want the creamy potatoes or the speckled sausages taut in their skins, I want wine. Patrick migrates down toward my end of the table to be nearer the sausage platter. I watch him bow his head and mumble before eating and I feel a strange kinship with him because he, too, has one foot in the imaginary.

"Is it hard to remember all those complicated prayers?"

"Repetition," he says. "I don't have to remember them. They're an invisible ladder I climb to the Lord. I don't have to build the ladder; it's centuries old."

"But you *do* have to build the ladder, don't you? You have to say the right things."

"Look. If you're a Lutheran, for example, you have to make it up. 'Hello, God, it's me, Sven. I'd like to talk about my sick horse.'" Huh, they never teach you *anything* about Protestants in Catholic school? It's like he knows advanced trigonometry but no basic algebra. "I don't have to do that," he continues. "I have an exquisite ready-made verse that takes me there. It's transcendent."

"That does seem cool," I say because I have found the same thing, looping around and around in the same fantasies, the same sparse script that I can climb like a glittering net to a place of ecstatic near-contact with one man. Confused, hungry, a little drunk, I remember we're combatants, Patrick and I, aren't we? I add, "I mean, everything you believe is insane and made up, but I like the idea."

"Is it? You don't have to believe, Jean. God loves you anyway."

"Oh Jesus, here we go."

"Him, too. This whole world is organized by his love."

"So God is like an old man leering at me? It's unwanted attention from an old white guy who works on his pecs and has good hair."

"You want to make it dirty, but that's your mind, Jean, not God's."

"You don't know the half of it, Patrick." I lean toward him. "My mind is *disgusting*," I say, and find it completely remarkable that in our little grotto of irony and antagonism I am telling Patrick and Patrick alone the truth. Patrick has no doubt heard my foolish lie about my past but has no idea how diabolically I am willing my future.

"All I can say is, good luck to you, Jean. It must be very difficult. To have no principles, no beliefs, no rituals, no guiding power."

"Well, I have myself."

"How's that going?"

I don't know what to major in, I have no career ambitions, I've never had sex, and I just spent two and a half hours imagining my teacher pounding me into a library door with a merciless cast-iron erection. I lied to everyone about having an abortion, and I wish my flesh would melt off me and leave me all bone like Judith or that dog I saw in the dumpster.

"It's going great."

Better that than eating Jesus jerky every Sunday, I should say, but the fight has left me. There is something about Patrick's religiosity that I like. A feeling that he's not out for himself, and also, that his decisions have already been made, opinions formed. So I can say things like:

"I'm really enjoying getting drunk here."

"Great."

"Do you drink?"

"Not to excess."

"I never did before! My mom drinks too much."

He doesn't care. He looks away from me, sitting with a straight back, scaffolded by rectitude. Maybe he's left our grotto where I burn candles to all the martyrs whose vaginas God covered in iron panties or shields of gold or cascading head-hair or a thousand frogs, the place where his conviction and mine meet, where I plead for penetration with the passion that his faith created. The Jean that hovers above me, monitoring myself for David, chimes like an angel, and I look up: There it is. I haven't had it in so long, not since the church where I lit the candles. David watches me intently, lost, unaware, and when I catch his gaze, the proof that it contained something it should not is that he snaps away to a senseless alternative: He looks with sudden intensity at a sheep. Oh god, now I believe again, now I believe. All the candles are lit again. *I want you to come to me, I want you to come to me, I want you to come to me.* The words repeat, over and over again: *I want you to come to me, I want you, I want you.* I climb the ladder of the repetition, I feel its rhythms in me, on me, like they'll break my bones, my bed. And David, courageous now, looks at me, for just a moment, the power of my prayer pulling him up, the seraphim I created lifting his chin, and I know it is in him.

Chapter 35

The next day, Saturday, is as lazy and empty as all the others, but it goes fast. I take a walk with Judith on the castle grounds and talk with a casual confidence that surprises me about my imaginary abortion. "Maybe I'll have kids someday," I say. "It just wasn't the right time." The Jean who thinks only of David has colonized my mind, leaving little else, but as much as I trust Judith, something tells me not to share those thoughts.

MONICA: Smart.

So the fake events surrounding my fake boyfriend and our fake unprotected sex and its fake consequences are a green pasture right now, and even Judith finds it easy grazing.

"You can still have kids someday," she says.

"Totally. You can still have kids after an abortion." I haven't actually researched that, but, like, all our moms had us, right?

"I hope I can have kids," says Judith. "I think I might have messed myself up too much." She says it so quietly that I sense I shouldn't follow up, but I also find that I'm intensely curious—not because it's revolting or weird but because I want to know more. I can imagine, for the first time in my life, that giving back all the food you take is pleasurable, is rewarding, but I don't know why, and this is what I want to hear articulated.

"How long have you been doing it?"

"A long time, on and off. Like seven years."

"Why?" We walk on, following a little path through the woods. She's wearing Converse high-tops and khaki shorts that could be from GapKids she's so small, even though she's twenty-three. She has beautiful nut-brown skin and green-gray eyes, but her face is so drawn that her skin wrinkles like plastic wrap when she smiles or laughs, pulled between her hard chin and her cheekbones.

"I can't explain it," she says finally. "I know exactly what's in me. What I'm made of. When I start from scratch. I'm not an A student or a Harvard student or whatever my mom and dad think I am." She sputters an odd, childish laugh. "I guess it's a bad feeling at first, or a gross feeling, but actually when you get used to it, it feels *good.*"

"I can sort of understand that." To be selfless, the opposite of greedy—light and small. To take control of who you are exactly, to cut yourself into a new shape. I don't want to be hurt, but I want an impossibly small waist. It's as if my body has always just been in English, obvious and overfed, and Judith has the keys to its Latinate translation, its Romance conjugation. With her knowledge, I could give the thick, thoughtless typeface of my body a gothic twist, a calligraphic attenuation. In this light, to refuse food seems artful, adult—not so different from smoking cigarettes, it strikes me, an acaloric pleasure, possibly fatal and a little filthy but feminine, French.

"I have to stop. It's really not good for you." She senses that I'm interested, and she's pushing me back, pushing me away from it. Her face is distant, eyes casting ahead in the fields, but she grips herself lovingly, again, the way she did in our bedroom. We come out from the trail in the woods and arrive at Jojo's vegetable garden. She has her secrets and I have mine. I turn us around.

✦

When we get back, all the chairs in the salon downstairs have been moved to face the TV-VCR and everyone but David, Neary, and Patrick is watching *Beverly Hills Cop.* I watch some of the movie with them, but soon I slip out and gather my notebook and my pen and books from my bedroom and look at myself in the mirror very carefully through what I imagine to be his eyes. Bootcut jeans, a Weathervane striped T-shirt over the balcony bra that was something like $36 but that my dad had to buy me at Filene's. My mom didn't want to take me shopping and he was too embarrassed to make a fuss. That was all another lifetime. That person's knowledge of the world, her wants and desires, the people she once considered kin, are dead to her now. The only thing that matters is how good her chest looks, and it looks very good.

I progress.

I push—the door swooshes and squeals—and David is in there. I wave quickly and soundlessly as if we are at a large public library full of people and walk to my desk.

He looks up from his desk.

"It's Saturday night, Jean."

"I don't like the movie they're watching." The last thing I want is to seem desperate. For reasons I don't understand, it's essential to my success that I hide my desire. "I might as well work on my term paper."

"Indeed," he says, disappearing back into his homemade alcove. I hear the muted clicks of his typing, the sound of papers shuffling.

I try to stay focused on *Early Romanesque Statuary*, but I get the impression that all my cells are pushed up against the side of my body closest to him. There are hints of life outside this library, occasional gunshots from the movie or the shuffling of the sheep. But everything melts against the force field of our shared concentration. No noise can compete with our intermixing breath, screamingly silent. I take dry notes about stone arches, and my abdomen is a metal vessel of warm oil.

"Jean," he says after some time.

I have been desperate for his voice.

"Mm-hmm."

"You don't happen to have a spare one of those cigarettes you and Yoni spend all day smoking, do you?"

"Oh, yeah. Of course." We've never done this before. I've never known him to smoke.

We descend the stone steps. I hear his footsteps behind me, soft, chasing. We get to the ground floor and pass in front of the salon, walking furtively: I glance behind to see him with a finger at his lips. We slip out the giant front doors of the castle. I hand him a Camel Light.

"Let's move off to the side," he says. "I don't like being seen to smoke. I don't smoke!"

I follow him down the front steps of the castle just around the corner, to a patch of wall covered in ivy. We lean against the wall, side by side. I like this pretense that we're mechanics, brothers. The casualness of it gives us shelter to connect.

"Are you ready to do a song and dance?" he says, turning his head to me. Something hoots in the field and flaps its wings. I cock the lighter for him, he bends toward me, and the cupid's bow of his upper lip stretches as he inhales. He says a slightly choked "Thank you," flashes his dark blue eyes up at me, courtly, decorous. When he exhales, he holds the cigarette up and studies it with a passing kind of wonder.

"What do you mean 'song and dance'?"

"A group of American philanthropists is coming next weekend. The people who've paid for all this—the flights, the food. And the prince is finally going to grace us with his presence, I'm told. We have to show them that our work is worth their money—we hope they're going to give us much, much more."

"Oh thank god. I thought there was gonna be a talent show or something."

David laughs and taps his cigarette. He's a good smoker; he must have done it a lot, a long time ago.

"What would you do at a talent show, Jean?" He looks at me searchingly, teasingly.

"I don't have any talents."

It was a pathetic phrase, and he gives me a slightly theatrical pout. "Some people," he says, turning his head away to look at me askance, "simply have a talent for being." He pauses, enjoys his cigarette. Then, with new energy, "You're a very talented cook." I want to show him Jojo's garden—it's so good in the evening there, a pleasure I've wanted to share with him: the way the fruit holds the day, the tomatoes hot to the touch. You can smell the skins of everything, damming back the swell, that baked skin smell like a hot pan. And we can lie down in the garden together and— "Why *is* it you can cook?"

I don't want to launch into the empty evenings at my house, how I fed myself. Or tell him about my dirty canteen next to the men's showers in Hampton Hall. It wouldn't fit this moment, that particular truth. And besides, I want him to lift me out of my life and give me a new one: soon none of that will matter.

"Recipes," I tell him. "You make them enough that you memorize them, and then it becomes second nature. Patrick said that's how Catholic prayer works." David shoots a smoky laugh out his nose. "Patrick?" He looks at me pointedly, intrigued, talking through a lopsided smile. "Patrick uses *recipes*—the Lord's Prayer is his lasagna." He laughs again, shaking his head. "It's wonderful," he says. We each take a drag, release together. "You talk to Patrick?"

If our conversation has always been somehow dancing, light, this question passes between us like a plate going from the dishwasher to the shelf, like we've gone through courtship and straight into marriage. We are two people who spend every evening together, tidying, talking, making plans.

"Sometimes." Our cigarettes are almost finished. I don't want them to end. "I like Patrick," I say. I turn to David, my shoulder against the wall, and he does the same toward me.

"Of course you do," he says. He lets out a heavy breath.

I'm calm. I will get what I want. He looks at my lips. I can feel before even moving what his hair will feel like in my hands—brushy and coarse—how I'll move the cotton corner of his white collared shirt aside; I can feel that I, virgin, teen, student, fool, possess a complete and unquestioned competence in opening my mouth and letting him in. All I need is for it to begin.

Then there they are, all of them, tumbling down the stairs holding glasses by the feet and a wine bottle by the neck, Sigrid singing the *Beverly Hills Cop* theme song, imitating a synthesizer, crouching like a stalking cop. David and I roll away from each other against the wall and I pull out another cigarette, as a cover.

They catch sight of us and Yoni says, "David, I didn't know you *smoked.*"

"Hi, guys." I hate them. I hate them all.

"Because I *don't,* Yoni. It's a rare sighting, like Halley's Comet," he says, tossing the butt on the gravel and squashing it underfoot. "It'll be another seventy-five years before my next Camel Light." With that he shuffles off from the crowd. They gather around me and someone goes back in to get me a glass and there is some stupid chat, but my head is not in it. I can't go back up to work in the library with David—it's too late now; it would be embarrassing to follow him up there. We've been cleaved in two, me and David, and now I'm back with the kids.

A few minutes later, lying out on the lawn, Yoni asks, "What were you and David talking about?" Ruthless Jean knows that Yoni, keen analyst of people, may have picked up on something; that he will turn the others on to a juicy possibility and they will, smelling our sweetness, buzz about me and David for the three weeks we have left here. I can't have that. So Ruthless Jean says, "David told me there's a big event happening next weekend. We really have to impress these rich Americans. And the prince. We'll have to do presentations and everything."

There. They've been set off for the night now. Speculation whizzes, loud and circular like a Roman candle. I can sink back into myself and smoke and taste the memory of how close it came, and plan my next move.

"Hey Jean, what's for dinner tomorrow?" asks Brice.

Something good.

Chapter 36

I wake up in the middle of the night and see stars, the golden stars painted on the underside of the canopy above my bed. Sigrid and Judith are gone. I push my covers off and I'm in a white nightgown, thin like a veil. I pad down the corridor barefoot and take the stairwell that leads to the library. This is where everyone was a few Saturdays ago, watching Brice and Sam kick each other in the crotch. I suspect they must be up at the window again. The door squeals its familiar puppy squeal and I feel warm, full of the anticipated satisfaction of David's company. I see he's at his desk; he leans back to greet me from his alcove.

But it's not him, it's Neary.

"I knew it," he hisses. "You have to leave David alone."

"What do you mean? What am I doing?"

Neary has his flask, he's full of a fiery truth, he sees right through me.

"You are trying to distract him for your own silly girlish experiment. Have you no shame, nothing more worthwhile rattling around in your little brain? Don't do this to David."

"I'm not doing anything," I say, a liar. Look at me, my body, its dark centers of interest, all on display in this thin cotton nightgown.

"Just leave him alone. Find someone else to satisfy your vanity. He has demanding, important work to do." His eyes travel down my body with scorn for and maybe even fear of how compelling, how dangerous it is.

I turn away, and the library door bangs shut behind me. As I go downstairs in the dark, my nightgown tangles around my legs and I reach for the banister but it's no longer there and I tumble forward in the dark and—

I wake up in my bed, sweating, my T-shirt twisted around my torso.

I'm so relieved. I never did anything wrong. I never touched him.

Chapter 37

A LIFE OF SAINT THAIS, COURTESAN, FROM *The Golden Legend*

✦ ✦ ✦

Thais the courtesan was a woman of such beauty that her lovers frequently fought each other at her door and covered the threshold with their blood.

When news of this came to the ears of a holy father, he put on layman's clothes, provided himself with some money, and went in search of Thais. He offered her the money. She took it and said, "Come with me into this room."

He was invited to climb into a bed with precious coverlets, but he said, "If there is a room farther in, let us go there." She led him through a series of rooms, but he kept saying that he was afraid of being seen.

Finally she said to him, "If you are afraid of God, there is no place hidden to his divinity."

When the old man heard this, he asked, "If you know that, why have you brought so many souls to perdition? You will be damned."

Thais heard the man, prostrated herself at his feet, and then brought everything she had earned by sin and burned it in the center of the city while the people looked on.

Then the holy father shut her up in a narrow cell in a monastery of virgins and sealed the door with lead, leaving a small window through which bits of bread and a little water could be brought to her. Thais asked him, "Father, where do you want me to deposit my water when nature calls?"

"In your cell," he answered. "That is all that you deserve!"

After three years, the holy father had a vision of a bed with precious coverlets, watched over by three virgins: they represented Shame, Righteousness, and the Fear of Punishment. The holy father went to release Thais, but she asked to be allowed to remain enclosed. "Just as breath has not left my nostrils, so my sins have not left my eyes." He led her out of her cell and she died a fortnight later.

The holy father went to convert another courtesan the same way. When this woman tried shamelessly to entice him to sin, he led her to a place where there was a crowd of people and said, "Lie down here so that I can copulate with you!"

"How can I do that with all these people standing around?"

"If you are ashamed before men, should you not be much more ashamed before God, who reveals the secrets of the dark?"

The woman walked away in confusion.

Chapter 38

The Neary of my nightmare was right: It is just vanity, this *silly girlish experiment.* I want to lasso the moon that watches me and bury her back in the crater she left in my mind, but I don't know how. What's so charming about David anyway? Stupid perfect pants, the way they fit. Sometimes, without warning, he will wear a SNEAKER instead of brown leather oxfords and that is infuriatingly hot, the tiniest atomic residue of a teenage readiness to get erections and play basketball. How to forget the feeling when his attention is so fully on you, so sunny, and comes directed at you by his beautiful eyes, trapezoidal and mineral blue and set off by the gray hair at his temples? There are handsomer people! A young French man with balls so active you could smell them in his neck kissed me last week! I should want *him*!

But it is useless—even if I *will* myself to think of other things, I see myself seen by David. Like a surveillance device implanted in me—when? When was it installed? How to rip it out?—I can't not watch myself through his eyes. It is as if I see myself for the first time; I am new. I am amazed to discover with an architect's pleasure the harmonious distances between my features, to note with a baker's satisfaction that my skin has gone gold in the country sun. I hold my shirt up and turn sideways: I am losing weight; my periwinkle shorts used to squeeze me at the tummy but not anymore. I hear my voice, too, for the first time, as if it were a stranger's. I sing sometimes and when I sound good, when I work up a little vibrato staring out at the lake on the lounger listening to the Indigo Girls on my headphones and humming all the Emily harmonies, I think how seduced he'd be, how his ears would prick up at the sound and he would want to lay his head in my virgin lap like the unicorn.

✦

I will disappear into the kitchen, focus on my work. When Victoire asked what I needed this week, I told her butter, just butter. Because I knew there was leftover chicken, and there was the garden. And I am an economical cook. But something else is happening to my cooking, I can tell: it's lifting off, going places, becoming my own. I'm moving away from the scripts I had memorized—I have this idea for a savory bread pudding with leftover baguette and the ends of all the cheeses and the herbs from the garden. Along with my salad last Sunday, I did a thing with breadcrumbs and anchovies and artichoke hearts whose crockery they fought to lick. To cook here, for all these people, is first to imagine the experience they will have, to taste things for and through them—it's an exercise in fantasizing about other people's senses. I'm exceeding myself, but I needed them. Him. David. It's his pleasure that pulls me most out of myself, makes me want to dazzle.

I start prepping at lunchtime, and people come in and out to make sandwiches, to visit me and chat. We've become accustomed to this, to everyone dropping in on Jean as she putters around the kitchen of a Sunday. My fingers are frittering away in a wide bowl of flour and diced cold butter when David comes down. I was lost in my work a moment ago, but now my heartbeat stumbles and I am overcome with alertness like a standing hare.

"Are you making *pastry*, Jean?"

"Kind of."

Sam and Brice look up, interested for the first time. "You know we're in France, right?" says Brice. "Where there's world-class pastry on every street corner?"

"You'll see what I'm doing."

David rummages in the fridge for a moment and turns around holding some packets and a jar.

"I wouldn't doubt Jean, guys." He walks around the kitchen island and whispers to me, "Pardon." I step away from my station for a moment so he can reach the silverware drawer. He pulls out a knife and knocks the drawer closed with his hip. A lizard runs from my heart straight to my vagina. David assembles a cheese and pickle sandwich.

"Hey, you two," he addresses Sam and Brice. "I need you to pick your two or three most impressive drawings. We'll have them blown up and put on posters for the funders event next weekend."

"Awesome," says Brice. Then he and Sam fold in toward each other, like band groupies of themselves, to rank their awesomest drawings.

I glance up at David, who tucks a wedge of Gruyère back into its wax wrapper.

"What's *your* talent?" I slide the question across the table to him, not quietly enough to be a whisper, but in a little envelope of my voice just for him. The thread of this conversation began last night over cigarettes in an intimacy that only he and I know about; one that, on the surface of things, does not exist.

"My talent," he says, pausing, looking at me. I make myself a pleasing sight, crumbing butter and flour in my fingers with gentle concentration. "My talent . . ." He watches me, his eyes fixed on my fingers, finding the little cold cubes and worrying them away into pale yellow sand. I think he will not finish the sentence. He is in my hands now, like a rosary bead passing through my fingers. *Just don't leave, eat here, sit here with me, for ever and ever.* "My talent . . ." He snaps out of it suddenly, breathes heavily with frustration and says, "My talent is being late." He gives me a collegial smile, grabs his sandwich, and twists out of his seat. He stops at the fridge and throws all his lunch things back in messily. "Bye, guys," he says. Sam and Brice wave and I look at the crumpled back of his khaki pants as he leaps up the steps to the kitchen door and slips out.

✦

Later that night, I serve the chicken potpies, humble in their mismatched ancient stoneware, savory jets steaming from the slits in their crusted lids. Everyone has taken their seats and I'm holding the knife high to slice the first pie when someone says, "Where's David?"

Neary replies, "He's gone to Paris for the week."

No reaction plays on my face. "Who's first?" I say, slicing neatly.

"Lucky fucker," says Sigrid. But there's a silence otherwise that suggests to me that everyone besides Sigrid is a little bereft, everyone chilled by the same passing cloud.

"Why?" asks Judith.

"Sources," says Neary, filling his wineglass to the brim. "For his book." We all nod, aware of the pressure on David, nervous for him.

"Hey," says Yoni. "Is there a chance *we* could get into Paris? On this trip?"

"Hay is for horses, Yoni, and yes, I've already considered that." Cheers erupt. "We've three weeks left. I think we can spare a few days for Paris during our final week. We'll do Notre-Dame together, perhaps a few other sites, and then you can pursue whatever it is you consider interesting."

I make eye contact with Patrick across the table. "Time I did some *dildo shopping*." Yoni, next to me, adds: "I need all new drugs." Patrick shakes his head slowly, takes a bite of chicken, and spits it out immediately with a "Hothothot!!" He grabs his water glass and chugs, and I feel guilty for not warning him, guilty that my food has hurt him, guilty that I have been excessive and needy and dangerous and obvious and made David run away.

Chapter 39

My body is changing in ways I thought only happened to movie stars and models. At first it just happened. I ate less here than at home. At home in the summer, there was nothing to do half the time but put Hooters hot wings in my gut, literally nothing. I was below the legal drinking age, so there was only hot sauce, or candy worms at the mall, or Bertucci's Pizza, where they give you a ball of raw dough to play with while you wait for your order and sometimes you nibble at it like an unsupervised toddler. And the whole time, you never think about your body. When you are a teenager roving the highways of Monmouth, New Jersey, your body is a thing that you sleep inside, a backpack holder, a marionette that gets diarrhea *a lot*. And then I didn't want to be seen by David eating birds' bodies like a caveperson and it's been hot, and I have had these fantasies inside me, so nourishing and wild, that all I've wanted was to drink pink wine and steal sideways glances at David and feel something southerly go *ding* like a cowbell.

Like magic, with no effortful dieting, my face is narrowing. My chipmunk cheeks, which were always so red with pastrami juice and atomic hot sauce and Sour Patch sugar, are hollower now, only flush with good health, and garden nutrients, and maybe the recentness of a homemade orgasm. And under my boobs, which I still have to hold with both hands when I walk down stairs even in the good Filene's bra with the underwire, it's flatter now, where it used to be just roundness upon roundness, like a snowman. And I like it. I don't just like it, I cling to it; I think about it in almost all my spare moments, in the car, falling asleep. If I'm not picturing David, I'm tracing the winnowing lines of the body he sees, the body I'll serve him. But now I want to help it, I want to accelerate it, and I know exactly how.

It is early Monday morning, and when I wake, Judith is still asleep. Sigrid is out running. I walk down to the kitchen and find Sam alone.

"Hi, Sam."

"Hi, Jean."

"Why are you up so early?"

"It's not that early." It's clearly kind of early, so now I wonder what I've caught Sam at, why she had to lie.

"I like to have a little time alone in the morning," she says. I thought she was reading, but now I notice that her book is a diary and her pen is in the crack, marking a pause in her writing. This doesn't seem like the Sam I know—the idea that she has some interior weather to record in a diary, that she's making herself available for company without Brice. Ruthless Jean does some advanced math deep in my brain and whispers, *She's hoping for contact with David.* I almost can't believe I'm saying it, but Ruthless Jean sees no downside, no cost, only information for her campaign.

"Do you have a thing for David?"

Sam freezes, raises her eyebrows but gives nothing away. She holds herself very still. And when she speaks, she places each word down between us like chips bet by a person with a winning hand.

"I. Don't. Have. *Things*. For anyone."

"Oh, OK." I shrug and try to think of something to talk about that will make me seem less nosy and childish. The kettle comes to a boil with a rushing gurgle and click. I make myself a tea and sit at the table with Sam. I scan the counters, but we're so early, Victoire hasn't brought baguettes yet.

"Do you mind if I sit here? I'm just waiting for Sigrid," I say.

"Let me tell you something very important," she says. "I hope someday you remember this. All that matters," Sam says, looking at me with her pretty, joyless Heather Locklear face, "is the work."

"The work?" Oh no, is this a Christian thing? Does she mean work like *good works*? I imagine her handing ten-pound Bibles to skeletal children.

"Work. What do you want to *do* in this life, Jean? What do you want to think about, or make, or change, or be an expert in?" She *is* smart, no soft religious moron but a scientist who has pierced my empty nucleus instantly with a sharp scalpel. "Nothing else matters. Marry the person who gets you there, live in the place that gets you there, study the thing that gets you there. I come from people who never did anything, and it sucked. They sucked. They didn't know what to make a priority. Partying? Renovations? Money? Affairs? It all rotated." Her hands chase each other in a wheel and then come to a sudden stop. "You need a point. A point of orientation. *What are you going to do?*"

I shrug.

"You care about whether I have a *thing for David* because you have no point. You don't know what to care about, so you're an empty vessel, so David can pour in, or whoever else."

"So you just stuck Brice inside you like a cork?"

"You know what? Kind of. I'm fine with that description. I'm done with that part of my life. Boo-hoo. But do you know what makes me passionate? Alive?"

"Jet-Skiing? The Macarena?" She will *never* like me, so I don't know why I'm trying to be fun. I am a flailing yellow tetherball in this conversation and she is just here to pound me and leave.

"I'm going to keep some of the most historically and aesthetically significant monuments ever made by human hands from crumbling. I'm going to keep them standing. I'm going to know their bones like an osteopath."

"I don't know what that is."

"There's a lot you don't know. So let me help you. The work. That's what lasts; that's what matters. And you mention David?" I listen intensely now. "He should take my advice, too."

"What do you mean?" She raises her eyebrows at me. I feel thrilled, hopeful. Is she about to confirm that David—

"Maybe David should make his work a priority, too." She stares me down. I can't help it, I can't help my sick little smile. She shakes her head at me. Of course, Sam knows what's happening between me and David—she's the first proof that something *is* happening—because Sam feels what I feel. Sam wants David, too, wants to touch him, wants him to look at her, but is losing to me, losing at a game she won't allow herself to play. She is being disciplined; she holds herself together, focuses on her husband. And now I understand: She married him so they could share books! So they could think together about naves and transepts! That's why it doesn't matter that he's a douchebag! And assiduously, dutifully, every time the little green sprout of some crush cracks through her, she pulls it out, she stomps on it. Because she's playing a long game of success and integrity. But the possibility of what she's saying is too delicious, so I push further.

"What, do you think, is distracting him?"

"David cares too much about the present, and not enough about—"

JEAN: The future. She's right.

There's a loud BANG as Sigrid bursts into the kitchen, bright red and damp, her blond hair in sweaty streaks, like a chick's wet feathers revealing the pink skin beneath.

"YO." Goddammit, I didn't want it to end there with Sam.

"You went running already?" asks Sam.

"So hot these days. Gotta go early. It's already like twenty-four."

"Twenty-four what?" I ask.

She taps her glistening temple. "I trained myself early to think in Celsius."

"Sigrid," I say. "Can I run with you sometime?" Her reaction to this takes me completely by surprise. She was in the process of getting herself a glass of water, but she freezes at the cabinet and spins around.

"Duuuuuude." Then she lunges toward the table and I find myself in a damp, salty embrace. "OF COURSE," she says. She squeezes me further, shaking me in some kind of wrestling move. "You want some of that SIGRID POWER?" I feel like my entire body is inside Sigrid's armpit and I don't want to breathe, but I am also wasting a lot of breath squealing. "You wanna tap the POWER OF THE 'GRID?"

"Yes!" I gasp. "The power—" I'm plugging my nose, and I don't have enough oxygen to speak. "The power—"

"GET ON THE 'GRID, BABY!" She's still holding me and shaking me. I hear the door creak open and Neary shuffles in.

"Sigrid, please don't kill Jean." In a foggy and illogical search for bread, he moves a bowl of bananas, lifts the kettle. "Wait until David gets back, anyway. I've got a lot on my hands without him. Morning, Sam."

"Morning, Professor."

"Sam, your elevation sketch of Sainte Mazerine showed an asymmetry across the transept that I'd never noticed before. I think you might have helped me figure out how they constructed that tower. Come find me after the site visit today; you'll want to see this."

"Sure thing," she says, looking only at me, as if this exchange is further proof of what she said to me, of the rightness of all her values. She closes her diary and slips it off the table with the deft minimality of a sleight-of-hand artist. She disappears through the kitchen door and I know I've seen part of her this morning that she never shows anyone, that I will likely not see again.

Chapter 40

I ran with Sigrid for a little while, but right away I started panting. It wasn't long before she sketched out a complex route for me in the air with her hands, and assured me that if I wasn't back in half a day, they could track me with Robert the terrier. Then she jetted off ahead until I couldn't see her anymore.

Maybe because I expected to be Sigrid's buddy, I find myself suddenly, intensely alone in a dense wood, a royal wood where no one goes. I can't believe how much happens in this forest I never bothered to enter, just next to the castle—can't believe the way the birds talk to each other, furious, manic, their throaty whistles piercingly loud, curling, licking from their beaks. Their noise drips like a liquid down from the canopy. The thickness, the greenness, the different greens, of all the trees. Now I come to one particular tree, bigger than the others but not creaky or grandpaternal, just strong and crazily alive in every leaf, the light coming through its bushy branches like fizzing sparklers. Far from any church, I can believe I am in the world of the dinosaurs. I feel myself to be on a planet, so suddenly and strongly that I have to stop in my tracks. It feels good to stop running, to acknowledge gravity, to feel pulled, wanted, downward. It takes so much energy to get even a few inches off the ground. All these churches tricking you to look up, all the skyward imagery—Christ evaporating, Mary ascending, piles of fat-assed babies floating up like party balloons, what a lie! Look *down.* Stay down. Feel everything sucking down—how good this is. How honest. How *obvious,* when you enter the wilderness, that this vegetal, wet, shrieking world has no will to ascend, to behave—doesn't need your guidance, your Good Book. Sap flows, vines push, little insects like black raindrops live for the time it takes a raindrop to fall, buds pop and hope to be sucked, slugs like yellow tongues lick up the dead; I watch the whole world sway and chirp and pulse and absorb and decay and that's all this is.

And then a funny thing happens. As I stand here, a guest of nature's completeness to itself, I suddenly want to share this moment with David. I imagine that he is seeing me, that he is waiting behind a tree, that he came here to think alone and was startled by me, by my speed and beauty. And although one second ago I was nailed to the earth, all of a sudden I find I can run, I can lift up off the ground—I'm sprinting, leaping. My lungs fill with this excellent air, pure and vivifying. I touch down and spring up like Robert himself. I don't need the hunting dog; I *am* the hunting dog, purposeful and joyful in motion, weightless, fleet, tearing down this path for my master. God, it feels good, to move beautifully and to imagine David seeing me move this way, my torso twisting, my long legs sweeping forward in turn. I burn through that burst of speed and my lungs sting and I return to my weighted jog, slower now, depleted, but still blazing with the muscle memory of my flight.

Flight—it flashes in my mind: one of the portals we've seen, a carving of Adam and Eve sprinting out of the forest, and God, bug-eyed, craning down from the sky, witnessing them. For the first time, I think I get what they lost: the bliss of acting unseen, like a slug. How petty and human am I, that I can't imagine such bliss for long, that what I need is someone to run for.

I hear rustling to my right, and I see some animal move maybe twenty meters away through the forest. It sounds like it has the heft of a deer. I stand still. I want desperately to see a wild animal that lives in secrecy behind the green curtain of the forest. It stops. It moves into a clearing. It's wearing blue shorts. It's Sigrid. She sees me, too. She smiles one of her bookie's smiles, and soon her whole face lights up. She marches to me across hostile terrain, casually picking over brambles, her smooth thighs flexing in the dappled light. When she reaches me, her arms fly up and she looks all around us. "Are you getting it, Jean? Do you *get it*?"

We embrace, sticky and limber. So this is where she gets her power. She comes here to move unseen, to be for herself, an animal. Maybe, in time, I can be like her. We high-five so loud it scares some crows and I trail her back to the castle.

Chapter 41

It's Friday. Every day this week I have woken up hoping David will come back from Paris, and every day he has been absent. Jojo drove the second van in David's place today and told us tales about the prince, who arrives this weekend. He has dated Princess Stéphanie of Monaco and Sporty Spice and Naomi Campbell; he has multiple degrees from Oxford; he could have gone to the Olympics for skiing, but he declined—too much time away from charity work. We all nodded, rolling our eyes furtively at each other and pressing Jojo for more.

"How many languages does he speak?"

"Oh, nine or ten, fluently."

"Does he know Bill Clinton?"

"They've worked together many times."

"Can he rap?"

"I think so."

"Does he have children?"

"Not officially!"

"Has he ever shot anyone?"

"Of course!" Then he told a very racist story about the prince protecting a supermodel from a beggar in the streets of Rio.

But there was one question that stopped Jojo in his easy, obsequious tracks.

"Will he ever be king?"

A heavy sigh, a clenched fist. A bone to pick with long-dead men in tattered pantaloons who put democracy above the heart, mind, and murdering gun of Prince Germain de Hoult de Bourbon de Saxe.

"It's not impossible, eh?"

I recognized in Jojo a fellow fool.

Chapter 42

I have my headphones on and am deep into the never-ending strummy, twangy baffling regressions of Dave Matthews with my eyes half closed in the late-morning sunshine when I see Yoni on the lounger next to me put his book down and look up. Judith, sleeping on the grass on her stomach, gets up onto her knees and looks over our shoulders.

I take my headphones off. Car doors slam.

"He's back," she says.

I put my headphones on again. I start the track over. The relentlessness of the thin, tinny drumming is urgent and even though I don't understand what Dave Matthews is saying ("celebrate wewwo"?), it's about me, for sure; it's about me and David. *We cannot chaaaaaaaaaaaange* is sung truly as if from the deep red throat of an aqueous demon who's just taken a bong-rip at a Vermont-based university, and it is the cloying absorption I need it to be. It keeps me from popping up, running to the driveway like Robert the hunting dog, who wants his nipples touched.

I am the last to leave the lawn, acting as if I couldn't care less about David Harwell. I'll see him at the event this afternoon.

Judith, who has been to greet David, scampers back to me, her arms shaking at her sides. "He brought his *wife*!" she says, giddy with the news like a little girl.

Ah, but now I see that we are both little girls. David's wife's arrival puts me in my place firmly, as if I'd been playing make-believe grown-up but now I'm back in my pinafore in the nursery with nothing but a dirty face.

"Did you know she was coming?"

Judith shakes her head, wide-eyed. "No way."

Something impossible and delicious that was never going to

happen has been taken from me. Nothing has changed—no contract has been amended; there's been no turn in the weather—only I have been struck down, whacked atop the head like a leering little mole in an arcade game.

Two weeks left here: It's over. His wife has shut the door.

"Why doesn't anyone *tell* us anything!" I say, the complaint of a powerless child.

On the upside, though, I wonder if she'll go away now, the Jean who watches me as if through his eyes, who takes pleasure in me if David would. Maybe I'll be free, restored to myself. But a few minutes later, I'm in front of a mirror, painting my lashes and lining my eyes because Ruthless Jean, desperate, smarting, rummaging through her armory, told me to.

Ann Harwell is neat and small. She looks like Jodie Foster, with a sharp nose and penetrating eyes and unfussy shoulder-length hair. She's wearing leather loafers and jeans and a floral silk blouse. She's skinny in an effortless, God-given way—she probably never thinks about food, and I bet her fingertips smell like pencil-wood and Woolite. David gave her the tour, his hand on her lower back, gesturing at oil paintings in the salon, Ann following keenly. "You have to see the library," he said, and their eyes met in happy anticipation. They like libraries. They like to write books in libraries, where I like to sit on the quavering theremin of my vagina pretending to read.

I'm in a dusty-blue linen J.Crew summer dress that I got for my cousin Ed's high school graduation this June, before I came to France, when I was as unitary and concentric as an egg. It feels appropriate to put the dress on again now, reduced as I am to little Alice, indignant and childish, battling fantasies no one else sees. There's kind of an Easter feeling, everyone milling about, setting things up, in clean shirts and ties. Some of our church studies—Brice and Sam's plans and elevations, Patrick's photographs of sculptures, Sigrid's sketches of capitals—are displayed on easels around the garden. Suddenly I become aware of a very small gay clown leaping around finding everything "Perfect! Perfect!" in a strong British accent. This, it turns out, is the prince.

No one has actually introduced him to me, but he is obviously royal, his features delicate, his sandy hair blown back from his restless face, his hazel eyes. The materials he wears may be earth-toned, but they are sumptuous, velvets and suedes and dark rich corduroys that suck up the light like thirsty moss. Turns out a modern prince is not a roving tumescent tenor like Disney would have it; he's a living handful of the world's best soil.

I wander up to easels bearing the architectural plans of churches, beautiful in all their blue, bird-boned detail. *So this is what Sam and Brice do,* I think with some admiration, following the hair-thin lines with my eyes. None of my aperture measurements were included on any of the plans, even for the churches where I'd accomplished the measuring. It was busywork, a waste of my time, I realize with anger. And though I spoke forgivingly with David about it in the library, now I feel cheated that there wasn't a more dedicated plan for my education here. Looking at these lines, my hand twitches; I have an aching sense of my own wasted potential. If I can understand the infrastructure of a language, how it bears weight, how its pieces interlock, could I have been good at this?

JEAN: Yeah, give me a worksheet! Give me a fucking quiz!

I'm glad I broke their stupid church. I imagine in retrospect that I did it on purpose, that I'm an iconoclast, someone who knocks churches down to their godless materiality in an uncompromising obsession with truth.

"Is this your work?" asks the prince, approaching the easel.

"Yes," I say, compromising my obsession with the truth.

"Brilliant. Absolutely brilliant," he says, and I smile like a professional thief. *What is this place doing to me?*

✦

Two new couples have joined us here: the rich Americans. The husbands are both fat and the wives are both thin. Neary, standing by one of the couples, signals to me with a herky-jerky wave. He's desperate to delegate the burden of entertaining them. I walk over to their group. "This is one of our wonderful undergraduates—Jean," he says, scanning a hand in front of me like I'm a washer-dryer on *The Price Is Right.*

"Wow, this must be so exciting for you! Living in a castle with a prince!" says the wife.

"Oh, this guy?" I gesture at Neary. "He's just a professor."

The couple bursts into laughter and Neary, deafened by anxiety, mirrors their laughter for no reason.

"You know who he reminds me of?" The husband and wife chase each other into an inane conversation about a movie no one's seen, and James Neary's smile is so forced and oversize that he looks absent and dissociative. Jojo ambles by with a tray of champagne and I grab a glass for myself and one for Neary, who drinks half of it in a gulp and says under his breath, "Well done, Jean."

Yes, well done me. I made a stupid joke and plucked champagne from a tray. If this is what gets me rewarded, then let's have more of the same. I ask Jojo if he needs help and he takes me to the kitchen, where we fill another round of glasses on trays. *"Allez, vite,"* says Victoire to us both with a quick grin and we all three hold up a glass for a wordless toast and down the champagne—"It's good, that," she says, clapping her floury hands, which go back to pressing goat's cheese into pastry discs. I go out with the tray. Everyone is happy to see me: I'm the champagne girl.

Maybe Sam is right; maybe all I need is to work, and everything will fall into place, desire will be flung down by industry. So with a purpose, with a job, and with the alcohol hitting my empty stomach, I sidle up to David. We haven't spoken since last week, and the sensory specificity of his newly shaved face, the cut of his body against the green lawn, the sound of his voice, it all hits me at once as he turns to me with the freshness of good news.

"Champagne?"

"Jean," he says. "Have you met my wife, Ann?"

"No," I say. She stands next to him and looks around with no free smiles for anyone.

"Champagne?" I offer.

"This is Jean, and she's doing a very good impression of a cocktail waitress. But she's a brilliant student."

"What do you do here?" she asks.

"Champagne," I say, making a robotic face.

"Jean is one of our undergraduates. She's never done any medieval history before."

"What is it you study?" asks Ann.

"Champagne!" I say.

"Stop it, Jean!" he says, laughing, but Ann stares at me. "Jean studies languages."

"Modern? Ancient?"

"Both," I say. "But I might major in history."

"We'd be lucky to have her." He turns to his wife and says, "She's quite a reader." He intuited this fact from how *Belle et Sébastien* made me cry in the kitchen. He extrapolated something about me in his spare time, and this tiny realization heats up all the liquid in me so that I simultaneously want to pee and sleep. The tray rattles in my hand.

"You don't want to study literature?" she asks.

"No." I give her nothing more. I like stranding her conversationally. I like how she looks dull in this instant.

"OK," she says, volleying the dullness back at me.

"You gang are so lucky to have Ann here. She's going to show us around an old convent this week."

"Cool." I nod and smile like I'm trying to find it cool out of generosity but no amount of my kindness will change the fact that knowing about convents sucks.

"It's a very exciting place, actually. And Ann knows more about it than anyone *in the world*."

"I wrote my first book about the nuns who lived there," she says.

My first book. She's so self-obsessed.

"How did your research go?" I ask, turning to David. "In Paris?"

"Fantastic," he says. "Spent some time with a key manuscript. I think I'm— I think the end is in sight."

"Well, that's something to celebrate," says Ann.

"Champagne?"

"Jean!" Aren't I a scamp, a playful little scamp at the heels of this dignified couple. They talk about abbeys and *key* manuscripts. I make stupid jokes and I'm friends with the groundskeeper and I sneak booze and have filthy dreams in which this upright and educated man, so proud of his wife, whimpers in disbelief as he sinks inside me. I'm a bad person. I suddenly crave—

"Patrick!" I see him a few feet away, alone at a tall table.

He jumps. I excuse myself, leave David and his wife, and careen toward Patrick, who's sweating in a navy suit and a silly fishing hat that protects his virginal skin.

"What?" (Terrified.)

"Nothing. You want a drink?"

"Oh. Uh. OK."

I stand next to him.

"What?" he asks.

"What?" I say.

I put my tray down on the high table and hold my place next to Patrick, like a dutiful wife, sipping intermittently.

"I'm never sure what to do at these things," he says. He takes his hat off and then puts it back on.

"I think you're just supposed to seem smart and promising." He nods. "Are you afraid you'll say something weird and Catholic?"

"No," he says, but I bet he is. I bet that's a fear, when you're religious in a secular world. "Jean. Almost everyone here has faith. Why do you think those rich Americans want to fund the program? They're Catholics. Maybe Episcopal. *Maaaaybe* Evangelical. Anyway, *you're* the odd one out."

"I'm trying to get in!" He looks at me with a warmth I don't think he's in control of, a little accidental affection, and shakes his head. "When you go to confession, do you tell the priest *everything*? Like what if you pictured boobs *one time*—"

"Oh come on." Now the warmth is gone and he's twisting his face away from me as if I'm sneezing or spitting.

"No, I want to know!"

"You want to mock. It's easy to mock. It's hard to believe. But you get something for belief in the end. What do you get for being a jerk?"

I look at the side of his face, at his block-shaped head and his rusty-brown beard, his fish-belly skin scattered with freckles in a pattern of ash, as if someone tapped a cigarette over his nose. But he would be OK with that, wouldn't he? I picture his mammy saying happily, touching his speckled little nose, "Our faces are the Lord's ashtray, Patrick," and him nodding, because everything God made is good. He is not one of us, he's some other kind of being; he holds some other kind of office. I want to confess to him my suffering, confess to him that I live every second in an involuntary and acute awareness of David Harwell, where he is, what he's seeing, and whether, in time, I might eat his breath like the cats that kill babies. I notice that my high heel has stabbed a clump of sheep shit, so I stand on one foot, lean on Patrick, and remove my shoe. Patrick shrinks from my touch.

"Just let me shake my shoe off!" I say. "I'm not gonna *molest* you." I whip my shoe toward the grass and the shit goes flying.

"You know what you need, Jean? A spiritual life," he says.

Maybe he's right. He's probably right. But I have a spiritual life: I'm Team Devil. I'm with the jerks, the glorious jerks! *What do you get for being a jerk?* You make your mind a marble run for inappropriate desires that skitter along its channels and plunk through its holes, which is pretty fun although you have to agree to feel guilty and deluded and small. But you get to be with the other jerks, laughing and experienced in all the dark arts of lust and lying and being very cool.

"There's sheep poop on your hand," says Patrick calmly.

Chapter 43

David and Neary now sit at the sides of the long table and it is the prince who takes his place at the head. Jojo and Victoire stand to the side, Victoire wiping her hands on a cloth that hangs from her waist, Jojo beside her with an arm around her shoulder. The prince is making a toast: "To the unparalleled richness of the Bourbonnais; to the distinguished scholars who have come to help uncover that richness; to the *partners* in this project"—partners, code for money—"supporting that knowledge; and finally"—the glass lifts a little more—"to the students, who bring such marvelous energy."

"Hear hear," David says, and Neary just drinks, and Yoni and I exchange criminal glances about our "marvelous energy." The prince, sitting down now and plucking his silver from beside his plate, says in a voice both piercing and effortless, a voice trained to carry nonsense through ballrooms, "I'm going to get to know you *all* before you leave!" His eager eyes dance around our faces. "Who's the *troublemaker*? Who's the *clown*? Who's the *star*? Come on, you're guests in my home, I've got to know the gossip!"

We laugh uncomfortably—gossip? The gossip is, Sam and Brice are choads, everyone else is fine, Judith's sick, the sheep are unpredictable, and Neary's mean. A week ago I would have said that everyone was a little in love with David, but now the razor-sharp presence of David's wife has weed-whacked the creeping vines of our affection. I can tell: David is lost in conversation with her, and no one is trying to get his attention. We've come back to ourselves. David's charisma is channeled now, appropriate, spousal, not leaking and spilling and corroding us. I feel disconnected and demoted, even from the kitchen: For tomorrow, Sunday, they've hired a caterer since the American donors are still here and there will be a banquet in the formal dining room, attended by a symbiosis of (as the prince said) "mayors, who like to open champagne, and priests, who like to drink it."

If I've been demoted, the prince is making demotion look desirable: He hates being with the grown-ups and keeps squeezing himself between us at the low-status end of the table, his antennae out for excess.

"When you go to Paris," he says, "I'll tell you all the clubs to go to."

When I introduce myself, my name is distasteful to him. "I refuse to call you Jean." He pronounces it as I do, like the fabric. "It's a boy's name! That's 'John'! You're not a man, you're a woman! Be a woman."

"Or just be John," offers Sigrid, helpfully. But the prince isn't done with me yet.

"Do you know what?" He puts his wineglass on the table and before I know what's happening, he grabs my jaw with his hand, rotating my head slightly and looking at me with a collector's eye. "You might be pretty when you're older." To the others: "Don't write her off!" When he releases me, I can still feel his fingerprints around my mouth, as if I've been slapped or scolded. I'm stunned. I feel an immediate rush of anger at how he touched me so nakedly, so possessively, but my anger is half of a hot thrill: A prince foretold my beauty, gave me a golden ball I can play with in my heart when all seems lost.

He turns to Yoni.

"*You,* sir, you're a sly fox." A moment later, Yoni and I are taking turns in the small spider-filled toilet attached to the kitchen. Through the door, he says, "He thinks I'm *sly*. He has *no gaydar* so he just thinks I'm like a spy or something."

"But—he's not gay?"

"No! Isn't that crazy? He's just a European party animal." I hear the ancient toilet flush with the sound of a steam train leaving a small brick station. Yoni emerges with at least seven visible spiders on his button-down.

Back at the table, the prince has moved on to Judith, who sits in awe of his prowling big-cat ego. "And you!" he says. Judith smiles.

"What an honor to have the daughter of Myra Meier here. I'm a huge fan of your mother's." Most of us look perplexed, but Sam almost drops her wineglass.

"Your mom is Myra Meier?!"

"Wait, who's your mom?" asks Yoni.

The prince replies. "She's a Pritzker-winning architect. I was at the opening of her opera house in Luxembourg in ninety-four. My friend the grand duke cut the ribbon. With his *sword.* Almost killed a schoolgirl. Should *we* go to Luxembourg? It's three hundred kilometers; we could be there in three hours. You'd have to ask your daddies." He glances in the direction of David and Neary at the far end of the table. "I suppose they'd say no. No churches there, only banks. Too bad." He puts a cigarette in his mouth and Sigrid's hand is suddenly there, bearing a flame.

Within a few hours of the prince's arrival, Sigrid has become his wingwoman, his bodyguard. She knows where his lighter is, his driving gloves, his blazer. I don't think they ever even spoke about it. I think it was just metallurgy, chemicals: He, in his mercurial madness, pooled toward her toughness and consistency. Does she like being subservient to the prince? Sigrid, whom I admire so much for her inner-directedness—yes, she does like it. Sigrid has voluntarily become a bondswoman to this confident, rich vessel of landed power, and it makes her feel good.

The strongest, the smartest, the most independent—even they need to please someone. *Maybe your dignity,* reasons Ruthless Jean, *is not worth protecting after all.*

Chapter 44

A LIFE OF SAINT PELAGIA, WHO DIED IN 290, FROM *The Golden Legend*

✦ ✦ ✦

Pelagia was the richest woman in Antioch, and the most beautiful. She was also ostentatious, vain, and licentious in mind and body.

One day while she was walking through the city to display herself in gold and silver and a variety of perfumes, she was seen by a holy father, Veronis, who began to weep bitterly. He wept because Pelagia's care for her appearance and for pleasing others was so meticulous that it put his own devotion to the Lord to shame: "In comparison to this harlot, we give little care to pleasing our heavenly spouse!"

Pelagia heard him preach and was stricken with remorse and asked to see Veronis, who, knowing her beauty, was afraid to see her alone so he asked her to bring others. She came with a retinue and said, "I am Pelagia, a sea of iniquity cresting with waves of sin; I am an abyss of perdition; I am a whirlpool, a sink to catch souls." He baptized her, imposed penance on her, and sent her to Jerusalem, to the Mount of Olives, where she donned the robe of a hermit, moved into a small cell, and lived life as a starving man named Brother Pelagius.

When she died, the clergy and monks gathered to give solemn burial to the holy man, but when they prepared the body and saw it was a woman who had starved to death, they marveled and increased their worship of God.

Chapter 45

The temperature has spiked and it's become humid, but the Church of Saint Gonzague, in a no-place called Tiers-la-Grotte, is blissfully cold and, to cite the guidebook I am writing with Yoni, "very Nieman Marcus"—white stone, beautiful carvings, little by way of tacky plaster saints bleeding out or showing their sores, a simple stone altar that is almost modern, like a rich person's kitchen island. We sit in the pews in the nave, Neary and David doing a back-and-forth with a lot of architecture words *(transverse arches, quadrant vaults)* that hammer me to sleep. Ann is off exploring the church on her own, not tied to us needy children. As David and Neary lecture us about the church, Ann motors up to David and whispers, "Great little crypt," with the intonation of a lover holding lingerie.

"Such dorks," I say under my breath.

"What?" whispers Yoni.

"Nothing," I say, but Neary has caught me.

"Jean."

"Oh no," I mutter. Judith, at my other flank, cringes for me.

"Why don't you give us a reading of this building. We're nearly five weeks in. You should be able to produce *some* knowledge from your observations."

I glance around. *The bricks have a pearly gloss, like buttercream frosting.* On the spot like this, I can't suddenly access all the things I've learned; that's not how my mind works. Think, Jean, think! *Not buttercream, really more of a Swiss meringue.* While Ann watches me with a detachment slowly curdling into disappointment, David gives me little nods of encouragement. *Of course David's won awards for his teaching, not Ann.*

"Come on, Jean," says Neary. "Before Jesus himself comes back to explain the place."

"Well. . . ." I have nothing to say.

"Look from east to west," David hints, pointing in front of us and behind us.

"Ohhh," says Yoni. "I get it." But before he can say anything, Brice has stood up to face east.

"That side," says Brice, "is gonna be eleventh century. Heavy capitals, thick columns, rounded arches. That side"—he pivots—"is . . . twelfth? Thirteenth century?"

"That's exactly what I wanted you to notice," said David. "But I'm afraid your dating is wrong, Brice."

"The cornerstone was laid in 1157," says Neary. "And construction was continuous. It was built within fifty years."

"Do we know that for a fact?" asks Sam.

"We do," says Neary, and for once I savor the dickhead side of Neary, his willingness to punch Sam in her button nose with a rock-hard denial.

David, head back, jaw sharp, Adam's apple indecently visible like the start of a boner: "It shows how fast the knowledge of vaulted support was spreading—that they changed tack within just a few decades to incorporate this new style."

"They were so eager to build more perfect buildings," says Patrick, confident, enjoying the western side with its streamlined arches and their little tulip tips.

Patrick's comment sits badly with me, partly because at dinner yesterday the cap popped off a bottle of ketchup in his hands and ketchup got on everyone but him, which I took as theologically airtight proof of Catholic God's love, and I've been thinking about how to get back at Patrick ever since. But there's something else—I don't know what I want to say, but I can't let Patrick's smugness end this conversation.

"Hi," I blurt, to the group. Yoni makes a confused face and turns toward me.

[Monica laughs.]

"Yes, Jean, did you want to add something?" Neary says, hoping that I don't.

"She didn't say anything to begin with," says Brice.

"I just want to say that I don't think the later part is *more perfect* than the earlier part."

"Go on," comes David's voice. This is one of the little fish bits we seals bark for, one of David's loveliest treats. *Go on* means you've found something interesting. Even Patrick pulls himself around in his pew to face me now.

"Well, just because it gets pointier doesn't mean it's better. It's just later. Like, I happen to *like* the more Romanesque style with the heavy capitals. Those"—I gesture at the big mounds of sculpted stone, boxy and richly carved: a rangy leopard with falcons' wings nosing his twin, curly mazes of sculpted vines like tangled tagliatelle bearing their meaty fruit, and funny faces with rubbery chins and big ears, split across the blocks, or seeming to meet at their corners—"are some jazzy capitals."

"Jazzy," agrees Yoni. "Very jazzy."

"No offense," says Patrick, "but no one cares what *you* personally like or don't like. The medieval builders thought they were evolving toward a more perfect structure."

"But didn't Brice's fuckup just show us—"

"Jean, come on," says David, unamused but gentle.

"Sorry. But didn't you just say that sometimes these styles were basically simultaneous?" I continue. "They were testing out different things at the same time. Like, what if the explanation is that they wanted a building where one side had all this cool storytelling in the sculpture, and the other side had the windows—"

"Apertures!!!" squeals Yoni, elbowing my ribs.

"Oh my god yes, *apertures*!" Yoni and I bump fists. Brice rolls his eyes, but I see a smile scamper across Sam's face. "Apertures that let in all this light. Maybe there was an idea here: let the light illuminate the capitals." Neary looks confused by the possibility that I've had a good idea and squinches his face to look directly at the light coming from the west side and how it falls on the east side. "And if you think that all history is progress, you're going to fuck up like Brice."

Neary and David: "Jean!"

"Sorry! I need another way to say *fuck up*, but I don't have one." Yoni laughs uncontrollably behind his hands.

"Um, error, slipup, misjudgment. Or just mistake," offers Judith sweetly. Brice stares at her.

"Jean, it's a church," says David. "More important, we're losing the thread of your thought here, which was valuable." Ha! Point for Team Devil! "What Jean is getting at, and correct me if I'm wrong, Jean"—*I won't; I'll let you explain our mind to those who live outside it, let you alone dredge the elegant ivory from the milk of my eyes*—"is if everything moved inevitably toward the end point of the present, we'd miss the flux of the historical moment, the messiness. Structures, events, alliances existed, for themselves, in their own time, and not merely to be defeated or cast aside by the victors of history."

"That's *exactly what I was saying*."

Brice blows air out of his mouth past his disgusting soul patch and says, "Yeah, right."

David goes on. "Western Christianity has in the past few hundred years undergone what we could call a modernization. Its doctrinal chaos has simmered down; its institutions are centralized and powerful."

"It got its story straight," says Neary.

"But the openness, the conflict of the early years." He's really into it now. "I mean, look at that corbel." He points east. Corbels—the sculptures *underneath* arches and things, like bookends rotated upward, bearing weight. I think I was gesturing at corbels earlier when I said capitals, but David got my point anyway, didn't get hung up on a technicality, let me shine. "You've got two little humanoid beastie faces coming together to kiss at the corner of the corbel." Everyone turns to see how profiles that look alone viewed straight on meet another profile at the edge—a kiss revealed by your own movement as you walk around the corner of the block. "Then not far away"—he twists ninety degrees and flings his arm out toward the front doors, and our heads rotate together like a tennis crowd—"you've got Adam and Eve harangued out of the Garden of Eden by a very angry God—for the same thing!"

"I thought they got kicked out for eating the apple," says Yoni.

"It's not about stealing fruit," says Neary. "The apple is the dawning of self-awareness." Then, sighing as if it were a big headache for everyone, "Sex."

"So . . . In the same building, part of its very structure, holding up its walls and doors, you've got a representation of profane, human love *and* the rebuke of that love." David smiles lightly, entertained by this moment that I opened the way for. "Christianity's paganness, its Hellenism, its . . . confusion about women, about the nature of Christ. . . ." He pauses here, chin in hand. I wonder if he might be vetting his own thoughts so as not to offend Patrick. "If we assume that the streamlining of the church progressed apace toward the present"—here he gestures up at the pointed arches—"then we might miss what's messy and interesting about the past." His eyes come to rest on me, satisfied, joyful.

"Or messy and interesting about the *present*," says Ann, who has quietly rejoined us.

"Mmm," says David. It was my point, but Ann got the final "mmm." *It's OK, Ann. I don't need it anymore. You can eat my dessert.*

Chapter 46

The weekend's festivities are over and the rich Americans have left, but a celebratory atmosphere hangs about the prince like expensive scent. Jojo and Victoire thrum with satisfaction at having him in our midst. Tiny hard salamis with their intestinal casings twisted at the ends like candy wrappers are set out in terra-cotta bowls before dinner. Wooden boards with glossy, oozing cheeses appear after. The prince leaps around so much I'm not sure how much he eats, but he's gracious with the compliments, even demonstrative. One night he gestured at Jojo, who was running to the kitchen in a stained apron: "He's like a dispossessed brother to me." His hand floated to his heart as he said this, although he did not sketch out a plan to restore Jojo's possessions. I looked down to the far end of the table, where I could read Ann's lips as she said *I'm so tired* and yawned and put her head on David's shoulder. *She's not one of us,* I thought, proud of how the rest of us had grown together into tough, absorbent winos.

"Are you going to work on your paper tonight?" Yoni asks me. Ann and David have both been in the library in the evenings since her arrival and I've kept my distance.

"I'm taking a break."

"Should we get a drink, then?" he asks.

I nod.

The prince looks electrified. "Which bar?"

"Oh, I just meant the backyard," says Yoni.

"Have you not been to the local bars?" the prince asks. Yoni and I make darting eye contact with each other, knowing that our Bastille Day outing was a violation of royal rules. "I shall take you to the most adorable little nightclub in a field," he says, and jumps up. He sits back down. "Oh pity, never mind, it's Monday. Only open on weekends. You have to be careful because once a month they bring in some *exotic dancers* from Moulins. Disaster. The whole place gets very *sticky*, but it's also full of *hay*, so by the end of the night, you feel tarred and feathered. But on a normal night, it's like being taken into the bosom of a kind, poor family. We'll go this Saturday." I have a feeling that by Saturday, he'll forget. He has the same feeling: "Sigrid! Sigrid, remind me Saturday!"

I'm relieved when Neary calls the prince back over to the grown-up side of the table. I need Sigrid.

"What's the deal with Ann?" I ask her, just discreetly enough that everyone starts to listen.

"What do you want to know?" says Sigrid, as if she were opening a trench coat full of informational stolen goods—medical history, family life.

"What makes her such hot shit?"

Sigrid pauses to collect our full attention. "Nuns."

"Nuns?"

"Nuns," says Sigrid. "In her book, women aren't only saints and martyrs. They're artists, makers, people who controlled their own destinies. It's like a whole field that Ann created."

"So that's why she's taking us to the convent."

"Whoever makes the first joke—" begins Yoni, but he's cut off by Brice:

"Get thee to a nunnery!"

Yoni sighs. "Did someone save a receipt?" A tired hand points at Brice and Sam. "Like, can we return these two?"

"Yeah," I add, "if anyone finds a Sharper Image receipt from a mall near Princeton, hold on to it."

"You guys are mean," says Sam, and I feel some compunction. Is it so bad, what they want? To care about success and achievement and doing things properly and being on top? They don't want to make gazillions of dollars or wield power over others. They care about the dusty bones lying under our feet, about "Western culture" as a thing worth understanding. This shared faith with David makes them begrudgingly sacred to me—in them, I can dig underground toward David even though they're superior and dismissive and maybe too smart for human company. Sam knows how beautiful David is, and I bet that her eyes, like mine, want to latch on to him like curved talons when he's standing there in his olive pants talking about Roman grout, and this makes her like a sister to me, a mean older sister who only wants to distance herself from my sloppy affection.

"Ann basically invented a category of visual culture," continues Sigrid. "She looked at textiles, little small-scale things, amateurish drawings. The things women made for themselves. Not like fancy illuminated manuscripts, but everyday things. Nobody had ever really looked at them before Ann."

Brice leans over the table, glancing briefly in the direction of Ann and David. He talks low.

"OK, *here's* the deal. David is trying to say something *new* about major, traditional subjects, which is much harder. See, you either have to have a totally new way of looking at the same old stuff or you have to find new stuff. So there's more pressure on him to be original. Meanwhile, his wife is reveling in all this new material. She doesn't even have to *try* to be original."

Judith sniffs the latent insult. "So she isn't . . . she isn't writing something original?"

"She's a perfectly capable scholar," he replies. "She's really a tactician. Writing about nuns right when, you know, *gender studies* is the hot new thing." He rolls his eyes.

"Have you read her book?" Sigrid asks him.

"No."

"It's . . . the most cutting-edge research to come out in the past decade," says Sigrid.

"You *would* say that."

I catch Patrick smirking. He sees me and quickly bites into a big hunk of baguette and runny cheese. He looks like a toddler eating a craft project made of cotton wool and Elmer's glue.

"And why would I say that?" Sigrid's glare is ice-cold. Brice doesn't answer. "Because I fuckin' read everything?" She looks at

Patrick, who is still mashing fat around inside his smirk. Brice looks out into a field. "I thought so."

"I tried to read Ann's book a little," I say. "The pictures are crazy."

"Oh yeah," says Sigrid.

"The crucifixion with the two nuns on either side?"

"Oh sure, from Cologne. With all the blood?"

"Yes! They're pulling Jesus off a cross, but his wounds are gushing so much blood into their faces that they can't see anything. It's like something out of Mortal Kombat."

"And a nun probably drew it, like in her cell, *hot in the chops* for Jesus." Everyone but me and Sigrid seems confused and appalled. "*Gushing*," continues Sigrid. "But what Ann does with that image is amazing. . . . The idea of blood in your eyes, of wetness. It's not completely blinding, it's more like blurring, and it helped the nun drawing the picture to go past vision, past seeing into feeling. A kind of bloodied, material vision as a form of intimacy? I mean . . ."

"INTERPNENETRADING!" says Yoni, drunk, poking Sigrid with a cake fork.

"Big-time," says Sigrid, not sidetracked. "These nuns are like, 'You, holy fathers, have told us a story of passion, ecstasy, and *love*. You told us the Savior loves us. And guess what, it's fucking mutual. We're feeling the passion in ways you didn't foresee and can't control. And we're gonna make some fuckin' art about it.' "

"Like, Jesus dolls," I add, remembering the pictures in Ann's book.

"All kinds of stuff! And all this intensity of feeling, without a priest present, with no one there to mediate. I mean, that's *insane* for women in the thirteenth century."

Patrick, now washing his cheese down with water, looks only bored.

"Have you read this, Patrick?" I ask. He shakes his head.

"I don't do this niche stuff. It's a subcategory of medieval history, not mainstream Christianity—it's a couple of freak occurrences. Great for Ann that she's been able to make a career of it. Congratulations to the gender people, the race people, but it's not, you know, the most important stuff."

"Oh, you *wish*, Patrick," says Sigrid. She shakes her head so hard, her floppy blond hair falls on her face. She jerks her thumb toward him and scans our faces. "You *hear* this chump thinking he knows more than an Oxford professor?" I love Sigrid right now, steely, full of facts, small and stout with her German boy's bowl cut, ruddy in the face with wine but delivering every word with lawyerly precision, her eye contact wielded like a mallet, her mind like the reliable library it is. She tucks her hair carefully behind her ears and fixes her eyes on Patrick. "The devotional images and practices developed by these bitches locked away in their cells, illicitly, illegally, aroused by Jesus—"

"Like, actually *aroused*," I add. I remember reading these words, sitting up in the library, feeling like they came from me, like I was warping the text with my own fantasies. "They wanted to make out with Jesus—they write about wanting to taste his lips."

"OK, but *so what*. A couple of lonely nuns," says Patrick, still chewing.

"A couple of lonely nuns? There are nine hundred million Protestants in the world today, Patrick. People who think they can talk to God directly."

"So?"

"So these lonely, locked-away women in European convents in the Middle Ages just nursing their passion for Jesus paved the way for a billion people, for a devotion that doesn't need—maybe even *rejects*—patriarchal management, the middleman of the priest."

I hear Patrick whisper, "Bullshit," but it's barely a word, it's a unit of anger.

"They carried that through from early Christianity to late."

"Wow," says Judith, her chin in her hand. "That's amazing. Just some lonely nuns."

"*Passionate* nuns," says Sigrid, with a finger up. "Lit the way. Nothing 'minor' about this. You stay a benighted dipshit if you want, Patrick, but what Ann accounts for isn't a 'subcategory' of anything. It's fully fucking human, and it's rampant in the varieties of devotion you don't care to understand."

Brice shakes his head. "I don't know if that's been proven. The link between Protestant devotion and medieval nuns."

"You don't know because you haven't read about it," says Sigrid, decisive.

Sam has been silent during all this, following the thread acutely. Sam the draftswoman, Sam who has a bruise on her thigh from the sharp crescent compass that lives in the pocket of her cargo shorts. "Does David have the book up there?" She gestures at the library. "I'd like to read it." Brice's face hardens, and I think how delicious it would be if Sam's commitment to hard work and high ideals was upended by a book about nuns.

Chapter 47

The prince drives so fast that we've left the other van in the dust, and I wonder if anyone else's French is good enough to know that he's swearing with intense vulgarity at drivers doing nothing wrong. All the other grown-ups are in the other van. I recall looking back through the rear window at Neary's worried face as the gap between our vehicles lengthened, putting more distance between the steady paid scribes and the capricious lord. Although it's morning, it's shaping up to be hot, and the humidity hasn't broken. We were instructed to cover our shoulders and knees to enter the convent, so we're already sweating inside the legs of our jeans. The windows are open and the radio is on, so everything has to be shouted twice.

"On our Paris trip, I want to go to Buddha-Bar!"

"You want to gobble dude a WHAT?"

"BUDDHA-BAR! IT'S A BAR!"

But suddenly the prince shuts us all up, waves his arm wildly behind the driver's seat, and then cranks up the volume of the radio. There's some vocabulary I don't know—"*procureur*" and "*conseil spécial*"—but I understand "*liaison sexuelle*" and Bill Clinton *("Beel CleenTONNE")*. It's the Lewinsky thing, surfacing in France, filling the vacuum left by soccer. The prince turns his head way too far around for a person driving and shouts, "It turns out your president is a man!" Then he starts laughing. "A *French* man!" This story has been consistently in the news for five months, but anything truly salacious has only been glimpsed behind a veil of legalese or hinted at by side squabbles. The prince's enthusiasm suggests we're going to get some red meat. We all pipe up with questions: "What are they saying?" "Did he admit to it?" But the prince shuts us up—"Shhh!"—his arm flailing again, and we listen to the newsreader: *"Le président a quitté Washington pour une réception payante à East Hampton chez l'actrice Kim Basinger, afin de—"*

"Oh, Kim," says the prince. "Lovely woman, bit bonkers. Helping with his legal bills . . ."

"He's gonna have to come clean now," Yoni says, turning to me.

"What do you mean? Why?"

"She got immunity! She got her deal. And he got subpoenaed. They're closing in on him." Yoni looks totally alert, attentive. He seems confused that I don't share his enthusiasm. "I can't believe you don't read the newspaper. You're missing out. This is the president of the United States we're talking about. Having sex with some random intern and perjuring himself? Bad news for Billy."

JEAN: It's so embarrassing that I didn't read the news. I was such a twat. My dad subscribed to *The New York Times* and I'd go straight to the movie reviews.

MONICA: Why didn't you read the news?

JEAN: I didn't think it was for me. Political reporting seemed like some kind of clockmakers' manual: the clocks would always be right and keep time, and if you wanted to read about the grinding of the inner cogs, you were welcome to. But I just trusted that things worked. I didn't even know who my congressperson was.

MONICA: You'd think that of all the people in the world, you should have come to my defense, understood me in my suffering. But how could you have known what I was up against, Jean, if you had no idea what *you* were up against?

The reporter babbles on, and the prince listens keenly, shaking his head in deeply savored disbelief before breaking into laughter again at something he's heard in the report—*contact bucco-génital.*

"HA! *Contact bucco-génital,*" he repeats. *"Ah bas dis-donc!!!"* We look at him quizzically, and in full Fräulein Maria mode, he says, "A blow job, children," while turning at top speed into the parking lot of a convent.

✦

The convent has two parts. One consists only of thick gray stone walls and looming pillars capped with moss and ferns. The morning was still dewy when we arrived and the old ruin was dotted with snails, nearly as big as tennis balls and striped like neckties, their webs of slime glittering in the new light.

It was druidical, magical, the mist clinging to the grass, everything still but the bulbous snails slowly pumping across the damp lichen. Ann clearly loved it, felt at home there, looked up at the sky with her lips bent in a shallow canoe of a smile. David watched her, breathed like she did, looked where she looked. I had the tiniest sensation that he was imitating her, that maybe he even envied her belonging here.

"This," she said, pointing to a stone archway, "was the door. The one door. When it was first built, the convent had no other doors. You entered when you professed and you exited when you died." Sam, leaning in the doorway, suddenly looked around and backed up, as if she might be sucked in and trapped. "Now," Ann continued, "that door always faced the altar. So here's where the altar would have been." Ann walked to the spot and put her hands out as if they rested on a table before her. "On the other side of the altar would have been the choir, where the nuns sat in their choir stalls—those were wood and burned a long time ago, but look, here's a hint." She gestured up at a lone standing column, topped with a weathered carving of a woman's face, her mouth gaping in a wide O. There was a collective gasp when we all saw her—as if she'd suddenly appeared. "Perhaps she's singing, as the nuns would have done."

"Or she's waiting to receive the host," said Neary. Ann nodded in agreement.

The prince's fine-linen elbow swiped my side as he whispered, "Or hoping for some *contact bucco-génital*?" I chomped down on an involuntary smile while he snickered like a weasel.

"So," resumed Ann, "if the altar is here, and the choir is here—then there's something wrong." It was true. I was beginning to imagine the nuns sitting on the other side of the altar in their benches like a nest of black sparrows chirping for their blessings, but then between the altar and the choir stood—

"A wall." Ann clapped her hand down on it, a wall a few feet taller than her, of gray stones, with two rectangles knocked out, one in the middle and one higher up, like a socket. "What's this doing here?" she asked.

"Security?" offered Sam. "Keeping them in?"

"No."

"An unfinished renovation?" said Judith, screwing up her face as if it were the most outlandish suggestion.

"Nope."

Then came the gravelly certainty of Patrick's voice: "It's to separate the nuns from the altar."

Ann's eyes grew wide, and she scanned our faces. "Did you all hear that?"

"*Separate* them?" I said. "I thought it was their whole job to go to church." (I wasn't even looking at David, but off to my right I felt his smile go like a heat lamp from low to medium.)

"In the thirteenth century, the convents swelled with nuns," said Ann, meandering around the wet wall, keeping a hand on it as if it were an animal she'd trained, a swaying elephant that warmed to her touch, "and the priests became fearful of them. You had nuns like Isabelle of France becoming objects of worship, epidemics of fasting and starvation, reports of visions. The bishops needed to get control of the nuns' devotion; it was taking on a life of its own, an outsized passion." Standing where the choir would have been was Judith, issue of a rich and powerful family, self-denying and intense, and it took no work to put her in black robes in my mind, to have her spend a lifetime with her mouth in an O, singing, unwashed, leaving porridge in her bowl, desperately in love with the masculine ether. "So that's what these cutouts are. The upper window—that's where the nuns could see the bread lifted as it was blessed, becoming Christ. Then they filed past the lower one; it's like a—what do you call it? When you get McDonald's from your car?"

Fancy bitch. "Drive-through," I pronounced with the authority of a trial judge.

"Wait," said Yoni. "That window is so they can *see* the communion bread held up for one second?"

"Yup."

Sigrid, with sinister precision: "They give up *everything* to celebrate Christ and then the priests put up a *wall* in front of the altar."

"That's right," said Ann.

"That's so shitty," I mumbled; I didn't think he could hear me, but David pinned both eyes on me with a passing severity. I caught the look—a scolding only, intensely, for me—and in the space of a second, I aspired to be more articulate and self-controlled while at the same time I felt a hot coin deposited in my underpants.

"Imagine the priest's experience," said Neary, with a diabolical twinkle. He walked over to the site of the altar, raised his arms in benediction, closed his eyes. "The enclosed nuns sound wonderful, like a host of cherubim, not women. To him they are voices only, a decorative harmony for his own connection to God." He opened his eyes and looked around at us with a crooked smile. "He's having a *marvelous* time." Neary obviously enjoyed this pantomime of a wall between him and his flock.

"But now we know why the nuns did what they did," said Ann.

"What did they do?" asked Judith.

"Did they burn the place down?" asked Sam, arms folded, selling it as a reasonable solution. Brice, who had displayed a languid kind of boredom this morning, shot her a quick look of concern.

"No," said Ann. "They went off and wrote stories and drew pictures and made objects, carved bodies of Christ they could hold and adore, assembled portable altars they could stash away in their cells, touch, look at."

Yoni, skeptically: "So they gave up their lives to attend a concert, but then it turns out they can only make-believe-watch the concert footage later in their rooms on cardboard TVs they crafted from garbage?"

Ann thought for a moment. "I guess you could put it that way."

✦

Now we are in the other part of the convent—newer? better built?—under a wooden roof in a long hall, walking in a troop behind Ann, who is, thank Christian God, in an unflattering boxy blazer and shapeless long skirt. Next to Ann is an actual nun. She's in a black habit with a close-fitting white collar that descends to her shoulders and makes me think of a tube of toothpaste squeezing out her fleshy face.

As we march behind her down the hallway, the nun pulls up short. Ann keeps walking a pace or two, stops, and turns around. *"Non, je suis désolée,"* says the nun. *"Ça, non." No, I'm sorry. Not that.*

"We've come all this way," Ann replies (to my dismay, her French is quite good). "No photography, I promise. Just"—she swings an arm out toward us—"for the students. I'd love to show them." What I know about nuns is that they've devoted their whole lives to prayer and good works. But this particular nun, a six-foot tower of black cloth with a cross Mr. T would envy dangling between the Costco turkeys of her bosoms, looks at us with no love, and her loveless eyes roll like snow tires back toward Ann.

"Non."

Suddenly the prince wiggles up from the back of the crowd in his immaculate linen and pulls the nun off to the side. I can't hear him, but he is shameless, holding his pretty little hands in prayer at his chest, smiling like an old friend over an old joke, and—oh gosh, he's pouting. Is he going to cry? The nun looks away from him, but he just keeps it coming—he has enough charm that, like fire-hose water, much is meant to be wasted—and when she looks back, he's still going, pointing to his chest, opening his arms, dropping them . . .

"What's going on?" Yoni asks Sigrid.

"I have an idea," she says, but when we ask for more details, Sigrid shushes us. "Hold on. I want to see this play out." The nun softens finally, nodding, even at one point saying something with the intonation of a businessman's joke—"You ol' so-and-so!"—and touching the prince on the arm. The prince and the nun rejoin

Ann, and we are all finally ushered to a wooden door covered in carved medallions in flower shapes with animal faces protruding from each one. The nun inserts a big jailer's key into the door's iron lock and we are invited to sit at a sturdy long table. We wait. Neary and David wander around the library, whispering, looking at all the shelves, drawing each other's attention to liver-colored volumes.

A few minutes later, we are all gathered around a book, carefully placed on a stand so that it opens just enough for us to see the pictures, like a breathing mollusk, but not so much that the book flattens, straining its binding. Our heads are nearly touching as we try to look. The nun delivered the book with bare hands; Ann received it in white gloves.

"Here it is," Ann says. "A page of *The Devotion of Sainte Odette.*" The book's cover is frayed, and it seems each page is a different color of fawn or tea. The picture she wants us to look at has four square panels. "We start here," says Ann. We are approaching noon now; I'm hungry and sleepy and the room is hot and it's just another boring Jesus, nailed to his boring cross. Also in the picture is a guy in nice clothes kneeling on the floor and praying to Boring Jesus.

"This is Geoffroy de Bellemer, the founding donor of the convent. And what is under his feet?"

"A dragon," says Sam. It's a funny creature, under the rich guy's pointy slippers—a dog-faced thing with claws and a scaly body.

"So he's modeling himself on Saint George," says Patrick.

"Fine," says Ann. "All normal. Next panel."

"Oh," I say, "did the dragon escape? It's on the other side of Boring Chr— of Christ." The beast has moved from under the rich guy's feet. Now you've got Jesus at the center and then below him on either side you have the kneeling rich guy and this dog-faced, lizard-bodied gremlin, in a kind of a triangle.

"Exactly. It escaped," says Ann. "Good word for it," she says, looking up at me from under her sandy brows.

"Is that common, iconographically, in the thirteenth century?" asks Brice.

"No," says Ann. I catch Patrick shaking his head almost begrudgingly. "Just wait," she adds, her eyes beginning to sparkle. Sigrid looks like a person who's been to this magic show before, anticipating the wonder that we are all about to experience. I glance around for David and Neary, but I don't see them and then with a shudder I realize that David's behind me. He's looking over my shoulder. All of a sudden, from an imperceptible vessel of consciousness, my body becomes hard and material to me; afraid my sour breath might reach his air, I breathe shallowly and get lightheaded.

"Now," Ann continues, "on to panel three."

"Well, that's a straight-up nun," says Brice.

"Exactly. Fine. So now it's the nun, and Geoffroy—her confessor and patron—and Christ. And the hybrid dog-dragon is gone. All makes sense. But can you read anything else in the image?"

David leans forward. I hear him make a little "mmm" noise. His crinkly sky-blue button-down brushes the back of my arm and it is like something moves from his body into mine, like a fish swims from inside of him to inside of me through the tunnel of our contact. I turn my head slightly to see the outline of him. My attention is so heightened that my untrained hand could reproduce the slope of his brow, his cheekbone, his chin perfectly on paper. His eyes are fixed on the book.

"Wait," says Judith. "I don't know, maybe I'm just making things up . . ."

"Try us," says Ann. Her dry way, her short words, her adequate, mechanical eye contact make ideas feel important. We're not here for her—she doesn't need our affection, our gratitude. We're here because she thinks this piece of paper is remarkable, is world-historical, and should be known and attended to.

"Well," says Judith, "the nun looks like the dog. There's a kind of visual rhyming. Look. She has a funny rounded snout, and her wimple folds just like the dog's ears."

I hear David mumble "Good, Judith." It's a morsel of appreciation that he uttered to himself, but it lies like a scrap on a table and without his knowledge, I steal and savor it.

"I see it!" says Sam. Brice comes in closer.

Yoni gasps and hits me. "Total dog!"

"And her drapery?" pushes Ann.

"Oh my god!" I see it clearly now, too. "The way it falls but she pulls it back, it looks like scales. Like the dragon's scales."

"Nice, Jean," says David.

The fish that swam into me is now a hundred fishes, silver noses pushing into every channel they can find.

"Wait, so"—Yoni puts his hands up—"this nun was a dragon? Is she saying she was secretly a demon the whole time or something? That's crazy."

"Well, let's move into the last panel and see."

I don't need the others. I know exactly what the last picture is. Geoffroy has disappeared. The floor has fallen away from where he had kneeled and the nun and Jesus inhabit a blank page, a no-place, a formless void. Christ holds the Eucharist, but the nun wants more than a stale little cracker. She has floated up and put her lips to his.

"That's definitely not allowed, right?" says Yoni. Ann smiles. I feel a trickle of sweat move down my back like a snail. I notice the nun who guided us here sitting in a chair at the side of the room, diminished, waiting, no longer commanding. She rests her eyes on the spines of the books in the library, as if we are not here; as if our presence has humiliated her.

"No, Yoni, it's not allowed."

Chapter 48

In the gap between church and dinner, we gather on the back lawn. Our drinking has become increasingly early, and increasingly princely. The prince has taught us all to drink Martini & Rossi red vermouth on ice with little strips of orange peel. The orange, casually flayed, rolls between us on the long table, and the peeler goes from hand to hand. Patrick often drinks milk at this hour.

MONICA: Stop it. That can't be true.
JEAN: This is where I lose you? The milk?
MONICA: Ugh. Go on.

Neary and David are off collating data, filing pictures, putting away tools. The prince has the rest of us taking turns standing guard on the front lawn—Brice and Sam are there now—because he's expecting the cable company to come install a box. He's become crazed about this Lewinsky thing and the French news isn't covering it adequately. He wants CNN and Sky News the way his ancestors wanted Flanders and Alsace.

"Oh, the things I've convinced people to do," says the prince. "I took Sporty Spice to the *opera*."

"So how did you get the nun to let us in?"

"I told her a story." The prince smiles, lights a cigarette. For no discernible reason, he's changed brands. Now it's something called a Stuyvesant that smells like a forest fire. "When I was a little boy, I loved only one thing. Cognac." None of us is surprised. "Cognac was my pony." This *does* make more sense. "Well, he was actually a dwarf version of a Western Holsteiner, sort of like a semi-concert baby grand piano." No one knows what kind of horse or piano to picture. "I told the nun that as a boy, I cared only for Cognac, Cognac, Cognac. And nothing for Jesus."

"I see where this is going," says Sigrid, and the prince points at her with his cigarette fingers and winks.

"And then one day, I was shown a picture of Jesus, coming in to—wherever it was—on a beautiful chestnut horse like Cognac, on Palm Sunday."

"Jerusalem," exhales Patrick.

"Oh dear, I think I said something like 'Bethesda' to the nun. Where is that?"

"Maryland," says Yoni.

"Well, anyway, I said, 'Seeing Jesus on that horse was all it took to unlock my heart to the goodness of Christ. And you never know what these students will see in the images you, Prioress, possess here.' "

"Is that true? About the horse picture?" asks Judith.

"Did you enjoy your time in the library?" retorts the prince.

"Absolutely."

"Well, then it was true, my little Jewish princess." He taps the top of her hands, which are folded on the table. "You're welcome."

"But why did the nun need convincing?" asks Yoni.

"Oh, it's the same with art dealers and jewelers; you always have to convince them to show you the best stuff," says the prince. "Speaking of the best stuff! I think Jojo took a lamb."

Jaws drop all around.

"What do you mean *took*?" I ask.

"You didn't think they were pets, did you? Mark my words, you'll tell me later tonight it's the best thing you've ever tasted."

Judith looks like she might cry.

The prince pats Judith on the shoulder, looks with sympathy into her eyes, and says slowly: "Now, now. Victoire is going to do a nice *caper sauce*." He turns toward the castle. "Which reminds me, I should check in with Jojo. They *love* when I take an interest. See you all at dinner."

We wave as he slides elegantly off the end of the picnic bench straight into a trot and disappears through the side door to the kitchen.

"They *killed* a *lamb*?" says Yoni. "There's a butcher shop ten minutes away!"

"It's about possession," says Sigrid. "They call it husbandry for a reason. Must give you a hard-on to eat your own lamb." I catch Patrick lifting his eyebrows in a *maybe.* Yoni is still disgusted.

"We caressed them," says Judith. "We *knew* them! I wonder which number it was. . . . Oh my god, remember Twelve?" We all smile as if we do. "I *loved* Twelve!"

The dead lamb does not scandalize me; I'm only scared it will eclipse all the things I've cooked. I wasn't given animals to kill for David. If I had been, I would have killed them, of course. I would have asked Jojo for the freshest, deadest, most delicious creatures, done things with the livers, the hearts. You can sneak a little liver into a Bolognese and no one will know. They'll think they like the upstanding expensive parts, the healthy thick parts, the *chuck* and the *rump,* but what they will love without being able to name it is the dark vitamin density of the organ, the rare interiority of it, the taste of it like breath from the back of the throat.

"Sigrid." She looks at me. "Why didn't the nun want us to see that image?"

"It's not some piece of scholarship to them. It's not ancient history. They still worship with that image. It's *private.* They never expected Ann to publish it."

"They were mad at her?"

"Furious. That wasn't for the public to see."

"Can they sue?" asks Yoni.

"They're *nuns,*" says Patrick. "They don't fight."

"Don't they *famously* beat children?" says Yoni.

"It's a million years old, it's public domain," says Sigrid. "Once Ann got her digital camera in there, it was game over. But she never asked permission. For Ann, the lives of these women were an important story—and that story was erotic and challenging. But the nuns still *live in* that passion. It was violating for them to be described by outsiders. To be seen as a story."

I feel a rumble, a wind: I look at Monica, who closes her eyes and breathes deeply. She gathers her strength for what is about to happen.

Chapter 49

Ann left earlier today to go back to Oxford. David is working in the library, but I won't go there. "He can't have your company after a week of Ann—punish him," says the calculating Jean I wish would go away, and I tell her, "He doesn't think of me! He won't feel it as a punishment. He will simply work, not noticing my absence." Ruthless Jean is so self-important. She believes she can pull a planet off its orbit with her will. She believes that someone as poised and established as David Harwell would ruin his life to touch a potty-mouthed junior in tomato-stained short-shorts who (he thinks) goes to Student Services to get her sloppy pregnancies ended. "Yes," she says. "Precisely." I swat her away, ashamed of her grandiosity.

JEAN: But, Monica, am I here to try to rid myself of Ruthless Jean? Because—

MONICA: You like her. [Monica smiles.]

JEAN: I mean, she wants me to be plowed by my teacher, which is a bad idea, but she multiplies my capacities. She thinks so highly of me.

MONICA: You've come to think of desire like some sort of hormonal spill that will only lead you astray.

JEAN: But won't it? Didn't it lead you astray?

MONICA [frustrated—eyes cratering with hurt]: I thought you were a good reader, Jean. Lucy and Anastasia and Agatha and Thais and Pelagia, they spell it out for you, in blood behind the text. They are warning you. You can be the most virtuous woman in the world, and you'll still carry the blame not just for your desire but for everyone's desire. I paid a price for mine, Jean, but I was tortured for his.

In the middle of the day, I find Judith in our bedroom cowering, her jaw locked open again.

"Oh no," I say. She covers her mouth with her hands, and this time she has tears in her eyes. I open my arms and she crawls in for a hug. "I'll tell David and Neary you're not feeling well." She feels so strange against me, scarily like a doll with her uncushioned bones and her long, wiry hair and her mouth held open as if for a spoonful of make-believe soup.

But this time as the day wears on, her jaw does not click back into place.

The last thing I see as I fall asleep that night—maybe eleven or twelve hours after I first found her upstairs, gaping—is Judith, so slight under a knit blanket, in the darkness with her mouth still open like an old woman starved to death.

Chapter 50

On Sunday morning, I wake to see Judith sitting on the edge of her bed, her huge eyes sunken, the fear and shame now replaced by exhaustion. Her mouth is still open.

"Did you sleep?" I ask. She shakes her head. "Oh my god, Judith. Has it ever lasted this long?"

"Yunch." She holds up one finger. "Un hime."

"One time."

She nods.

"What did you do?" She comes over to my bed and picks up my notebook, thick and wrinkled with all the notes and stories I've written in the library. She scribbles on the inside cover, STEROID INJECTION.

"Ih workhh."

"It works?" She nods. "OK. Do you want me to talk to Neary? Or David?"

She looks at her watch.

"Gnaygee waih—a yiyyul."

I'm learning to speak broken Judith: "Maybe wait a little?" She nods. "OK, and you'll just hide here?" She shrugs.

✦

Within a few hours, word is out that something is wrong with Judith. As she lies in bed dozing after her long sleepless night, the rest of us mill around in the kitchen speculating.

"She did it to *herself*," Brice says. "Crazy."

"We don't know anything," says Sam.

"Dude, I had a friend who got tetanus, seized up, couldn't open his mouth. It's no joke."

"It's not tetanus, Sigrid," I say. She seems to have no room in her worldview for self-harm, wants to grant Judith the ridiculous dignity of tetanus.

"It is crazy," Yoni says to himself, but when he realizes that Brice said the same thing, he quickly adds, "I mean it's sad."

By midafternoon, I'm in the kitchen, preparing for my second-to-last Sunday—only two meals left with which to dazzle David. Yoni and Sigrid sit at the big table, watching me pick leaves off a heap of basil. Judith is still upstairs, weak, worried, her dry lips still frozen in a gaping O.

"They can't leave her like this," says Sigrid. "There's a duty to care." Occasionally she reaches into my pile of unwashed stalks and slips a leaf in her mouth, working it in her cheek like tobacco dip.

"How can you possibly use all this basil?" asks Yoni.

"You'll see," I say. There was a hard sheep's Tomme in the fridge that Victoire had forgotten to put out on the cheese board. The minute I saw the unused waxy wedge, the economist in me remembered the superabundance of basil in Jojo's garden and began to envision a pesto—I'll produce a whole jungle-green tangle of garlicky spaghetti, and Victoire won't even need to shop.

JEAN: Why am I so obsessed with cost-effectiveness? I'm not even paying for the food here.

MONICA: You've really forgotten? Your forty-year-old self thinks it's degrading to make food; you see the kitchen as a trap for servile women. But when you first discovered it, you knew it was the work of the mind, too.

JEAN: *Cuisine Économique.* The certainty I could survive on very little—in style, dessert included. That mastery of raw materials.

MONICA: Look upon this red-knuckled forager, this user of scraps, this magician of the margin, and tell me you don't need her in your home, your senate, your school, your conquering army!

JEAN: Wow. You feel really strongly about this.

MONICA: Because I am here to protect the difference between *giving* and *being had.*

I go to get the Tomme from the fridge now when David shoves the kitchen door open, rushed. "Has anyone seen the van keys?" he asks, scouring the countertops and patting his pants. He carries a windbreaker over his arm. We shake our heads.

"What's going on?" I ask.

"I'm taking Judith to the hospital. I have to. She can't go on like this."

We gasp.

"Hey," says Yoni. He points to a spot next to the whiskey bottles on the counter. "Your keys."

"Goddammit," David mutters. "Neary . . ." He thanks Yoni and runs out. A few minutes later, we are all in the entryway of the castle, wishing Judith well and seeing her off, when David, at the threshold, turns back and points at me. "Jean," he says. "You should come with." Judith looks up at me with a little light in her eyes. I'm wearing shorts and a tank top. "Do you have a raincoat or something?" He wants me to cover up. Even though it's a humid summer day, I'm embarrassing, I'm not wearing enough clothes, maybe a reminder to him of the story he heard, a confirmation that I'm slutty and incautious.

"I'll go get it." I run upstairs for the khaki coat I wore to Newark and haven't worn since. Soon we're in the van, Judith in the back and me in the passenger seat.

"There should be signage in Moulins for the A&E—what is it here?"

"Urgences."

"Right, of course. Still, we might need this." He hands me a folded road map. "Can you read a map?"

"Yup," I say and then, "Oh no" as I suddenly remember the state of the kitchen. I gave no one instructions. I was lifted from cook to first lieutenant so fast, I didn't have time to train a replacement.

"What is it?" says David, his words compressed by stress as he knocks the gearshift into reverse.

"Nothing. It's fine. They'll feed themselves just fine," I say.

"Oh, right. I'm sorry, Jean. I think I need you more than they do tonight."

Horses. Horses run through me. Fences break. Hoofprints in my organs, churned like lane mud.

"It's no problem," I say.

"Hank ooo, Gheeen." From the bench behind us, Judith's little paw brushes my arm.

Judith is asleep next to me, her head on my shoulder. David is sitting on my other side, occasionally popping up to get an update on the wait time. I don't care how long it takes. We watch old French people cough, young French people cry. Some are depressing, like the old woman who's had a fall and whose middle-aged daughter holds paper towels to the blood coming from her head; she gets seen quick. The boy in the tracksuit top with the sleeves tied in a knot like a straitjacket, a displaced shoulder underneath, he's been waiting a while. His mother is furious because he did something she told him a thousand times not to do and now he says, "Mommy, how much longer?" and she says, "You be quiet."

But in my mind, there might as well be a single candle dripping onto a Chianti bottle between David and me because it's our first date. I always knew it could be like this, if by some miracle we had the time. For four pressurized weeks we could only talk in snatches, with excuses—that one time, a little expansively, over a cigarette—before he got ripped away. But now . . .

"They were both musicians." (His parents). "They played in orchestras in London, and they had pupils."

"So they were teachers, too."

"I suppose they were. I think there was a combination, in their lives, of intense solitude, when they would practice or learn new pieces, and then the interaction of teaching to balance it. Maybe that's why academia seemed—normal to me."

"Is it not normal?"

"Well, it's . . . strange," he says.

"Would you recommend it?"

"Would I *recommend* it?" He laughs, then considers a moment, then seems almost surprised. "Yes, I would. It's a profession that lets you *think*, in fact requires you to think deeply. To go beyond the normal ways of thinking, to be theoretical, speculative, profound." He glances around this plasticky room full of normal people who, for the moment, make normalcy look infectious and dangerous. "God, that's rare."

"What did Ann's parents do?"

He sidesteps Ann. "Neary was raised by priests. By a priest, I should say. He lost his mother quite young. And I think his father— Maybe he drank. I don't know the whole story, but he was outwardly this caring deacon and then privately not very kind. Must have made young James think critically about the gap between doctrine and life—become a scholar, in short. And he got to know the architecture, of course: He actually lived in a church."

"I bet that'll mess with you."

"Well, I don't know if it—"

"Is he a believer?"

"That I don't *know*." It's a question David has thought about a lot, a problem that lives deep in a thicket in his mind that he shows nobody. But I can miraculously wander into it, the thorns pulling away. I was born to talk to him. "Isn't that funny? Fifteen years we go back and I don't know whether he believes in any of it—the way I somehow do." He scans me quickly for signs of shock or mockery, but to me David's faith makes sense, is proof of his weakness for whimsy, charity, decency; I nod reassuringly as my butt warms up at the thought of him in a good suit in the gold light of Christmas candles. "Why don't you ask Neary?"

We lock eyes and smile at the comical impossibility. The very idea of me, a student, asking Neary anything personal.

"You know," he continues, "James Neary is a deep man. Brilliant. And caring. I almost think that's why he has so little patience—so little tolerance for the everyday. It's exhausting, seeing people fully the way he can. What he's done for me and my career, I can't begin to tell you. He saw talent in me I didn't know I had. I probably would have drifted off into . . . I don't know, the law, something sensible. Don't tell anyone I said this or they'll take away my British passport, but I love the guy."

"I like him, too."

"Of course you do. Whom *don't* you like? Gosh, that's horribly gossipy." Gossipy? *Whom don't you like?* is basically the framework of all conversation at the castle, but you, you good man, you recoil at its ugliness. "Whom could you *possibly* dislike?" he says. "You were worried those clowns would starve tonight. Or perhaps it's a brilliant bit of subterfuge and you dislike *everyone* and you go about making us all happy, collecting little spiteful notes in secret." He looks at me squinting as if through a jeweler's loupe. "Hmm?"

Making us all happy: Ruthless Jean plucks that from the air and puts it in a ledger for me to savor in the fullness of time. "My notes? My notes are all about the books you gave me." It seemed a logical joke: *I'm here for school, remember?* But it's disastrous. Now Ruthless Jean is furious, shrieking, spinning. He straightens up and pulls away from me. *Why did you remind him of school?* Now you've chastised him for his warmth and ease, the extrascholastic chat, all this true communion, this line of heat that you sense has the power to slice your formless, senseless world into the shape of a woman.

A nurse calls Judith's name.

✦

The next thing I know, we are in the doctor's office and I'm speaking French. "My friend says this happens to her occasionally. There's an injection you can give her, in her jaw. A steroid?"

"A steroid?" repeats the doctor.

"Yes, yes, a steroid."

Judith nods with gratitude and relief at his recognition of the word. "Yech, chkewoid."

The doctor's tone remains consistent, efficient, but his words take a sharp turn. "It does not exist."

"Surely it exists."

"Yes, of course, steroids exist, but to give her an injection? It makes no sense. Tell her I will have to use force."

Judith sees the surprise in my face.

David follows the conversation, but he is a reader and not a speaker of French.

"What do you mean 'force'?" I ask.

"I mean you're going to help me hold her and I'm going to push her mouth shut."

"That's crazy. Why did we come to a doctor? Don't you have medicine?"

"Duh he hag ge chot?"

"No, he doesn't have the shot."

"Non non non," says the doctor. He stands back with a terse, frustrated laugh. "It *doesn't exist.* There's *one* solution here. You want me to use it or you want to go home?"

The doctor is middle-aged and has a ring of white hair around the back of his head like a chief surgeon on a TV program, but he is telling me that all he can do is punch the patient in the face.

"Just wait," I say to him. I explain to Judith what the doctor proposed. She cries and shakes her head violently, "Gnognngnnogno," and the doctor says, "Then go." He points to the door.

"Judith. He doesn't have the shot. He says this is it. I'll hold your hand." I turn to the doctor. "Can you give her some painkillers or something at least?"

"After. I will, after."

"He's going to give you something after."

She whimpers, she shakes her head, but she knows this is the end of her furtive, private self-harm. A man she has never met before will bring it to a violent climax, will rip the power she exerted over herself away and grab her muzzle as if she were a bad dog. She's still making the gesture of a shot with her hands and barking her incomprehensible pleas.

"There's no shot, Judith. It's this or he sends us home. It's up to you. Will you let him try?"

Her whine fades into a pale silence and she swallows and looks up at him and finally nods in permission. "Hold my hand," I say, and she does. She squeezes. The doctor instructs me to stand close to her, so that her head is pressed against my chest. He comes up to her from the opposite side and wraps his hairy hand, ungloved, around her jaw and leans into her, his belt buckle at her face, his hand squeezing. Within seconds, she's moaning, but that's only the start. She releases a gut cry, unshaped by her open mouth, just a noise. The doctor mutters, "*Putain.*"

How long does it last? I think we are killing her, me and a stranger, for several seconds. I think we will wring her neck. I think I was duped by this man into wringing her neck with him. Why did I believe him? Why did I trust the authority of his waxy head, his firm commands? He's a fucking murderer. Then with a horrible bone crunch, her jaw snaps shut. "There we are," says the doctor, like a nice dad who's just opened a jam jar.

I try to look in her eyes, but they're blank with pain.

"It's OK. You'll be OK," I tell her. I find I'm holding her, almost all of her, collected in my arms on the examination table. I feel her heart through her chest like a bird in a paper bag. I pull away just enough to look in her eyes, to search for recognition, for her to land safely in herself after the pain. At some point, I look up and am surprised to see David Harwell. He is standing against the back wall, next to a trolley of disorganized supplies, covering his mouth with his hands. For a few minutes, for the first time in six weeks, I had forgotten him.

✦

Judith is passed out on her side, curled up on the middle seat of the van, the seat belt missing her tiny crumpled frame almost entirely. The doctor gave her a muscle relaxant and a prescription for more, and said, in a surprisingly caring way, that he didn't want to see her again.

Now there is only, finally, relief. It's ten o'clock at night and the sun has set, but there's a lingering dark blue light and it's still almost as warm as day, the air heavy. We haven't eaten since lunch, and stress has torn through our energy reserves. David hasn't buckled up yet, nor have I. We just breathe.

"Crazy," he says. "The things you never expect to see."

"She's so sweet to everyone." I can't shake the memory of the doctor pushing her, of her head pushed into me as if she were livestock. I somehow want to confirm that she's a person. "And she's so smart."

"Mmm," he says. "I know it." He looks at me and smiles. It's a tired, unaffected smile, a gift for Judith that will be lost in the mail, that she would have loved to receive. "We need some food."

"I'm starving."

"It's forty-five minutes back to the castle. We'll see what we see before the motorway." Forty-five minutes is all I have left of this crisis-born intimacy. Then we'll go back to our places, miles apart. He'll go back to his important book and his thin wife and I'll go back to making casseroles and masturbating. Forty-five minutes.

"You were wonderful, Jean." His hand is about to turn the key, the other hand on the wheel. The seat creaks as he leans forward, facing me in a suspended moment of noble, cool appreciation. I am, in his eyes, more than I ever dreamed: strong, competent, good. I'm happy. This is all I should want, all I will get, and maybe it's enough.

✦

"Go on," he says, "see if they'll take us." I run into the pizzeria and back out to him, like his fine falcon.

"They're closing, but they'll do takeout."

"Great! Here." He hands me cash from the inside pocket of his jacket. "Get us whatever you fancy and we can eat in the car park."

We stand side by side leaning against the van, the pizza box resting on the passenger seat, the passenger side door hanging open. We each hold folded slices in our hands, angling our heads to eat.

"There's so much good food in this country," he says, chewing. "I'm sorry to feed you this." *Feed you.* Tonight I am his to feed.

"I don't care," I say, exhausted. "Any pizza's good pizza."

"Mmm. That's worthy of a proverb."

I do a silly baritone: *"Omne pizza bonum pizza."*

He laughs. "I forgot. All your languages. Why aren't we putting them to use here?"

"You are," I say, and I jam my thumb toward the interior of the van, like a hit man with a body in the trunk. Something about that is so funny to us suddenly, the way I jerked my thumb at Judith, the way she's dead but not dead, a gisant in the van behind us, the passing casualness of my reply, as if I did this all the time, fought with French doctors over the bones of my friends. David and I both burst out laughing, and I double over and come up gasping, his body, too, rocking with laughter.

"Oh god," he says, finally catching his breath, and the memory of what we saw at the hospital comes back, the horror of it. "Poor Judith." He looks deep into my eyes, shaking his head, wiping his mouth with the back of his hand.

The sky rumbles. It starts to drizzle. We've finished eating. It's time to go. Our hands are greasy, and there is a prickly chemical wash of Diet Coke in my mouth. He holds a palm up to gauge the rain, looks at the sky. I walk to the trash, toss in the Coke can and shove down the pizza box, and walk back to him. The town is empty and gray and there is no one around but the teenager in the restaurant wiping down tables. I watch David watch me return to him, his falcon tonight, a loyal animal who saved a life. His eyes hang heavy on me. His hands are in his pockets. He is still. I stand facing him.

Suddenly there is a pause. Someone should say "Let's go back" or "Ready?" but no one does. The world is a formless void; nothing's been invented yet. Then his hands are under my coat, on my ribs, finally, finally squeezing them as they have yearned to be squeezed, pulling me toward him.

✦

If I was a human in that instant, I can't tell you. I felt myself to be a sea creature with no eyes, nothing but a pink spineless will to wrap myself around him and feel. And although I had been ashamed of her, tried to shake her, tried to ignore her, now I spoke to the Jean who had brought me here, the Jean who calculated all her moves as a function of David Harwell's vision: *You believed, you believed, and it paid off. There were no signs, there was no confirmation, but you knew, you knew he would come to you. Your faith did this, it wished for this meal and now you feast. Now you are full of him.*

PART III

✦ ✦ ✦

Jean of Hoboken

Chapter 51

Stillness, in the great marble throne room. Only cool. The water in the tub is transparent now, and I see the bottom of the basin curved and waiting like an ear. I don't want to move; David's kiss is still peeling off me like a priceless vapor. Monica studies me.

"Why did we leave?" I ask her. "It was just getting good."

"That's why."

"Should I not feel the good stuff?"

"Oh, no, on the contrary: the good stuff is the point." She rises. "Come on."

She takes my hand and leads me to a door in the wall I hadn't noticed. She pulls the handle and colors flood in. I recoil until my eyes adjust to a wide sitting room, where picture windows tessellated with gem-toned glass throw streaks of ruby and lapis across the beige sofa and carpet, and through the shafts of color I see that the walls are covered with floor-to-ceiling tapestries.

From a distance they're busy scribbles, but as I approach the central tapestry I can make out a terrifying scene, a swirl of prancing, grimacing men and women all piercing Monica's skin with sharp, dirty claws; she hovers in the center of the cloth under the red letters ILIA FEMINA, blood streaking down from the wounds in her contorting, naked body: "that woman." Her eyes loll upward in pain, an inaudible cry twists her gaping mouth. The only words belong to her tormentors—one of them, a grinning goblin with a huge malformed chin and a distended potbelly, barfs a scroll that reads "Monica Lewinsky has gained back all the weight she lost last year. In fact, she told reporters she was even considering having her jaw wired shut, but then, nah—she didn't want to give up her sex life."

Her *sex life*, imagined like a primordial tar, bubbling in her abdomen, where good men get stuck. I have it too, this dangerous ooze that David discovered, that pulled him in, that he had to fight his way out of. I trace the stitched blood that meanders out from her wounds like the footprints of a hundred beetles and the words in my mind are not "How can I avoid this?" but "Here I come": I will follow you. I will feel this. I rest my forehead on the tapestry, on the red lines, longitudes of a map I'll use, raised scabs that I'll pick with the painted nails of a silly teen. Onward, forward—that's what she wants, right? Isn't that why I called her? To bleed again, bleed together, because I know that her world-historical public degradation can swallow my private shame like burgundy swallows pink.

And yet: that kiss. David's hands finding my ribs. All I feel is hope. After these five weeks in France with little Jean, I'm suffused with the sweetness of what is brewing between me and David. Ha! I've learned nothing. I've gotten *dumber,* fallen back into the fog, lost my way again. Is that what she wants me to know? That I'll shimmy right up to the sales counter and buy David again and again, at the cost of my confidence, at the cost of my future?

"I don't think I'm getting it." I sink into the sofa, and Monica settles in beside me. A blue-toned light from the window slices into my vision and I close my eyes.

"What are you not getting?"

"Well. I'm—I'm no wiser now. I love him again." I meet her eyes with resignation, and she only smiles, thank god. "If you want me to see that it's not my fault—I see that. All I'd known was confusion and drunk parties and boys my age who still wore puffy coats with mittens attached and pushed whole chicken tenders into their faces from start to finish like their mouths were log chippers. Then, *that man? That touch?*"

"He was sexy."

"He was a *man,* which used to be a synonym for *human. This smart, strong man is our best specimen, the top of the line,* you think, and you touch his collarbone, the canvas of his skin stretched between his jaw and his cheekbone like some ingenious sail, every part of him strong and meant to work, and working. And everything tells you that you should be taken! Every ad says 'Be more enjoyable!' 'Wear *thongs*! Ask your asshole to actually *eat* your underpants before you'd spoil the spectacle of your butt with panty lines!' "

"The worst," she breathes.

"And messages aside, the very fact of your body coming into beautiful form—your boobs are so squishable, should they not be squished?!"

"Here we go."

"I get it! It's not my fault the trap was set, but still, I wasn't smart enough to avoid it."

Monica's face falls. She stands up and moves toward another tapestry, a life-size portrait of herself resplendent in her cobalt gown, a frieze of hands reaching up to her hem from below—I hope she can't read my thoughts because I'm thinking this picture looks like bad hospital art, and that whatever image of grace and consolation it offers feels cheap and distant. Does she want me to think this is all great, a rollicking good time? Is she in the end some flinty fairy with no appreciation of the *years* of wasted energy, the deep-rootedness of my attachment to this hurt? She's not the only one who can time travel—eventually when David discarded me, he went back in time and made my *first cell* feel worthless.

"I know what happens next, Monica," I say with more grievance than I can control. "Spoiler: It's not good. What, I'm supposed to be grateful for David?"

She whips back around to me. "No, I never said that. But Jean, do you remember why you called me?"

"No. I don't." I don't remember the adult I became. I'm a nineteen-year-old basking in affection.

" 'I don't want to live my life anymore. I have no conviction. I'm dead.' "

"Then it's too late." My eyes travel up the wounds stitched into her body, and my own skin itches. "Send me home. I'm sorry I don't have the guts to go through what you did, to watch myself get mortified. I want to go back to Jersey and hide in my little life. I'm never going to heal."

"I never spoke of healing," she says lightly and returns to sit next to me. She is so close to me that I see the black and cream of my bad office clothes glow gold in the aura of her halo. "You called me because you saw me resurrect myself, with purpose and grace. That's all you want. Come, Jean, don't lose heart now. I will tell you—the life you return to, that sense of going through the motions: You can't bear it much longer."

She says nothing for a moment, but her tilting face exudes seriousness. Then, brightly, she shakes it off.

"Should we have a little palate cleanser? Do you want to see Kenneth Starr roasting on a spit in hell?"

"No."

"You sure? It's very rewarding. He genuinely looks surprised. He's like, 'But I'm a Christian!' It's hilarious."

"Is he in pain?"

"Oh yeah." Monica glows a little brighter. "It's a hot, hot fire."

"Monica, can't you change what happened?"

She exhales, takes my hands in hers. "That's not what I'm here for."

What is she here for? She's the vaporous embodiment of women told only to be beautiful and then damned for being hot, told only to be nurturing and then damned for being sluts, told their hearts were the devil and their bodies were a trap. Goddam all the confusion, all the gray area: Is it not time for a crystal-clear act of defiance? Sure, I'm kind of meek and super friendly and I don't do any strength training, but with Monica at my back, can I be firm and heroic? Surely this extraordinary intervention requires extraordinary action—didn't Saint Margaret come to a farmer's daughter and ask her to wage war?

I meet Monica's gaze now with new vigor as I meet her challenge in my mind. I eyeball the gruesome figures stitched before me, insulting Monica, bleeding her for crass jokes.

"I know what you want."

"You do?" She leans toward me, wide-eyed and hopeful.

"Vengeance. Kenneth Starr is getting his comeuppance—it's David's turn!"

"No. Kenneth Starr is in his own theological bind; that's not my work."

"Well, in my case—I know how it ends."

"Ends?"

"I'm supposed to go to David's party . . ."

"OK . . ."

"And kill him."

"What?"

"I know, it sounds crazy! But this is what faith is for, right? You're the Margaret to my Joan of Arc, exhorting me to great action!" She's about to reply, but I've found another clue: "And I know why you chose me to do your bidding."

"I *don't* want you to do this."

"It's my knife skills! I'm the perfect vehicle!"

"Your knife skills are for carrots, Jean! Don't lose your way here!"

"You want me to be the actor in my own life. That's what you said. I know how to do it, how to reclaim center stage."

"Jean, what I want for you is so much better than vengeance." She is not winking at me. There is no subtle saintly semaphore; no dove appears behind her, carrying a gun and nodding suggestively. In fact, she looks legitimately alarmed and is hemorrhaging nos. But maybe this is how it has to be: I have to go on faith. I can't simply take orders.

"I'm your foot soldier, Monica! I'll do this for *you*! For everyone who insulted you! For me! For all who were used and abandoned and shamed. You can't say it, but you want vengeance!"

"No, Jean."

"But no means yes?"

"Jean."

"I can do it, I swear to you."

"JEAN."

Chapter 52

"JEAN."

My eyes crack open and I can make out Michael, close to me.

"JEAN, are you OK? Were you *drinking*?"

"What?" I have no idea where we are—there's a confusing taste in the air. It's too bright. I bury my face in the darkness. When my eyes open again, my lashes scrape the fabric of the futon, which I recognize, though it's blurry. I adjust to the light and turn slowly back to Michael.

"Jesus, Jean, you almost burned the house down."

Michael wasn't there; he doesn't know. "It's not food, it's Kenneth Starr."

"It's *what*? It's *farfalle*. You tried to make pasta. Drunk. And then you fell asleep."

"What are you talking about?"

"*What happened to you?* Last thing I know, you've had another breakdown in court and you're leaving early. You tell me you'll be on the PATH train in twenty minutes, and then you don't come home, you don't answer your phone. I was out of my mind, calling all your friends. I guess you came home drunk in the early morning and tried to make some food and passed out."

"I was in France. In the Bourbonnais."

"What?"

"Monica, tell him." I look around frantically. I listen, my eyes scouring the room for a sign.

"Monica? Who's Monica?"

"Monica Lewinsky."

"Monica Lewinsky lives in California, Jean. You don't know her."

"No, no, not the human lady. The all-powerful numen they created when they tried to destroy her."

"Do I need to take you to the hospital?" Michael is genuinely distraught, tugging at his hair, then covering his eyes to think. I feel like I haven't seen him in weeks—I've been with David. I miss David. Michael looks at me, searching. "You're freaking me out. I mean, are you just drunk?" He says this hopefully. If only I were drunk.

"I was never drunk! SMELL ME! Do I smell drunk?"

"You smell terrible."

"I must have been sweating a lot." I look at my clothes, my court clothes—a fake silk blouse tucked into black pants, sensible flats, the fucking timid outfit I used to wear before I became JEAN OF HOBOKEN, CRUSADER, KILLER, AVENGER OF WOMEN. One of my boobs is half out of my bra, and my pants and shirt are smudged with dirt, like actual earth dirt. I look past Michael at the narrow IKEA mirror propped up against the wall that I never installed because everything felt tentative and equivocal before I had a FIERY PURPOSE. "Holy shit," I mumble: My face in the mirror is streaked with gray, like I'm an ensemble member in *Cats*.

"You smell like smoke."

"Oh, the votive candles." I think back to Trinity Church. "Also, I smoke cigarettes sometimes."

"You do?"

"Yeah. And I'm having a hard time, even though I was never molested. It was an affair—well—an inappropriate—see—"

"I know you're having a hard time. I don't understand it. Is it this thing with your teacher from ages ago?" I suppose the answer is yes, but it doesn't feel accurate: "your teacher" is such a small designation, better suited to Mrs. Kawasaki in second grade laying out art supplies; and "ages ago" has no purchase on the way it is always recent, how David has always just walked out of the shower somewhere in my mind and left wet footprints across my day, across whatever I wanted to do. I thought that his residence in my mind was my secret, that I could cry in the cracks without anyone noticing, but now that I have washed up in a heap and nearly burned down the house and Michael is asking about my "teacher," I realize he is seeing, and maybe has always seen, how haunted I am. "This isn't new, Jean. It's been happening in cycles since I met you, when you couldn't be around kitchens anymore. You just get erratic and you want to throw everything away and start again. And I think I was one of those fresh starts for you. And the translation work; it was all going to be stable now. But then the new life that you started—you'll want to throw that away pretty soon, too." Then, quietly: "When are you going to throw me away?"

I let myself take him in: olive skin, two-day beard like a promising crop, cargo pants, soft stomach, a water bottle I assume is for me. "You're so nice." *But you're not enough; you're some nice pussy who feels safe and who won't ever abandon me, but actually I'm in love with David and now I have to go to France and murder him.*

"There's a lot going on behind your eyes, Jean."

Chapter 53

SATURDAY, APRIL 20, 2019
HOBOKEN, NEW JERSEY

Since I woke up back at home, I have been drifting in and out of naps, and each time I wake I am disappointed to be in my own life, my own home, and not in the Bourbonnais with David. Nothing is happening here except that Michael says I'm not well and has taken off work to look after me and I have decided to roast a lamb leg for dinner—the kind of big-project cooking I haven't done in ages.

I take a narrow but strong boning knife and stab the leg. In and out, quick. *Could I do this to a person?* I wonder as I thrust. I send the lamb spinning. It slides off the table onto the floor with a loud *thwack. I can do better, Monica; just wait.* Michael rushes in.

"What's going on?"

I am half out of my chair, leaning across the kitchen table with a knife in the air.

"Making dinner."

Michael shakes his head and hoists the joint off the floor, groaning with effort. "This is a huge piece of meat for us two."

"Just being an economical cook." I wink for Monica.

"Why are you winking?"

"I'm not."

"You are."

"I got blood in my eye." He hovers for a moment and turns to go but then turns back.

"Was that lamb on the chair? Were you having coffee with the lamb?" I begin to say no, but he goes on. "Were you talking to the lamb? You can talk to *me*, you know."

"I'm just making dinner! I really have nothing to talk about!" This is not a good time to tell him I have spent $2,200 of our savings—destined for a down payment on a house (talk about delusional!)—on a flight to Paris in a week.

I look around my kitchen, weighing my own life like an emperor: a brown banana, onions molting, garlic ready to slip its paper and stink me up. A Springsteen poster. Cheery, affectionate Christmas cards, which have only ever made me feel bereft and unaccomplished. A stack of stained cookbooks. A bowl of keys, batteries, and the free mints they give you at Maggiano's. This is a small life. It would not be such a shame to throw this life away, if it meant one blazing solution to a muddy, intractable problem. Didn't I throw it away a long time ago?

I keep practicing, but more carefully. It's to show you, Monica, to show you what I can do. I close my eyes and I imagine, with all my power, that this is the living flesh of David Harwell, this hard bone his sternum, his rib, that his meat has the density of lamb, which I have no doubt it does—it's one of those funny biblical truths, that all creatures seem molded from the same clay, all of us lizards and lambs and professors are leather purses full of tomato soup. I hold the handle of the knife and I pull my arm back and *zip,* in I go again.

I stop and listen for your approval, your voice, but I hear nothing.

In each slit, I place a sliver of garlic. Twenty, forty cloves. Garlic, garlic, how I always stunk of garlic when I cooked in my dorm, or even later, as a pro—how it's good in the moment, good when it's fresh, but inevitably turns into an embarrassment, a rancid trace, distasteful, low-class. I learned how to avoid skin contact, bashing and scraping it with a blade, but now I let myself go, pinching the ivory bulbs in my naked fingers, halving cloves in the air deftly, saturating my skin with the overwhelming burn of it. A burning without flame. Immoderate, staining, leaving traces of its oily fuckness. Garlic is pervy. It is naked and lobed under its cosplay bridal veil. You plant it in your food like you plant a desire. You can sweeten it but never stamp it out. Garlic shows its thong, tenfold, twelvefold. Garlic stays in your throat, whispers from your throat to everyone about the pleasure you had, and why not? Why not, Monica? I inhale deeply: Is this what you want me to say, that pleasure stinks? That desire stains? That I just have to accept it, and move on? But how, when the rancid trail follows me? I think about David, his fine fingers, long, proportioned like his legs, on my waist, squeezing me like he'll pop me out of my paper.

✦

"This is really garlicky." Michael eats approvingly. He chews slowly and slurps wine to cut the funk. "But *great*." He moves David Harwell's flesh around in his mouth. "What's this sauce?" He gestures to his cheek with a knife.

"Capers. Can I ask you a serious question?"

"Of course, baby." Still chewing.

"Do you think I'm capable of murder?" Michael stops chewing. Swallows. Drinks a glug of wine and poses the glass with a heavy hand.

"*No*, Jean." His earthy eyes, middle-class-wooden-furniture-color, varnished, stable, born to look with dignity upon people in states of undress and disrepair. "You're obviously not capable of murder. You are one of the kindest people I've ever met. Always thinking about others. It's your favorite thing. You go on vacation and you spend the *entire time* trying to find some rare tea your dad likes. You make me a perfect Manhattan and when I take my first sip, *you* get tipsy on how much I love it! It's a *superpower*. You should appreciate it! You watch me eat this dinner and you're almost laughing, you're so happy."

"Well, that's a bit different because I was imagining killing this—"

"Jean. Did someone hurt you? Can you just talk to me?"

Did someone hurt me? Did David hurt me, did he love me, did he make me, unmake me?

"I don't remember." I *don't* remember. Monica is right. No one remembers the history, really: they only hold a dry record of who won. Like David said, in the stony hodgepodge of that church: "Alliances existed, for themselves, in their own time." But why, and how much garlic I used, and whether I should be killed for it, or whether he should be killed, or whether we should be killed together, our bodies left to the sun, to the dogs, are all questions I still can't answer. *Fine. Let's watch me open all my doors and be taken like a fool. But I reserve the right to get my vengeance.*

A pigeon lands outside the kitchen window, its iridescent blue throat swelling. "I'm coming," I whisper. Michael's head rotates as he traces my laser gaze to the bird. Worry multiplies on his face.

✦

The next morning, I brush past a custodian at the door of Trinity Church.

"Can I help you?"

"Headed to the crypt," I say like I work here.

"We don't have a crypt."

"Yes you do."

Moments later, Monica draws a finger across the surface of the water and we watch the ripples dissolve: There's little Jean, lying on a white blanket on a canopied bed, hands on her abdomen, like a duchess of the Bourbonnais, dead or waiting for her baby to grow.

PART IV

+ + +

Summer 1998: Doors

Chapter 54

CHÂTEAU PLAISY, FRANCE

I woke this morning with the exact same name, same clothes, same schedule, but after what happened with David last night in the car park, I'm a completely different person.

On jelly legs, I enter the kitchen. Sigrid was gone when I woke up and Judith still asleep. My heart almost bursts as I open the kitchen door, but David isn't there, only Patrick, reading a book, eating plain bread and drinking coffee.

"Hi, Patrick."

"Jean." He glances up and back.

"Can I have some of that?" I ask, pointing to his cafetière.

"Be my guest."

Patrick is about to bring his book back up to his face when he asks, "How did things go—at the ER?"

"The doctor fixed her, I guess." They are strangely intermixed in my mind, the out-of-body panic of holding Judith on that doctor's table, and the out-of-body pleasure of holding David by the van.

"Good. It was good of you to go along." *You don't get to give awards for goodness, Patrick,* I think, and then, remembering my amazing sin, *PS, you suck at it.*

Yoni steps into the kitchen, sees me, and speeds over to us.

"Oh my god, is Judith OK?"

"She's OK. But it was intense. The doctor just"—I shudder remembering it—"shoved her jaw into place."

"He what?"

"Yeah. I wouldn't go to a French country doctor for anything serious. Probably remove your cyst with a fork and a knife."

"Fuck." Yoni scans the kitchen, and his face contracts in sudden confusion. "Why doesn't the prince ever have breakfast?"

"I bet he has it brought to his room," I say.

"By Sigrid," adds Patrick, beaming with self-satisfaction. It annoys me that Patrick's right, that a creature so beautifully weird and wild loves to please the prince. But I can't let Patrick take digs at her.

"And do you bring Neary his?" I ask. Patrick squints at me, and Yoni makes a hissing burn sound.

"And do you bring David his?" Patrick cradles his mug and speaks casually. I flush with alarm but also excitement, to feel my connection to David enter the world, to hear it in another's voice. It doesn't completely surprise me that Patrick, and not Yoni or Judith, has called us out: He is attuned to the higher things.

The door swings open and David and Neary descend the steps side by side, mid-conversation.

". . . That's what I figure. Bourges is about a hundred kilometers, so on the motorway, that's—"

"Surely not more than an hour and a half."

"I think we can easily make Paris after that."

They patter on, David facing away from us now as he fills the kettle at the sink. He turns around. I'm not sure I'll survive this moment; it's like going over a waterfall. He looks strangely into the middle of the room at no one in particular and says, "Hi, guys." But then his gaze drops out of its odd suspension and falls on me and we make eye contact and it's self-aware, manually directed, not automatic. At the same time, he doesn't seem ashamed. He can look at me; I can look at him. We were our true selves, our breakfast selves, in the night, not drunk or lying.

Last night: I remember Judith's body twitching to life on the middle bench as we left the pizzeria. "Jean?" she bleated. David and I had separated by then and were stepping into our sides of the van, in unison.

"How are you feeling?" I asked her. I twisted around and touched her knee as she lay across the seat and David got the van moving.

She thought for a moment, her hand rising to her face. "That doctor was *crazy*, right?"

"That doctor was an asshole."

"That doctor was probably a vet," David said, quietly, looking out the window at the field on the other side of the road and at the cows, far from us, immobile, guts draped between bony haunches like complicated camping gear. David shook his head and rolled down the window, letting the cool air and the animal smell pour in. He turned to look at me, at all of me. His left hand covered his mouth and his right hand rested on the wheel. Half a smile spilled out from under his hand and I knew it was me, that I was drawing it out of him even though he was also scared. There was a revelation in that half-smothered smile: He had wanted this. It was not a momentary spark, a tired accident, a trip-up. Like me, he had wished for this and doubted himself.

He drove us back to the castle in silence—not an awkward silence, but a silence like the ones in the library, static but patterned, full of frantic, antic connection, like a busy, bestial tapestry, and when we got home, I took Judith up to bed and didn't see him after that.

Of course even though I had felt reassured in the van, when I found myself under the starry canopy of my princess bed, where I had practically seared my pillow with fantasies of our bodies mushing together, I wondered if the next day there would be a talk: "Look, that was a mistake." Maybe I would be blamed: "You've clearly been sending me signals . . ." And it would end. And that would be the right thing to do, the Sam thing to do. Set ourselves on track, have integrity. *Integrity:* everything integrated, the story simple and true from every angle, no hidden pockets, no lake under the floorboards, no alchemical haze that turns wrong to right. No need for scholars, for the furious exegesis, for the search for the word that might open the book to the sky.

But now something tells me that there won't be a talk, that he hasn't lain awake all night fomenting a thousand regrets. And if last night wasn't a mistake, then . . . The Jean who calculates knows that something has been put in motion and if it is not stopped by external forces, it will go on.

"Planning our trip to Paris for you guys," says David.

Cheers, nods.

"Finally," says Yoni, and Neary says, "Yes, finally, you can have your pockets picked."

"Can't do *that* in Bressac-le-Puteaux!" says Sigrid, and she and Yoni high-five. My breath, when I exhale, doesn't end but wiggles down in some muscular convulsion—is this world as good as I had hoped? Do you push your spoon down and find treasures in the soup, will there be chocolate in the mail, a kiss from the king? Will Paris be for us? David's smile is tossed across the group, a scattered blessing for these young scholars excited to scamper and play, but again, his dispersed gaze condenses out of the air and fixes on me, and I know that a magical season is upon us, that anything is possible, that I might be given gifts, that I might be visited and transformed.

"Bet we could find some really Eurotrash jeans in Paris," says Sigrid. Yoni levels her a serious look.

"Bitch, believe."

Chapter 55

The excitement about going to Paris in two days has sapped Yoni and me of any energy we might have mustered for these last few Podunk churches. The others are under an Orangina-themed sun umbrella at a local café, drinking coffees and Cokes, waiting for lunch, but Yoni and I have pulled our chairs into the sunlight and sit silently in our sunglasses, baking like the lizards we scare off church steps.

"What's going on with you?" he says, unmoving.

"What do you mean?"

"You're being weird."

"No I'm not."

"Yes you are. You're really spaced out."

Do I tell him? Do I tell him about Moulins? When I test out a narrative in my mind—*David and I made out in a parking lot*—it doesn't seem right; it doesn't seem promising and beautiful. But at the same time, I do want to tell Yoni, want to see him throw down his notebook and go "You WHAT?"

"Nothing's going on. Guess I'm stressed about my paper."

"Oh, I almost finished mine."

"You WHAT?"

"Yeah."

"I haven't even started!"

"It's a ten-page paper! Bang it out."

I think of my tangle of notes, the way they digress into diary, how hard it is to read about Cistercian abbeys or ivory trade routes when a glance up at the back of David's neck will fill my body with fighting eels.

Through my half-closed lids, I sense that David has separated from the group under the sun umbrella and is approaching us.

Even with our glasses on, we have to squint to see him between us and the midday sun. I can't make out his facial features, but his shape is crisp, his earlobes, the signature scribble of his hair. He is not mine but is known to me differently now, like a cup I once drank out of.

"What did you think of the church today?"

Yoni and I say, "Nice" and "Not bad" at the same time.

"Can't wait to read your guidebook."

Yoni holds up the red spiral notebook we have scribbled in during our site visits, tattered, ashed-on, with a pen drawing of a church with two cartoon dicks for bell towers. "This baby's solid gold."

"Yeah? What if we took a little random sample," David says, plucking the book from Yoni's hand and flipping it open to a few pages from the start. He reads, " 'Saint Roche. This one not so hot. Extra-gross sores. Mary sad.' " He looks at us coolly. "Mary sad?"

"You had to be there."

"It was a super sad Mary."

"It usually is, Yoni."

He flips further and reads again. " 'Saint Martin in Mauriac-le-Bretel. Cubed stonework and thick walls suggest no later than eleventh century'—well well well! I'm impressed, guys!" Yoni and I shrug minimally. "That cubing technique that you picked up on is a proper carryover from the Romans."

"Romanesque," says Yoni, lifting his arms like he's graciously solved a major problem for David.

"Indeed." David surveys us as a gardener might survey a patch of very small vegetables among a lot of healthy weeds. "Look, I can tell you both are a little churched out. But in two days, we're going to Bourges."

"I thought we were going to Paris!" says Yoni, sitting up.

"Bourges is on the way—we'll stop there in the morning and be in Paris by evening."

"Oh, good." Yoni goes back to his anesthetized slouch.

"It's *stunning*, one of the biggest cathedrals in the world." No reaction.

"I'm really over Jesus," says Yoni in his shades, a celebrity being mean about other famous people.

"When we get back, you two can skip the last couple of churches, OK?" David tosses the notebook back to Yoni. "I'll let you stay back and polish up this masterpiece."

"Send it to the publishers," says Yoni.

"Oh god, if your book is published before mine—"

"Well, you better hurry," I say, and now we are somehow the teachers and he is the whining student.

"I'm almost there! Something's happened this summer." He looks at me and then away, over the road. "I think I'm ready for new ideas."

Chapter 56

The hierarchies so well established over the first five weeks here are disintegrating as we approach our last ten days. Jojo has begun spiffing up the whole castle, taking an oil can to every hinge and varnishing every floor, because while we're in Paris, the prince is hosting a fundraiser for what will officially be called the Château Plaisy Field School, and this has given Jojo the authority to yell at us right and left. *"Reculez! Marchez pas là!"* This evening, Victoire occupies the seat at the head of the table, irritated at something in her shoe. She brushes off her naked foot, which is protuberant and yellow-gold like a baked good.

Yoni is in polished adult mode. "So, David, tell us a little about your book."

"Oh." We've chattered about it behind his back, but in five weeks, no one has wanted to bring up David's work in front of him—we know it's a source of stress. But Yoni pulls it off, not as needling but as country-club chat. "Well, I'm interested in sound."

"Sound!" I hear myself saying. "So you're not into buildings, either!"

"No, no I am very *much* into buildings. Remember, they were once filled with sound, designed for it. The oral liturgy—then all that sacred music."

"Aw, where's Caitlin when you need her?" says Judith.

"Giving hand jobs in Lubbock," says Yoni out the side of his mouth and I start to laugh when Neary steamrolls us both.

"Methods that David has developed for studying church acoustics here have been adapted by people all over the world. It's really cracking work."

"We always look at these buildings empty," says David, eyes downcast, a little embarrassed. "We lavish attention on the outside, the surface. But as soon as you imagine people in them, filled with breath and song"—he looks up—"it all just comes to life."

"Can't wait to see the book, David," says Sam.

"Yeah, me, too," says Judith.

"If it's along the lines of your paper on Chartres, it'll be amazing," adds Brice, shoving a ladle into the stew.

"Well, you won't have to wait long. I have a few last sources to check in Paris and then it's off to the press." David doesn't look at me; what he says makes sense, sounds true. Yet *I believe*, I believe that I'm being whispered to, that signs are being given just to me.

"So you're not coming with us?" asks Judith.

"I'll drive up there and back with you guys, but I'm going to have to bury myself in these manuscripts while you're out gallivanting. It's fine. Neary's the Notre-Dame expert anyway."

"You run along," says Neary, waving David off with his hairy old hand. "Finish your manuscript. We'll be fine."

✦

Later that night, Yoni and David and I are in the library. Yoni grabs a book and heads to his room, and I decide I shouldn't push things.

"I'm heading out, too," I say once we're alone, but as I make for the door, David springs up from his desk.

"Look, Jean. About Paris." I stare at him, everything about to capsize. "Neary—it'll be a fabulous site visit." Is he dumping me? Is he afraid I'll try to follow him? "But if you wanted to make your excuses to the group and meet me, that'd be no problem." Now I am immobile, like some kind of bandy doe; if I even twitch, I'll knock what I think is happening out of its fragile becoming. "Excuses— I mean, you can't say . . ."

"What— You mean—"

"I'm asking whether you'd like to meet me in Paris." He's got a surface nervousness but also a rosy bloom pushing him from within. Warmth. He wants this.

"Oh. Yes. I can easily tell Neary— I mean, I have a lot of family living not far from Paris. I could say I'm meeting them."

"Of course, your family," he says. Now it's a game, the two of us believing my fictions.

"I've seen Notre-Dame anyway." A complete lie.

"I'm sure you have." I'm turning down a guided tour of Notre-Dame with the world's leading expert on it, but in this moment I might as well be dodging a visit to the town dump. Thank god I've escaped.

[Jean smacks her forehead.]

MONICA: To be fair, *no one* expected that place to burn down.

"I'm sure *you'll* be the guide once we're in Paris," he says.

"I don't know." I think I have said something else, but I haven't. I recall the bliss of the waiting room in Moulins—just to have open-ended time, all the time in the world.

"It'll be fun," he says jauntily now that it's decided, like ours is also a school trip, just a smaller one. He goes back to where he was working and then returns, swiveling his hips like a dancer to wend around the scattered desks, holding a glass of wine and a map of Paris, which he shakes open. "Probably against the rules up here," he says, lifting the wine, "but occasionally a scholar's aide."

"Mmm," I agree, thinking of the fluid erotic monologues I draft here drunk.

He tilts the glass toward me with a lift of the eyebrows.

"Sure," I say. I sip the warm red, barely taking it from his hands, and give it back.

"This is what I'm thinking. We'll all drive up Thursday and get there in the evening. Then Friday morning, you can meet me around ten?" I come closer to look at the map, laid out on a leather-topped desk. "I need to go here," he says and points to some nexus of lines and squares, totally meaningless to me, "but we'd be free to have lunch or a walk after. Then Saturday we could meet here and walk down toward the Marais, where there's a bonkers little museum I think you'd love."

A whole itinerary. Conceived for us.

I'm not really looking at the map. I'll go wherever he tells me to, I don't care. I grab his wine again and sip the last of it, looking at him over the rim. And without having done it on purpose, I get the upper hand; that gesture made me the hot party girl to his road-trip-planning dad. He has to prove something, get his youth back, his coolness, in this instant or he'll be an old loser forever. I'm almost nervous I'll humiliate him just by standing here, just by being my age and my size and my niceness. He grabs my wrist with one hand and takes the glass with the other, holding my gaze and revealing a wolfish smile I've never seen on him, accompanied by a strange shrinking of his eyes. It's a transformation, a chemical thing, a cloud around him, but when he's held my wrist a moment, the cloud lifts. He's succeeded, put me in my place, thank god. I hear the foot of the wineglass land on the table. I look up at him. He still holds my wrist with one hand and the other one must be in the air, sailing toward me, some part of me, his to choose. I imagine he will punch through my ribs and pull my organs out like a fistful of sausages, and I squirm with anticipation.

"Jean." The way he says my name, low and serious, halfway to "Jesus" but ending in pants. He looks at me in a practiced way that hurts me a little, that tells me he's done this before—maybe not a lot, but that he's been in love, held hands, gone together to Greece or Italy in white slacks, had it all reciprocated. Unlike me—I don't have a look of love, and I fear that what he sees is a kind of freckled hungry owl. He puts the wine down and is moving toward me when—

SQUEEE—the door screeches open. At the sound, we jump apart, arms flying toward books, maps. The wineglass, empty, topples, splattering a few droplets on the desk but not shattering.

It's Sam.

"Oh, sorry," she says.

"No, no, it's fine. I shouldn't have wine up here anyway." David dabs at the desktop with a tissue he's pulled from his pocket. He rights the glass, folds up the map, and then turns around. "What's up?"

"Any chance I could borrow Ann's book? If no one's using it?"

"Which one?" he asks, with a comic self-pitying sigh, as if to say, *My wife, all her books.* He's a good performer; he recovers fast.

"The nun one."

"I was using it, but you can have it," I say.

"Great," she says. I pick it up off my desk and extend it to her. She doesn't thank me as she takes it and seems almost peeved to be getting my hand-me-downs. "Dinner's in a minute," she says, looking at each of us in turn, reaching for the door again.

"We know." I hear it immediately: my terrible, terrible misstep in using *we,* in sounding possessive. I see him stiffen, annoyed, and I flush with shame—as if I thought we were an established couple, as if I could speak for him, salt his steak, count his pills.

"I'll be right there," David says, grammatically detaching himself from me.

I'm reeling too much to feel hurt by his sudden detachment—I will later—but for now I say to Sam, "I'll follow you down."

"See you guys in a sec," says David, burying his head in a book.

Sam and I slip out. She stops in the stairwell and looks around at me with hateful cat eyes. My hands are in my shorts pockets, raking through cold coins that I'm now convinced I stole.

Chapter 57

I have barely seen Sam all day, or David, for that matter. Yoni and I got excused from the day's church to work on our papers. David was just leaving the kitchen this morning with Sam and Brice when I trotted in, and he ignored me, held eye contact with Brice, dug into the point he was making with well-timed intensity. I shrunk against the wall in the corridor as he passed, trying not to exist. I'm paying for my gaffe, for "we," backpedaling furiously. I fear that I've been horrible, a lech, a psycho, when I know I'm the opposite.

MONICA: But you *are* a psycho!
JEAN: I am?
MONICA: Well, what do you mean by "psycho"? Obsessed? Hyperfocused?
JEAN: He doused me with attention and then went cold.
MONICA: You'd be perfectly cool if you could tap him on the shoulder and say, "Hey, are we on or off?" Instead, look at you, staring up at him in the hallway with your soupy eyes: You look like those pictures of me in the receiving line, "obsessed" like a mystic scanning the stars for a sign. Yes, you're unhinged, because this situation has taken a hammer to your hinges, to the normal joints and bridges of mutual affection.

Chapter 58

A LIFE OF SAINT JUSTINA, VIRGIN, KILLED IN THE YEAR 280, FROM *The Golden Legend*

+ + +

The virgin Justina was born in Antioch under the reign of Diocletian and was long pursued by a certain Cyprian, a magician. He invoked a demon to come to him and enable him to win the virgin. "Can you make it possible for me to have her and work my will with her?" The demon said, "Sure! I can let you have one mere girl and let you do what you please with her. I will come and set her heart on fire for you." But when Cyprian arrived, Justina made the sign of the cross and the demon disappeared. So Cyprian called the devil himself, who said, "I will inflame her spirit with hotter passion and spread hot spasms throughout her body. In the middle of the night, she will be yours."

So the devil transformed himself into a handsome young man and came into the room where Justina was lying in bed. He leapt on her and tried to envelop her in his embrace. But again Justina made the sign of the cross and the devil melted.

Cyprian changed by magic into a woman, or sometimes into a bird, to be permitted to come near her, but always near her his magic failed. One time he became a sparrow and watched her from a ledge, but when she looked at him, he became Cyprian again and then he was just a man stuck up high on a ledge. Justina was afraid he would fall and break his bones, so she brought him a ladder.

Cyprian gave up and converted to Christianity and became a bishop and sent Justina to a convent. One day a local prefect, hearing of the fame of Cyprian and Justina, asked them to sacrifice to the pagan idols. When they refused, he had them boiled with wax and sap. This only refreshed them. A pagan went near the cauldron and called out to Jupiter and Hercules, but the flames leapt out and consumed him. Finally, Cyprian and Justina were beheaded together; their bodies, first thrown to hungry dogs, lay rotting in the sun for seven days, and then were transported to Piacenza, where they lie at the heart of a great cathedral.

Chapter 59

BOURGES CATHEDRAL

All day yesterday I waited for a sign, a sign that it was still on, that David hadn't come to his senses. Finally, contorting infinitely, I thought, *Maybe no sign is a sign.* Then, after dinner, as I dried plates in the kitchen alone, he slipped me a piece of paper on which he'd jotted down *Metro Saint-Michel, 10 a.m.*, and said, "Think you can manage?" I could breathe again: Sam hadn't really seen anything in the library, and we'd be far from her eyes, far from them all in Paris.

My own giddiness this morning was easily disguised among the group's liberated insanity, everyone singing and shouting about their Paris plans during the ninety-minute drive to Bourges. We were all so hot, crowded in the vans, then climbing up the cobbled hill as the cathedral came into view, vast and complicated but also wounded-looking with its buttresses fanning out like fancy crutches. Now inside, it is so deathly cool that the sweat all over us prickles as it dries; the real world, the hot world, is instantly historicized by this place like an ancient way of life we strain to imagine.

And I know David is in architecture heaven and I know Neary sees a thousand things to lecture on and Patrick's Mets cap is in his hands as he looks up in pure astonishment. But something about this place makes me want to laugh. Gaudy chandeliers dangle twenty meters from the ceiling and two meters off the ground so you almost have to duck to avoid them. A phalanx of a thousand empty chairs is inhabited by a lone woman with an Umbro brand T-shirt and a mullet, looking nervous. A pigeon-toed white-haired tourist stalks slowly like she's trying to find the pace of significance. People who would have looked unremarkable at a café look like broken imbeciles in this cathedral.

Yoni also finds the soaring ambition of the cathedral—the incalculable heights, the softening echo—a perfect comic foil for everything actually human. We pass a faded photo of Mother Teresa, looking like Beetlejuice with a referee's pants on her head, and that's when we stop to marvel.

David, who has taken the circular racetrack of the ambulatory in the opposite direction, comes into sight. He diverts toward us and whispers, "Remarkable, isn't it?" His eyes travel up to the vaults above us, boned like bats' wings. "Just the scale!"

"Mmm," I agree. "But you kind of get used to it."

His face falls with an involuntary, defeated sigh. "Do you, now?"

"Also," adds Yoni, "I feel like they could use some uplighting. Those chandeliers are *offensive.*" He gestures at a wooden box with a slot on top. "I'm'na leave a comment."

"Please don't, Yoni. That's for alms." David cruises on and just as we're about to continue, Sigrid emerges from behind a pot of poinsettias.

"C'mon," she says. "I'll show you the butt."

"The what?"

"The butt." We shrug and follow Sigrid toward the crypt, and along the way we pick up Judith.

"Where are you guys going?" she asks.

"The butt."

"Ooh." Judith falls into line.

A moment later, we gather around a wall-mounted sculpture of a juicy pair of butt cheeks, just butt cheeks, held apart by two floating hands to show the deepest center. Judith's mouth hangs open, but when I look at her in fear, she snaps it shut with a reassuring smile.

✦

Later that afternoon, the whole gang stands outside the cathedral listening to David and Neary summarize the place as "sophisticated" and "coherent," and Yoni and I feel we must intervene.

"You guys know there's a straight-up asshole on the wall, right?"

"Yeah, Yoni and I found an asshole."

Sigrid nods with solemn approval.

"Jean," says Neary, "must you—"

"This isn't my fault! I'm saying what it is!"

"She's right, James," says David.

"But she's *loud.*" Neary looks out from under his furry brows at the Girl Scouts next to us on the steps. "Yes, there is a sculptural *arse.*"

"Arse?" I whisper to Yoni.

"Is that, like, the *medical* term for Robin Hood's anus?" he whispers.

"What are you guys talking about?" says Brice.

"I did not see a *butt,*" says Patrick, who is almost postcoital, exhausted and limpid from his experience of the cathedral.

"On the way to the crrrrypt," I say, rolling the *r* to emphasize the use of the correct scholarly word, "the most *important* part of the church, where the *relics* are kept and only the *holiest* people can go"—I wait for applause, but none comes—"there is a butt carved into the wall. Like, a life-size butt. It's supporting an arch."

"It's the kind of thing scholars didn't focus on for a long time," says David.

"Wonder why," says Yoni.

"It didn't fit people's ideas of what a cathedral should be."

"I'd forgotten it was there," says Neary, almost dreamily. "Of course, the Bourges Bum. Didn't what's-his-name write a very good article on this?"

"Yeah, Dennis Clare, at Chicago," says David. "Exciting stuff." He gets bashful, looks down. "It dovetails nicely with my work on song, actually."

"Is it a singing butthole?"

"No, Yoni. Sadly, it is not a singing butthole. But you can't understand its presence if you don't understand how people actually used these spaces. And there was a carnival season when the seminary teachers would become the students and the students would become the teachers—and this bum probably had to do with that time."

"How did they use the butt?" I ask.

"We saw a little kid stick his finger in there," says Judith, disgusted, "and then the *mom* did, too!" Everyone laughs, not only at the story but also at Judith's scandalized telling of it in her high, naive voice. It strikes me that Judith is unmistakably more present recently—she has vim. With sudden horror at what she's been through, I realize she must be keeping her food down. She's scared to go back to the ER. This is what she should have always been like—energetic, outspoken, burning fuel like everyone else. There *is* a price to pay for self-denial, measurable now in Judith's volume. If starving makes you better than everyone, it also makes you less than yourself.

JEAN: Monica, what happens to her? Was that it? Did that fucked-up doctor fix her?

MONICA: No. She'll relapse. She'll struggle for a long time.

Teen Jean sees, just as the others see, that Judith is better, *more Judith,* when she permits herself basic nourishment. But Judith doesn't see it. Her own robustness upsets her. When she imagines her mouth full, her stomach full, she feels repugnant, excessive.

JEAN: I wish . . . I wish I could make her something so delicious it would change her mind. Like magic. She would eat it and the worry would go away.

MONICA: Isn't that why you called me? I see you the way you see Judith: I tear my hair out wishing for your appetite not to feel like a vice. I wish you'd soar and hunt and kill and eat like a remorseless hawk, shrieking with iron innervation and enjoying your needs.

JEAN [perking up]: You want me to what?

MONICA: No, no, no, I don't want you to kill anyone. That was poetry, Jean.

"We don't know exactly how the bum was used," says Neary, "but there was a season when the body—grotesque and base and constantly at war with spirituality—had its day. It's a joke, you understand, to put an arse where you'd ordinarily see a face."

"Professor Neary's absolutely right; the punch line is right there in its placement," says David. "Face, face, face, *arse.*"

"Arrrse," Yoni mouths at me, chomping down on the *r.*

"Hilarious," says Brice, drily.

"Look, it's not *The Late Show.* But it wasn't just a bit of fun." David actually seems moved by the butt. "You can't understand holiness or perfection or righteousness if you don't define its opposite. It was good for the dominant values of the church that once a year, for some small window, everyone could have a laugh at their arseholes, stop perfecting themselves, become fools."

✦

A few hours later, Yoni, Judith, Sigrid, and I are at an Ibis hotel in Montmartre, drinking tiny bottles of hard liquor from the mini fridge over ice in plastic cups on twin beds with matching floral bedspreads, doing impressions of Neary and David ("Face, face, face, ARSE!") when suddenly Yoni props himself up on his elbow and trains his attention on me.

"Wait, why aren't you coming with us tomorrow? What are you up to?"

"I'm meeting my aunt Pauline. She lives in Brussels. She's coming in to take me to lunch." I do have an aunt Pauline. She's a pissed-off piano teacher in Leuven who would never take me to lunch. Yoni squints at me but is too tired to pursue whatever suspicion has scurried through his mind.

"There's no room service in this dump," he moans.

"Jean!" barks Sigrid, on her back in the neighboring bed. "Cook us something!"

"Sorry, guys," I say. "I'm on vacation."

Chapter 60

I am standing on a thick stone bridge. I don't know its name, but David does. He looks over the bridge down the bank at Notre-Dame, which from this angle seems tucked into a forest. For some reason, even though everywhere is always full of people, there is no one else on the bridge. Just like God kept ketchup off Patrick, maybe he cleared us a bridge. This morning, I parted ways with Neary and the others, dweebs off to sightsee as I headed toward the metro. I came up at Saint-Michel—a big stone fountain, a huge bookstore—and all the people there were in their twenties and thirties, as if Paris had graciously picked the perfect gradient of person to blend my age and David's. David found me at the fountain and led me through Place Saint-Michel, down the quay to the bridge, not talking much, smiling plenty, knowing we'd have time.

We lean over the bridge, watching the water slosh up against the thick stone legs as it passes. He looks up from the river and puts a tentative hand on my back. I get the sense it is a test, not of me but of him: Will he be able to do this? I want to draw attention away from us, to make it feel less huge and new.

"Serious current," I say, staring down at the paisley pattern of swirls on the surface. He retracts his hand.

"Mmm." He turns around and leans his back against the bridge, resting on his elbows. He crosses one leg lightly over the other. "Can we agree—" He squints at me, bites his lip, pauses. "Can we agree that this isn't good?" I suddenly feel dizzy. "I mean, no, it's *good*—it's just. You know, we *lied.* I'm a rule-follower." He looks down at the stone beneath us and then up at me, his blue eyes locked on me, brow furrowed. But this confession has put us more firmly together at the center of slippery intentions.

"I am, too. I think it's . . . OK," I hear myself say in the voice of a cartoon flower. He picks up one of my hands and studies it as if it's been brought out for him from an archive.

"I can't tell you what you do to me," he says. He must be talking at a normal volume, but I have never heard words like this in real life, so they sound weirdly loud, like they came from a trombone next to my ear. *What you do to me*—I feel an impulse to say I'm sorry. He's still holding my hand; he traces things on it, looking at the Seine, and I feel my body changing shape, my gut a foundry, my inner beams suddenly soft, glowing bright orange. From a primitive, pragmatic structure, I am smelted into some art nouveau railing, given new luxury. He looks up at the rest of me with astute assessment for a moment, as if he, too, knows I'm being reshaped. "I mean, what you do to me—it's hard not to be happy around you." I don't know what to say. I actually feel like there's a cage over my mouth, like I'm a Doberman in an airport. He drops my hand; his go in his pockets. "OK, here is what we'll do. I have to swing by an apartment to pick up some books. It's walking distance."

"OK." I can't stop to think why, but this simple chore seems loaded with thrill or danger—whose apartment? What aspect of David's private life will I see?

"And then we'll get lunch."

Lunch I can talk about. "Lunch isn't bad."

"Lunch is never bad."

"Lunch is sacred."

"Lunch is classic. *Via trita, via tuta.*" His smile broadens. We both love these games; love to talk in quick confirmations, like-minded scholars; love Latin. "And then maybe we can just . . . have a wander. Tomorrow—oh, will you be able to meet me tomorrow?"

"Sure." Haven't asked yet, but of course I'll pop out a perfect bright new lie for Neary like a gumball machine.

"Tomorrow I'll take you to my favorite museum in Paris. Then you'll have to return to the group. I'll rejoin you all for the drive back."

"What museum?"

"We'll keep it a surprise, shall we?"

"Is it the medieval museum?"

"Am I that dull to you? A die with the same number on every side?"

"Seemed like a good guess."

"Suppose it was. Suppose I *am* quite dull, really." I nod my head sadly in agreement, an acid hunger dripping behind my jaw. "Dull, dull, dull," he says, coming closer.

"Dull" has the force of both a joke and a truth, because his attention makes me feel almost *too* alive, like someone in a bag of bugs on *Double Dare* and because at the same time I release him from dullness in his own life, from weariness, from the fear of repeating himself, of being totally known, of the present conforming obtusely to the past. I can tell that I pull from him, like poison from a wound, some kind of anxiety for which I possess a magical antidote. The way he spoke to me and Yoni about his book—how he's ready to finish it. I made him want the future. Without my doing anything, the parts of me that were a problem before—interest without focus, intellect without ambition, a meandering appetite for pleasure and a novice's hope for connection—were precisely what was called for, were the rare herbs that could cure his fatigue, his self-doubt. I'm beginning to understand that as he gives me specificity, I release him from his.

I was going to make a joke—*Yeah, you're such a bore*—but again I find I have no voice. He's too stunningly close, and then he pushes my lips open and I spin on my heels as he moves into me, moves me against the bridge. When it happens—twice now, he's kissed me—I am filled with a kind of terror; some paralysis seizes my brain as his soapy man smell envelops me and the tongue that he talks with enters my mouth discreetly, gently, Britishly. And when he pulls away, I feel relief at my unobstructed breath, my mouth returned to me, the little private fruit bowl that has always sat on the counter of my consciousness. Then all I want is to be choked with him again.

Later, we walk by a café and a glass shatters, the sound followed by the sharp *s*'s of a Spanish family scolding their child, and we hear the waiter say, *"Oh putain, je veux pas savoir"*—"Oh fuck, I don't want to know." I don't want to know, either. I don't want to know what it's like to be locked into familial relations. I only want this relation, forming itself, hot with formation. Who is David here? What will he do to me?

✦

As he twists the key, the lock shudders with ancient, heavy mechanics and the door creaks open. We are both panting from the climb.

"It's the apartment of a friend," he says. My eyes begin to skitter from one unusual shape to another—objects, beautiful objects everywhere.

"Oh my god, it's like a museum in here."

"Yes. Occasionally at Cambridge you meet people who benefit from extraordinary . . . good luck." Did I meet people at Rutgers who had good luck? Yeah, they tanned well or got allocated a dorm room with a river view. They didn't have marble panthers in their hallways. Whoever this person is, his lamps wear nicer jewelry than my mom. "He's lovely, though. *Wildly* generous," adds David.

Just as he says "wildly," my eyes fall on a stuffed swan in a glass bell and I imagine the generous friend lending it to David and I say, "But what do you need with a swan?"

David looks confused for a moment and then sees the swan and laughs and is about to respond when he loses himself in looking at me with amusement and a flat, clear kind of happiness. I sense just then that maybe he *loves* me; maybe he loves me best of all the people he's ever known. And maybe he alone understands what there is to love—other people see me, a blundering, sweet puppy. He *hears* me, has the imagination to hear breath moving through me with invisible dignity and rigor and promise. Maybe what we have is real, not the vulgar satisfaction of needs but a precious, rarely occurring element, as incidental as a gemstone burped up by the desert.

"Two shakes," he says. "Don't nick anything." He smiles and trots off to find whatever he has come for. I roam around the apartment, walk up to the arched double window and look out at the expanse of blue-gray roofs, pigeon-colored, with rows of terra-cotta chimney pots. Through the cracks between the buildings, you can see a park, pedestrians, but I suddenly panic that I've wasted even a second on the exterior when the interior is so crazy. I turn around and examine a marble table. *Purple-brown* marble, veined in red and gold, with porcelain figurines dancing on it, next to a little clever balloon doggy like from a child's birthday party but somehow metal, maybe gold? I pick up the doggy because I want the fun of feeling how unlike a balloon it really is, but I stain it with foggy fingerprints. I put it down and hustle to the other side of the room, to a big messy painting of a lady in an oversize hat.

I peek down a hallway that ends, terrifyingly, in a bedroom. The door is ajar, revealing a simple white bed, the covers rumpled. My heart leaps in fear. Where is she now, Ruthless Jean? She brought me this far, but now I need courage, I need certainty, and she is quiet, her calculations spent. I glance again bravely at the bed. Will it be the making of me? This scenario, this place, seems like something out of my fantasies, but then why is it that when I picture myself in that bed, legs up, legs around him, I feel nauseous with worry? Why is it so chilling to imagine the first gestures, how he'll have to pull my shirt up over my head, how he'll deploy the hand I know by heart and watched all summer gesturing up at vaults or tapping his manila folder on a café table, how he will slide that hand into my pants and I will have to let him, help him, unbutton myself, tilt my hips for him. And then it will be my turn.

But perhaps this is it, this is why I feel so scared, because it matters, because it feels scary to be melted from sand into glass, feels scary to be hammered and polished into something beautiful, feels scary not to be a balloon animal anymore but a sophisticated golden toy people will forever want to touch. Hadn't the prince foretold it? I will be beautiful someday. Now I must give in to my own carving, my own piercing.

Still, I quickly shuttle back over to the far corner of the room—I can't be seen hovering close to the bedroom hallway, like some eager dog pulling at the leash. I will be ready; I am planning it out now, reminding myself of all the steps, of the order in which our clothes will come off, of the places I will put my mouth. His penis might taste weird, or look weird, but it's all part of the process. *You have to just do it,* I tell myself. *You'll probably like it. It only seems weird from the outside. You'd think cotton candy is* asbestos *until you taste it! Diet Coke is toxic waste and you fucking love it! Lots of things like that!*

"What's wrong?" He comes back into the room with a tote bag full of books.

"What's wrong?" I say. "Nothing."

He approaches me and looks closely at my face. "Sorry it was a bit of a hike up these steps. Are you quite wilted? Shall we get a drink downstairs? And then pootle off to lunch?" I don't respond, but I realize that my mouth is dry. Yes, maybe that was it, maybe I wasn't scared of growing up, maybe I'm not a pudgy adolescent unworthy of connection, just dehydrated. I think about my mom in recent years, dating and dieting, always with a huge pitcher of cucumber water on hand, slurping and sloshing. Maybe if you want to call sex down upon yourself, you keep your mouth wet, you water your tongue like a succulent, misting it a little every day. I've neglected mine and it's gone dry like a sponge in a sink in a house where no one lives. "It's a stunning apartment, but it's a bit scary, isn't it? You're afraid you'll sneeze and knock over some Limoges shepherdess."

"Mmm," I agree, relieved that we are moving toward the door and maybe a café and some water but also aware that I've failed, that we've hovered over an exquisite opportunity without diving down to capture it. There was a bed waiting for us, an afternoon cleared; we were among ancient careless Aphrodites and onyx cats carved for the purpose of standing by with unseeing eyes while wise men fuck eager girls. Perhaps *I* have failed to do something, to send a signal. But I can't figure out in the moment how it happens. Feeling desperately ashamed, my regret rising in hot patches on a face I don't know how to arrange, I walk out into the creaking hallway in front of him.

It takes him a moment to lock up—I watch him struggle with the clunky key. We've never discussed it, but I gulp in my dry throat and worry I might cry thinking of the abortion story that he heard and probably believed. Maybe he is scared of me, maybe he is taking me under his wing to be kind, but it never *crossed his mind* to—to—and *now this poor deluded woman has the wrong idea and desperately wants me to take her clothes off and take her to the bedroom and—oh god, how embarrassing.*

I feel my desire for David hung out like a scarlet lobe of curing meat, pungent and twisting, visible from every angle. And look at David, the bag of books on his arm, tugging his white collared shirt away from his neck as he wrestles with the lock. This is what he came for: *books.* You are here because you are a companion, nice, affable. There was never any question of love, and he was never going to perform some maniacal sweaty act of devouring you, you crazy—

"Dammit. This ancient thing." He sighs, gives up. The struggle with the lock has used up some crucial measure of will. Now, without saying a word, he flings the door back open and turns to me. The world disappears from under our feet. He reaches for my shirt and pulls me against him. I brace myself with my hands out, and then I hold on to him. A thud as his tote bag falls to the floor. In a tidy soccer move, he kicks it behind him, into the apartment.

His mouth is on mine again. He dissolves into touch. I am stricken with panic. It feels like there are ten of him, like he's a car wash, like his fingers are in my ears, like I'm the size of a nutcracker doll. I want to know which way is up again, I want to pull away and breathe, but of course I hear her: Ruthless Jean, thrumming, content. *Don't listen to your fear,* she says. *This is a good fire—walk toward it. You're welcome.*

The door shuts behind me.

Chapter 61

Saturday morning. We are at David's favorite museum: a hunting museum. Oil paintings of wrinkly beagles, rooms full of stuffed oryxes and tapirs and minks, a little armoire whose surface is entirely covered with owls' feathers that coalesce cruelly into their whole faces, beaks and eyes and all, glued to the walls like pretty flowers as if they'd never had brains inside their heads. I can see why David likes it here: These things are gorgeous and silly but not important. Pressure's off. The notebook is stored in his bag.

We admire a shelf of mice, spotlit like they're about to sing.

"So, what are you going to do with your life?" he says.

"Well . . ." My eyes fall on a hawk in leather shorts. "I was going to work at Red Lobster, but now I just want to be a rich person." He nods, endorsing the choice. "I think I'd be good at it."

"I think you would too, Jean." Smiling but sincere, he takes my elbow gently in his hand. "This way."

At first when I saw David this morning outside the museum—a cashew-colored townhouse—I didn't know how to behave. I have never had a day like yesterday. There has never been anything like it.

MONICA: You don't know how to describe it, even to yourself. Already, no idea how to remember it.

JEAN: Because it can't be described the day after. It can't even be held in thought.

MONICA: Don't you think that's important, Jean? What happened between you and David didn't just evaporate in your memory; it was an evaporation you lived through.

JEAN: Maybe that's why you have to have it, why you want it again immediately, even if it was scary or confusing. Just to try to see if what you half remember is right.

As David and I amble through the museum, flashes of yesterday cut into my thoughts—of the tasseled emerald-green sofa beneath us (we never made it to the bed). Of that energy that is completely absent from daylight transactions, that weird rage. But today my mind keeps working it, keeps wanting to study it. His fingers at the buttons of my sleeveless gingham button-down, I started to feel afraid again, about how he wasn't there anymore, how he became sharp and purposeful. His decorousness gone, I was overwhelmed by a kind of herb and alcohol smell off his chest, his throat, that I wanted to breathe into my last cell and also escape. Watching myself become undressed, it was all running away beyond me, it was all too fast. I had to grab it and stop it.

"Wait wait wait," I blurted. And he did, he stopped. And I said I was scared. Because I had always just said what I thought, and it had always been OK.

He paused.

"Yeah." But it was flat, his *yeah.* Our legs were twisted, my jeans unbuttoned and unzipped. Maybe that's what I sensed, maybe that's what I knew was next. He panted. Stayed still, his upper lip dewy, his body still threaded through mine. So close and so beautiful. He combed his hair back with one hand. And instantly I regretted what I'd said. I'd made him self-conscious. We'd been floating up, floating away, and I'd pulled us down to earth. I'd been small-minded and unartistic. I had lacked vision, spontaneity, joy—all the things I promised.

"Sorry." I said this quickly, alert, as if we could go back.

"No, you're right." Heavy sigh. "You're absolutely right." I took his agreement like a punishment. Now he would retreat. Could barely look at me. The heat between us escaped and wafted up to where we couldn't touch it, like incense. And of course enter Ruthless Jean, storming, stomping like the coach of a team who's suddenly squandered a lead. *What are you doing?*

"No, just . . ." *Maybe slow down,* I wanted to say. *Maybe just give me a moment.*

"No, you're right. I don't want to . . . I mean . . ."

But you deserve to fuck her, said Ruthless Jean, talking right over me, in my mind.

As if he could hear her: "Trust me, I *want* to . . ."

Ruthless Jean again: *Say something to him! You can turn this around!*

"Should we go, then?" he asked, with a regretful look down my body, a contradiction between the casualness of his tone—as if we were with the whole group again—and the dramatic fact of my breasts, white and round and damp, surrounded by the mangled straps and cups of my bra like two shivering fish shocked, agape, and dying on a deck.

"OK . . ."

Don't give up so easily! He's got a boner! If you put his penis in your mouth, he will *change his mind, trust me!!!* But I didn't know how to do anything Ruthless Jean wanted—it seemed too late—I had failed, I had broken this. Instead, I sat up in the quiet and fixed my bra. He looked away. He neatened himself as well. I caught him chewing the inside of his mouth. Worried. This is not what he'd wanted, not why I alone had been invited here.

At the threshold of the formless void, I'd called back the world.

✦

We left the apartment and descended the stairs in silence, turning, turning, the threat of tears just under my skin. Ruthless Jean coaxed the tears back inside my face, soothed me, pointed to the future, where everything could be repaired. *You had faith before; don't lose it now. Stay focused and you will have each other again, you will find your way.* I passed a door with a finger-painted sign on it and a child's scooter by the welcome mat, and I felt disdain for the wholesomeness of the scene, pity for children and their primary colors, their ignorance, their lack of purpose.

Then it hit me: *It's the place; the place is all wrong.* What I realized was, we need the library. Only in the library. There is something about the library. For him I am connected to his thoughts, his ambitions, his work. He likes me in the library. He needs me there. Even though it's where we were almost caught—if it hadn't been for the ancient door squealing its warning. But it did warn us, it looked out for us, made the library even more a place for us, where the very beams and joins were on our side. *Bide your time, Jean, stay cool. You can make it up to him. And when you get back to the castle, he will have you in the library.*

"Let's get a drink at the café on the corner," he said behind me. He was back in control, cool and caring, soothing the emotional student with breezy talk and a Coca-Cola, like the time I broke the church. And I wanted to go to the café and remember to moisturize my tongue like a sexual woman, so next time someone was about to take me at the feet of a marble panther, I'd be ready.

JEAN: I don't know if I can keep going with this, Monica. She's so pathetic.

MONICA: I'll tell you what you never knew, could not have imagined. Just as a part of you broke off in response to David's attention, David, too, is split. He told himself that he only needed to fetch a book. But another part of him—let's call it Ruthless David—moved all the pieces into place that day so that you two would be alone in that apartment. He thought it would be so obvious, that you would walk in there and just jump into each other's arms. But then you looked precious to him, not like an expensive object but like an ecosystem, chains of fresh little worries cycling through you so visibly, delicate and damp.

JEAN: Look, some people sweat. I sweat.

MONICA: David is building a reality that is incompatible with his life. You two inhabit a fanciful blueprint, a temporary structure. Like his work—

JEAN: *Theoretical, speculative, profound.*

MONICA: He's lying; you're living.

JEAN: I lied about the abortion thing.

MONICA: You did! And he heard. And he knew it was a lie.

JEAN: How?

MONICA: [Laughs] Jean, you'd never had a conversation with a forty-five-year-old in your life—

JEAN: Where would I have met one? Crashing PTA meetings? Lurking at office parks?

MONICA: But his entire professional life took place among nineteen-year-olds. You were a species he knew. He heard the desperate debate tactic in your abortion story; he knew it was all made up.

JEAN: So that's why he picked me? Because he knew I could play make-believe? *She doesn't know how to have sex, but she knows how to lie.*

MONICA: You know that's not it. Remember, David is conflicted. Walking out of that apartment, he didn't think he'd ever cross the line with you again. But you knew better.

JEAN: How? How did I know?

MONICA: Because, Jean, you are very loving, and very smart.

Chapter 62

We left the hunting museum and settled in like habitués at a crimson bistro David knew. David knows everything, but I am better at French, so I am like a Seeing Eye dog, a speaking-mouth dog.

"You do the ordering."

"You!"

"Don't humiliate me, Jean, please." *Please.* Yesterday's failure at the apartment has bruised us, but it's not unpleasant to push on now; to have hurt each other a little is promising. A pigeon flutters at our feet. Paris is absorbing what happened yesterday. The women in big sunglasses and the men in expensive army jackets having sexy arguments—it seems like *everyone* did the same thing yesterday, fumbled and erred on exotic upholstery. We are all playing a game of temporary resistance, gentle pain, pouty resurgence. As we wandered down gray streets on the way from the museum to the bistro, through puffs of other people's smoke and rivulets of spoken French, bubbling and pouring, a healing substance that springs to their filthy blameless lips and pools in their wine-stained mouths, I didn't have to make any decisions. I could just say what I thought.

"Do you want to see something?" he asked.

"Yes." He ripped me by the hand out of my seat on a bench and we were suddenly before a mural in a little chapel that no one cared about but us. The mural depicted Jacob wrestling the angel, but I'd never looked at a picture that way: Jacob's back was knotted with muscle, and the angel's wings were chicken bone and dog fur, and their wrestling was not some abstract parable I was supposed to learn but palpable energies I already knew.

✦

Over lunch, I tell him rambling, expansive stories about home the way I never could when we were stealing little sips of time together.

When they have cleared away the gristle from his bavette steak and my salad bowl and there are crumbs and napkins between us, I tell him about how in Ath, my mother's village in Belgium, there is one day every year when all the children switch names with their neighbors. When she was little, my mother, Christine, switched names with Laure, the neighbor girl. But she found she loved being "Laure" so much that she tried to keep it and her family got in a huge fight with the neighbor's family.

My mother wasn't playing by the rules of the town game, and then more people in town got mad at her, as if she would break the game. As if the whole town would cease to function because Christine had been selfish and greedy in her desire to be a different person. But she *really* liked being this new person, "Laure," and she looked at herself in the mirror in the morning with an open-endedness: What would Laure wear today? What would she do? New, thrilling things, even if they were what Christine used to do.

"My mom was *happier* as 'Laure' than as Christine. But most people refused to call her 'Laure'; they insisted on Christine even if it crushed her, even if they had to slam her old name down her eight-year-old throat."

David shakes his head, captivated. "So this is a proper schism. It has all the makings of a citywide vendetta, the Ghibellines and the Guelphs."

"I don't know what that is, but *yes*!"

"The Ghib—"

"And some good people defended Christine's right to her imagination, and they called her Laure."

"Ah, 'good people'—so you're team Laure."

"Absolutely! Why?"—with horror—"You're team Christine?"

"Well, I see the villagers' point!" He leans back confidently, arms crossed over his chest. "We can't all go changing our names all the time, can we? We need *some* stability, no?"

"But . . ." Never in a million years did I think he would side with the Christines. It seems so obviously evil, so obviously mean to tell a little girl she can't rename herself. "Yes we can," I say, but without the well-reasoned argument I would have given if I were

Sigrid or Sam or David himself. Can't we change names? Aren't we doing that right now? Aren't we being different people, not ourselves but our invented neighbors, unmarried, peers, at complete liberty? If he believes we can't just change our names—my mother has to be Christine, and cannot call herself Laure—somehow this also means that David must be married and must abandon me at some point. To follow the rules will require cruelty from him, the same cruelty he now shows to my mother. *We lied.* I cannot be his companion. I will have to give David back at the end of the day, or all the villagers will be mad at me. I am telling a story that breaks their story; my game will break their game. There is a dominant truth, an objective truth, and David belongs to it, and must return.

It was a lesson my mother learned young—they will let you have your wish for a holiday, an exercise, a pageant; you can have *everything,* as allegory; but if you try to hold on to it, try to use the powers of the queen they dressed you up as, you'll bring down their anger, you'll count as crazy. Maybe that's why when she grew up, she only cut loose, only inhabited other selves drunk, which is a form of imagination that comes with the time limit you need and the punishment you deserve.

"Did you like your salad?" he asks, which seems like a conventional question, but he's already cracking up at the response I'll give, partly because everything I say amuses him, and partly because my salad *was* hilarious.

"It was mostly meat, right?" I say.

David is rolling in a surf of shallow delight. "It was. It was really a heavily garnished charcuterie platter."

"I tried to be healthy," I say, pointedly lighting a cigarette and shrugging.

Chapter 63

SAINT ROSE OF LIMA, VIRGIN, WHO DIED IN 1617,
FROM *Butler's Lives of the Saints*

✦ ✦ ✦

Rose was of Spanish extraction, born in Lima, the capital of Peru, in 1586. Hearing others frequently commend her beauty, and fearing lest it should be an occasion of temptation to anyone, she rubbed her face with pepper in order to disfigure her skin with blotches. A woman happened to admire the fineness of the skin of her hands and her shapely fingers, so she rubbed them with lime, and in consequence was unable to dress herself for a month. By these and other even more surprising austerities, she armed herself against external dangers and against the insurgence of her own senses.

Her parents tried to induce her to marry, but she took a vow of virginity, moved into a hut in the garden, and wore on her head a circlet of silver studded on the inside with little sharp prickles, like a crown of thorns.

The last three years of her life were spent in the home of a government official and his wife. In their house, she was stricken by her last illness, and prayed, "Lord, increase my sufferings, and with them increase thy love in my heart." She died on August 24, 1617, thirty-one years old. She was canonized by Pope Clement X in 1671, the first saint of the New World.

Chapter 64

I rejoined the group at the Ibis yesterday around five, and David showed up twenty minutes after me, grease on his lips, no one the wiser, and I got in Neary's van for the three-hour drive south. It's our last Sunday, but dinner is not on my mind; Victoire is cooking, graciously, since we got back so late last night, but also: I don't need the kitchen anymore.

As our return to America approaches—only two nights left—David gathers us against the eastern face of the castle for a group photo. The ivy tickles our necks as he sets the timer on his Nikon and hustles in to join us. He puts himself as far from me as possible. He has kept his distance from me today, but I understand; I have had plenty of him and will not be greedy.

Evening. Harder and harder to be OK with this distance, which I have to convince myself is not a cooling off; he is not losing his taste for me. Must remind myself: His pretending not to care is a sign that he cares.

I have become an animal. I don't understand words, the content of conversations, but I'm hyperattuned to tone, to mood. I'm aware of where everyone is, of who is speaking to whom. As I walk out to dinner, from across the lawn the vinegar in the sauce bathing Victoire's duck thighs comes at me with the high clarity of a string section. But this is all information, not food for me to eat; all factors, all part of some Last Supper chalk sketch, with David alone at the center, painted in, fleshed out. I am good at looking around, moving my gaze from the castle to the trees so that it passes over him with a quick lick.

"This chicken is the bomb," says Brice, and my ruthlessness has sharpened me, elevated me, polished me to such an extent that I don't even retort "It's duck, dummy"; instead, my gaze picks its way to Sam on spider's legs, and when it lands on her, she brushes it off, furiously, because it was a naked acknowledgment between us that her husband sucks. It is the cruelest thing I've ever done, this cold stare, actually, and it makes me think that I must now be capable of sex, that I am cresting into a comprehensive set of adult powers. An explosion of laughter at the far end of the table makes me look over. Neary and the prince are cackling at Sigrid's impression of some academic from home. David is part of the group but not laughing as hard, because, I know, his mind is elsewhere.

Chapter 65

When I come downstairs for breakfast this morning, hungover with fleshy fantasies, I'm pulled into the salon by the sound of the TV, with its new big black cable box sprouting ugly cords along the creamy salon walls. The whole setup is incongruous with the porcelain lamps, the soaring mirror, the oil painting of a fancy boy on a horse—of course, it's the prince, alarmingly identical to his adult self at age eight or nine, astride his beloved Cognac. Neary is in the salon in a large fauteuil, Patrick leaning toward him holding up a heavy book, and giving an opinion that Neary takes like a flu shot. Brice has Sam in some kind of headlock of love on the sofa, and Sigrid is on a footstool with a napkin on her lap holding a three-foot-long buttered baguette up to her mouth, the far end still on her knees like one of those Swiss mountain horns. (By now I know she's "carbo-loading.") Judith wanders down the steps behind me.

"What's going on?" I ask. I see a CNN World logo in the corner of the TV screen. Soldiers in padded gray jumpsuits run around in rubble.

"Clinton deposition yesterday, top story," says Yoni, legs crossed, espresso on his knee, engrossed. I screw my face up at the footage of men with guns ducking behind cement. "Oh, that's Kosovo. Just wait."

"What's the story?" I ask.

"He addressed the nation after the deposition. They're gonna play the statement in full."

"What depo—"

"Ssssh," he says. Brice and Sam shoot me annoyed looks, too. "Sit down."

I guess the prince is back. "DID I MISS IT? DID I MISS IT?" he hollers, hustling into the salon with a mug in his hands.

"No, you're fine," says Yoni, businesslike.

"Oh thank god," says the prince. He settles into a love seat, and I drop down next to him. He turns to me as if we've been chatting for hours. "When I studied at Harvard, obviously the food in Boston was shocking, but I did leave with a taste for these large coffees." He narrows one eye at me as if I have shown him my thigh through a deeply slit dress.

At some point, David wanders in and sits next to Brice and Sam on the sofa. I don't look at him.

"Here we go, here we go!" says Yoni, craning forward.

We see Clinton, bags under his eyes, dark suit: "I misled people. I deeply regret that." With high-strung music, the camera cuts back to the anchor, a stiff blond guy with an Australian accent. "After months of denial, United States President—"

The prince nearly spits out his coffee. "Who is this lifeguard? Go back to Bondi Beach! Australians can't have *gravitas.* Ted should know that!"

The footage jumps to Clinton moving through a receiving line, and there is Lewinsky, full cheeks, a deep black V-neck, her eyes pinned to him, pressing her mauve lips together.

"Woof," says Brice and a few people snicker. No Helen of Troy, no Marilyn Monroe—the president fell for an unpolished nobody with puppy fat and a frizzy blowout.

Voice-over: "After hours of embarrassing testimony, a stunning confession. He never said the word 'sorry,' but he did admit to a relationship with a twenty-something White House intern."

Clinton again, hangdog and serious: "It was wrong. It constituted a critical lapse in judgment and a personal failure on my part." More footage of a receiving line, and this time Lewinsky is in white, again with the full lips, dark-rimmed eyes, mouthing an intimate *Hi.* You watch her lurking in line, demure, nervous, looking down, and then when he passes, just doing his presidential job, she lights up hungrily.

The voice-over continues: "But Clinton was clear about the legal case: 'At no time did I ask anyone to lie . . . '"

"Well, you did ask her to *lie down,*" says the prince, over the rim of his coffee cup.

"The president asked for a return to personal privacy: 'Now this matter is between me, the two people I love most, and our God.'"

"Ha," puffs Patrick. "*Our God.* These people are such phonies."

"Now for reactions from around the world . . ." continues the anchor.

"Oh come on, just play the statement," says Yoni.

David looks at his watch, annoyed. "Guys, it's our *last church.* Let's focus and get in the vans."

"He knew he had enemies. But he still couldn't stop himself," says Patrick.

"Do you think he'll be impeached?" Judith floats.

David folds up his road map neatly, tucks it into the manila folder, and taps the folder on the table.

"They just gave the poll numbers!" the prince says. "America with its puritanical self-image and Jesus on the five-dollar bill and it turns out, *nobody cares*!"

"That's not Jesus, dude, that's Abe Lincoln," says Sigrid. The prince *loves* being dude-d by Sigrid. He visibly shivers with pride.

The TV is on mute, but we lazily watch a commercial for a water park in central France in which a hot model pretends to be a mother of five.

"I don't know, man. Monica's such a dog," says Brice, shaking his head.

"She's gross," Sam adds.

"*Apparently*—I don't know if you've heard this," begins the prince, as if this is palace gossip, information whispered to him by the lady-in-waiting who laced his corset. "Apparently she'd done this before, with a teacher at her high school, also a married man." He looks around the room, reading our faces for appreciation.

Sigrid, with bread in her cheeks: "She showed Clinton her thong! That's how this whole thing started! She's hungry for that D." She waves the remaining half of her baguette in the air.

"That's, like, so *skanky*," says Yoni. "It's the Oval Office! You're not at Kappa Kappa Gamma."

The commercial break ends and the prince unmutes the TV.

Even though David does not seem as enthralled with this scandal as everyone else, I am conscious of wanting him to see me as informed and political, like Yoni who reads the paper and the prince with his gossip. I should have an opinion, too. The receiving line footage is shown again, Lewinsky's eyes widening in real time as her lust surges up to meet its target. I race to do the *Psycho* soundtrack: "Wah! Wah! Wah!" It gets a laugh.

Patrick shakes his head, perplexed at the existence of such creatures. "She's a nutjob and he's a womanizer, perfect storm."

"OK, that's it." says Neary. "TV *off.*"

"They're about to play his statement—"

"I don't CARE!" he roars. "OFF!!!" He stands up and there's something strange about him, his head jerking toward each of us in turn, his mouth tight in some kind of rictus I haven't seen before. "LISTEN to all of you!" Eye contact is administered like a spoonful of poison to each of us, one by one. "Do you hear yourselves? Have you learned NOTHING through your precious educations?" He is silent for a beat, nostrils flared. "Do you come in one door and spend all these years memorizing dates and writing essays and then leave through the same door no wiser? No more human? Do you apply your brilliant analytical minds to these crumbling buildings and then the minute you encounter real life, history building itself under your feet, you become venal cretins? A jeering crowd? Incapable of seeing human lives with complexity, beyond the uses to which they are put? *Think!*" He stomps, looking down at the plush pile carpet, fuming. Then, looking up at us again: "For god's sake, you're quick to throw the girl under, aren't you? Week after week of this, church after church, beast-headed man after man-headed beast after Adam and Eve in their shame and morsels of Mary Magdalene's sinning flesh in a crystal bowl in the crypt . . . After all of it, you want to sit here and call her a *smank*?"

"Skank," mumbles Yoni.

"I don't even know what that means! Explain how to be perfect. Explain how always to walk the clear path. Put all the goddam priests out of work, you priggish popes and sniggering cardinals!" This is true Neary. *Priggish popes* is the moment he was born for; he gleams with a sober rage that reminds me why he drinks, because the anger strains his eyes and makes his hands red and his back hunched like he's some kind of recoiling hole-eyed cave eel, about to lunge.

The prince sits very still like a schoolboy at a tiny desk.

Neary continues, "You lot have put yourselves above all the human—the human—"

"Interpenetration," says Sigrid, with the intonation of an "Amen."

"For chrissakes. Get your goddam tools together and be in the van TEN SECONDS AGO, and I hope I see you extract every ounce of truth and knowledge that today's church can offer with HALF A CURSORY GLANCE at it since you're all SO GOOD AT THAT." We stare at him, frozen. "Well, SHAG ASSSSS!" he roars, and everyone but the prince and David shoots vertically in the air and sprints for the doorway.

Now, in the empty salon where David and the prince look down at their hands and Neary stands shaking his head, the scene becomes still and suspended and the room goes church-dark. Monica is no longer by my side but in the scene, weaving between the love seat and the sofa. She proceeds toward Neary, her cobalt raiment shooting off a glow like a rippling lagoon. She puts her hand on the side of James Neary's face and she kisses the top of his head where the lone little hairs sprout through the liver spots. She kisses him sweetly, serenely, with love and gratitude, and I realize I have seen the blessing of a good king that history forgot.

Chapter 66

SAINT MARIA GORETTI, VIRGIN, KILLED IN 1902,
FROM *Butler's Lives of the Saints*

✦ ✦ ✦

Maria Goretti was born in 1890 at Corinaldo, a village in Italy some thirty miles from Ancona, the daughter of a farm laborer and his wife.

On a hot afternoon in July 1902, Maria was sitting at the top of the stairs in the cottage, mending a shirt: She was not yet twelve years old. A cart stopped outside, and a neighbor, a young man of eighteen named Alexander, ran up the stairs. He beckoned Maria into an adjoining bedroom: she refused to go. Alexander seized hold of her, pulled her in, and shut the door.

Maria struggled and tried to call for help, but she was being half strangled and could only protest hoarsely, gasping that she would be killed rather than submit. Whereupon Alexander half pulled her dress from her body and began striking at her blindly with a long dagger. She sank to the floor, crying out that she was being killed: Alexander plunged the dagger into her back and ran away.

Her last hours were most touching—her concern for where her mother was going to sleep, her forgiveness of her murderer (she disclosed that she had been going in fear of him but did not like to say anything lest she cause trouble with his family), her childlike welcoming of the holy viaticum. Some twenty-four hours after the assault, Maria Goretti died.

Alexander was sentenced to thirty years' penal servitude. One night he had a dream in which Maria Goretti appeared gathering flowers and offering them to him. From then on, he was a changed man.

In 1950, Pope Pius XII canonized Maria Goretti in the piazza of Saint Peter's, before the biggest crowd ever assembled for a canonization. Her murderer was still alive.

Chapter 67

It's our last night.

I am drunk, but a sharpness in my focus bends the alcohol to my will, like a sea I command.

Wearing my dusty-blue J.Crew dress. Roaming around. Jojo and Victoire got a long extension cord and put a record player outside on a footstool, and one by one they brought out not the prince's records but their own, mostly a gravelly voiced folk singer whose songs are sometimes jokey and sometimes sad but always about prostitutes. The music bumps along between two chords, in a rhythm that we all slap our thighs to and even the sheep seem not to fear. We eat a final meal, Victoire's best, a honeyed tagine made from the legs of our dead pets, and talk about what we are returning to: Neary groaning about class prep and admin, Judith not as joyful as you'd expect about joining her mother in Berlin for some fancy junket. Yoni's going hiking in Aspen with his parents and his brother. Sam and Brice will keep visiting churches in France. David will spend some time with Ann in Oxford before they have to separate for the term, before he's cast down to the purgatory of Rutgers.

"And what about you, Jean?" says Sigrid. "You gonna come to New York and train with me? Marathon's in November."

"Probably just hang out at my mom's house until school starts, I guess." There's a beat of confusion and then general acceptance of—maybe even appreciation for—how simple this is. "I'll drive around." Heads bob. "Go to the mall. The shooting range at the beach."

"The shooting range *and* the beach?" says Neary.

"The shooting range *at* the beach," I repeat.

"You'll have to excuse Professor Neary," says David. "He's never been to New Jersey." But David has—David alone knows my greatness-adjacent, addictively salty mozzarella stick of a home, and in this moment, this intimacy is not like a secret that stays in France but a promise that comes with us. I am going back not just a changed person—skinny, skilled, a newly minted history major who knows about thousand-year-old arches and forty-four-year-old boners—but to a changed place. Campus will open, will welcome me. I go back knowing a professor, knowing my place, finally. Knowing what I'm good at.

MONICA: What is she good at?
JEAN: Delusion.
MONICA: Come on.
JEAN: Catering and delusion.
MONICA: You knew it then, and you refuse to see it now.

We drink more. I don't know if we cleared up from dinner. It's getting darker earlier now and we are all pinballing around in the same darkly luminous blue evening I remember from the parking lot with David. Occasionally I'm swept up into a dance by Jojo, or I extend an arm toward the person with the bottle. Neary stays out with us, too, and I see him give Patrick a little splash of his whisky, with some measure of warmth, or at least resignation. More wine and then David is dancing, too, wrapping an arm around Judith's waist and spinning her. Judith's smile, it goes all the way to her throat. You'd think Ruthless Jean would want to intervene here, but she has her kindness, too, her generosity. She is a millionaire who can put some change in Judith's cup. Then David hooks arms with Yoni as they twist in a little jig before unhooking and spinning into the field. Sigrid stomps and claps and Sam and Brice are ballroom dancing like assholes, but at one point, Brice spins Sam out and she falls into David's arms and for the one arc that she lets him lead her, Sam looks far over David's shoulder, avoiding his eyes, avoiding his face. He releases her back to Brice.

The romance of it. The incredible beauty of this place. The heaped ancient ziggurat of the château now dark behind us and the lawn blue as a ballroom carpet. I was always bouncing around, always at the margins of my own life, until I came here and moved to the center. I was challenged, had faith, persevered. Crowned, found, rewarded—the reward is coming, I know it.

I am gulping white vermouth that isn't cold anymore, but it anesthetizes my throat nicely between the cigarettes that I enchain as I sit on the bench at the long dining table across from Neary and Patrick. I watch the dancers, but I'm afraid to get near David and show too much in front of everyone, especially Sam, who expects me to fawn over and follow him. I enjoy the distance, the public performance that I don't particularly care about him, any more than I care about Neary or my warm vermouth or the sheep that shuffle by me that I never got the chance to kill.

"David, we *do* have to face this at some point!" Neary shouts toward the dancers. David twirls around the record player holding a wineglass in the air—not tripping, not undignified, but sort of wide in his orbit, moving fast, getting everyone else twirling, too. He slows to a halt and puts his arms down.

"No, you're right." He breathes for a moment, looks at the grass. "We'll be grateful to ourselves later."

"Come on." Neary slaps his thighs. "I'll pack up the Cambridge loan equipment and you start in on the books." David salutes and comes and plops down next to me at the table.

"Let me just catch my breath and I'll head up to the library."

"Rightio," says Neary, who heaves himself off the bench and moves toward the castle. Brice and Sam volunteer to help Neary and maybe now that we're all leaving and he won't have to be nice to us forever, he feels the freedom to warm up a little; maybe he's just happy to have anyone but Patrick by his side. He thanks them with a new smile—one that fits his face, is almost handsome.

David leans toward me. With a cold swell, I think he has forgotten himself and is coming to take me in his arms, but instead he grabs my cigarettes off the table, shakes the lid open, sees three left. Raises his eyebrows at me. I gesture for him to go ahead.

In his lips, the cigarette. The click of the lighter in his hand before he flings it back onto the table. When he smokes, I no longer feel I'm seeing a prior David, but a new David, a changing David, younger, careless, caring for me. He faces out, elbows on the table, left ankle on right knee, swaying gently with the music. He looks up at the navy blue night. The endless visual interest of his face, the curl of the lip, the cross-hatching under the eyes: I cannot look away. I drink him in. I feel the sight of him in my mouth, like I'm sucking a pastille in the shape of his profile. I sit with my legs piled under me, perfectly still, taking him in with the heightened focus of my narrowing eyes. He turns to look at me, assessing me. Smiles.

"You look like a cat."

"I feel like a dog."

"Hmm"—it's not a laugh, not a word, but the sound you make when something is right, when someone has given you a startling new fact that you are happy to know. *Hmm.* And it's accompanied by a look that cannot bear to hang long on me, that is too much for this place, for a picnic bench and a folk dance, and has to come over me quickly and then be shot safely into the night like a flare. He finishes his cigarette, neither of us speaking, both of us smirking, raps the table twice with his knuckles to indicate a new seriousness of purpose, and disappears into the castle.

Jojo and Victoire move the record player back inside. Bottles clink as they're collected. Judith walks like some slow tidal bird scanning for prey as she plucks butts of cigarettes she didn't even smoke from the lawn and puts them in a cut-glass ashtray the smokers ignored.

I see an opening, and I take it.

✦

You can hear the thuds and thwacks from the hallway. I push open the library door and David is on the edge of a chair, tossing books from piles on the floor into an open suitcase. He looks up.

"Have you come to help me?" he asks. I nod. "OK," he says, his attention fixed on the books. "Anything modern, basically, is from home, but if you're not sure, check the inside cover for the ex libris." He opens a book jacket and shows me the Rutgers stamp.

He stands up to move to a different desk, trips over a book, and catches himself along the shelved wall. "Whoa, Nelly. Careful when you move around here."

We pack without talking for a while. We're focused and efficient. At one point, he zips up a suitcase and tries to lift it and can't. "Oh dear," he groans. "Far too heavy. These can only be half-filled with books. I'll put my clothes in the other half." A suitcase half-filled with medieval literature and half with David's dirty shirts, intense with the myrrh of his body, takes shape in my mind as something so rich it could feed people, like a roast, or be auctioned at Christie's. He crouches near me and starts to unpack what we just packed. My foot dangles near him in a white Keds sneaker. He looks at my shin and pauses and shakes his head. He closes his eyes, and when he opens them, they are still fixated on my leg, but something is different. I feel it now; I feel it like the French did when they won the World Cup, history turning like a lock in my fingers, history not a sequence of past events but an exhilarating coming-undone, an unraveling that will free up the threads for unimaginable new patterns, for the rush of new work. For progress, knowledge. We are making possible a future.

I am scared, but I believe. I will do the right things. Parts of me I never knew I had will unfurl for action, like wings.

JEAN: Please, please can we stop.

MONICA: You're afraid.

JEAN: I don't want to experience the culmination of my stupidity.

MONICA: You were treated cruelly and unfairly. You know it, and you knew it before you called to me. But there is something you forgot, something trampled by language and distorted by memory, that belongs to you, only to you, and that David cannot take from you and that you wrongly believe he put there. Listen to me. You possess a power.

JEAN: A *power*? The power to fuck up?

MONICA: No, Jean! You can see it in how terrified they are of it. In the telling of our lives, it is diagrammed as an error and flagged as a danger. It is what the holy fathers told us to kill in ourselves, to make impossible with scarring and starving and self-denial, to ignore and repress, because they can't control it, they can't touch it, they can't own it or sell it or use it for their own gain. Oh, they'll try—if you want to see my sexuality exploited, read the *Starr Report,* or don't. It's no kind of truth. Who would *ever* use those words—"he fondled her bare breasts"; "she performed oral sex"—to describe the consensual acts of adults? Gossips, pimps, and moral authorities.

You've always known that there's a mismatch between the language and the spirit, the inside and the outside, the *vita* and the life. You have always found it impossible to say what you did because in what happens now, you left this earth, you were a consciousness in the dark, a candle flickering inside your mind. There were no separate parts of you. What prig would focus on the holes; what pragmatic butcher would want to separate fingers from toes from necks from lips from the heart from the sex? We won't cut you up, we won't hang you out, we won't apply words to you that only the leering observer would use.

JEAN: But I *will* be observed and hung out—

MONICA: That's all you remember, and I understand why—humiliation is so *loud,* so deafening. And it becomes the whole story. But there is a moment before, or maybe beneath, that story, in which, far from being pained, belittled, hurt, you discover a source. It's *yours,* and you still have it, and I want you to know it. Trust me.

No noise from the lawn now; everyone has retreated to their bedrooms. I turn completely to this learning. An incredible amount of information, knowledge of an entire person's body, how much he weighs, how strong his legs are, how hard his hip bones, wide and flat like a snow shovel. But also myself: I am conjured now with new specificity. From a savage cave to a pretty house to a full church, I am now inhabited, appreciated; breath moves in me. I am generous, good, hilariously gobbled up, gnawed at and never diminishing, like some biblical bread.

I feel a book in my back and I like it, I like its corner in my rib, a little pinch that appetizes me for getting split, burst, killed so that I can be a new person. My muscles incant *Come in, come in, come in.* Finally not caring about "my body" as some shape that needs work, some flawed image; my body is gone, and I'm a thousand fingertips, a sea creature again, my brain dispersed along my iridescent jelly surfaces. What we do has no relationship to procreation, to porn, to anything anyone has ever done: I entered his mouth like a vapor, dispersed myself in his mind; I see Bourges now, not from where I walked but from the heights, where there is no air that is not vibrating with song, no molecule unpatterned by breath. I see David's book; I am inside the argument of David's book. I see all the images from this summer, separately and at once, and I understand them, I understand that I will swallow grapes and be swallowed, that all it takes is the energy of a line to turn woman to bird and back again, that with his breath in me I can skate upward against the pull of the earth, that I can die and live again.

You can have this. It is real.

It is not a story, or an allegory, or a picture or a prayer. It is your life, and it is good.

Another pain now, delivered rhythmically, like the daggers aligned in the mosaic floor, a black stripe in the sky next to all the blue and the gold, you feel it in your inner ear, where a wet snail has come to live, and behind your eyes, which are made of stone.

In, in, in. Up, up, up. Further we go.

Thank god I wanted this.

Thank god people want to bang me, and they should! They should come here, one by one they should line up and I'll do them all, it would be my pleasure! I sense an infinite generosity in my squishing cellular energy, that it could do this forever, always welcome, connect to literally *anyone*—men, women, old, young. Out of nowhere I imagine Ellis Island; the phrase *huddled masses* pops into my head, and instead of a bronze colossus it's just me, in my J.Crew linen dress, ready to make out with everyone, ready to have the *best time,* ready to welcome them to America. *This* is what my languages are for! For telling people from far away that they can have me, for asking them where they want to start and telling them not to stop. I'm *so good at this,* I realize, and also my snaking, orgasmic imagination has run amok and I'm seeing fiddlers and peddlers with paper bag pants around their ankles and folksy sausage dicks in my mouth, and I'm bubbling with laughter now and I'm aware of David seeing my laughter and swallowing it back into himself, where it surfaces as a smile and he says, "What, Jean?" because my thoughts are in my body, which is made of thoughts, and David can absorb them like a current. David, David. I want to tell him how ready I am for all of it. How complete my competence, how infinite my space.

This is my term paper.

Religion is right, and faith is worth it, and heaven is horny. The holy fathers were perverts, and so am I.

David! my body shouts. *I have news for you! I have good news for you!*

✦

My eyes are closed. And then I turn my head and my lids flutter open and we are not alone. Patrick stands there, motionless, holding the door open. It must have opened without a noise. Of course: I flash back to Jojo with his oilcan, greasing and varnishing for the fundraiser. I look up at Patrick from the floor where I lie on my back, at the underside of his chin, his terrible eyes obscured by his cheekbones, his boots too close, and defeated, undone, all I can think is, *God really does love Patrick.*

Chapter 68

AUGUST 1998

MONMOUTH HEIGHTS, NEW JERSEY

The blinding light off the surface of the pool, the smell of chlorine and fried food and something gross coming out of the changing rooms where earlier this morning Eunice's older sister, Grace, said, "I *told* you you'd be pretty if you ate less."

I've been meting out a story for Eunice in little coded bits: I tell her I dated an older guy over the summer. His name was Cyril. He was an aristocrat, a friend of the prince's.

"Do you miss him?" asks Eunice, wide-eyed, slurping the blue bottom of her rocket pop like a child. I've left her in a prior era of development, where she still snacks all the time and has upper-arm fat.

"He's gonna come visit." School starts in three weeks. My stomach drops when I think of it.

"He's coming to *Rutgers*?" She thinks he's a Provençal marquis.

"Well, maybe we'll meet in New York."

Eunice aches with envy. She earned buckets of money at Red Lobster, but she had mean, tired co-workers, crazy customers, long days on her feet. In contrast, the summer I had had with David—or "Cyril": red vermouth, the Pont Saint-Michel. Sex. It almost isn't fair.

"Cyril" and I parted with passionate, legal kisses. David and I parted on the floor, under Patrick's laser gaze of piggy-eyed disgust. I woke up the next morning sore, aching in a period way but knowing it wasn't my period, hungover, running the night through my mind over and over. Everyone was frenzied, moving fast—suitcases schlepped downstairs. Van loaded. A sequence of goodbyes, numbers exchanged. At every moment, I feared I would get pulled aside by Neary, or even by some imaginary higher-up dispatched to fire David and kick me out of school. David was severe and maniacally preoccupied with packing up—a good excuse to barely look at me. On the curb outside the airport, he said, "It's been a pleasure, young man," to Yoni and shook his hand and then, to me, "See you in the fall, Jean," with a quick wave. I knew he had to play the part of the teacher this morning, which, after all, he was, but all I wanted was one second, one second in the kitchen or the toilet or the wine closet with him so he could ask how I was, hold my hand, tell me it was good.

Everyone else made talky, vague plans to get together in the fall—the Chinatown bus, maybe New York for fall break—but Patrick didn't say good-bye to me. He couldn't look at me, couldn't be in the room with me. Yes, he'd seen me on the floor with David. He'd seen more of my skin than he'd seen of any woman's. It made him rattle with pale anger, how scared he was of me. I thought about something Ann had told us in the convent. Nuns on their period couldn't come near the priest, or take Communion. That morning, Patrick knew that I was in some bloody season, that some flush female thing was turning over in me. It was bigger than him; it was real, radioactive with elemental change, and he couldn't bear to be near it. Or—had he told Neary? Maybe he wasn't awed and afraid; maybe it was just the classic shame of the tattletale.

But Neary gave me a nice good-bye—"You've done well here, Jean"—and then, back home, there were no emails from the dean, nothing. Just the usual information about orientation.

✦

Eunice watches me aerosol my legs with a can of Banana Boat. She coughs, waves her arm to clear the air of coconutty toxins, and then with her blue-stained lips she says, "God, you are *so* lucky."

Chapter 69

NEW BRUNSWICK, NEW JERSEY, RUTGERS CAMPUS

Early September. David's office, a place soaked in David's quiet work, his valuable time. Walls eloquent with museum posters (a metal bird with a red "The Met" logo), bracketed bookshelves groaning with volumes. A raffia basket full of pens, highlighters.

"I wanted to talk to you about two things." He has only begun speaking, but something is off. *Two things.* In France, we existed in unmarked space, we could connect infinitely; why would he ever itemize? I'm wearing a white eyelet sleeveless button-down so fresh from the Gap, it still has a new car smell. My mind races, trying to set us on course—maybe he can't smell my old smells; maybe it's like how you're not supposed to touch baby birds because your human smell will mask their bird smell and then their bird families won't love them anymore. But if New Jersey has changed my color or my scent, it's still me; and it's still him, his face, his voice: Can I not trust the continuity of something as basic as human consciousness? I try to stare into his eyes, but they won't permit extended contact; they run away from me, to places on his desk, to his hands.

"The first thing is that I should apologize for perhaps allowing our friendship to become . . . that I allowed us to be friends outside the normal bounds. I think that wasn't fair to you."

Of course Patrick, so eager to ingratiate himself with Neary, must have told him. And surely David denied it, and I'll deny it if anyone asks. It's over, and I accept this instantly. I will be a good citizen of this situation. I nod, with real vigor and pursed lips. We will solve this together.

"I understand."

"OK, great. And I'm sorry— Yeah, we are just figuring out the Field School and obviously, maybe, we needed a little more structure."

I continue nodding, like he's a business genius and I'm taking dictation. As if a tighter academic curriculum would have operated like a chastity belt, focusing me inward, warding him off. I glimpse the possibility that he's right, that the energies that flowed between us could have been channeled differently, channeled *at all*, to carry ideas around in my brain instead of soaking it like a fourth martini.

But before I can make sense of this image rising in my mind—a pattern of canals that I never built; a flooded settlement, roofs askew—it dawns on me that he was sitting at his desk when I arrived at his door. He had emailed me about coming to his office hours, but he did not get up to greet me when I arrived, trembling, knocking quietly. He has kept the door open. Someone walks by and I hear "Hey, David," and he says, "Welcome back, Samir," and this is the moment, when I hear the warmth, the old David warmth, that he affords his colleague, in contrast to his metered, defensive treatment of me, that the sadness begins to swallow me and the flood becomes real, where my head sloshes with hot, foul water that might spill out of my eyes, my ears, my nose, if I move.

"The second thing is. I read your term paper. And Neary did, too."

JEAN: No he didn't.
MONICA: Of course he didn't.

"You and Yoni did a great job with your guidebook, and you did master *The Golden Legend*, I know you had a great time with that stuff." *Had a great time*—had my learning been undermined by my enjoyment of it? "But your paper was a chance to go a little deeper, and I guess we both feel that you failed to think about the *historiography*"—a term I had never heard him use, or at least not with any emphasis, over the summer—"so we're going to give you a C for the paper and a B for the class, and I think that's fair."

JEAN: This is insane. Don't listen, Jean! Talk back! Tell him he provided no rigorous coursework! Tell him he never defined the terms for you!

MONICA: I've read your paper. It was a *classic* B+. This is bullshit.

He's having both sides of a conversation. I have no role except to observe. My attention is focused inward, on containing the rushing sadness. "But what I would say is, I don't think it's a particularly promising foray into medieval history or, more generally, *history* as a discipline. I think maybe literature, you know, English, would be more suited to your . . . way of thinking."

I'm pretty sure we both know I've only taken foreign language classes—or else this is proof that he's already begun deleting information about me from his mind. It's too late for me to major in English. But I see what he's saying. English is for girls. English is for people who like to have sex on old carpets with the wrong people. English is for women who swear too much and light up at the adjective "three-cheese" and get hot before they get critical. In the English department, there are no timelines, no Great Action, no consequences; you can read about love stories between a boy and a dog on a faraway mountain. You can lose yourself forever in "Only connect" while David and his kind map alliances.

In the end, he says, very softly, listening to make sure there are no footsteps in the hallway, "Whatever you do, I have to ask you, as a favor to me, not to take my classes."

"Yeah."

"It's really important."

Outside, I watch two returning students in terry-cloth shorts hug on the quad. Everywhere you go, there are warm reunions, people picking up where they left off. *Whatever you do* is the part I hear over and over, and each time, a freezer-cold ice cream scoop scoops through my stomach.

Chapter 70

NOVEMBER 1998

NEW BRUNSWICK, NEW JERSEY, RUTGERS CAMPUS

I keep seeing posters around campus for a visiting lecture on caricature in late medieval sculpture, with funny little apostles carved in wood, with big noses and bad teeth, arguing, bored. Something in my brain fizzes at this picture, finds in it what drew me to medieval art in the first place—the grossness in the high purpose, where the holiest men have the donkeyest breath. I noted the date in my binder, but as it approached, I doubted myself: Am I really interested, or is it just Ruthless Jean, who's melted into a blood-borne confusion, pulling me into David's path? I can't tell. I'm not scared of looking psycho; I'm scared I *am* psycho. Twice now I have split from the drunk girls late at night and wandered the walkways around the history department alone, so wasted I don't even remember those wandering hours, or how I got home. So I don't trust myself, don't trust that I want what I want for the right reasons.

Now, as I approach the lecture hall, I catch David, unmistakable from the back, about six people away from me, holding a briefcase and chatting amiably with a male colleague. I feel instantly criminal, like everyone here will turn to me and tell me to leave him alone. *But I just thought I might like these funny wooden faces,* I would say in my defense, and everyone would say *Yeah, right* and tell me to go join the truth-or-dare slumber party of the English department. But David, above all, he'll see me; he'll think I'm there to be near him, which I probably am, so I turn away and leave the lecture. On my way home, I bump into a group of people headed to an off-campus party on College Ave. and it's a noisy, welcoming alternative. I get blackout drunk, rip myself away from a disgusting hookup, barf in a sink, and wake up wishing I were a deer or a bear who had never met a human, never had a drink that wasn't water.

JEAN: I recognize this woman. She's the person who called you; I never grew past that season, until now. You've carved back the dead parts and you've shown me I'm still green, and I will go back, able to grow again. But I want to go home now. Do you know what it does to me, to see just the back of David's head again? It liquefies me. It terrifies me. I'm not going to France to hurt him, to hurt myself, to make a stink.

MONICA: Is that all you want, a private revelation? You are satisfied to put your one little life on track?

JEAN: It's all I can do.

Monica's attention on me intensifies, her eyes no longer brown but pure, hot fire. And then—

Blackout.

Chapter 71

I am in Monica's throne room—I see the tub, the sinks—but it is almost unrecognizable. The lights are out. The floor is wet. My feet slip beneath me. There is only a faint silver light on the surface of the tub. It looks like a vat of tar.

"Monica?"

There is no sign of her. I nearly wipe out, catch myself on the rim of the tub, which is overflowing, out of control. Monica is nowhere.

"Monica?"

I hear a bang. The bathroom door has blown open. Moonlight limns the sitting room furniture in ghostly blue.

"MONICA?" I move slowly, my arms out in front of me, into the sitting room. One of the big picture windows has swung open, and an icy wind tears through the room. The tapestries buckle and whip like loose sails against the walls. In the center of the room, on a pulpit, rests a thick book, its pages flipping frantically. I fight my way to the window against the furious wind and slam the pane shut and twist the handle. I hold it down, my hand against my cold, damp cheek, the room now still.

"MONICA!"

No response.

I pull a lighter from my pocket and light one of the extinguished votives on an iron rack. The flame picks out the raised seams in the tapestries that I know so well—Monica's wounds, her giddy torturers. Where is she? Was it all a trick? Where have I been led? Did I die for real? Panting, I shelter my candle and carry it to the pulpit and in the quivering light I read the buckling pages where the book rests open:

Jean of Hoboken was a child of divorce. She was beautiful but damaged and needed attention. She attended a great place of learning, where she was instructed by a wise scholar whom she cajoled to lie with her and to take her one and only sacred virginity. After this, the scholar repented, cleansed his soul and his memories of Jean and her voracious unholy needs and her fatty entrées, and dedicated himself to a great career of learning. On the site of their sin, he built a school, where many bright lives were shaped. Meanwhile, Jean did not have the discipline or intelligence to get over her lascivious desire for the scholar; her grades declined and she left college with no distinction, drifted between jobs for most of her life, married an airport ham sandwich named Michael—

"Hey!"

—and blamed her lack of success on the scholar whose attention she had once so desperately courted. To rid herself of the hot fiery devil that turned her from the productive and virtuous life she should have lived, she denied herself food, feared pleasure, and one day, exhausted by dragging her useless and defiled body around this earth, she prayed to the Lord to take her to his bosom—

"No . . ."

—and to be the husband she deserved and he did and she finally found Eternal Joy, dead and buried at the age of forty-three.

"No! NO! I want to drag my body around! Let me keep it!"

The window whooshes open again and the book slams shut and I see the cover that I've seen so many times before: the praying monk, the floating saint, radiating peace with a knife in her throat. *The Golden Legend.*

I scream the silent scream of epiphany: I am not afraid. Take me, Monica; take me to the present. I will go to David's celebration. The truth is not for me alone: They must hear it.

PART V

✦ ✦ ✦

Miracles

Chapter 72

FRIDAY, APRIL 26, 2019
CHÂTEAU PLAISY, FRANCE

I step out of the taxi onto the gravel, just touching the circumference of the giant green oval of the front lawn before the castle. There are more cars than I ever saw here, more people, some in white shirts, holding trays, rushing down the path to the kitchen. But the castle is the same—twenty years was nothing to her. Glowing, golden, luxuriously furred in ivy, rippling and sensate in the wind. I hope I look OK. I'm underslept, alone, wearing too much eyeliner, my rumpled khaki dress flapping around my pale legs.

I enter the castle through the open front doors, and I could be nineteen again, returning from a site visit. My heels tap on the broad stone steps. I pass through the salon, half expecting to see the prince's prized TV with its cable box and wires, but all of that is gone. The room is scrubbed up, white-walled, turned into a place for talks, workshops. There are rows of chairs and a lectern. Along the walls, posters advertise past speakers—a "Decolonizing the Codex" series and a paper on "Empress Theodora and the Politics of Birth Control," which strike me as worlds away from anything I was taught. I'm too manic to focus on them properly, so I pretend to read with my unseeing eyes, leaning in demonstratively, postponing my movement toward the double doors that open onto the back lawn, where he must be.

"Jean!"

I leap in the air and yelp. Even before recomposing myself and turning to face her, I recognize that hair, that height, that way of emerging from behind an easel.

"Sigrid!" Her arms lock around me. "My god, it's been so long,"

I lie. She is almost completely unaged apart from some fine lines across her forehead. The smart linen suit over the running shoes seems like something she will rip off in a hilarious reveal.

"You came!"

"You expected me?"

"I'm the reason you're here."

"You work here?"

"No, I'm at Princeton. I'm department chair for now."

"Is that good?"

"Well, it takes me away from my research. But I have some discretion to get funding behind the projects that deserve it." She moves her hands around like she's working a craps table. "That, I like." All those years ago, when I watched her bend to the prince, it was only a first step, an apprenticeship to power and not a spineless deference to those who had it.

"How did you invite me to David's party?"

"Well, they invited all the prior students, going back to the first year at the château, our year. But then I noticed that they'd left you out. So I made sure David followed up with you."

"He did."

"After our year, they stopped taking undergrads, so most of our alums are architects, academics. You're—what?—I had to look you up—"

"I'm a translator-interpreter. Spanish and French."

"Cool."

It's not. I'm hiding from myself in my own life.

"Why aren't you a famous chef? To this day I've never met anyone else who can make magic out of nowhere like that. You barely broke a sweat. We still talk about it. David's always like, *Where can we get another Jean*?"

Thunder rumbles from a perfectly clear sky. "Weird," she says, looking up.

She rotates toward the back lawn. We saunter down the steps into a midday sun so bright and direct it feels like warm water, climbing over my face as I descend.

"I don't know what you remember of our summer here—they were still figuring things out."

"I *do* remember that."

"But they did it; they really built something. Hundreds of students have trained here. They've produced scholarship that's changed the field. And we were part of building that." She squeezes my shoulder. "Germain is thrilled."

"Who's Germain?"

"The prince."

"Oh, right. Is he still around?"

"Big-time. He's taking me out-of-season hunting later. Wear something bright if you go running. You still running?" A shy smile, a reference to our own long-ago intimacy.

"Yeah."

"My woman," she says, beaming. "Me too."

We walk out onto the back lawn, which is busy with a croquet game, circulating waiters, and students chatting in clusters, a striking, instantaneous sign of progress in that they are not all white, and not all smoking. Lastly, I recognize, because they look like Victorian matrons laid out in their coffins, a lot of priests.

"What's with all the priests?"

"Gotta keep 'em sweet. They have to be flattered and included so we can keep studying their churches. The prince takes care of most of that, but still, they need a mini quiche and some bubbly every couple months." Dutifully illustrating this fact, two men with placid hammy faces in ankle-length black frocks and gold brooches pass us cradling mini quiches like baby birds in their palms.

"Who's here that I know?" I focus on Sigrid intensely, something she enjoys and returns, her eyes sharp, pink cheeks up in the kind of smile you usually have to earn with a long, dirty joke. Talking to her stabilizes me, shields me from the awareness of David on this lawn like a pesticide misting through the air—I'm slightly nauseous, my skin prickly.

"Well, David, obviously. Without Ann—they have some kind of arrangement. Ann's a serious scholar; she needs to be at Oxford. David published that first book, but he hasn't really published since. This is his thing: fundraising, dealing with students, hosting conferences. And he's good at it."

"Is Neary here?"

"He's still ticking but too fragile for the trip. Sam made it. You remember her? Like, sad Soviet Heather Locklear?"

"Definitely. And Brice?"

"Who's Brice?"

"Her husband."

"Oh, I forgot about him. She must have axed him ages ago. She's a big-deal archaeologist now, gets all these grants, is always in the papers. She discovered a ninth-century Turkish port that some bridge-building project was about to blast, saved the whole thing."

"Wow. She got what she wanted."

"You remember Yoni? You guys were tight."

"Yeah, we're friends." That's an exaggeration—Yoni and I found each other online a couple of years ago and we've stayed in touch in that modern way, with little internet jokes, by distantly liking each other's choices. And I *do* like his choices: he's a lawyer at a big New York firm, married to a hot doctor he seems to adore. No kids, interesting art, trips to Croatia and Cambodia.

"He's actually given some money to the center over the years. We tried to get him here, but he didn't have time."

I wish he'd come. I would give anything for his counsel. I guess everyone would. I guess that's why his counsel costs $750 an hour.

"Is Patrick here?"

"Who's Patrick?"

"You don't remember him? The really religious guy? Rust-colored fur?"

"Oh, of course! *That* doofus. Fuck that guy. You know he tried to transfer to Columbia for his PhD?"

"He didn't get in?"

"Are you kidding? The chair of the department was Elise Rackoff, the most prominent feminist poststructuralist art historian in the world. His reactionary ass wasn't getting through the door anywhere prestigious."

"Where did he end up?"

"Works for a congressman." A gust of wind flips a table over.

"Is Judith here?"

"I wish. We tried to get her, too, but she's teaching."

"She teaches history?"

"No! She's a super famous poet." Sigrid shrugs. "Like as famous as a poet can be."

Sigrid squints at the sun and then chooses this precise moment to pull an SPF 75 broad-spectrum sunblock stick from her blazer pocket and swipe it over her whole face. The old Sigrid never would have done that, would have just fried and molted and littered her cast-off face on the ground like a burger wrapper. Maybe even Sigrid, in some small way, realizes how little we understood our own worth back then.

With a shock to the heart, I spot David out of the corner of my eye. I know it's him, although I sense the inevitable changes—he's heavier, and his hair is grayer. But I can't turn to look at him. I need Sigrid to stay with me.

"So what do you work on?" I ask her.

"Western Christianity and the Ottoman Empire, fourteenth, fifteenth centuries. Exchange with Islam, that kind of thing."

"You learned Arabic?"

"Yup." I feel the sting of regret—I have to accept that I lost real things because of David. I gave up on Arabic in my junior year; it was too difficult for a hungover wreck. "I've slowed down a little since having kids," Sigrid continues, "but . . ." Now I sense David moving between groups, and it squeezes my brain. I almost can't hear Sigrid; I'm a cardboard cutout pretending to listen. She stops talking, and I register that she said something important.

"Wait, kids! How old are your kids?"

"I've got six-year-old twin boys, Manny and Lou."

"Wow. What's the age gap?"

"They're twins. Are you OK?"

A server comes by with a tray of drinks. I grab a white wine and as I raise it to my lips I glance over the lawn and David is staring at me idly while in conversation with some people. He looks away.

Someone comes up from behind me, shooing me.

"Inside, inside!" I hear the prince urging. *"Allez, au salon s'il vous plaît."*

"That voice, it hasn't changed." And then I see him. "But my god, the face has."

"Yeah, he's addicted to fillers." Sigrid shrugs. "I think it's harder to just let yourself age when there are, like, marble busts of you out there."

Robert the hunting dog is long dead, but the prince seems to have absorbed his spirit as he scurries up to each group in turn, barking to corral them into the castle. "We have a ceremony to start!" No one is moving very fast. I finish my wine in a few sips—it's only noon and I haven't eaten, so the alcohol is working like a Xanax—and refill my glass. The wine somehow accelerates time, and the next thing I know, Sigrid has pulled me over to David.

"You remember Jean, right?"

"Hi, David." The world feels plastic, small, material. I have been a fool. He's no god, this object of a long-held desire, this foundational presence in my mind, just a polite and average old man, with the little wobble of skin under the chin, the slight puff over the belt. He does not come in for a hug. He might have shaken my hand, but his hands are full, coffee in one and pastry in the other.

"Gosh, Jean, of course! Were you— Well, how are you?"

"I'm fine!" What seems to be happening is that there is a complete contradiction between the people we were and the people we are—this man would never kiss me, and I would not dream of touching him. I have spent thousands of hours since 1998 fantasizing about David Harwell, and all the while David Harwell was busy becoming someone else. He is an old academic and administrator; I am a forty-year-old lady in a fast-fashion shirtdress; we are at a party. I smell his coffee and I smell the paper of the cup.

"Tell me, what have you been up to?"

"Lots of stuff." I shrug.

"Yeah, I bet. Were you—were you in France?"

"When?"

"I mean, just now."

"Oh. No, I flew here."

"Wow, for this?"

"It seemed fun." I swish my wine around and act breezy, but it's crazy for me to have flown to his retirement party and he knows it and he's worried.

"Well—thank you." I shake my head, like *It's nothing.* "It's a great place. We've done a lot with it. I'm proud of, you know, everyone." We seem unable to say anything even vaguely sensible. But now something strange is happening, distinct from the words that we say. Some historic link between us is coming alive for me; some cord of warmth, some ineluctable liking is reoccurring. I like his face. I like to look at it. I like him. The way he carries himself. I'm sorry that I'm making him nervous.

"It's really impressive." We stop talking. We look at each other, David holding a pinched smile. And look who's here, hopeful: Ruthless Jean taps me between the shoulders. I stand up straight, suck in my tummy. She wants me to look stunning, desirable.

Thunder rumbles again and David looks up.

"Hope the weather holds."

"It will," I say. "It's not real thunder." He's obviously not listening because he acts like this is a normal thing to say. He's very aware that we are loosely standing in a group of grad students. "Guys, this is Jean. She was part of our first cohort in 1998." He says this with exaggerated appreciation.

"Actually, I wanted to talk to you about my grade." The grad students perk up.

"Your grade from twenty years ago?" He tries to roll with this like it's a joke.

"You gave me a B for the summer and you told me I wasn't good at history, which I don't think is fair."

He knows he has to get me out of earshot. "Well," he says, looking at the grad students with a *yikes* face and handing one of them his empty cup, "step into my office." He gestures at the lawn, and the group chuckles. He leads me away from them, to an empty pocket of grass several meters away.

"You gave my paper a C and you said I hadn't dealt with the historiography, even though you never taught me what that meant."

"Are you serious?" He's confused but listening in a way that tells me I am hitting him in a place he cares about: his professionalism.

"Yes. Yoni and I co-wrote our guidebook, and you gave him an A."

"What is going on here?" I can see him considering playing dumb about Yoni.

"I know you remember Yoni; he gives you money. You gave me a C on my term paper, which was on feasting and fasting in medieval iconography, with a very nice conclusion about the harvest imagery at Bourges. I actually had a friend look at my paper—she's *really smart,* she has a PhD in, like, literally everything—and she said it was obviously a B+."

"Jean, I'm sorry. I have a million guests here, and speeches are about to start. I don't have time to"—he scoffs gently—"to reassess your paper right now. It's really great to see you. I'm so happy you're thriving."

"I never said I was thriving. I'm not thriving! You gave me an unfair grade just to discourage me, to keep me away from your department and your life." The crazy thing is, I don't want to score points; I don't want to fight with him. What do I want? I want—I want us to understand each other.

"I honestly have no recollection of your paper, but that doesn't sound like something I would do. I really think you're remembering things wrong." He is nervous; he shifts and wipes his brow and tries to laugh casually, a degraded whiff of the adoring laughter I used to elicit from him effortlessly.

"No, this is exactly what happened. You had been such a good teacher, such a lovely guide to the beauty of this world"—I gesture toward the castle, glowing in the sun—"and it was seamless when you used that same authority to make me feel small, to make me disappear. You did so with the same authoritative ease, and I believed it. For life. Can you imagine how much you mattered to me? I mean, we were close. We made out; we had sex."

"Excuse me?" Oh, he's going to pretend it didn't happen.

And if Monica had not come to me, had not led me back, I might even believe David now. I might doubt my own memory. But it is all so fresh that David's denial stings, baffles me. As he confirms again that no such thing occurred, I instinctively look down, as if I'll see a crack in the lawn between us and his side will be a verdant green carpet and mine will be parched and unkempt. He must hold to his reality. My story breaks his story. The village will be mad at me if I insist that our little pageant was real, if I say that we broke the game together, that we did it willingly, that he should have known better. Our *vitae* compete: It's not a mere fact that we are fighting over but a *life*. Mine or his.

"David. Look at me." He does, with unseeing eyes, chalked over with fear. I want us to compare truths, to admit to mistakes, to walk into our imperfect past like it's a squat stone church whose east side doesn't match its west side, but I know from his eyes that we can't. "It's sad, isn't it? For you and me to understand each other would take a miracle."

The crowd has finally moved inside, and the prince, standing at the threshold of the salon, makes an impressive whistle with his fingers in his mouth.

"Take your seat, David. They're ready to start!"

Chapter 73

JEAN OF HOBOKEN,
NOT A VIRGIN, NEVER KILLED

✦ ✦ ✦

There was once a castle in France that had been converted into a great center of learning, at first called a "school" and later, although no one knew why, renamed a "hub." The director of this center was to retire and so a great gathering was held, to which all former students of the center were invited, as well as all the priests from the churches in the region, hosted by a munificent prince. Many students attended because it was a beautiful and meaningful place in their lives and many priests attended because priests love quiche.

Among the students invited was a woman named Jean, who was stricken by this invitation, for many years earlier she had lain with the director, who then had only been a scholar, and who awakened in her a demon who made her hot and fiery but also filled her with shame, because after he had been carnal with her, the scholar had treated her like a pest, a curse, pretended never to have known her mind or body. This sudden shift had driven her mad and incited a period of starvation. Her breasts disappeared and her ribs rose on her chest like runes. The suicidally festive atmosphere of American college life had absorbed or obscured much of her derangement so that she appeared to be just another "drunk party girl," but she alone left the crowd and wandered in her blackouts to the history department hoping to see the scholar, praying that God would put him in her path. Once, she believed that God had answered her prayer, but it was a raccoon in a trash can and from two feet away, so ardent was her hope that she persisted in calling it the scholar's Christian name.

So twenty years later when she received this invitation to France, Jean in her profound distress prayed to Saint Monica, who showed her that her heart had been and still was a miraculous organ, a restaurant of many open chambers where anyone might dine, noisy and restorative, coursing with wine. Why should she close this heart? Why should she pull it from her chest and live without the noise of clashing cutlery and the stains of oil and garlic, only because one man so long ago had left without paying his bill? Fortified by the saint and fired by a hope that she might leash her demons like dogs and follow them to feasts, Jean traveled to France, although at many points in the journey from New Jersey she wanted to turn back, for who would enter the dilapidated port of Newark Liberty International if they did not have to? But Monica filled her with a stinging courage: "It is not for you alone that we do this." Jean did not know what she would do at the great party, but she brought her chef's knife with her in case she felt like killing the scholar, although Saint Monica said many times, "That is not the vibe here, Jean."

Now when the scholar saw Jean, he was shocked, for he had initially held back the invitation that the alumni office had prepared for her so that she would not attend. They exchanged words that were meaningless and polite, but under these words a torrent of fear flowed from him, for he knew that he had wronged her as a person and as a student, diminishing her achievement so that she would not pierce his virtuous orbit, bearing with her in her very body and the searching affection of her gaze the evidence of his desire and the truth of his misdeeds. But there, on the great lawn studded with priests and sheep and badly dressed young people who were experts in reception theory, pilgrimage badges, and ivory caskets, she rebuked him for his cruelty, and as he did not consider himself dishonest, he lied.

Then a ceremony began whereby many former students

were to read tributes to the scholar. One by one, the students rose to speak at the podium. But as they opened their mouths to deliver their tributes to the scholar, it was Jean's *vita* they recounted: "Jean of Hoboken," they began, their faces going rubbery with huge surprise. But try as they might, they could not recite their prepared remarks and instead narrated Jean's arrival in France in July 1998, her eagerness to study, the efflorescence of her talent in the kitchen, and her growing attachment to the scholar; the power of her faith, the intensity of her wanting to be shaped by him. And they described how David had taken her in his arms, undressed her, kissed and caressed her, and how uncertain and afraid she'd been, and also how trusting and joyful. The speakers' words, which were more than words but like feeling itself, greatly moved the audience, even the priests, whose own desire for transcendence swelled from within their tight dresses.

One by one, the students rose, ready to get the event back on track, to speak of the professor's kindness and goofs and to make art-historical jokes with punch lines like "That's not what a plumb bob is for!" But one by one, ever shocked, they took up where the last had left off: Jean wandering for so many years after that summer, taking a husband but feeling a shadow alongside her commitment, always dreaming of an apocryphal self who had not been sloppy, slutty, drunk, distracted, easy. The scholar at several points wanted to leave, to stop the proceedings, and gestured for help, but even the stronger country priests could not unglue him from his seat, nor his seat from the floor. It was observed that the scholar, stuck to this position of honor at the front of the room and listening to the *vita* unfold, began to cry as he let the points of Jean's *vita* into his heart, as he suffered with her starvation and wandering and doubt. His emotion went beyond the usual for a touching departure; it was clear that he was fighting rivers of tears and then fought no more until he was weeping openly, so forcefully that he could not form words of thanks. Finally, the scholar was so frenzied with soulful bawling that the prince said, "I think the Festschrift is over," and a guest who was vaguely familiar to many of them although they could not place her, a woman with long brown hair in bright blue lederhosen, leaning against the far wall, said, "Oh, *das* Festenschrift has just begun."

When all the students had spoken, and all was brought to light, the scholar was suddenly released from his seat and stood to make a closing speech, wanting to explain away all that they had heard, but he could not open his mouth, for it was fused completely shut at the teeth as if with forged lead. Then it was observed that the priests began to cry, blotting their eyes with oily napkins, and the students, too, not for the scholar but for the unguarded lovers, for churches with no glass, for doors that howl open, for robberies that a house enjoys—for who appreciates a home better than a thief?—until it finds itself too bare to inhabit. No one paid attention to where the scholar went as the arguments he so wished to make were transformed by the private apse of his mouth into a fitful, plangent song, ideal, Saint Monica thought, for some inward contemplation.

The priests went to the cocktail table, and the students found each other and agreed that they would redouble their efforts to dismantle the patriarchy with their work on reception theory, pilgrimage badges, and ivory caskets. No one even bothered to pull the cotton drape off the oil portrait of the director, which was poised on an easel in the salon. It was not until later that many observers, laypeople and priests alike, saw the two spots appear on the drape at the level of the scholar's sapphire eyes, and drip in wet streaks to the floor. (For many years, the portrait leaked until it started to damage the parquet floor and the prince quietly had it moved to a barn.)

Jean did not see the mass weeping in the salon, for she had descended to the kitchen in the belly of the castle, where she found the old cook and groundskeeper, who remembered her fondly and embraced her. She saw her face reflected in fiery gold in all the copper pots that lined the walls. The couple was separating rabbits into pieces, and Jean took up their work with them. *This is what my knife is for,* she thought as she watched her left hand close around the silken thigh and bend it back, watched her right hand do things for which she had no words, only joy in her movement, intuitive and just and angled. After some time, some wine, and some typical cooks' jokes that involved positioning whole rabbits suggestively, they parted ways and Jean walked out through the side entrance to the kitchen and wandered in the direction of the setting sun, her knife in her hand, a few lambs following, mouths open, shouting questions in men's voices from their guts. She had no answers for them. She watched a thousand small black birds lift together from the trees and the hedge and the lawn into the sky in one great cheerful armored body, which swelled this way and that with total caprice before a pink sun in the fresh air. Jean breathed deeply, and exhaled: *Dear Monica, dear Monica, dear Monica,* she prayed, *thank you.* Jean felt suddenly alone, alive, and very hungry.

Acknowledgments

As of writing this, I have never met or communicated with Monica Lewinsky, but I would nevertheless like to thank her. In the public life she did not ask for, she has again and again chosen to advocate for more humane and fully dimensional consideration of distant people we may not know but whom we have the power to affect. Her grace and altruism have moved and inspired me.

We talk a lot about people "believing" in us, but I think this story required a leap of faith from my agent, Sarah Bedingfield, especially when I thought I might be writing a play (yikes). In order to edit this book as she did, with majestic patience and extraordinary vision, Lee Boudreaux was game to put herself through a whole catechism in the inner workings of my mind, and she deserves not only my eternal gratitude but also maybe a white dress and a party with a local DJ and a golden medallion of her own beneficent profile and the words *ut fabula movens*—keep the story moving. Thank you also to Maya Pasic for insightful work on the manuscript and to everyone at Doubleday who contributed their talent and energy to this book, including assistant editor Sarah Perrin, production editor Melissa Yoon, managing editor Vimi Santokhi and managing editorial assistant Kirsten Eggart, cover designer Emily Mahon, publicists Elena Hershey and Julie Ertl, marketer Jess Deitcher, and designer Pei Loi Koay. I thank artist Catherine Vaesca for her beautiful illustration of Château Plaisy.

Nancy Thebaut's sharing of sources, ideas, and enthusiasm has been, at every phase, essential to this project and, moreover, a total joy. I have to thank several important draft readers: Priya Swaminathan set the course with perfect questions early on; Elayne Oliphant told me not to pull punches; Kate Cortesi entered so thoughtfully into the questions at the heart of this book with me and gave me notes I returned to again and again. I am deeply grateful that Katy Hays exists and that she made time to pull me up out of a last-minute crisis of confidence with a generous read. Thanks to Alison Ray for her brilliant research into images. I am grateful to Adam Shapiro for telling me where Yoni should hike (and for other support, big and small). Thanks to Mei Chin for talking through every possible ending so many times that any other friend would have changed names and numbers to avoid me.

For help with foreign and dead languages, I thank Hanna McCloskey and most of her family, Martin Patience, Grisela Ruiz Marti, and David Rundle.

I was trying to write these acknowledgments in a sober and concise manner, but I gave them to my husband to proofread, and he said the part where I thanked him read like "agreed wording from a divorce settlement," which is typical of the inadvertent hilarity of his every breath and also the uncompromising nature of his feedback. But because he can't lie, when he loved an early draft of this book, it filled me with hope, and when he gave me the time and space I needed to finish it, he earned my undying gratitude, my ever-deeper affection, and fifty percent of the house.

It would be impossible to thank all the academics, researchers, and curators who gave me the tools I needed for this book, but I should say one important thing. I studied art history as an undergraduate at Columbia University, received my MA and PhD at the University of Chicago, and then held a postdoctoral fellowship at the University of Oxford. At no point in this academic career did my supervisors or instructors behave inappropriately toward me. On the contrary, I am lucky to have spent so much time among people dedicated to thinking deeply within bracing rules of truth and transparency. What still astonishes me is the imaginative richness that those rules can produce.

SOURCES

The churches in this book, with the exception of Bourges Cathedral, are fictionalized amalgams of real Romanesque churches in the Bourbonnais region of France. Likewise, the scholarship referenced by characters in the book is fictionalized—I found that academic discourse in all its precision could not be imported intact without crushing the story. However, I did draw on the work of real scholars of medieval art and history. I would like to cite in particular the following: Peter Brown, *The Cult of the Saints: Its Rise and Function in Latin Christianity* (Chicago: University of Chicago Press, 1981), Caroline Walker Bynum, *Holy Feast and Holy Fast: The Religious Significance of Food to Medieval Women* (University of California Press, 1987), Michael Camille, *The Medieval Art of Love: Objects and Subjects of Desire* (Abrams, 1998), Cynthia Hahn, *Portrayed on the Heart: Narrative Effect in Pictorial Lives of the Saints from the Tenth through the Thirteenth Century* (University of California Press, 2001), and Jeffrey F. Hamburger, *The Visual and the Visionary: Art and Female Spirituality in Late Medieval Germany* (Princeton University Press, 1998).

Saints' lives were adapted from *The Golden Legend: Readings on the Saints* by Jacobus de Voragine, translated by William Granger Ryan, volumes one and two (Princeton University Press, 1993 and 1995, respectively) and *Butler's Lives of the Saints, New Concise Edition,* edited by Michael Walsh (Burns and Oates; Collins Dove, 1991).

A NOTE ABOUT THE AUTHOR

Julia Langbein is an art historian and a writer. She is the author of an academic study of hilarious French art critics (*Laugh Lines*) and the novel *American Mermaid.* She has written about art, food, and travel for a number of publications and received a James Beard Journalism Award in 2024. A native of Chicago, she lives with her family outside of Paris.